OUT OF COMPETITION

OUT OF COMPETITION

A novel by Lew Collins

JEF BOOKS

JEF BOOKS 99
Arlington Heights, Illinois, 2024

ISBN: 978-1-884097-99-7

ISSN 1084-547X

Text design and cover - Lew Collins

Out of Competition

9.10 AM

'OKAY SHAKESPEARE DIDN'T SAY now is the spring of our discontent but maybe he should have.'

Clinging to a jar of jam Annie looks like she's going to drop any minute Larry studies his assistant staring at him as he sounds off, with his burgundy pyjamas and fluffy bone-white hotel gown half coming off him. He lowers his voice:

'Who else knows about this?'

'Only the author's estate.'

'Keep it that way.'

Larry throws his gown off and stands holding his chest. 'And Bella?'

'They took her luggage in at 5.30 am. Five vans worth.'

'You were there?'

'Your spy was.'

Larry grunts his approval. 'At least he's doing something.' He totters along his balcony breathing hard, gripping an iron railing. 'The word's out on Edgar?'

'Everywhere.'

Dropping the cellphone on the glass top he throws his arms dramatically up in the air. 'He's got to think before acting. This is a foreign country.'

Larry pours coffee. 'It's cold.' He downs the whole cup. He needs the caffeine. Grabbing a croissant, he stares at his diary, flicks through the film magazine pushed under his door. 'There's nothing. Maybe we caught a break.'

'It's going in tomorrow.'

'Nothing is nothing even if it's nothing. Do I need this. This meeting with the South Americans, cancel it.'

'You promised them three times.'

'Jesus. Pencil it for after Bella. I'll talk if they tone down their damn politics, if Bella comes through.' Larry lowers his voice: 'Who from the author's estate?'

'A lawyer in LA.'

'Get him on the phone.'

'Her. It's night. She won't answer until after four.'

'We made a deal, Annie. I swing it with Bella we fund the South Americans and give the author's crowd a bonus. Come back at four.'

Annie places the jam jar down with a hard clink on the glass and flees the suite. Wiping his brow with a serviette Larry turns back to the Mediterranean.

'What's wrong? The waters are sapphire. The sky's cloudless. The sun mopped up the rain puddles by the old seawall. Annie found my favourite jam. I slept most of the night.' Larry empties some juice, spreads Annie's jam on a croissant. 'There's always chapter 11.' Wondering now if any balconies are listening in. Just what he needs more gossip. He has chest pains. Breathing hard, he nearly tips over the railing. That'd be perfect Larry spreadeagled on the breakfast terrace. Shading his eyes he watches a swimmer's progress across the bay. 'I gotta lose some weight.'

He smothers his croissant with more jam and shoves it in his mouth whispering his mantra: 'Get the money.'

Twenty minutes later in his rumpled grey linen suit Larry treads carefully down the hallway. Taking the anonymous stairwell he hikes fast across the terrace not looking left or right. He doesn't need to come face to face with some bad deal, worse see his body dead on the tiles. Making it into the nearest public space, Larry gulps in sea air. Steadier now, he texts, On my way.

He's in a better mood. Upping his speed he heads towards the South Americans hotel on Rue d'Anglacés. If Bella brings her boodle maybe. She texts back: Nails being done. Dont be late Larry. I'll use them... That gets his first laugh. He sends: NEVER. He heads into a store thinking he'll buy her gloves. Looking around it's a bookshop not a gift store. He hasn't been in a bookstore in ages. Hovering in picture books, he flips through black and whites of La Dolce Vita, grabbing his chest seeing a photo of Dino De Laurentiis, Federico Fellini, Marcello Mastroianni in the background.

'And did De Laurentiis lose on that.'

Moving on to foreign dailies he finds nothing on Edgar's antics. It's a relief, his phone shaking in his pocket. God, she's cancelling. 'Hell-lo,' Larry says softly.

'He's not here.'

'Semi, is that you?'

'Three journalists and no Edgar.'

'The publicist?'

'No.'

'They promised they'd sort it out.'

'Annalise somebodyoranother wants to know if you're coming.'

'Call Annie.' Voices in the street swing him around, Larry grinning at the woman at the desk. 'I gotta go. I have a meeting.'

'Yeah, here.'

He switches off, grinning again at the woman. 'Problem?'

'Juste des gamins.'

'Kids,' he whispers walking outside. She doesn't return his smile. He didn't buy anything. Blinded by the sun Larry sees a mass coming down the road, voices bouncing off buildings. 'DIX ANS C'EST ASSEZ! DIX ANS C'EST ASSEZ.'

He tries speed walking away, catching his left foot, nearly going in the gutter. A hand grabs him. Two kids are by his side. He grins. 'This a student thing?' Looking around it might not be that simple. 'You want a donation? Ten bucks do?' Larry tries getting a hand in his jacket pocket but they won't let go. Staring up at the sky he sees seagulls. People on the sidewalk are clapping. A man shouts 'BRAVO.'

'What's this all about.'

He's marched into the middle of the road. He tries to catch the eye of a kid reasonable enough to start being reasonable with. 'I tell you what...' The kids drown him out with, 'DIX ANS C'EST ASSEZ.'

'Ten years for what?' Walkers are enjoying the spectacle. Larry smiles. 'I have a deal to close. I'll do that and come back and join you after I promise.' Nobody's listening to him. 'Why me?' A boy alongside stares back at him.

'Because you're in films dummy.'

Larry blinks. 'What movie we talking about? They can't all be good.'

Larry shouldn't have been within a hundred meters of the damn bookshop. This town should ban bookstores if people are accosted by street criminals walking out of one. Larry should be riding an elevator to Bella's rooftop. He and Bella should be out inking their deal in the sun, a twenty-first century mogul's mega-plan, Bella clinging to a post-breakfast flute of champers waving the document in the bright-air. Two movie moguls making history. No mogul worth the threads he's standing in goes into a bookshop before signing a deal. Larry tries to slap his forehead, but he can't get an arm free. 'GOD WHERE'RE WE GOING.'

'DIX ANS C'EST ASSEZ.'

'Are you sure you have the right Larry? Maybe you want

Lennie. I'll give you his mobile.' Larry tests their grip again. It's solid. 'Am I the only one you could find?'

There's always someone who hates a Hollywood producer. Larry Linsteeg defending Hollywood against the world. Famous, rich, or was, and American, the only defender of Hollywood the kids could find. 'Nobody knows how hard it is to carry the world on your back.' Nobody's listening.

They wheel him right then left, Larry seeing where they're going. 'WHY ARE YOU DOING THIS.' It's revenge for his director. Edgar's enemies are Larry's enemies. 'Edgar only hit the deputy, a complete nobody for godsakes.'

Larry's sweating. Bella's getting him out of the way so she can sign with someone else. Squashed in the middle of this rabble Larry can't rule anything out. This crowd is ten times bigger. 'Who's directing this?'

A man rushes up shoving a tiny digital in his face, Larry's grin turning into a yell: 'I'M LARRY LINSTEEG THE PRODUCER.'

The protesters yell: 'DIX ANS C'EST ASSEZ.' A news photo with his mouth wide open Larry knows what it means. Evidence he's one of them. The kids drag him to the Bâtiment. A line of blue is out in front. Larry knows what's happening now. He's going straight to a French jail.

BEWARE THE TIDES OF MAY. Les méduses in the bay. Media outside the bâtiment. Everything floating in focusable distance, inspiring Zucca to get close and shoot wide.

Pushing through onlookers he gets a cinemascope closeup of an old protester, his mouth wide open. Zucca's instincts tell him he has something he can sell. The nude snaps of his new girlfriend sprawled asleep in the Hôtel Sublime will probably end up on Youtube. He left a note saying he was heading for breakfast at Coffee & Cakes in Place de la Mer opposite Notre Dame des Bonnes Pensées.

Sipping coffee he heard chanting then saw a mountain of kids wheeling down his way. Zucca didn't need a town hall briefing to tell him what was up. He stuck his lens in the face of numero uno and pressed the shutter multiple times. Now he's going with them as they charge a cop-line. Zucca's seen the like of it maybe once before in his time as he prepares himself for a bang-up of bloodied faces.

Only no blows happen. Not even a short shouty standoff. The cops step aside, leaving the bâtiment to its fate, and after a bit of argy-bargy security step aside and let the demonstrators right into the building.

A MAN SHOULD BE ABLE TO DIE MORE THAN ONCE. If Bella has her way Larry will. She's said goodbye to her manicurist, still no sign of him. Sitting on her Grand Hôtel des Belles Sables rooftop deck she stares at her cup of green tea going stone cold. She tries his mobile again. No answer.

What she's seen so far she likes. The movies suit her finances better than Bitcoin. She's even ready to make an offer on this rooftop.

Renne-sur-Mer is more than okay. Only where the hell is Larry? She trawls her messages. Nothing. He rings her constantly, sends her champagne, chocolates and flowers, gets her to fly half-way around the world, now the day of the big deal where is he?

Another boyfriend with cold feet. Well Bella won't be ignored. If Larry walks out on an idea she agreed to do, the one she made him think was his, she'll kill him.

Life's best imagery is but a sleeping shadow of a sudden ripple of street applause for the professional responsible for Ivan Dzerzhinsky's party sounds. The LA-based American audiovisual expert and putative film producer Jack Kimmelon, arm-in-arm with his stunning wife, Merryl, the still gorgeous fashion model, a now wildly famous pair walking out into a spring sun from the Casino de Monte-Carlo CCTV flashback security cameras capturing their wide-eyed surprise at finding officers, police cars and flashing lights—another jewel-thieving pair caught after a decade on the run. Jack's eyes spring open.

'Hell,' he moans softly, 'where am I.'

Glancing to his left he sees Merryl still fast-asleep. Parking another of his dreams filled with disturbing images deep inside his head, Jack slides from the bed, managing to get upright without waking Merryl, staggering on numb feet down the corridor to the boat's galley. Few know that Alex Zanayev gave Jack his Sunshine Coast free of charge for the entire festival. Even fewer know the Russian also let a fellow-Russian Ivan Dzerzhinsky have Zanayev's belovèd Soraya for the same period. Who knows where the money comes from to prop up Zanayev and his luxury Monaco lifestyle or what his connection is to Ivan Dzerzhinsky. And why should Jack care. Alex Zanayev is just another Monaco-based well-boated Russian oligarch living the good life, another of the taxless territory's financial mysteries. When an English clothing billionaire whispered in Jack's startled ear that Zanayev actually began his working-life as a contract house painter in Siberia, Jack at first began to protest, mumbling something about everything he's heard about Alex Zanayev being unverified rumour. Jack got it early on that entertaining tittle-tattle about a Russian oligarch who just loaned him a boat wasn't in his best interests. So what if Alex Zanayev is rich enough to bet on any market and never lose. So what if he is able to kill people with impunity. As long as corpses with Zanayev's DNA attached to them don't drift near Jack's borrowed boat, no local or international cop will get anything out of him. As far as Jack's concerned it's all straight from the realm of a whodunnit novel.

That his benefactor Russian oligarch is mysteriously alive, marvellously afloat, fabulously rich and miraculously out of jail is all Jack needs to know. Everything else is blind gossip generated by a smouldering fire of envy and dismay at all the money Alex has. All the terrible things he's said to have done, deeds dead and buried because everyone who knows anything about them is dead and buried as well, adds up to the what about where which Jack is simply not investigating. Any negative image of Alex Zanayev adds up to nothing.

Jack was lucky enough to have met a man who is lucky enough to call Monaco home. He's not deconstructing the oligarch's bona fides. Any investigation into Alex Zanayev or his life ended when Zanayev became Jack's employer. Jack's not about to elevate any conjecture to a truth-exposé. Why should he. That is all that needs to be said.

Finding himself staring at recently-ground coffee in a jar that he is holding in two idle hands, Jack looks out at the morning sky recalling the moment another new friend, Rob Le Riche, introduced Zanayev to him and Merryl.

On the back of the Russian oligarch's yacht, lounging on the largest cutting-edge technology super-boat currently on the planet—he was told—that afternoon made for a wonderful moment. Jack's life took a turn toward the stars when the Russian began filling him in on the plans he had for upending Monaco's cultural scene, streamlining it internationally. Jack is blessed with a sixth sense when not to probe for details about any famous rich person who is paying him so well. So it is a month since he first met Alex and a day since he and Merryl motored down the Côte d'Azur coastline to weigh anchor in Renne Bay in Alex's first floating home, the grace and favour bonus payment for Jack's reorganisation of the on-board entertainment system of Zanayev's current main home, the Soraya.

If Zanayev's main boat is not the biggest yacht ever built, who cares. If the Soraya a three hundred and twenty-four-foot welded steel and aluminium moulded fibre-glass ocean cruiser is a key asset a firm of Dubai based London-trained lawyers are trying to prise from Zanayev's grip, being legal representatives of two of Alex's ex-wives, how is this any of Jack's business.

If the Soraya is the ocean-going part-solar-powered ship cruiser listed in an alimony payments petition currently before Le Tribunal Suprême de Monaco, who the hell cares. It's none of Jack's business. That's all for Zanayev's ex-wives to sort out.

A burst of helicopter rotors in the eastern sky has Jack spilling the coffee meant for the Sunshine Coast's espresso machine.

'We being attacked?' he half-yells, then regrets raising his voice as he woke Merryl up, her moaning coming down the corridor to him.

Running outside in his silk pyjamas Jack sees a chopper silhouetted against the rising sun. What's he looking at? A promo-stunt trying to get the festival's attention? He's seen better on small-country TV. After watching it crossing the bay he heads back inside Zanayev's first floating home to finish making the first steaming Jamaican brew for the day. Ah, Montego Bay, the coffee brand named after the place where Jack hopes to park his own ocean-going luxury yacht pretty soon. Once he's become a major producer making movies like Titanic, anything with a box office to make his daydreams come true.

SHAKESPEARE MIGHT SAY we know not what we may be and Edgar Gordon Olles doesn't. Staring at 09.28 on his bedside digital clock, he knows nothing of where he is or should be or what people are now probably saying about him for not being where he should have been nearly twenty nine minutes before. He stares at the clock until it flips 09.29.

'Fuck. The press conference.'

On two sore feet Edgar runs around a small apartment calling: Rob, you there? Finding no Rob or any bed slept in, Edgar keeps calling out. No answer.

Running around in circles Edgar gets himself ready, grabs his bag with a camera inside and staggers out into a corridor. Nearly falling down some antique stairs he finds himself in the black and white marble lobby of a waterfront hotel.

It dawns on him it was his suite up there. Wandering light-headed outside still having trouble staying on his feet, a passing silent scooterist nearly runs him down.

There's no press tent anywhere. Weaving his way towards the waterfront going by a merry-go-round he says over and over, 'Larry'll kill me.' He agreed to help Semi handle their first press-do, but seeing only film magazines on a seawall, he sits heavily and flicks through one cover to cover. Finding nothing of any note he stares out to sea re-hearing Rob yelling against the noise the night before.

'You are living in terror of getting your cinematic ass kicked. It's a common directorial dilemma, Ed. There is too much to say. Nothing's believable. How do you line up the facts in time to get cinemagoers hooked before they don't start saying: WTF, I'm outta here?'

Rob le Riche a.k.a the snake was sounding-off in Edgar's ear in whatever bar they were in, Edgar unable to get a word in edgeways. 'Il y a trop de mauvais films,' Rob shouted.

Many in the game don't get Rob's drift and only a few appreciate Different Styles, his weekly Youtube rants, yet for some inexplicable reason millions subscribe to Rob.

The sky's cooking Edgar's hangover, the bâtiment fracas coming back to him in technicolour, Edgar murmuring, 'What's the point.'

His right fist is curled into a ball, the one that connected with the festival's deputy.

'The competition's getting you out of the way, Ed.'

He can't remember much about the moment and deciding to go down a concrete ramp to the beach he ploughs through sand over to the sea's edge where he stands recalling even less of Rob's advice on how to handle it all from here on in than he did two minutes before. Swaying a few moments, Edgar stands on one leg trying to pull off a boot. Falling backwards he removes the other. He stares for a long moment at his feet as if they are to blame for everything. Struggling up he wades out, his head as tight as a drum.

'The mêlée won't be forgotten.'

Rumour has a life of its own in this town. He's lucky he missed the press thing. He would have been crucified. A burst of rotor noise in the east gets him squinting, his ear guiding him to a thing above blue and yellow umbrellas, pine and palm trees and sand-coloured buildings against a rocky backdrop. A second helicopter rises with something underneath. His eyes scrunched into two thin red lines Edgar follows its progress.

LORDY, WHAT ARE THE FOOLS DOWN THERE DOING. With so much thumping on glass happening Annalise de la Forêt is not wondering if the protesters will get in but when. She knows only too well Daniel doesn't have the whatsits to handle this crisis.

Morale went through the floor when Léo disappeared. Checking her watch, she hovers a moment by the escalators wondering if she should dash up to the press room, raise a general alarm, help out with evacuations, or simply get out the back way alone. She has never heard anything like what's going-on. A security guy tossing his walky-talky and running up the escalator yelling 'JE NE MEURS PAS POUR CE BOULOT,' snaps her out of it.

She manages to stay a few paces in front of the heavy breathing man, running full-tilt into her home away from home, the bâtiment's press office, journalists clinging to hot cups, looking up wide-eyed at her as she bursts in. 'We're under attack.' The guy behind her yelling, 'Les communistes ont pris le contrôle de la ville.'

A mug's contents goes into a lap, inspiring a scream which lingers as the cup hits the floor and breaks as the main doors cave-in down below getting a colleague to observe: 'Au moins, nous avons l'histoire pour aujourd'hui.'

LARRY'S LATEST WRITER is on a hardwood stool inside the Bar du Poisson fiddling with a pen that isn't working, though the ink is already dry on much. Today began way too early. Bella Fibben moving in. Staring down at his notes he can hear Larry's assistant's voice saying Larry is driving her crazy, the change to a Hôtel Royal Mélodie her latest nightmare. Scribbling she hates him. He crosses out ~~she hates him~~. He can't take sides, as Bill Goldman said, 'No matter how much shit you may have heard or read, movies are only about one thing: THE NEXT JOB.'

Larry's writer has no next jobs on the horizon. Two things are in mind, what's next, what's on the table, which is added to what's he doing here at all? Recording what's going on whispering 'by being here.' His dithering brings the barman down. 'Que puis-je vous offrir d'autre, monsieur?'

'Une bière s'il vous plaît.'

A third coffee is better, but Larry's writer won't retract the order. He's doing what spies do, blending in, saying nothing, seeing without being seen. And so far he's failed on all three. What is there to see anyway? A man at the back is leaning against a mirror, his head in a newspaper. A blond walks in, drops her bag on a stool right beside Larry's writer just as the toilet flushes down back, Larry's writer admiring her blue satin-lace push-up bra under a black lace top, pegging her size at 40D, her retro-look reminding him of Marilyn, a faucet squeaking, a door clattering open, releasing a bone-white faced man, a middle-aged burgher-sort ambling back to his stool saying: 'Ah Charlotte, Tu es là!'

'Bonjour, Charles.'

Not much to see you might say and you would be right. They kiss each other's cheeks. Charles points at the beer pump. The barman nods. Charlotte asks for a coffee and Larry's writer listens in to her going on now about a Russian's boat.

'Tous les bateaux ont cettes choses en haute maintenant,' Charles says calmly.

'C'est vrai, mais à quoi servent-ils?'

'Ils sont juste pour le spectacle,' the man against the mirror yells.

'Tais-toi, Bernard.'

Charlotte's dismissal of the man at the back is enough for Larry's writer to write: Were they an item? Charlotte goes on to how big yachts are show-off expensive military-lookalike toys. Military fashion statements.

'Alors, Léo est-il vraiment parti?'

'Hier.'

'Où?'

'Nobody knows.'

Larry's writer looks up, seeing Charles staring right at him. Gathering intelligence is the art of mining gossip not being noticed. Larry's writer has been fingered.

'Léo est soudé à la structure du bâtiment. Il ne peut pas y aller.' Larry's writer scribbles a shorthand-description of Léo's indispensability to the festival. If you are wondering if he's wasting his time you are on the money. He looks up and sees Charles is staring again, the barman producing a coffee for Charlotte, Larry's writer looking at the space where a wrist-watch could be, his face too warm for the early sun. A man runs in breaking his lack of concentration.

'QUELQUE CHOSE EST ARRIVEÉ.'

'On sait déjà, Simon.'

'Tu sait déjà sur le requin?'

'Quel requin?'

'Un requin est tombé du ciel.'

'Quoi?'

A shark falling from Renne's skies stimulates discussion. Is the time ripe for Larry's writer getting himself out of there? You bet.

'Est-ce que c'est une promotion?'

'Quelqu'un est mort.'

Writing this last thing down Larry's writer pulls notes from his pocket only to drop one as he makes a right meal of paying his bill.

'Anglais.'

'Moi?'

'Vous nous quittez?'

Larry's writer sees how many notes he tossed onto the bar-top. Together with the other that is on the floor all his calculations are wrong. He thinks of retrieving the floored one but as it's wedged under his stool it's too late. He grabs his bag and leaves.

'Get what you wanted?' Charles calls out.

Larry's writer doesn't look back, running now towards the beach. 'HELL,' he says at a pair of silhouetted faces. They clear from his way. He doesn't know where he is going. Day-two of his assignment his cover is blown.

ZUCCA STAYS WITH THE KIDS shooting everything he can focus on, especially the big guy looking out of his head with fear at this point. The demonstrators collecting below shout at each other as they run up an escalator, breaking glass still sounding somewhere.

Zucca shoots three of them unfurling a poster going up with a black on white painted Gruppo dell'Apprezzamento del Film. Captions appear in darkrooms. Zucca is thinking the big guy has to pull off something or else why is he here. Maybe he will go big last minute. Right now he looks crazy. Zucca's seen many types, inspired to bonkers. Few are the real deal. Most are not. But Zucca's counting on this guy, hoping he has an inspiration.

Zucca needs a defining shot. It could it be a psycho-political introspective leader inside an action scenario. It could be a scenario inside an introspection. Really, Zucca doesn't know. He needs a front-page pic, one for the whole world. Could bolshy be the one? Is he a meal ticket, photo-historian of the year, Time Man-of-the-Year portrait? Zucca's last breadwinner was a fizzog he had to throw away. Zucca needs a payday. 'Come on big guy.'

Zucca can't afford to keep losing them, small or big. He's convinced he saw something in the guy's eyes. He pegged the guy as a pilgrim. Zucca pushes further up in through the kids barging their way through the doors of La Salle Truffaut now, a sign saying a Directors on Directors Directing Genre session is on, the white-haired startled audience looking up almost with one face. Zucca scans around for a perfect position. Wherever his subject goes he's going. So far, nobody looks fazed by the intrusion, a woman telling everyone: 'It's improvisational theatre.'

'Let's hope not,' someone behind her says.

When the protesters parade their leader in front of the screen the audience falls silent. A black and white film still running goes white. The projector judders to a halt. A kid yells through an intercom, 'Stop phony festivalism,' his high-pitched voice and message not really carrying or going over that well, but the audience gets the drift. This is unscheduled and disruptive and is going to take time to resolve. Many sit shaking their heads and sighing, the first woman saying loudly again, only with a little less conviction this time: 'It's street theatre.'

When the house lights come up a big intruder is on stage blinking out at people his own age, everyone caught in a type-situation. In the over-heated cinema everyone is sweating. 'It's showtime big guy,' Zucca whispers, hoping the unimpressed faces all around won't multiply. A voice says: 'Larry Linsteeg, gimme a break.' A man laughs.

Zucca's heart sinks a notch. A backlash is close. The lights in this Larry's eyes. Not only is he looking under-confident, he's beginning to look like a true phoney. Those closest to the stage glare at him. Some grin. Zucca's brain does a rethink and when the kid with a banner Gruppo dell' Apprezzamento del Film forms the acronym GAF, Zucca's about to give up. Titters spread as more demonstrators pour inside, tipping the numbers in favor of the protesters for the first time. Big Larry springs to life, raising himself up.

'Friends, comrades, film lovers. I come neither to praise Léo nor to bury him.'

Zucca isn't the only one with his mouth open. Larry moves to the edge of the stage dragging his minders with him. 'Friends I was here in 1968. My first year. I was an ingenu in film but I understood the error authorities made in removing Henri Langlois as chief of the Cinémathèque Française.'

Zucca is stunned by how clearheaded Larry sounds. His voice isn't shaking. The mood change has guests in front vacating their seats, Zucca's photo opportunity staring out at what he seems now to believe is his own private captive audience. At least by the look on his face. Silence lingers in the room, some hanging on to what Larry's next words might be, grinning nervously as if they're half-expecting a stand-up experimental theatrical comedy routine might break out, audience members being asked to come up on stage. Among those who get that Larry might now understand the power he has, are smiling with Zucca, who's quietly urging Larry not to shut up. The photo op he thought he had only minutes before is back on the agenda. Many in the audience are on the edges of their seats, some by their faces looking like they're getting ready to make a run for it. When Larry lifts his arms into a V everyone sees this is no bathroom rehearsal by an amateur. Larry's in the zone. Zucca sees the eyes of a man with only one way to go, forward. Slipping into Gregory Peck's voice, taking on the actor's steely gaze, Larry's voice fills the silent auditorium: 'I have joined this protest to stop another mistake being made with the removal of today's Henri Langlois—Léo Stern.'

Protesters all-around are stunned.

'I am a producer aware of what people want.'

Even if his grasp on the facts might still be a touch dubious his confidence is suddenly sky-high. Larry seems to be channeling someone stronger than himself. Mike Douglas at the end of Traffic? Throwing his arms up into another V, Zucca sees who Larry is playing. 'This protest deserves a place in history. 68's protesters demanded Langlois' return. I say bring Léo back. Bring back the great white shark of 21st century film.'

'Léo is a great white shark?' a white-haired woman asks near the front. Larry probably meant great white hero but even the truly great make some mistakes. Let's not get hung-up on detail, Zucca nearly shouts. Larry is in the zone and he's staying there. 'Langlois championed Welles—Bergman—Kurosawa. Léo championed Spielberg—Coppola—Campion—Almodóvar. Who could force Léo out?'

'You're trying to save your tanking film,' someone shouts. A voice tells the speaker to shut-up. Scepticism is now dead officially in this cinema. If Larry's a fraud he's the best fraud Zucca's seen. 'Go for the throat!' he whispers, 'Avanti!'

'Political controls are the enemy of art,' Larry shouts at his audience.

'YES,' the kids shout: 'And the jury and management must resign right now!'

Larry's learned the ropes of what he has to do, and he seems to know he must do it fast. He's enjoying himself, a good sign, most in the audience and all the protesters now clearly with him. It's remarkable. Larry the faux leftie with a tanking film stands sweating and enjoying his power. When a woman holding a walker stands up and shakes her fist, shouting, 'Yes!' Zucca snaps her doing it and swinging back gets his subject's grinning face. Zucca would vote for Larry in any constituency. He's a candidate with a workable quorum anywhere right now. Larry could win a seat in any parliament. Zucca's even ready to shout 'Democracy Now. Jury Out,' more loudly than these kids. Larry's pumped. So too are the kids. 'Stay cool, Larry,' Zucca whispers. 'Don't you lose it now.' A Jean-Luc Godard moment is at hand, Larry now demanding that the jury president come down and face the music, yelling: 'THE JURY'S THE PROBLEM.' Kids throw their fists in the air and yell 'DEMOCRACY.' Zucca's even shouting now: 'If the képi fits wear it, Larry. Your die is cast. Cross your Rubicon. Don't look back.' Larry looks straight at Zucca as he says it, Zucca repeating the words so Larry doesn't miss a syllable, aiming his camera at Larry's forehead. 'Godard and Truffaut are on stage with you,' he continues, Larry's eyes going as wide as they can go hearing this. Larry the leftie is raising festival hell, pulling himself up to his full five-feet-eight inches from where with his arms up he could easily be over six feet. Arms aloft, his voice hoarser than Jack Nicholson in A Few Good Men, the kids' winner on fire takes aim: 'IN SOLIDARITY WITH MY

FRIENDS TODAY I AM TAKING DEATH AT INTERVALS
OUT OF COMPETITION.' Zucca got him in that moment—
The Definitive Portrait. Larry the Leader with his arms aloft
in vintage Charles De Gaulle style.

TOGGLING THE REMOTE in the living room of Elena's
Belle Époque apartment on Rue des Nations-Unies Viktor
Andreyevic stares at the replays of the fracas on television
with protesters flooding again and again into the bâtiment.

'What on earth is going on?' he says to an empty room.
The Promenade des Rois is only a short walk away but he's
not going near it. Switching off he stalks around on Elena's
polished boards scuffing her Persian carpets furiously
rubbing his forehead.

Viktor has no information on this Larry Linsteeg, what
he wants or represents, who he is even. In the past Viktor
would have received a character file inside five minutes,
with a thorough summary of his weaknesses and strengths.

Turning to a photograph of Tolstoy Elena has in her
entrance Viktor asks the dead author if his enthusiasm about
being in Renne is misguided. 'Things are bad.'

On the TGV to Renne, Viktor told himself all he had to
do was peddle his vast experience in intelligence to various
producers, convince people what a great film he has to make,
explain how many Rubles they'd make together, then stand
around in cocktail parties telling Russian jokes. Bingo the
wheels would start turning. Well, they are turning now, only
in ways Viktor never imagined. He walks around in circles
stopping to face Leo again telling the author that Ivan's
reliability as the money-man is now up in the air, his past
as a porn operator known all over town. 'God knows who'll
be in power after this mess. The people of Renne will force

us to leave. The dream is gone Leo, all in a day.' Viktor's brow is saturated, his breathing shallow, everything around suddenly so remote to him. Sighing, he heads back into Elena's sitting room. Falling hard on the sofa he manages to hurt his back and pointing the remote he stares wide-eyed at the images: Protesters barging by security, taking over the bâtiment, charging into a cinéma.

'Where the hell were the police?'

Blinking at the scenes Viktor bangs his nose with his fist, the buzzer sounding. Leaping up he runs to the intercom his heart fluttering as he says, 'Hallo.'

'C'est moi.' Viktor presses the button, sitting himself down in a chair by the door and clasping his knees. His palms are sweating. Hearing Elena's footsteps on the marble stairs he stands up too fast putting a hand on a wall to steady himself. Rubbing both hands on his hips, trying hard to smile as the lock turns, he blinks at Elena's blurry figure coming inside.

'Uff,' she exclaims putting down her bags. 'Ça va? Tout va bien?'

'Speak Russian Elena. This talk everywhere what do you think it means?'

Straightening up to the full 5'5'' height the former cabaret-dancer often boasts is actually more, she stares back at Viktor. 'What talk? I bought you some nice things.'

'This is not what I expected when I came here.'

Elena frowns at his tone.

'People are saying this American's a communist sympathizer.'

'What American Viktor?'

'They are calling him the new Trotsky, Elena.'

'The French always talk about communism at this time of year.'

'I don't mean ...' Viktor looks around himself, then whispers, 'It's not just the French, Elena. German Dutch and English television are talking about it.'

He follows her inside the kitchen watching her say over her shoulder, 'I see you've been busy.'

'This will become big.'

'What will Viktor?'

'This ... thing.'

'Viktor what thing? It is just French sociologists talking.'

He rubs his head, blinks and grimaces. 'I'm telling you communism is a major issue.'

'You said communism was dead.'

'Listen to me Elena. French intelligence will soon be all over town if they're not already.'

'The intelligentsia are always at the festival. It's just academical talk.'

'I said French intelligence, Elena, not intelligentsia. I thought with the changes in Russia, my new passports, my travel itinerary through Turkey, I could escape any attention. But with this mess I can't avoid scrutiny. Maybe I should give this whole idea a miss. Wait for another time.'

'Viktor you are seventy-five. What other time?'

He goes back into the living room banging his forehead, staggering on the carpet and almost falling.

'You're very pale.'

He sits down, puts his face in his hands.

'You are getting all worked up about this. It's nothing.'

He stares up at her. 'Damn festivals. Friends turn out to be phony then get nasty inside a day. Everyone is so competitive. Petty jealousies rivalries commitments dishonoured. The dressing up and social games you have to play. I am certainly not learning modern dancing Elena. I simply can't fathom these explosions of irrational behaviour.'

'The KGB wasn't irrational?' Elena says walking into her kitchen.

'We had rules Elena. We behaved ourselves,' he calls back.

'Behaved, that what you call it?'

'I have dipped into bad politics before, but this is completely idiotic, plain stupid. Shallow. Impossible. Vain. Dishonest. Disloyalty in my world always had good form. Here there are no rules. Even dishonourable politics has a structure to it. Here everything is upside down. People not only don't mean what they say they tell all these lies as if they believe the lies were true all along. At least we knew when we were lying. The people here cheat on the simplest things flip ideas beliefs in seconds.'

'And the KGB was different?' she calls back.

'Elena, we had controls.'

She comes back inside the lounge room. 'That's what you call it. When I left you were fine, what's happened? Has Ivan pulled out of the deal?'

'No. This whole bâtiment thing Elena. That's what just happened.'

'I don't see anything to worry about.'

'I've been trying to tell you. This chaos at the bâtiment.'

'Every year I have been here there's been chaos at the bâtiment. It's normal.'

'Well, this time it's real chaos.'

'Coming back I heard some noise. I thought some celebrity must have arrived.'

Viktor stands up and switches on the set. 'Look Elena, there are police outside the bâtiment. A huge crowd is there.'

'It's festival time Viktor.'

'This Larry Linsteeg character has taken over a cinema.

He's taken hostages. He's locked the doors..'

'It's called an audience. A captive audience. It's probably just a genre discussion.'

'A what?'

'You are very pale. I'll make tea.'

Viktor wrings his hands watching her going out to the kitchen.

'I was promised that there wouldn't be any politics. Now the festival chief has gone. Where? Nobody knows. This Linsteeg has lost his mind. In my world a man steps out of line like this, dishonours the power that put him where he is like this you stick a gun to his head and renegotiate his priorities. If the French find out about me I have no FSB friends here. I'll be removed in broad-daylight Elena.'

'Have you taken your pills?'

Viktor wrings his hands mumbling again as he walks out into the entrance hall. 'If intelligence here doesn't know about this I'm a monkey's uncle.' He paces back inside the big room, Elena following him around with a tray with a teapot, cups and a plate of strawberries on it.

'Sit down. Have some tea. Aren't these strawberries wonderful? Viktor the fruit here at this time of year is heaven. I got those wonderful biscuits you like. You're getting yourself all worked up over nothing. Maybe you need some vitamins.'

Viktor keeps pacing. 'Elena, they will see me as washed-up wannabe trying to reignite old glories. Worse a never-was. A never-can-forget-his-past kind of guy. A hopeless case on a pension. How humiliating. This whole free-for-all set off by this bloody Larry me-me whoever he is. He's going to explode everything in to a thousand pieces. The French will think I'm part of it.'

'How?'

'There are so many Americans here, Elena. Any one of them could be from Langley. They might even decide to take me and Ivan out.' He points his index finger at his head.

'You're sweating.'

'Of course, I'm sweating. In Moscow temperatures like this in May it's called high summer. Here it's spring. There's no air-conditioning. The fan isn't even working.'

'The man is coming today.'

'Fat chance with this mess at the bâtiment.'

'What mess? I don't see anything strange.'

Elena stares at the screen completely perplexed trying to comprehend what she is missing. 'I'll get you a glass of something. There's something you're not telling me.'

'Isn't this enough?'

'Maybe you ate something. I'm sure the blueberries I bought yesterday were okay. Did you have any more? I hope you washed them well.'

Viktor walks into the kitchen, wipes his face on a tea towel staring at Elena's collection of fridge door reminder cartoon character magnets. 'Get a grip,' he says to himself furiously. Walking unsteadily back inside the living room he sits down and pours some tea.

Swallowing he splutters the drink all over himself as it goes down the wrong way.

'You put vodka in the tea?'

'I'll make another. You should lie down. Or go for a walk.'

'A walk? Did you see all the armed officers? Turn up the volume and listen. Listen to the TV Elena. Listen.'

Grabbing the remote she stands listening to a journalist speaking. 'It looks like a protest.'

'Elena, it's a revolution.'

'People in the market were talking about something going on and they don't usually care about the festival. Someone said an American producer was leading something.'

'It's what I'm saying. This Linsteeg fellow's leading a major revolt.'

Elena stands trying to grasp what Viktor is saying. 'What's so awful?'

'It's nineteen sixty-eight all over again that's what's awful. They've occupied the bâtiment. Linsteeg is leading it.'

'I didn't know these Americans were so political.'

Viktor grins in spite of himself.

'The French love a protest.'

'Remember Prague, Elena?'

'I was a little girl. What do I know about Prague?'

'Well, I saw it. I was there. I don't forget.'

Viktor stands up, both eyes wide, his mouth open as he stares at the TV remembering Prague as if it is happening in Elena's living-room.

'That was another time, Viktor. Times have changed.'

'Plus ça change plus c'est la même chose.'

'I thought you said we had to speak Russian. You really should lie down.'

He obeys her this time feeling suddenly exhausted. Leaning his head back on the couch he stares up at the mottled ceiling, allowing her to take off his shoes.

'Your heart pills Viktor, where are they?'

'In my small black shaving case on the bedside table.'

He looks at her face filled with worry, following her with his eyes as she rushes into her bedroom. Staring back at the TV screen he listens to her go into the kitchen, pouring water and coming back again.

'Here take this. She hands him a glass and two pills.'

'What's this?'

'Your pills.' He stares at them. 'Viktor ... they are your heart pills.'

'You don't see what's happening because you've never experienced it. You think these are French kids just being kids. It's not. This is how it all begins.'

'How what begins?'

'This on the TV. They were talking about Linsteeg and Trotsky.'

'Viktor, Trotsky is dead.'

She studies him staring back at her.

'There's something you're not telling me. What else has happened?'

Viktor puts his hands over his face. 'Ivan's shark fell from a helicopter.'

'WHAT!'

'I told him drawing attention to himself like this was a very bad idea. He said that's why people come to Renne every year, to draw attention to themselves.'

'What happened?'

'He was in the speedboat right under where it was being lowered to the platform. The wires broke and the shark came straight down on him and the driver. Ivan nearly drowned but was saved by some young director. Federico's disappeared.'

'Disappeared?'

'He was driving and the shark landed right smack on top of him. Swallowed him.'

'Oh my god.'

'The shark's gone too.'

'Where?'

'Into the bay.'

'I thought it was dead.'

'So did I.'

'Was this on TV?'

'Nowhere. It's all hush hush.'

'My god. How did you find out?'

'A crewmember called me. I went searching for some news and I saw this mess at the bâtiment.'

'So, this is why you're upset.'

'Elena. I think it is part of the whole thing. It has that feel to it. Two things happening together. A two-pronged attack. I've seen it before.'

'Viktor, take your pills. Okay. Now drink the water.'

STEPHEN KING IS RIGHT. Déjà-vu is a hallucination you can only have in French. Daniel Martin found this statement on the Web earlier this morning: Le déjà-vu est la sensation d'avoir déjà été témoin ou d'avoir déjà vécu une situation présente accompagnée d'une sensation d'irréalité d'étrangeté. The sense of being punched is with Daniel again and how, Daniel staggering around as if only half-conscious accompanied by an inner glow of the higher purpose associated with all current ambitions, defining the leader he always knew he could be in time. Pacing the floor in front of the picture window studying the Soraya, hoping his vision isn't too optimistic he does a little jig. One more luxury yacht at anchor is one more vote in the bank. A thought stops him—he has to keep his coup alive.

Opportunity came courtesy of a director's fist at the bâtiment. Daniel convinced Léo it was Edgar Gordon Olles's fault, or so Daniel is convincing himself now that he convinced Léo. Whatever the truth pans out to be he won't let this chance fly out the door. After examining every inch of the luck that got him to where he is right now, instinct tells him not to take anything lightly. Today is a day for getting things right. With fate on his side, Daniel can't do anything wrong. God wants him to run this festival and Daniel must do his level best to prove God's right.

First-up, Daniel has to organise this idiot producer into Daniel's God given plans. Turn Larry Linsteeg into a transformational agent. The sky is the limit if Daniel can manage this. His phone startles him. Picking it up carefully, he listens as his secretary tells him a police commander is still waiting outside.

'Tell him I won't be long.' Putting the phone down Daniel smiles out again at the Russian's boat. The ship of fools where punchy is hiding, punchy who has never done so much for another human with a single punch ever before. Gifting Daniel the blow that's changed his life. Whispering, 'Beware of the downsides. Ivan the Terrible must play his part in this. Stay savvy, join the dots, weld the director's off-the-wall biff into more than a one-off by a stupid director. This fool is your ace in the hole.' Daniel knows he must keep Larry Linsteeg and all the protesters inside Salle Truffaut for as long as possible. Combing his hair, he mumbles a prayer, and taking several deep breaths of the air-conditioning heads over to his door. Opening up, he announces brightly:

'Inspector, bonjour, I am afraid I still can't find him.'

'Chief inspector, monsieur. You tried his mobile?'

'There's no answer. He went swimming is all I know.'

'Swimming? Then send security out.'

'I'm afraid it's not in their job description.'

'Then write it in, monsieur.'

'I have to convene a board meeting to do that, inspector.'

'Chief inspector.'

The inspector's men are milling around over by an escalator, their automatic weapons catching Daniel's eye as the door closes, the inspector taking Daniel firmly by his upper arm, Daniel flinching at the hours the flic has spent in the gym.

'Television stations are saying we must go in.'

'Storm the Truffaut?' Daniel manages to get his arm free. 'People will get hurt.'

'Older guests in there will be at greater risk if we don't.'

'More at risk if we do.'

'The protesters are threatening people.'

'You have proof of that?'

'Televisions are broadcasting tweets from mobiles and computers of trapped participants.'

'I will decide soon.'

'Let's synchronize on that shall we.'

'Synchronize what, inspector?'

'Chief inspector...I suggest we find Léo.'

'He can't be located.'

'Then I suggest we wait five minutes, then go in.'

'I think it's best to negotiate.'

'We do that it is 1968 all over again.'

ALONE IN HER BÂTIMENT OFFICE Zeena Zatters in tears holds her head in her hands as she tries to figure out a last-minute festival invitation conundrum. In her intern role, the daughter of her more or less ex-dad Claude, stares at her computer in a deep panic. Claude, the renown Paris-based sex-lite rom-com director-writer-producer, who asked Léo Stern a week before for the favour for his practically-speaking ex-daughter, is not around to help her.

Léo being Léo agreed to do his old friend the favour.

Claude admitted that Zeena doesn't know her Fellini from linguine, but it didn't matter. 'The job's easy,' Léo said. 'She'll get the hang of it in no time.'

Except, getting the hang of it has multiple interpretations for Zeena right now. She finds foreign problems so difficult she's wondering if that's the only reason she got the job in the first place. No one else wanted it. The way things are going Zeena will still be in this office at seven tonight, and without her Dad in town she has no child-of-kudos to fall back on for fun party invites for afters.

She is shaping-up to be the year's princess zero. Missing the flying shark and the rescue of the porn filmmaker, tonight she will be taking the same dark road back to her crumby apartment on the wrong side of the tracks.

Hunched over her computer, she is currently trying to understand who Madame Morendo is. Zeena is unable to get a fix on the woman. For two hours, Zeena has been sitting here trying to resolve how two festival guests, Madame Morendo and Semolina Pynes, have been assigned the same room in l'Hôtel Sublime.

While Semolina Pynes is booked in, Zeena only has a Zurich address for Madame Morendo. To check her out Zeena googled the woman and found a Morendo listed as a top-floor occupant of an apartment in a company premises called Assisted Departures. Assisted what?

Zeena giggled at first then her blood ran cold. Madame Morendo's missing room is no laughing matter. So, Zeena wrote a long and lovely letter to her, then realized it wouldn't arrive in time. The woman was already on the train. She's arriving on the TGV this very night. And Zeena has no mobile number for her. So, Madame Death, as Zeena is now calling her, will arrive exhausted and find no room.

Panic is off the scale for Zeena right now. Then things really go haywire when Semolina Pynes phones suddenly from the Sublime Hôtel to say a Madame Morendo just called her asking why Semolina is in her room. First-up Zeena thought it was a joke. How could Morendo know what Zeena is still trying to work out? Then Zeena got spooked.

Hanging up she sat with an oh-my-god moment really sinking in. Morendo is Death for real and death knows everything. Zeena is now on Morendo's hit list.

Suddenly Zeena's phone rings again. Thinking it's Madame Morendo chasing her, Zeena lets it go to voicemail. Checking her messages, she finds it's only her mum calling from New York. Her hands trembling, Zeena calls her mom back and breaking-down hiccups out details of her nightmarish day.

'The festival will fire me. Dad will be embarrassed. Mom, this is the worst holiday I have ever had.'

'You are working,' Wanda reminded her. 'Calm down.'

'Mom, maybe Semolina is Madame Morendo after all.'

'Honey, Semolina was in Manhattan's Bellevue hospital last week. I know because I saw her. I delivered her première gown. She was having a cyst removed from her butt so she could wear her stripped own bikini on the beach. She's never lived in Switzerland.'

At this point Zeena begins crying uncontrollably. In between sobs she wails: 'The festival will blame me for this. They'll fire me. Then Morendo will track me down and kill me.' With her daughter in such a state, Wanda phones ex-hubby Claude on another line. Claude, who left Wanda for a seventeen-year-old stick thin Belgian actress a year before, throws his hands up in the air and rings Léo on another of his phones.

Finding out to his shock Léo is no longer head of the festival Claude yells: 'what the hell is going on?' Léo says, 'I'll tell you later.' Then Léo being Léo tells Claude not to worry. He'll fix it. And using another of his phones Léo resolves the dilemma by calling his former-deputy, knowing full-well Daniel will consider any favour done for Léo at this point in time as one worth three in the proverbial Provençal bush.

Morendo has now been assigned a new Sublime double room and another room charge is on the festival's tab. Léo rings Claude back with the news. Relieved, Claude rings Wanda back who rings their daughter back and calms her down.

'Zee, it's a win-win for all.'

Zeena's eyes are dry again.

'Buck up. Enjoy yourself. No more dramas.'

'No mum.'

'Get out and meet people.'

'Yes mum.'

Happy again, Zeena thanks her mum and ringing off says aloud: 'This job's not so bad after-all.'

She began thinking about her other festival problem. What the hell is she going to do tonight? Stay in or go out? Finishing off another small thing, Zeena sits staring at her screen thinking: why don't I just go on over to l'Hôtel Sublime and apologize to Semolina Pynes in person, tell her all about this little kerfuffle. Maybe I can apologize to Madame Morendo as well while I'm there, if she has already arrived. It could be a way of making two friends in one, get me out and about as mum said. And as her dad still says, her mum's always right.

LÉO'S SUDDEN DISAPPEARANCE had journalists asking what on earth is going on. The festival is Léo's life. He put in a new emphasis on cinema from so many lesser-known destinations. He downplayed the influence of Hollywood. Few journalists believe Daniel Martin's Léo swam away from his responsibilities fairytale. Léo's been swimming the bay for years. It would take a real catastrophe to drive Léo out of town. He's not going to just disappear out in the big blue. Seasoned festival watchers agree. A man so in love with his job, disappearance is out of character. Long-time correspondent Annalise de la Forêt says the real true blue know-alls at this festival don't believe a word of Daniel's tale. 'Did they poison Léo then?' some ask. Journalists are thinking the worst. Sinister events have a way of happening out to sea. Is this another one?

Whatever the truth, the bâtiment is in lockdown, the press office is closed, and Annalise can't even get her snail mail.

Without Léo everything's hopelessly out-of-hand, blame falling straight on the feckless usurping deputy. Another rumour, from a far from reliable source is that Léo may well have seen some hidden writing on the wall and taken-off to save his professional skin. When internet blogger Rob Le Riche says in The Snake's Daily Log that this may be the truth, the reaction isn't: 'Come on. Who believes this rumour monger? Did the snake mention this festival? No. I don't believe him. Nor do I.' No, the uncorroborated becomes corroborated within hours. Sooner. When it was first posted. Many now say this could well be true. Soon, experienced hands are quoting the snake's ideas, borrowing his in-depth backgrounders, weaving them into frontpage reports they send out about Léo receiving prior-warning of a protest from higher-ups.

At first, some Léo-loyal senior journalists refuse to believe a word the snake has written, then even they, one by one, with all the rest, begin agreeing that Snyder the Snake is probably right. His quoting of unattributed sources becomes the new probable. Then all's true, all within a few hours.

Weeks before, Rob wrote how a well-funded underground group with shady international connections was planning to disrupt a major Riviera festival. Back then of course nobody took any notice. Now everyone's believing everything the snake's ever said. Even his weather reports are gospel. The ideas that weren't considered plausible are now normal, life long held beliefs old hands always held. Everyone has been completely swept away. The take-away from the snake's influential post is this: Léo isn't the only one in jeopardy. An attack on French film culture is underway.

'A bunch of kids protesting about tickets is an attack on French culture? Are you serious? If the kids hadn't broken into the bâtiment we wouldn't even be discussing the snake.'

But they are discussing the snake and the kids are still inside the Truffaut cinéma.

'Security wasn't ready.'

'They're never ready.'

'I give the protest a day.'

'They'll be gone tomorrow.'

'They are all over social media.'

'The web forgets. Mark my words.'

'What do they want again?'

'Tickets to all the films.'

'Tickets, is that all? Then give them what they want.'

THE NIGHT BEFORE HIS DISAPPERANCE Léo called Daniel to say he was making him acting director, in order to keep the peace. Daniel didn't ask, what peace? No, he just saw an opportunity, and even without any written confirmation he's now peddling Léo's last words as if they are irrefutably true, a pristine truth, with one rider many find too ludicrous to repeat: 'If anyone asks, I've gone swimming.'

Léo went swimming. And, so far, nobody has challenged Daniel on this. Bracing himself for the coming trials Daniel sits at Léo's desk trying to think of ways of removing acting from his title.

Fiddling with his tie in Léo's mirror like the schoolboy he still looks like, Daniel mumbles to himself, rehearsing his spiel in a low voice: 'I am honoured to take on this responsibility. I'm privileged to represent this great festival and sell it to the world. I am up for the challenge. I'll leave no stone unturned. I am a stable genius.'

Energized by the sound of his own voice, even as a creeping dread makes his stomach gurgle again. He checks his hair in Léo's mirror again, pats his face, sucks-in a couple of quick breaths and flicking on a recorder switch under the desk he stands buttocks clenched in a final check of Léo's former-office. 'Be the part.' His assistant pokes her head around the door catching his last words, announcing wide-eyed: 'They're here.'

'Who's they?'

'The Biènville commander of tactical response.'

'The Chief Inspector?'

She points skyward. 'His boss. Général Henri something,' she whispers, 'with a man called F and the maire's aide.'

Daniel blinks, his stomach gurgling as he wrestles a brave smile up onto his face. 'Show them in,' he says his voice higher than he planned. His assistant grimaces, wringing her hands as a shadow appears behind her, the commanding officer of the Biènville tactical response group Général Henri Pilot of the Groupe d'Intervention de la Gendarmerie Nationale walking in, his hip grazing Daniel's assistant's shoulder. She runs back to her desk as Daniel ushers his guests inside trying hard not to look like an assistant himself. Seeing the round-faced mayoral aide appear they exchange brief schoolboy smirks. His older brother's sixteen-year-old twins scuttle inside and run over to two chairs by the window, grinning, as they pull out their pads and pens ready to record Uncle Daniel's first crisis meeting as acting-director.

Daniel's palms are sweating, ditto his underarms, crotch, forehead and backs of both knees.

'I hear you have been in the wars.'

Daniel is not sure what he means but doesn't miss the Biènville commander's ironic tone. The général touches his own face just below a cheek.

'All in the line of duty général,' Daniel says.

'Not what I heard.'

'It hurt for a second.'

The général gives Daniel a sceptical grin. 'I was going to a consultation lunch with colleagues in Biènville. This better be important.' Daniel nods his unconvincing gratitude the général's way, mumbling his thanks to the man for even turning-up. Daniel needs the général more than most, or at least thinks he does. Clearing his throat, he makes his first statement as CEO.

'Asseyez-vous messieurs s'il vous plaît.'

The général keeps pacing back and forth his face with its air of disbelief, rubbing his hands, then nodding coldly at the last man to arrive.

The greetings now complete, Daniel's guests each regard each other with equal dismay. Nobody moves towards the solitary chair. Daniel Martin yells: 'CHAISES S'IL VOUS PLAÎT.' His brother's twins get the message, leaping up in a blur of action to bring their chairs to the front of Daniel's desk. Placing them side by side they run back to their new window spots in the warm sun.

The last guest to arrive, F, from the Direction Générale de la Sécurité Extérieure, seats himself strategically opposite Daniel staring pointedly over the new director's head. The mayoral aide alongside him fiddles constantly with his phone and won't look at anyone. The général grimaces constantly as he stretches his right leg. Finally he gets himself seated. Daniel grins bravely around at all.

'Welcome.'

Nobody replies. It's hardly the grand start to his first in-charge meeting that he was hoping for but it has begun. Daniel manages to describe the day's events from the protest to occupation of a cinema without his voice trembling, glancing more than once at F's benign stare still fixed on a point somewhere behind Daniel's head. The maire's aide is mute. The général occasionally grimaces and stares anywhere but at Daniel. Then he breaks the ice.

'Where is Léo then?'

'He can't be found général.'

'Tried his mobile?'

'It's with his clothes on the ground floor.'

'Léo's been moved to the ground floor?'

'He uses a ground floor changing room.'

'Change room for what?'

'For his swimming.'

There's a silence as everyone digests this.

'He really went swimming?'

Tapping a pencil on Léo's blotter-pad on a desk that is

still clearly seen as Léo's by everyone in this room, including Daniel, he is painfully aware that his first meeting as CEO is close to spiralling out of control.

'Who found his clothes?'

'Security.'

'Nothing on the beach?'

'No.'

There's another silence in the room.

The général groans, getting up. 'Send someone to look more.'

'They have been very busy. That's an unruly crowd outside.'

'It's a riot,' F says, making his first intervention.

'A protest is not a riot,' the général barks, standing his full height.

'How would you describe a riot then?'

'It's not a riot F.'

'Have it your way. Let us say we are at the beginning of the start of an idea which could become a riot. We need to get reinforcements in before it does become one and closes down the city.'

The maire's aide flashes F an alarmed look. 'Madame Maire doesn't want any closures.'

'Tell her to talk to the général.'

The général sits down hard on a wooden side-board showing his teeth as he stretches his leg. 'Yes, tell her that.'

'We need to stop this now, général,' F says with a sigh.

'Messieurs!' Martin wonders if he should look exasperated as well. 'Stop it how?'

'Go in with armed personnel.'

'Special operations go wrong. I've seen many similar situations.'

'Under your command maybe général.'

The général glares at F. 'How on earth would you know? You work behind closed doors. You're a civilian. I work in the street, in uniform.'

Daniel Martin puts his hands up. 'Messieurs, s'il vous plaît.'

'The Mairie is prepared to cooperate, Daniel, but if this gets any more unstable then Monsieur F may just be right.' The maire's aide grins sheepishly back at Daniel's frowning face. 'Madame Maire suggests that we should find Léo and ask him back.' Daniel is a minute from ending a life-long friendship.

'We're looking for him. A boat came back just now. They found nothing.'

The général shakes his head. 'What boat? I thought you said you were too busy to look.'

'I kept it quiet.'

'From us?'

Shocked at how easily he trapped himself, Daniel darts plaintive looks at all three participants in a meeting that is already in a bad place. 'I didn't want to create consternation.'

'Consternation?'

'I mean I didn't want to create panic.'

Silence fills the room.

'We'll wait five minutes, then go in.'

'F, we won't declare an emergency until it's necessary.'

'The longer this goes, the worse it'll get général.'

'F, stop trying to stoke this up.'

'What's your solution then?'

Resourceful if nothing else in bad going ugly moments, getting out of the bar Larry's writer ran to the beach, where he received a very brief briefing of the shark-event, and learning of Ivan's ad-hoc survival celebrations he found himself a seat on a runabout taking early-bird partygoers out to the Russian's still-winding-up survival shindig.

Once on board the Russian's yacht Larry's writer did what he does well. He roamed. At first aimlessly, aimlessness being one of his tick-this-box personality or lack thereof characteristics. Still, he believes in the roaming, and it worked, because a chance meeting with Edgar occurred, apparently the man of the hour, and Edgar rewarded Larry's writer's aimlessness with "the story" first-hand so far.

So, with things turning up after his poor second start to his first day, in a bar, where he shouldn't have been at all, Larry's writer is feeling almost good about his choices now, staring over the water with Edgar at an empty wooden swimming platform wobbling in a stiffening wind.

Larry's writer has learned that the wood is covered in broken glass. He can't see the evidence of this but he sure as hell isn't swimming over there to check if Edgar is telling the truth. He's taking Edgar's word.

What Larry's writer believes he knows is that a half-sunk speedboat and a swimming platform form the site of Ivan Dzerzhinsky's art failure, though he's not saying those words out loud, and the waters all-around technically represent an as yet undeclared crime scene.

Technically it could be classed as a crime scene if a crime has been committed, which is not yet clear. So far nobody has declared it as one. Will that need to be done? Larry's writer writes in his pad, then corrects this note. What he can say for sure, if he can believe this witness, is that Edgar dropped his small digital camera on the sand, tore off his clothes and swam out, not thinking of anything other than saving a drowning man. Larry's writer wondered if Edgar really dropped his camera in sand but shrugged that off. The Russian by the name of Ivan Dzerzhinsky is the man he really wants to know more about. And so far in this action phase of the story, which could make a good opener for an article or film, or even an action-hero TV series episode à la Sea Hunt, Larry's writer finds Edgar a lucid and detail specific witness.

When Edgar got to the man, he wasn't moving. Edgar rolled him over, Larry's writer asking himself: Who would want to drag a corpse to shore? Two girls yelling from fifty meters away made the decision for Edgar and he headed with the body where they were pointing. Edgar said he had never done any lifesaving before, never dragged anyone through water alive or dead. When he arrived at the big boat he thought he would be welcomed but all he discovered were frantic crewmen yelling at him in Russian.

Two men jumped in the water, grabbed the shape from him and pulled it up onto a back-landing, Edgar almost saying, you're not going to blame me for this now, are you? He clambered up too, feeling miffed that nobody offered him a hand. The man he had saved looked stone cold dead. So, seeing the Russian crew running around in a blind panic Edgar did what he thought any sensible person would do under the circumstances, something he never knew he could do—he gave what he still thought was a dead man mouth to mouth resuscitation. It wasn't pleasant, but he's not going into that. The bare bones of the facts are this: he held a dead man's nose in his thumb and forefinger and breathed spent air into the shape as if his own life depended on what he was doing. At that moment he thought it did. As he recounted to

Larry's writer, Edgar thought the Russians would probably kill him if he failed. What seemed like ten desperate minutes went by before the Russian coughed-up muck all over him.

A crewmember gave what sounded like a woman's scream and ran off, coming back with a small tank of oxygen and a mask. Somehow still in charge of this situation, Edgar got the mask on, and started the oxygen feed, and after some tense TV drama moments, the Russian's chest began moving. Crewmembers put him on a stretcher, carrying him up deck by deck to the top, Edgar now fully realizing who it was exactly he had just saved. He brought Ivan back to life. The ship's owner. The Russian so many in town are talking about.

Hundreds on the beach saw it happen, some no doubt with binoculars, so word was probably spreading.

The details of all this, and before that, the snapping steel wires from a giant teacup hanging from a helicopter as it circled a swimming platform, only make Larry's writer's choices that morning seem even worse. 'It was too dark inside the cup,' Edgar kept saying. 'I didn't know what was inside until green liquid went everywhere and this thing fell straight at a speedboat.' Whatever it was hit the boat-driver flush, taking the driver over the side, the fallen-thing and him disappearing. That is all on his camera. Voices on the beach told him a shark had swallowed a boat driver and knocked a passenger clean out of his seat, the glass cup splintering everywhere hitting the platform.

'In the middle of all that two girls on the back of the speedboat somehow did backflips into the water and escaped. The helicopters disappeared, where to nobody knows. Another boat arrived, drove around a bit, then headed back here.'

Larry's writer sat blinking putting this all down, Edgar saying that if his camera is still on the beach he has the makings of a good film.

'You're a hero.'

Edgar waved this away. If he's a hero, he doesn't care. Girls call to him to come on down, a pair serenading him with Russian songs. It doesn't matter. So many girls in bikinis all around him and Edgar sits there staring into space, his eyes at times like a mummy on downers.

A DJ above began testing his equipment, blaring sounds coming from big speakers, 'We have a hero on board today' and somebody yelled, 'Grand Poisson for Death,' partygoers cheered, Edgar looked genuinely upset.

'It's going be a rough night.'

Edgar stared at his hands.

'Survival parties often are,' Larry's writer said. A crewmember went by saying in heavily accented-English: 'You're the man.' Edgar nodded as if he didn't believe a word of it. Still, he pumped fists with the guy and agreed to sign the man's t-shirt in his cabin, telling Larry's writer he'd be back.

Watching more runabouts arriving and Ivan's ship filling up Larry's writer is beside himself with fury.

'I was in a bar.' He still can't believe he got it so wrong.

Still, he did manage to record Bella Fibben's arrival. There is that at least. And it was a laugh. Leaning against a palm in the main boulevard at 7am sharp Larry's writer saw Bella's henchmen offload heavy metal trunks from a line of SUVs outside the Grand Hôtel, the boss in wrap-around sunglasses glancing Larry's writer's way as his workers, ex-soldier types by their size and manner, sweated over the load. Getting the hint he wasn't welcome Larry's writer hiked off down the boulevard going by Bella's fleet of twelve Mercedes 4 x 4s blocking the waterfront.

The town was barely awake and already a line of vintage cars stretched right out of town—a gridlocked 1975 midnight blue Lamborghini Countach, one 1962 three-litre V12 250 Gran Turismo Omologato red Ferrari, and a 1956 Packard Caribbean Convertible with reversible cushions and shark-skin interior. This gives Larry's writer a smile at least. At seven in the morning a vintage car rally was ruined by Bella's SUVs, flummoxed drivers seated in silk and linen tapping angrily at their steering wheels.

A girl appearing out of nowhere brings him back. Introducing herself as Ulyana, Ivan's assistant, she leads him upstairs, telling him Edgar wants him there to record Ivan and his conversation.

'This is a replacement for a Hôtel Sables reception.'

Without any background to the Sables gig none of what she is saying makes a lot of sense.

They find Ivan wrapped-up in a duvet, two huge pillows behind his head, speaking to Edgar in a state of vivid animation for someone who nearly drowned.

'You're worried about punching that guy? You think it'll wreck your chances? My guess it will do the opposite.'

Ivan coughs heavily, speaking hoarsely to all around.

'Day one this kid punches the festival's deputy. Day two he saves me. He's doing well. They don't want me here and he saved me.'

Laughing, Ivan pauses to study Larry's writer before coughing again. He stops finally. 'I hear you're a writer. What are you writing?'

'I'm recording what is going on.'

'You a journalist?'

'I write screenplays.'

'Any good ones?'

He shakes his head. 'Well, some maybe.'

'What films do you like?'

'You know Ace in the Hole.'

'You write things like that?'

'No, but I could. If I had been born before I was.'

This gets Ivan looking at him hard. 'You two crazies should do a story together.'

'We've been talking about it,' Edgar says quietly.

Have we? Larry's writer almost says.

'What the hell actually happened out there?'

Larry's writer stares dumbfoundedly back at Ivan Dzerzhinsky giving them both a heavy look.

'I don't know,' Edgar says finally. 'I was busy swimming.'

'Somebody must have seen something and worked it out.'

'It happened pretty fast.'

'You have enough for a film?'

'If my camera is still there and if I can get what the chopper shot as well.'

'They were filming up there?'

Edgar nods. 'I could do with what you have here on board too.'

'My security cameras.'

'You have a few.'

Ivan laughs. 'Take him in to the beach. You want to go?'

Startled, Larry's writer turns to go before Ivan can say anymore. Following Edgar and Ulyana, trying to walk as well as any actor he's seen, Larry's writer trips at the cabin door divide, going knee-first onto the deck. Struggling upright he hears Ivan having another coughing and laughing fit.

THREE HOURS INTO THE OCCUPATION Zucca's already unable to focus a lens in front of his face, hearing a far-off voice complaining: 'They've switched off the air.'

Zucca didn't notice it go off so how long they have been without oxygen he has no idea. It's so hot and steamy he finds concentrating impossible and has for quite some time. Completely absorbed in losing focus, only now Zucca realizes he's drenched in sweat. Down at the front on two numb legs he's been praying on bloodless knees for a perfect pic, the definitive shot of Larry. When the kid yelled out about the air being dead Larry's blurry sweaty face made complete sense. No hero on a journey to his political beatification is in front of Zucca anymore, the shot he was hoping for. Zucca's take on the big guy is now no longer paranoid Larry but a portrait of a man about to fall off the stage any second.

Zucca wanted a sharp political leader on heat kind-of pic, not a sweaty psychological puzzle play everyone stares at for ages to understand, only to give up trying and begin feeling sorry for the guy. Zucca's trying hard to be professional but if you asked him what he actually means by what he wants i.e. really needs right now he couldn't say. Whispering, 'Keep it simple, Zuk,' he's now trying to indicate to the big guy something of what he needs but Larry isn't looking down at him or into the lens anymore.

Larry asked if anyone would like to join him by pulling their film out of competition as well. There was no response. Larry's face fell at that point looking like it wasn't coming back up. 'This is your show,' Zucca kept on hissing. 'You don't need their say-so. You don't need any moral support from them. Who are these fools and what do they know anyway. You're the guy, the guy who's telling us, so tell us big guy. Get on board your own ideas.'

Zucca shouldn't be getting involved in the management of his subject's motivation of course. He's not meant to direct the thoughts of any subject he's shooting. That's professionally unethical. He sighs. So, he's unethical. For a moment he's staying on the floor praying someone will take up his point about Larry having to own this protest but all Zucca hears are voices yelling: 'Get the jury over.'

'Tell them to bring my medication while they're at it,' a white-haired woman near the front says again, older audience members murmuring their sympathy. A blinking Larry stands immobile, staring out at the audience, Zucca whispering: 'Be strong! This is your destiny! Play the part.' Zucca's wondering if his pics will add-up to a ten-dollar fire-sale now. Mobile phones are everywhere. Who cares what a professional photographer does anymore. Zucca's quest for a true portrait of a great man in a moment of truth is looking like another fruitless search. Damn the internet, Twitter and Facebook and the whole freaky-deaky world-wide-web probably full of images of Larry the Looney protester-layabout already. Grainy out-of-focus pics but who cares. They're probably all over social media attached to some half-baked commentary about this joker's stupid, nefarious deed, all filled in with how he came from some ugly unknown past, heaped into another bleak news-story that bleary-eyed on-liners stare at without comprehension.

The sceptical voice sounds again: 'The reason you're doing this Larry is because Death at Intervals hasn't a hope in hell of winning anything.'

Zucca watches more blood drain from Larry's head, the guy looking like he's ready to have a stroke. Zucca takes another shot of him. A kid comes to Larry's aid, yelling:

'Death's a great story, a truly great film.'

Silence resumes full-service. In the meantime, Larry has a new blinking fit up on stage continuing to stare out at a divided audience. Without someone handing him pages ten to sixteen of today's script he's flummoxed, beaten, snookered, a stage-struck actor who's lost his lines. Forgotten the plot and the lines more like it, in triplicate. Alone out on the boards Larry hasn't a clue what to do anymore. He doesn't even know how to get off this stage even. Support remains for him among the young marchers, but the oldies have him worked out, as a male voice yells: 'Is this just another promotional charade to sell your film?'

Zucca hisses, 'Larry, you're embarrassing yourself.' He watches Larry run a rueful hand over his scalp, smiling too hard to be believed.

Then the octogenarian Greek director George Pallas holds up his iPhone and shouts: 'We are on Greek TV.' Oddly, this perks everyone up. Then a woman yells: 'FRANCE 24 est en ligne.' 'BBC too,' a voice calls out. 'Danish TV now as well,' calls another. 'ARD in Germany.' The bâtiment break-in has Europe-wide coverage. It's taken the pressure off. People are smiling again. Larry looks very relieved. Zucca struggles upright again and takes another shot.

TUCKED INSIDE CREAM FLANNEL TROUSERS, fidgeting at a chain as he gees himself up for the moment, Jack Kimmelon motors away from the Sunshine Coast, heading towards the Russian's floating palace rehearsing what he's going to say along the way—'I saw the whole damn thing, the helicopters, the tank, whatever it was, that big fish falling from the sky.'

Tying up at the Russian's ramp Jack repeats his mantra for tonight: 'Don't blow it, whatever you do don't blow it.' Staggering upstairs he sidles through some young things falling prey to old habits almost immediately—a condition he calls CPSSS. Current Production Status Stress Syndrome. Whenever Jack develops it he loses general control of his hands, occasionally both elbows as well, giving way to his primal urges. In stress-filled moments he's prone to handling in the area especially when he's close to young sets of mammary glands. Patting the invite in his pocket, he knows he's probably on another errant fool's errand tonight as he silently recites his list of excuses. Poor eyesight. Lost my glasses etc. He staggers-on through another thicket of promising young flesh keeping his hands to himself so far, knowing Merryl is probably following his progress with the Sunshine's binoculars.

MERRYL REALISED EARLY ON she had to stop attending anything with him. Unfortunately, the bigger the feminine assets around him, the quicker Jack seemed to lose his way at parties. Recently she's been hard at filling his head with #metoo stories but Jack is a stubborn old goat. Merryl won't try to enlighten him on what he should do in places like Renne at festival time. She sighs and leaves him to run on his own impulses alone. He is free to manage his tendencies and deal with the consequences. By the look of tonight's crowd, there's plenty of young things. Using binoculars, Merryl has seen a couple Jack will need to watch himself with. If he wants to motor home with his skin attached to his body he better be at his sprightly best.

RECHECKING THE INVITE in his top pocket, Jack's reading Merryl's mind. Thinking he's out of her eye-shot by now, he gets ready to whip out his bona fides, silently re-rehearsing the old excuse—sorry darling, my think gland is on the blink.

The night's just begun and already Jack's brain is fighting fuzzy. He's forgotten his planned spiel twice, the youth of some of these beauties confusing him more than usual, getting him skipping every few paces, grinning as he grazes, softly uttering, miming really, stock-standard apologies one after another.

'There you go darling. Very sorry. I'm a bit clumsy tonight. Oops. Sorry dear.'

Some girls frown. One cupped an ear. A third took a swing with a free arm, skimming the limit of Jack's thinning hair. If he doesn't watch it he'll end up in the drink. His survival instincts are in overload, the sound system battering him into a stupor, the simplest things in life becoming impossible as heavy-metal and rap gets in at close quarters. Jack can't hear himself think let alone manage verbal responses. So he resorts to mime, elbowing his way, grinning, stroking and grazing. 'Is this the replacement for the cancelled shindig?' he sprays at one beauty as he liberally samples her chest, discovering a face tougher than the rest.

'One hundred euros old man. We can use the boat's loo.'

'WHAT?'

'You want to have a chat down on the back?'

'God, forget it.'

Can't she, or he, tell Jack's a man of cinematic stature, a cine-fellow who doesn't need to pay for his nocturnal sexual proclivities.

Furious at the slight Jack jams his invite further down inside his front pocket, nearly falling over as he wades less gracefully more elbowly through another promising thicket of female flesh a third his age.

'There was more space on deck at the end of Titanic,' he croons at a young blond, who rewards this chesty imprint of his right paw with a sharp near-miss right cross that grazes his forehead. 'Jesus,' he yells, 'sorry darling. Bad balance. I need to right myself on board now and then.' He grips his left knee to demonstrate the problem.

'Bullshit,' she yells back. Jack ducks but her follow-up left doesn't miss, leaving him with an excruciating pain in his right ear. What these girls can't do, the DJ will do for them. The rap is wrecking his brain, the guy up top hammering and tonging-away at Jack's jukebox street cred, as he manages to stagger away in time to miss a blow from the second girl he has his paws on.

Jack steadies himself this time to the good, but this girl scores a kick to his lower right leg. Limping away, he wears his frown bravely, and spying a new pair of jugs lunges involuntarily. This set is rock hard, and a handy Trans leaves him nursing a fresh facial-injury he'll really need to explain to Merryl. 'The boat lurched Merryl. I bumped my head.'

Jack's had some epic confrontations already tonight and he's only been at this party five minutes. He glares up at the DJ: 'Can't you give the gangbusters a rest, son.'

Moments like this have him regretting he ever got involved in home entertainment systems. Jack has seen less smoke at a biker's picnic. He's half-deaf and now dizzy from what the kids are toking. Jack's not averse to a bong or two but this lot will have him catatonic. Staggering on breathless he begins recalling his greatest film-party success of all time. The Bouzouki Bash, Dassin and Mercouri's Never on Sunday party that kicked Jack's career into orbit back in the 60s.

He got to dance with a famous Swedish blond a good head taller than him. She had a great pair. His hands operated in a different universe back then. Speak of the devil. Another blond has her eye on him. Even with his specs off she looks promising. As tall as the Swede too. Jack raises his elbows. 'This über-banging is detaching my cranium from the rest of me darling. They'll dump me at sea stone deaf before the night's over.' Deciding to postpone an errant elbow, he extends his hand. Trying a bit of verbal charm for a change.

'Jack Kimmelon at your service.'

'Don't you remember me, Jack?'

'Were you at the Never on Sunday party?'

'Ulyana. Monaco. I'm Ivan's PA.'

Jack stares at her, a long-lost grin appearing from somewhere in the back of his head. 'Of course! Sorry, I dropped my book things in the drink.'

'They're in your pocket.'

Jack's manhandles his own chest. 'Bingo. Well spotted! What's your name again?'

'I think Ivan would like to speak to you.'

'Have I done something wrong?'

Before he can get an explanation she drags him through a thicket of young things so fast Jack can't get a handful in edgeways, ducking his head the whole way just in case one of the young beauties recognizes him. He'll stay twenty minutes maybe, then head back, tell Merryl she was right. It isn't worth it. All the banging and clanging going on. Jack yells at the back of the blond's head, 'Maybe the DJ could have the rest of the night off. What do you think?'

'Wait here, Jack.' And she's gone. Jack covers his face with his hanky in case a girl he groped earlier goes by. Standing, his head still buzzing and ringing, he tries conjuring up some-sort of presentable introduction for Ivan. Why he is even on his boat? That'll do for starters. Jack doesn't want to get too complicated. Losing his balance, the hanky falling off, he latches a hand on to the shoulder of a Mark Ruffalo lookalike by his side. 'Hollywood Reporter right. You're on the cover.' The Mark Ruffalo lookalike squints at him. 'You're the guy who clocked the deputy.'

'Am I on the cover?'

'Don't be embarrassed, son. Everybody needs a moment of fame.' Jack scours his brain for more street cred jargon.

'What's your moniker?'

The guy cups an ear.

'YOUR MONIKER. YOUR NAME.'

'Edgar Gordon Olles.'

'Jack Kimmelon, producer.'

'Of what?'

'Godfather Four. Jaws Six.'

Edgar squints at him. 'You doing G4, J6?'

The DJ starts up again.

'What film you say you did?'

'I didn't, Jack. Death at Intervals.'

Jack cups an ear. 'Death at Innsbruck? That an action movie Ed?' The music stops right as he yells: 'I LOVE ACTION MOVIES.'

'It's not an action movie.'

The DJ's music starts up again.

'Based on a novel by José Saramago.'

His ears buzzing Jack squints in incomprehension at the young man's face.

'SIR WHO?'

THE OCCUPATION is beyond its seventh hour. With several bottles of a local prize-winning white wine empties and tawdry remains of a buffet-spread on an oak table getting staler by the second, any sense of camaraderie has disintegrated in Daniel's emergency control-group session.

The meeting's taking on a dogged atmosphere as it staggers toward night.

Two solutions are on the table—Go in—Don't go in—Daniel unwaveringly wavering in the middle, wondering how much longer he can remain in limbo and still be in charge.

When Madame la Maire Pietra Colombes finally arrived, pumped-up by her own well-oiled late-lunch elsewhere, one that rolled over into a self-styled brainstorming booster session over cognacs and coffee, her demeanour is clearly that of a politician on a career-defining mission. Anyone foolish enough to get in the way of her post-late-lunch designs, needs to look out. 'They're damn hooligans Daniel.'

'Not by their profile, madame.'

'Take those sunglasses off and look outside for godsakes.'

So far Daniel has congratulated himself on how little he has managed to see outside his new office. That and not joining anyone's agenda here today has been his main achievement. But with Madame Maire now shouting at him, showing sympathy for F's extremist positions, Daniel is growing more and more defensive, finding himself edging dangerously towards violence as the only solution for saving his own political skin, let alone for clearing-out an occupied cinéma. 'What do you think we should do?'

'Do what is necessary. You want this job then do it! Properly. Bomb the théâtre if necessary. Ram them with a truck.'

'It might be difficult getting a truck up an escalator.'

'Don't get smart with me young man.'

'I'm taking your views on board and I will consider them each in good time.'

'You don't have time to tie your shoelaces.'

F laughs. The standing général frowns. Given what Daniel knows of the state of the man's hip this is not good news. A gendarme général collapsing on his carpet is as unpleasant a prospect as an F-backed gung-ho shoot-to-kill team storming the Truffaut.

This bâtiment insurrection is about to tear Daniel's authority to bits. He touches the sweat on his brow, silently praying now his visitors don't join forces and turn on him. He seized his moment, stormed the bridge, threw the captain overboard, but now does he have the street smarts to hang on to this job? The wide-boy wannabe director of the Renne Film Festival is stuck inside the vortex of a growing crisis he didn't even really consider might occur before he launched his plan to force Léo out.

'What do you think général?' Daniel asks, his voice barely audible, blinking as he waits for an answer.

'Employing lethal force will turn this into a disaster.'

'It's already a disaster.'

'F, for reasons you aren't willing to share, you are hell-bent on fomenting violence.'

F glares back at the général. 'If it's the only way, it's the only way.'

Swearing Daniel to secrecy in the men's room just after lunch, F recounted how he is updating the Président, telling a shocked Daniel how he recommended bringing in the army.

'We are losing business every minute,' yells Madame Maire. 'These cineastes will be revolting as well soon. They spend money on fares and hotels, come here from all over the country. If your films don't begin again soon, they'll soon join in the actual protest making it ten times worse.'

Daniel notes F's grim smile as he nods his agreement

around to everyone. He has clearly enjoyed the Maire's inclusion into the debate, probably thinking her bringing up the cineastes is a master-stroke.

'Madame Maire is right. Let's grab this by the throat now, Daniel. We need to throttle this source of violence, or this village will soon be in the sea. Then no producers will come here next year or the year after that.'

'A few producers less isn't a problem.'

'Général, do your job. I'm here to do mine. So is madame maire. Arrest them.'

'Who's the ringleader?'

'We know who he is. Linsteeg. A well-connected international trouble-maker.'

'You said the Agence Nationale de la Sécurité des Systèmes d'Information has nothing on him. If he were connected to any organization, you would know.'

'We can't rule out international sabotage.'

'But you can't tell me anything about him. Either your intelligence gathering is defective or this is a nobody from nowhere who created a storm in a teacup, a lone American producer who by chance ran into a bunch of over enthusiastic kids who also grabbed him by chance on their way to make a small-time protest at the bâtiment.'

'Journalists are saying Linsteeg is working under cover.'

The général frowns hard at Daniel. 'Which journalists?'

'Some major ones.'

'One, journalists are never major, two, journalists always have to say something. That's why they're journalists.'

'There are things Linsteeg did years back.'

'Do you know what you are saying?'

'Yes.'

'Where did you hear this Daniel?'

'I hear things, madame.'

'Where?' Daniel shrugs.

'I have heard Larry Linsteeg could be acting on orders.'

'Is this true or a fantasy of yours?'

'Général I heard he could be a sleeper.'

'Like those sleeper communists they riddled the west with once.'

'F, you're mad.'

'Général I see Trotskyites everywhere out there.'

'You're out of your mind. The USSR dissolved thirty years ago. Trotsky was murdered in the 1920s.'

'He's still got hard-core followers.'

The général glances at madame maire to see if she is really with F on this.

'If this Larry Linsteeg has had Russian connections for years, you would know.'

'What about the FSB? They have launched new initiatives.'

Standing his full two meters the général continues trying to take weight off his bad hip. 'I sense something unplanned in all this.'

'Like a badly plotted film, général?'

'Worse, Daniel, no plot at all.'

'This town is about to burn down and you two are discussing films. As maire of this city, I have a responsibility for everybody.'

F bangs the table hard. 'I warned the festival.'

'You must have warned Léo.'

The maire throws up her arms. 'Let's get Léo back. He'll know who's behind this.'

'What do you mean?'

'Look at the films he chooses. Most of them have leftist messages.'

'My god, he chooses a film with a leaning towards improving societies all over the world and that makes him a communist sympathizer?'

'Général, let's find out who's behind these protesters.'

'We know who's behind them, madame. Leftist politicians have already come out in support of the demonstration.'

'That's a fig leaf, Daniel.'

'How do you know that, général?'

'Madame, please, they are mostly kids.'

'What about the jury tampering to allow the Russian entry?'

Daniel frowns back at F, wishing he never told him anything about the jury problem.

'Lock them up for godsakes.'

'Madame, we can't lock up cineastes any more than we can lock up the jury.'

'Who's this film director the jury are promoting?'

Daniel rubs his cheek. 'They're not promoting anyone.'

F slaps the table. Daniel flinches. 'This has all the hallmarks of an international conspiracy. A toxic mix of Russian pornographers and indigenous directors involved in a dodgy art film market making use of foot-loose cineastes without tickets or films to see, or any clue how they're being used.'

'What?'

'Open your eyes, général.' F stares at him and then at Daniel. 'So, what do you all want to do? If you really want to be in charge of this, tell me what you are going to do.'

'What do you want me to do?'

'Restore order. If not, the rioters will run amok tonight, then tomorrow until God only knows when. We need to send in a contingent of well-trained anti-riot troops in there.'

Madame maire nods. 'F is right. This will only get worse.'

The général squints at her, then at F, and then over at Daniel. 'ALL THEY WANT SO FAR ARE TICKETS!'

'No need to shout, général. They are occupying a cinema right now. We have been invaded.'

The général shakes his head. 'What if the protest is only on the level of tickets? Only that. You keep saying rogue elements are in there. I say they're just kids who like the sound of democracy.'

'Have you seen the videos?'

'F, they're kids.'

'Led by Larry Linsteeg who is not a kid. A man with a pinko past.'

'What pinko past? F, I don't see any leftist conspiracy here. On the contrary it seems opportunistic. If we go in hard, we'll turn a small thing into a big thing. We will regret it. The public will back the demonstrators. That's what happened with the students in Paris in '68.'

Daniel looks from madame maire to F then back at the général wondering what on earth led him to lust after Léo's job. Opening a drawer, he half tears a piece of paper pulling it out. He reads, his strained voice way too high: 'Les facultés, les usines, les gares sont occupées! C'est d'une envergure sans pareille! Et vous voudriez que cette action s'arrête aux portes de ce Festival? La radio donne nouvelles, heure par heure. Si on y annonce que le Festival continue il sera ridiculisé! Truffaut's very words in 1968.'

'Then you do want to stop the festival, just like Truffaut did, is that it, Daniel?'

'F, we have to think.'

'Think?'

'We can't stop the festival. Businesses will lose money.'

'Madame, if we go in this could spread everywhere.'

'Exactly my point, Daniel. It will.'

F slaps the table. 'What I thought all along. This is organised. Clear the cinema now before it spreads. The longer we leave these criminals in charge, the more we give them political kudos.'

RIDING WITH EDGAR into shore, Larry's writer for a few moments begins feeling as if he's truly part of the celebrity set. Have the drinks he's had gone to his head? For some minutes at least his life is looking up. Then it's looking down again, as Edgar finding his camera and gear disappears getting back to Ivan's boat, heading down inside a private section down a very private corridor on a very private boat, as stars do. Looking around Larry's writer realizes he's alone among freeloading revellers he doesn't know from a lamp post. The Russian's survival get-together is not so great after all. It's already well out of hand. He slips into critical mode and begins scribbling in his pad that the shorts and flip-flop brigade, around the time their third drinks kick in, are shaping up to wreck Ivan's survival party, yelling at Russian girls serving them drinks and reefers and pills to bring 'em on and hurry the fuck up about it. Why this crowd has turned aggressive this fast is a mystery for, or is it *to* Larry's writer. Larry writer's even forgotten his prepositions. He doesn't have time to organise a theory, but some facts seem clear. The freeloaders are in the majority. The host has few friends either on his own boat or in this town. Contempt for the Russian wannabe ex-porn producer is real. Larry's writer can't really fathom why Ivan invited all these people out in the first place. Of course, Ivan didn't invite them. They invited themselves. The freeloaders filling the decks, scoffing the free stuff and abusing the long-suffering girls in bikinis bringing them freebies simply hate the Russian. One English speaking freeloader begins yelling into his mobile about the shindig being so easy and trash talking his host, describing Ivan's shark promotion as just another art fraud insurance scam, and with a bottle in hand staggers around yelling: 'It's the porn artist's last chance café. The Sables reception was as dead as a doornail. The names wouldn't have shown up. The Russian's a porn filmmaker for crissakes, so he sets up the shark scam to get attention.' Larry's writer wonders how long before the pussy grabbing starts. Then it does. Looking around for some crewmen to help him, he sees he's completely alone. In a moment of moral panic, he takes on the freeloaders all by himself.

'You believe Ivan would scam himself and nearly get killed?' he says his tone filled with grit. At least he thinks so. His delivery might have been a touch shrill.

The group faces him as one.

'Well, Mac, if it quacks like a duck.'

'It's called PR, Mac.'

The speakers and their friends high five all around.

'His shark swallows his driver, how does he arrange that? He wants to kill his own boat-driver?'

'The rich kill their help all the time.' The group laugh as one again, the first speaker closing in on him. 'What's your point, Mac?'

Larry's writer holds his ground. 'He wouldn't destroy his own show.'

'You obviously know nothing about the art business.'

'I'm not talking about the art business.'

The drinkers stare at him, studying him through red-rimmed eyes, a couple looking like they are measuring the deck distance between him and them. Larry's writer begins wondering if they're thinking of pulling a Clockwork Orange on him. After a moment of tension, he turns and quickly climbs a set of stairs, a string of expletives attached to 'coward' following him. As long as they are not just behind him he'll take the insults. Still, he climbs another set of stairs just in case. Shaking, Larry's writer wonders if there's anyone he can alert. Seeing nobody, he wonders why he just did what he just did. His hands are trembling setting up a text, his fingers fumbling on the letters. What's Ivan's assistant called again?

RAIN CLOUDS THREATEN the sky out on the horizon, artificial lights suppressing the sun way-off in the Provençal hills. Two young partygoers sit on the back landing of Ivan's launch staring at the puffs of cumulus cloud and low charcoal storm fluff sweeping in with a rising breeze, watching the day slowly overcome by darkness.

The girl lost faith in Ivan's survival party early on. Unable to continue ignoring the abuse going on or listen to the electronic junk-rap-rock coming from huge speakers, the girl repeats she just wants to go. The boy's prepared to accept the party for what it is, an ad-hoc rave, but the girl is incensed with the DJ's choices.

The couple falls silent dangling their feet in the sea. The boy mentions a forecast for a rainstorm. She says she couldn't care less, their insistent bickering carrying over the water all on the girl's plan to swim to shore.

'Are you going to swim with me?'

'I'm thinking.'

'The longer you wait the harder it'll get.'

Ivan's survival party seemed a great idea at first but even

the boy is changing his mind on that. Though if swimming back was the end part of this deal he wouldn't have come out. 'Can't we take the boat?'

'You can wait for one.' She starts to undress.

'It's dark, don't swim.'

'What are you frightened of?'

'The next runabout for shore is leaving in less than an hour.'

But she's not listening to him anymore, and now stands before him nude, not caring if anyone anywhere is watching.

'Who's going to bring our clothes?'

'You will in an hour.'

'I can't if I swim.'

'Swim with me I'll carry them above my head.'

The idea of her swimming holding his clothes up over her head alarms him. Even if she is a far better swimmer.

'If you wait for me nude on the beach you'll be freezing.'

'Maybe someone will offer me a contract.'

He doesn't laugh, neither does she. 'I should be going with you.'

'Then get your things off and swim with me.'

He stares at her.

'Why are you so scared?'

'I was thinking we could take that dinghy there.'

'You take it.'

She dives in and swims towards shore. He watches her, hoping she'll stop and call back to him. She's doesn't. He looks down at her clothes then out at her. Studying the dinghy behind him he wonders if he can get it started.

He can still hear her rhythmical splashing. What will she do once she gets to the beach? He picks up her things and walks them quickly to the landing, staring down at the dinghy, studying its small motor. Turning around, he looks up at the decks filled with partygoers. Stepping down into the boat, it rocks from side to side. When nobody shouts at him, he places her clothes on a seat and sits himself at the back. Testing the rope twice he takes a deep breath and pulls it hard. The motor starts first time. He tests the throttle then runs to the bow and unties the rope. Without looking around himself or up to the decks he runs back down to the stern, the rocking motion nearly throwing him in.

Falling hard onto the seat he recovers and turning the boat away from the back landing, breathing hard, he accelerates. Halfway to shore, did he hear her shout? He slows down, cuts the motor. Looking around himself he calls out. He waits, then calls again but there is no reply. No splashing either. Nothing.

On top of the Grand Hôtel Des Belles Sables Bella Fibben stares at her big screen. The digitized scenes are mind-boggling. She howled with laughter when a woman called for her pills, the TV cutting to a studio presenter: Marceline can you hear me?

The studio anchor touches her ear. Marceline? I think we've lost connection. We have lost Marceline.

Watching cellphone-transmitted images of Larry, his little-boy-lost face matching his stumbling around in the street, then sweating up on a small cinema stage, Bella is wondering if her former boyfriend is having a nervous breakdown. 'I didn't fly halfway around the world to participate in a revolution. I flew here to make a film deal.'

Her manager standing at the back of the room says nothing. On screen a presenter sits upright in her chair shuffling papers.

'Dramatic events at a festival not seen since nineteen sixty-eight. We will try to re-establish the link. Meanwhile we have Pierre Soubriquet, a political scientist at the Sorbonne.' The image cuts to a man dressed in white chinos and a blue cotton shirt.

'Pierre, nineteen sixty-eight was led by Jean-Luc Godard, Milos Forman, François Truffaut and others. It was very political. Is this as political as that?'

'Quite political by the look of these protesters.'

'The demonstrators are being led by an American apparently with no apparent political profile. A man with a reputation for making politically unremarkable genre films. Why would he be out in front of this?'

'It's difficult to get a fix on Larry Linsteeg, what his overall intentions are, but it looks planned. I have received information from a good source that as an independent filmmaker Linsteeg had leftist sympathies.'

Severine perks up. 'So, he does have a political profile?'

'The information I have is he was a young communist in nineteen sixty-eight.'

Bella sits down hard on her sofa. 'There goes the deal with Fox.'

She grabs a large vodka martini, downing the lot, olive included, in a flash. 'Come clean, Larry,' she yells. 'Tell us the truth. What's this about? What's the deal?'

Bella turns to her security chief standing silently at the back of the room. 'He was just a pretend leftie, a student with a Trotsky t-shirt, Che Guevara's beret. For the look. Nobody took anything Larry said seriously, not even Larry. Why's he coming out of the closet now?' Bella stares at Jeff who is staring non-plussed back at her. 'This is utterly stupid. It has to stop. This is movie land. The Riviera. The French

Revolution happened ages ago.'

'About the time Australia was invaded.'

Bella throws him a sharp look. 'The word's settled, Jeff. And you lot did it. You're on stand-by. We might be out of here earlier than I thought.'

Bella knows her French Revolution history, Norma Shearer and Robert Morley running helter-skelter for the Swiss border. She lay in bed heartbroken for days after seeing that film. The French royal family guillotined in Bella's mind was horrific. Insurrection, coup d'état are only ideas for far-flung foreign places, desperate countries with desperate politics, places not to be taken seriously.

Bella grew up next to a well-managed mining pit. Her help is paid far too well to get political on her. Bella's country is holidays on empty white beaches stretching as far as her eye can imagine.

'Nobody thinks of revolutions in OZ.'

A screen filled with protesters only three hundred meters from her rooftop terrace has her very worried now.

'What do they want?'

'I heard it was only tickets.'

'Aren't there any spare?'

'They want them as a right.'

'Ticket rights? Like copyrights?'

'I don't think so.'

'How far is it to the chopper at the lighthouse?'

'You have to skirt all this. That'll take fifteen-twenty minutes. Then it's thirty klicks to the airport.'

'How many crates can you get in a chopper?'

'Three, maybe four.'

'What if these maniacs get wind of what's here?'

Jeff says nothing.

'They can't shut down a film festival just because they're jealous of people like me. WHAT DO THEY WANT?'

'Tickets to a film in a cinema.'

'Give them tickets for chrissakes. Who's in charge?'

'A man called Martin is the director now'.

'You have his number? Who's Martin when he's at home? I've never heard of him. Martin who?'

Bella squints out of her windows at the bay. She points south. 'It's that Russian's fault. All his bloody doing.'

Suddenly on screen the police are charging, throwing the doors open and running inside La Salle Truffaut their batons held high. 'YEAAHH. GREAT! FINALLY. HOORAY FOR THE CAVALRY.'

ON HIS KNEES Zucca didn't hear anyone creep up behind him. He was studying a half-lit Larry up on stage, focusing, getting ready to get a shot when he was dragged to his feet and bashed in the face.

'Hey!' he shouts as he scrambles his camera gear inside a carry-box, someone slamming the lid shut on his fingers as his other arm is grabbed. Holding his gear under one arm, his injured hand stinging, he's marched outside, his last view of La Salle Truffaut—a cop chasing Larry Linsteeg across the stage yelling: 'ARRÊT! ARRÊTEZ-LE!'

As the cinema doors swung open, Zucca heard a woman yelling: 'Get me my tablets.'

Frog-marched towards an escalator Zucca manages now to keep clicking his camera with his sore hand, the fixed wide-angle hanging on a cord around his neck getting waiting photographers pushing their cameras into his face. Zucca grins his best. Uniforms are at the bottom and more faces, some he knows, holding cameras up. Zucca calls out names but nobody answers. It is pointless to argue. His error is clear. He was with the protesters so he's one of them. Gotcha instant judgement, Zucca caught by automatic guilt by association. A professional photographer? What's that?

Heading for the street he sees a TV cameramen he also knows hovering near the doors. Zucca tries waving but the flics drag his injured hand down, pushing him faster towards a crowd outside, Zucca yelling: 'Is there a lawyer in the house?'

Faces press hard against the windows. The bâtiment doors are pulled open and what looked bad through the glass is ten times worse in the open air, the screaming and shoving so loud the tactical response cops pulling him through the mêlée are nearly knocked off their feet. Zucca can't make out anyone here in the crowd but he can't miss its size. He knows danger when he's in it.

The cops seem to want to use him as a shield, a woman yelling: 'MARCELLO.' Another woman screams: 'IS IT HIM?' One cop flashes Zucca a look as hands grab at Zucca's face. A women reaches inside Zucca's shirt trying to get at his chest hair. Another reaches for his crotch.

The cops are no match for this crowd. Surrounded, the face of the youngest is deathly pale.

Middle-aged women closing-in on him on all sides Zucca yells: 'Laissez-moi aller. Lasciami andare. They'll kill you both if you don't. LET ME GO.'

The youngest cop is knocked off his feet. Now he lets go of Zucca who catches a glimpse of the boy's stunned face looking up as the other flic grapples with his holstered weapon. The crowd surges forward, united it seems by a single purpose. Only Zucca doesn't know exactly what it is. Is it him they want? Or the flics? Zucca wrenches his good arm free, and still upright allows himself to be swallowed-up in a sea of wild faces. There's a bang and a scream. 'THE FLIC SHOT A WOMAN. GET THE GUN.' A woman by him says: 'Marcello, follow me.' She gets Zucca's agreement and full attention. Face to face with his only option: a middle-aged woman in heavy mascara, he gives himself up to her sense of fair play, letting the fan-maniac cover his head with her shawl. Once at the barrier he rips off her cloth not forgetting to thank the woman for her help. 'I have seen all of your films, Marcello. I have a room near the station.'

'Madame, Mastroianni has been dead for thirty years.'

The woman's eyes grow suspicious. 'Who are you then?'

'Right now, I don't know.' In truth Zucca does look a little like Federico Fellini directing Mastroianni, half a century ago, only with more hair. 'Madame I would love to discuss all this with you, but it isn't the time.'

She opens her mouth as another shot sounds, Zucca suddenly in Casablanca with Ugarte escaping from Ric's Café. Only Ugarte got caught. He doesn't want to end up like Ugarte or Peter Lorre. Signor Ferrari at the Blue Parrot maybe. The woman yells: 'SHOOT THIS ONE TOO.' Facing her, Zucca sees only hatred now in her eyes. Instinct kicks-in. Taking a quick pic of her he turns and runs.

SEMOLINA SQUINTS AT THE TV her hand over her mouth. Reports say two policemen have been shot, then it's one cop and a prisoner, then they don't know, Semolina shouting, 'As long as it's not Zucca.' A high-angle camera is getting most of the action. Semolina sees Zucca take a photo of a woman, then leap a barrier, the camera following him. Then he disappears. Is he okay? Has he been wounded? Semolina yells: 'RUN. ZUCCA. RUN.'

Sitting hard on her bed her hand over her mouth again, she does what she's convinced is a perfect rendition of a shocked girlfriend watching her erstwhile lover dragged down an escalator and out of a building by riot cops on either side of him. Her attempt at facial horror is ably assisted by Zucca's occasional grins of bravado as he is mobbed by women, one grabbing his privates, another woman yelling, Marcello. Semolina drops her channel-changer and shouts at the screen.

'It's ZUCCA, you fool.' Semolina saw a cop go down, then the other soon after. A shot rang out and the image cut back to the studio. 'This is serious,' says a presenter, her hands up to her cheeks. Semolina holds her breath, wondering if her Zucca is alive. She sees him again. 'RUN ZUCCA!'

GOING OVER TO A PORTSIDE GUNNEL, grimacing at the DJ's choices, Merryl studies Ivan's ship. She refused point blank to attend the party. Staring at all the paraphernalia up top and hearing this electro-muzak blasting in all directions, she sips red wine mumbling: 'It's some sort of Russian Psyop meant to drive people mad.'

The Russians are definitely up to something. She tried to warn Jack in Monaco but he wouldn't listen. Watching him motor over, Merryl debated in her mind if he still has all his marbles. The old fool left his production run way too late. He spent far too many years grumbling his way to small successes in his all-hours VHS sell-through outlet—with the 50% risqué content she told him to stock. He does his best, but he really didn't know what to make of anything until he ran into Merryl jogging down on Venice Beach. She sorted him out. From San Diego, she had just turned her back on clothes. She had had it with the fashion industry and right-off wearing practically nothing she found her thing in life.

Jack certainly liked what he saw. He shared her general disillusionment with life. Merryl offered to help out in his store and from week one serving customers at the front counter in her see through outfits, sales of his VHS sell-through-flicks went through the roof. Merryl told him to dump VHS for DVDs. Jack found his first paydirt. Then she introduced him to a man in fashion she knew from way-back who had forgotten more about audiovisual systems than most experts even claim to know, and Jack found an even easier way to make a killing. He made Merryl his business partner and two months later they married.

Merryl credits herself with the fact they're now enjoying the fruits of that cash up-front business. They bought a Pacific facing condo, raised the stakes of their social life and ran wild weekend parties. When Rob Le Riche turned up at one very smoke-filled shindig of theirs, he changed their lives, turning Jack's head toward Monaco.

A few days later Jack pulled plane tickets out of his jacket and announced they were off to France. Merryl said, okay. After a week doing the sights in Paris they TGV'd down to the statistically most-populous person per square-foot territorial possession on the planet. The tiny principality was as luxurious as they imagined, if a trifle empty and short on real style. Merryl walked in and out of the casino finding it boring. Still, they managed to shrug off their first-impressions and with Rob helping with introductions, Jack found himself with a whole new enterprise, servicing the Karaoke dreams of the super-rich. Meeting a Russian oligarch, Alex Zanayev, out on the man's spacious entertaining area on the top deck of his ocean-going cruiser, Jack began their friendship by saying the billionaire's sounds were in a state of terminal decrepitude, selling his first client a new entertainment system. 'Worry not Alex,' Jack said with aplomb, 'I can fix it.' Using Alex's cell phone Jack flew in installation experts. Building a super-sounds replacement system to inspire an immediate attack of envy in all Zanayev's floating buddies, in one feverish fortnight Jack served up a multi-screen dance and film night system the men in tennis-whites flocked over to ogle at. Every tax-dodger mooning around in that harbour was mesmerized, one even wetting his shorts. And of course Merryl was there to help out, her charms working on billionaire after billionaire. Jack got so much work from the idle super rich floating in that harbour the LA couple became permanent invitées at all the best soirées.

One evening sitting in a pow wow circle tossing back Alex's special Black Sea martinis they learned about Ivan Dzerzhinsky, Alex filling them in on Ivan's designs for film legitimacy. Merryl saw Jack's head go ding that day on Zanayev's super cruiser.

Brought back to the present by the rubbish music blasting from the very same boat, Merryl decides she needs a lift, maybe even a new horizon.

Heading back inside the galley, she pours some wine and tears off the cellophane off a pack of her little secret. Dropping three before she finally gets one into her mouth, she stands with her eyes closed lighting up, a grin spreading across her mouth. She smokes on the sly to avoid the aggravation of Jack's protests.

Smoke drifting south she whispers the magical name of the great continent she is facing across the sea. What would it be like to be on a steamboat going up a central African river. She did a catwalk in Cape Town once in a big whites only ocean-facing hotel, a shanty with a black woman with two kids in a carpark across from her balcony. Nicotine flooding her bloodstream Merryl exhales her shame out to sea. Suddenly her stomach's playing-up. She puts a hand on a guard rail thinking she's about to be sick. Then with a WHOOSH a thing comes out of the water.

'OH MY GOD.' Falling hard on her buttocks she wonders if she will ever be able to stand again.

'I won't touch you.'

'You're damn right you won't. We have a gun.'

'I won't hurt you.'

The sound of his accented English fixes her stomach. Looking at him and the state he's in she doesn't need any weapon. Climbing to her feet she rubs her behind.

'You scared the hell out of me.'

A naked middle-aged man comes up the ladder grinning, something slimy all over him getting the marine scientist in her squinting. 'What have you been doing'?

'You don't wanna know.'

'I do want to know.'

'You wouldn't believe me.'

'Try me.'

'I've no clothes on.'

'I'll get a towel.'

Merryl runs inside, grabs the first towel she sees. Not frightened anymore she helps the intruder on board. Staggering for a moment he collapses onto the deck.

Flat out and stark-naked, breathing hard, he's a helpless middle-age man with his floppy thing on full show. Merryl stares hard at all the cuts on him.

'Did someone torture you?'

The man lies breathing and blinking up at the sky saying nothing. She helps him up, and with his arm on her shoulder, walks him towards the boat's shower cubicle. Asking questions and getting only the occasional answer she hears bits of a very strange story.

He was swallowed by a fish filled with oxygenated balloons. She's heard worse lies and puts it all down to some kind of delirium. Then it hits her.

'Oh my god. You're that guy that got swallowed.'

He nods his head as he staggers into the shower. She waits until he finishes and hands him a pair of Jack's best pyjamas when he's dry. Walking him to their bed she watches him collapse on the duvet and fall fast asleep in seconds.

Hearing more of the heavy-metal banging-out over on the Russian's boat she decides calling Jack wouldn't do any good. In the galley she pours herself another glass thinking perhaps her guest would like one too when he wakes up. She pours another, leaves it on the table, then looking in on him realises he isn't waking anytime soon, so she drinks his wine as well, deciding she'll make a little search of his truth.

Getting into her wetsuit she asks herself whether she should dive after wine. It's only twenty feet. If there's a carcass of the show shark it'll be close to the boat. A quick drop to the ocean floor. Down and straight back up again. Merryl checks her torch and stares down at the dark water. Dead calm, no discernible current running. She's an experienced diver. She tightens the straps on her tank saying: 'Go for it.' Fitting her mask, she tests the mouthpiece for air and turning to the cabin says: 'I'll be back in two shakes of a seal's tail.' Giving herself the thumbs up she backflips off the stern. The water is cold. Swinging around two seventy degrees Merryl quickly gets her bearings, takes breaths on her mouthpiece and with the standard check-through done, begins finning in a four-beat rhythm down to the sandy floor.

Finding nothing there she heads left. Finding nothing left she goes right. Soon she has covered all the territory where the carcass of a dead shark should be. Finning further she finds no signs of it. Going further she tries picturing her guest backing out of a dead shark's mouth. Why didn't its teeth shred more skin? Merryl expected to find remnants of an airbag at least, anything to corroborate what he said and finding nothing now wonders about her new guest. How could he survive in a dead shark's throat? How could he get out of it backwards? Combing the area one more time Merryl abandons the search. The guy might not be lying but he might not be quite telling the truth either.

Merryl wants to believe him, enough to venture further out some more, but she's getting more worried every minute she stays down. She shines her torch upward, studies the Sunshine's hull. Everything is still. What's he doing up there right now, looking for their gun? Perhaps he sustained concussion and doesn't know the truth anyway. How could he survive a shark that size falling on his head?

A movement behind her makes her turn, a shape going by giving her a solid bump on the hip. Merryl stares at the tail fin of a shark ghosting off. The size tells her all she needs to know. It's not the same shark that swallowed the guy up top. This one's way bigger and alive. It's inspected her. Maybe her sudden turn startled it and it is circling her right now. Merryl hasn't much time, seconds only maybe. A great white and it looked like one doesn't usually investigate its prey. Merryl heads back to where she imagines the boat is. Surfacing she looks around.

The Sunshine Coast is a hundred meters away. Big sharks usually attack from underneath. She starts the longest, scariest swim of her life. Should she go back under? She won't dare. Seeing the after image of the huge tail going by again fear drives her to swim faster: Get out of the water girl. You won't get bumped again. Merryl senses something is just under her and swishes her fins harder. Head down, she swims as fast as she ever has getting across the surface in all her gear back to any boat.

OPENING HER DOOR Semolina's smile fades. She was hoping it would be her Italian lover. Instead, Edgar walks inside like he owns her room, accompanied by an oddly dressed blond, Semi extending a stiff arm to the girl.

'Who's this?'

'Ulyana.'

'You were supposed to pick me up at the wharf.'

'I got caught up.'

'You were too drunk you mean.'

'I was swimming.'

'Swimming?'

'We have been trying your mobile for ages.'

Semolina stares at her cellphone. Her battery is dead. She frowns over at her bedside phone, seeing it's off the hook. She thinks of offering somewhere to sit but with her clothes everywhere they can stand or sit on the floor.

'So, what's so important?'

'You didn't hear?'

'Hear what?'

'Larry's called off the première.'

Semolina drops her mobile on the floor. 'WHAT?'

Sitting hard on one of her dresses she stares gravely up at Edgar. 'Was it me at the press conference?'

'He's done it all by himself. It's off.'

'We're in competition.'

'Not anymore.'

'He can't do that.'

'He's the producer. He can do what he likes.'

Semolina buries her face in her hands, then looks up.

'Who told you, Larry?'

'No.'

Semolina's eyes widen. 'Then whoever said it, maybe they heard wrong.'

'Larry said it on TV.'

'Said it on TV?'

'He's on now.'

Semolina grabs her remote and switches it on. 'He did another press conference without me?'

'He's holed up in the Salle Truffaut with protesters.'

'What's he protesting about?'

Semolina remembers Zucca calling and leaving a message about taking pics of some guy in the middle of a mob of crazy demonstrators. 'God, what's he done now.'

'I knew you'd be upset.'

'Of course, I'm upset.' Semolina stares at the TV trying to understand what some journalist woman is saying to camera outside the bâtiment. 'There's no sound.'

Edgar grabs the remote, turns up the volume. They stand listening to a reporter speaking in French. Edgar switches channels but can't find any English commentary.

He switches back to a shot of the entrance over a cinema, Ulyana explaining that some protesters with Larry leading them took over La Salle Truffaut and barricaded themselves inside. Semolina listens to Ulyana but won't look her way. This is all too much for her. Her migraine is back. She's feeling nauseous. She can hardly breathe. 'Larry's gone mad. You hit that bigwig and you drove him crazy.'

'I pushed an official, barely touching him, some prick who can't do his job.'

'But he was an important guy. So maybe they're paying us back.'

'By driving Larry mad? It's got nothing to do with it.'

'But if Larry has gone mad, it's our film right. We can take it over.'

'Semi, we can't.'

'Are you sure?'

Semolina grabs the channel-changer off him and switches stations. Finding no English-speaking journalist reporting, she switches back to a woman speaking in French. Semolina stares for a moment at the screen rubbing her temples. 'What's happening? WHAT'S SHE SAYING?'

Ulyana studies her coolly. 'She is saying that some protesters are still inside la Salle Truffaut. Some tactical response police are in there as well. So far, the press hasn't been able to enter the theatre. She's saying that there is a lot of activity on social media about an American Hollywood producer Larry Linsteeg being the ringleader.'

'Ringleader of what?' Semi stares angrily at the girl. 'He's drunk or you are.'

Edgar points at the screen. 'Look at it. Listen Semi to what's being said.'

'IT'S IN FRENCH.'

'I thought you spoke the language.'

'Well apparently I don't speak enough.'

On screen the reporter is on camera speaking rapidly, Ulyana translating fast. Semolina turns to Edgar her eyes again wide. 'We can declare Larry is mentally incompetent. We can take over the film. Get a French judge to hand over the title deeds.'

'This is not a house, Semi.'

'A film's a commercial property, right?'

'Sounds complicated, Semi.'

'I agree with Edgar.'

'What? You agree ...'

Semolina squints at Ulyana as if asking herself why this girl is even speaking.

'My parents took my grandmother's money. They went to a judge to get it. So, we can too.'

'That's your family, Semi. Here, it's French law.'

'Larry can't do this? We have our rights.'

'What rights? Read your contract. In the end it's only a première.'

'Only a première. Maybe to you.'

'Calm down.'

'Me calm down. You calm down. Go down there. Speak to him. Slap him. Wake him up.'

'The advice is that you should talk to him. Try to get him to reverse the decision.'

Semolina stares at Ulyana, then at Edgar. 'ME? Whose advice?' Semolina glares at Ulyana. 'And when did this become your business exactly?'

'Stop it Semi. Ully is trying to help us here.'

'Her advice. Ully who? Her advice I mean, Hel-lo.'

'It's what a producer Jack somebodyoranother told Ivan. It's his advice.'

'Jack who?'

'Funny, that's what I said. Anyway, Jack whoever he is says he knows what should be done. He thinks you can talk Larry around. Unless he's had a nervous breakdown.'

'I'm having a nervous breakdown.'

'Jack says he has seen worse.'

'Worse than this!'

'Jack thinks Larry will listen to someone who doesn't threaten him.'

'I'll threaten him if he doesn't fix this now.'

'He thinks someone might have gotten to him and that you can talk him around.'

'Gotten to him?'

'Blackmail or something.'

'Blackmail. Christ for what? He's hasn't got any money anymore. What's Jack whatshisname got to do with this anyway?'

'He's producing my next film.'

'Don't you think you should concentrate on this one first, like one at a time.'

'That's what he's doing.'

'Oh pleeese, miss whoever you are.'

'Semi stop this. Get it in to your head. Ully's here to help.'

'By the look of that outfit she can't even help herself get dressed.'

'SEMI.'

'You can talk. Look at your room.'

'SHUT UP. SHUT UP.'

'I don't need this.'

Ulyana walks out leaving the door wide open.

'Ully wait.'

Edgar turns and points at Semolina. 'That was really stupid of you.'

'She your new girlfriend?'

'God. She's Ivan's assistant. Be nice Semi, okay.'

Edgar runs into the corridor going after Ulyana.

'WAIT.'

He gets to her just as the elevator doors are opening.

'Ully, stay. Semi practically had a nervous breakdown in our first press conference. It went badly. She doesn't know what she's saying.'

'Sounds like she knows exactly what she's saying.'

'Come back.'

'Only if she stops the abuse.'

'She will, I promise.'

Inside her room the whole thing is all too much for Semi. She falls straight back on to her bed, the room turning black. She opens her eyes and cranes her neck up to see a woman in a newsroom holding her earpiece.

'Our reporter Marceline Alles is on the spot right now. Marceline can you hear me'?

'Yes Severine. I'm here.'

'What's going on?'

'Well what began as a protest outside the bâtiment then went inside the bâtiment has just been broken up by police inside and outside the building. We believe the American producer in question Larry Linsteeg has been apprehended inside and they're bringing him outside. We're hoping to interview him.' The image shows Marceline jostled by a crowd of reporters as she calls out: 'Oh Mr Linsteeg.' Semolina staggers up to her feet, finding Edgar and Ulyana in her room again. Together they stare at images of Larry being taken from the building, his hands cuffed behind his back, riot police officers on either side of him, a cameraman following, swinging around to videotape Marceline pushing through the crowd to get to him, her voice yelling: 'Oh Mister Lins-teeg.'

Semolina stares at the screen rubbing her temples. 'What's going on?' Voices shout all around Larry, reporters pushing everywhere. Larry looks at the reporter then straight into a news camera. 'I am protesting for oppressed filmmakers.'

Marceline threads her microphone closer to his mouth. 'Mr Linsteeg, you took your film out of competition. Why?'

'It was my duty. My director is an indigenous Australian from an oppressed people, an historical situation that's been happening for more than two hundred years.'

Larry is dragged fast through a corridor of riot police. Marceline and her cameraman try to duck under the police cordon but their way is blocked, Larry calling back: 'My director Edgar is a persecuted man and the jury has been tampered with.'

'What? Edgar is being persecuted by the jury?'

'Shoosh, please let us hear.'

'Don't you shoosh me, dork.'

'Semi, we agreed. No abuse or we both leave now.'

Semolina folds her arms, squints down at the screen.

They watch two lines of riot police with their hands clasped above Larry as if saluting a famous figure as he's led away to a police vehicle, Marceline's cameraman capturing a tunnel image of the Hollywood producer turning and giving a peace sign to the lens.

'See, he knows what he's doing.'

'WHO'S RESPONSIBLE FOR THE PROTEST?' Marceline calls out, but she gets no answer, her way blocked again by officers as the camera pans to her.

'Larry Linsteeg has left the bâtiment.'

'Where are they taking him, Marcie?'

An arm bashes Marceline's head knocking her out of shot.

'Arrêtez de pousser.'

'Marcie, are you okay?'

The camera shot widens to show an angry Marceline rubbing her temple. Holding her face with one hand and the microphone in the other she frowns at the lens. 'I wish, Sevvie.'

'Stay strong.'

'As I was saying now. An American producer leading a group of young protesters has been taken away, where to we don't know. He claims the jury is corrupt. That's it. Back to you.' The shot lingers on Marceline gingerly touching the right side of her face. She is shoved out of frame.

'Stop pushing. What is wrong with you people.'

The image cuts to a high shot of the crowd as a police van drives away. 'I think we've lost Marceline again.'

INSIDE THE TOP-DECK LOUNGE adjacent to Ivan's stateroom, Ivan and Jack are following the day's events on Ivan's Samsung 100-inch NU9000 Premium 4K Ultra HD LED LCD smart wall mounted screen TV. Jack should know. He purchased the system from an online catalogue. The pair are knocking back vodka fortified juice combos made to Ivan's special orders like there's no tomorrow, Ivan and Jack taking turns to serve each other as they decide whose turn it is to speak, each expressing himself in longer and longer sentences, Jack at times getting up for a wander, his gait a touch unstable due it seems to sudden crosscurrents in surrounding dead calm waters. Jack manages to find his seat again, each time with more effort expended in the search, blinking up at the screen, confused at times, his mind in other moments lucid, as he speaks over what is being broadcast, or Ivan, nodding at his new business chief expressing himself on the likely outcomes. Jack wishes Merryl had accepted Ivan's offer to collect her in a runabout, bring her over to join in the discussion as well, with Jack feeling that being by himself without Merryl's subtle guidance he's well on his way to miming a bed sheet in a forty-knot gale. Who knows where he will end up. Some seconds ago, he could swear Ivan's vodka combos had transported him to Mars.

Luckily, most times Jack is getting Ivan's drift pretty well, appreciating right now how his host is agreeing with him that a major opportunity has arrived. What that opportunity really is, though, is far from clear. Still, sensing everything is closing in on some solution, Jack tries hard not to contradict any of Ivan's ideas, leaving any critique for the televised journalistic commentary, summarisable by what Merryl once theorized as a reporter's dilemma: What journalists think they know of the truth; what journalists can know of the truth; what journalists are allowed to know of the truth.

'It's the latter than matters,' Jack says sagely. One thing that he and Ivan agree on wholeheartedly, without question, apart from their general synchronicity throughout the unfolding of events, is how the commentators are quickly leaping to condemn Larry's behaviour. The fact that the cops are in a general meltdown over this protest has been forgotten it seems, together with any negatives looming for Renne, both Ivan and Jack, between gulps and sips, concurring that the lovely seaside village as Ivan calls it, is about a cotton thread away from slipping into total chaos.

'The authorities were totally unprepared.'

'They don't know what to do,' adds Jack, 'wherever they are at this moment.'

Jack repeats that he sees a clear and present danger all around them, with remedial options narrowing fast. A nodding Ivan agrees a crisis has arrived. They are also almost in full agreement on what the actual crisis constitutes, but as to what the actual remedies are or could or should be on the table is where they still diverge.

Jack wants the French army in on it. Ivan definitely doesn't. Still Ivan nods often when Jack speaks, seemingly impressed by Jack's various assessments, whatever they are on almost all matters, but says he still disagrees on that fundamental matter. 'This is not national, it's local, Jack. Let the local people deal with this. Otherwise there will be a revolution.' Wisely, Jack doesn't press Ivan on this. 'The very heart of my truest sentiment, Count,' Jack replies. 'Times have slipped into minus territory for everyone.'

'Jack, there are positives and negatives to be found in everything.'

'Absolutely, we need to be positive, Count I couldn't agree more. Chaos is the exclamation point writ-large in Renne right now,' Jack says staring at Ivan's blurred face. 'The greater the general state of dismay the greater the confusion,' he adds, as if he is suddenly in a tunnel, saying that he finds Ivan's analyses to be 'very, very interesting.'

WALKING INTO THE BÂTIMENT'S BALLROOM for a hastily convened press conference Daniel Martin trots up a set of steps to a dais to welcome all and everyone, announcing that the hostage drama is now resolved. Which comes as a complete surprise to everyone.

Cameras taping him, the acting directeur is confronted with an explosion of shouted questions, trying to convince everyone that he's right, as well as attempting to mollify the continuing journalistic anger over the fact they haven't been kept informed of what the authorities are doing, a widely held impression Daniel is not able to reverse. The assembled crowd of newshounds are furious, one journalist shouting: 'What the hell is really going on?' Daniel puts his hands up trying to quieten the room.

'We have secured the bâtiment.'

'Really,' Annalise de la Forêt yells back. 'People are saying the festival's finished.'

'All screenings scheduled from here on will go ahead.'

'Can you guarantee that? Linsteeg has withdrawn his film.'

'Linsteeg's Death at Intervals is on tonight.'

'When did Linsteeg change his mind?'

'Where is he?'

'Do you expect others to pull out their films?' another journalist shouts.

'I don't know and no.'

'How can you possibly know?' Annalise shouts which gets a chorus going: 'How do you know? How can you possibly ever know? How the hell do you actually know? What about the jury corruption?'

This last question seems to stun Daniel.

'Nobody mentioned corruption.'

'Well we are now.'

Putting his hand over the microphone Daniel leans back and speaks in a whisper to an aide. The woman whispers back in his ear. Daniel straightens up, taking his hand off the mike. 'I will have to get back to you on that.'

'Where is Léo? You have his job, but we haven't heard anything from him. Has he resigned officially?'

'He's taking some time off.'

'Has he resigned?'

'He's having a well-earned rest.'

'In the middle of a festival? Is he ill'?

'Not that I know of.'

'What's wrong with him?'

'IS HE ANGRY?' a voice behind Annalise yells.

'No.'

'Have you been in touch with him?'

'No.'

'What do you think he would do in these circumstances?'

'I have no idea.'

'Has he left town?'

'Is he on holiday?'

'I imagine so.'

'You imagine?'

'Is he coming back?'

At this point Daniel wheels around and walks off-stage, exiting the ballroom as a man calls out: 'Will you ban Linsteeg?'

More journalists yell out questions, one mentioning Lars Von Trier, but Daniel doesn't turn around, or answer anyone anymore, walking quickly down a roped-off passageway followed by armed guards.

IN HIS FIRST TELEPHONE CALL to her since her art piece disintegrated, M-iki finds Ivan calm considering his loss. Drunk but calm. She listens as he starts up on new ideas, new objectives. After an inaudible comment and a pause, he hands the phone over to someone called Jack.

'Jack's handling things now.'

'Jack who?' M-iki starts to ask, stopping herself as silence appears on the phone.

An old man, by the sound of his voice, comes on the line introducing himself as Jack Kimmelon producer of the upcoming Pulp Fiction 2, adding that M-iki's shark is still in circulation. Her patience is already slipping away fast, Jack sounding as if he's a sail or two to the wind as well. 'What do you mean by in circulation?'

'It has been seen in the bay young lady.'

Don't young lady me she nearly says. 'He's your shark. Well Ivan's, if it's still there.'

'Your shark seems quite social. It has attracted another one.'

'What on earth do you mean?'

'A bigger fellow has shown-up. And I hear there's a body in the Renne morgue.'

'What? I can't be held responsible for bodies in any morgue, and what a live shark thinks of a dead one is outside my contract.'

'Exactly.'

'What do you mean by exactly, exactly, Mr Kimmelon?'

'Call me Jack. The truth exactly.'

'The truth? What truth is your truth exactly? I suggest you talk to the helicopter pilot.'

'I have been brought in to advise. My wife's an expert you see. She is a marine scientist. She's just told me she's seen the new visitor. Actually, she felt it. You really need to get a handle on this rogue newbie.'

M-iki's heard enough.

'Mr Kimmelon, when Ivan's shark kamikazed from a helicopter it was already out of my hands.'

'Call me Jack. Ivan wants you to know that nobody is blaming you for what happened.'

'I hope not. Anyway Ivan is insured.'

'The insurance company is not processing anything until the police investigate it, so we thought you might be able to help with that.'

'How?'

'Make a statement to them.'

'What am I supposed to say?'

'Tell them the truth.'

M-iki takes a breath. 'You want me to go to the police and say a dead shark I used in an experimental art-piece I created for a Russian producer on a big luxury boat leapt from a cup hanging from a helicopter and swallowed one of his Russian crewmembers? You know what happens then?'

'What?'

'I am held on suspicion of criminal negligence and Ivan has gendarmes all over his yacht. You want that? I don't think Ivan needs the aggravation, do you? I certainly don't.'

'Don't get upset. I just wanted your input.'

'What with the body in the morgue or the missing boat driver or your wife?'

'No need to get lippy young lady. My mother always said if you can't say something nice don't say anything.'

'It's a bit late for that isn't it.'

'You're worried and upset. Ivan's upset too. I understand.'

'You understand what exactly?'

'Let's start again.'

'Please do. By the way I'm not upset or worried. I didn't choose to exhibit out to sea. I planned for solid ground. I wasn't in command of the helicopter. I didn't choose the site out in the bay. Ergo I'm not responsible for what happened.'

'Let's change the subject. What's happening with your new shark?'

M-iki closes her eyes, takes another deep breath.

'I found out it can be caught and on a plane in a few days. It should take at least a week to be here.'

'Make it two days can you? The festival will be over before it arrives.'

'I am not responsible for the efficiency of the shark catchers or international air cargo.'

'Once you have it and place it in a cup how long before you can have it on display?'

'Displayed where?'

'On the Promenade des Rois.'

'You are kidding me.'

'I was told the mairie won't object.'

'You believe that?'

'It came from their office. A man called Martin says the maire doesn't mind.'

'Who?'

'The new director.'

'There's a new director?'

'Just took over. He says if you want to put up more exhibits you can fill the Promenade with as many sharks as you like.'

'Last week they wouldn't give me the tiniest spot anywhere on any road. Now I have the whole Promenade des Rois? Anyway, it'll be a miracle if the shark and cup can get here in time.'

'So you're saying you can't do it?'

M-iki grimaces off at palm trees and other foliage lit-up in the distance.

'I tell you what I'll do, Jack. With insurance I have been through this, not exactly like this, but similar. I'm a name artist. I have a reputation with a brand worth preserving so the fact the festival reneged on an agreement to let me exhibit on the promenade, in a material way they created this incident by changing the venue. So, if you have trouble with the insurance people you could tell them that, and they can go after the festival.'

M-iki squints hard after saying this.

'There you go girl. When you put your thinking cap on

see what you can come up with. I'll tell Ivan. Let us know about the new shark soonest. I gotta go.'

Jack rings off leaving M-iki staring at her mobile.

CREWMEMBERS OUTSIDE Ivan's cabin yell 'TIME PLEASE' herding the last of the guests down to the back landing.

In the middle of recounting a pre-production story of how Jack could have had the rights to the fishiest tale ever told, Ivan fell fast asleep. So much for Jack's powers as a raconteur.

Realizing Ivan is out for the count, Jack leaves his name card on a table with a handwritten note of thanks. Exiting, he finds crewmembers sweeping up bottles, cigarette butts and paper cups everywhere on the decks, Jack hearing: 'LAST FERRY TO SHORE.' Sauntering down two sets of stairs towards the back-landing, he waves to the runabout leaving loaded with drunken partygoers.

Then he sees the truth. His dinghy is gone. Running down the last few steps, he calls out to the taxiboat to stop. Accelerating away to shore the driver can't hear him. Jack Kimmelon eminent producer of Godfather 4, Jaws 5, Dances with Wolves 2/3/4/5, stands alone on the Soraya's back landing where he is positive he left his dinghy four hours before. The last chance taxiboat is now one hundred meters away. It is either sleep on Ivan's deck or swim back to the Sunshine Coast. Jack yells some more but the runabout isn't turning around.

Then as luck has it, he must have been seen or one of the crew rang the driver on a mobile. Whatever the reason the taxiboat swings around and comes back.

Not believing his luck Jack clambers on board telling everyone the story of his stolen dinghy. The driver and kids stare blankly at him. Sitting on the floor of the boat he starts re-telling a girl the same story. She just shrugs.

'My boyfriend stole my best friend.'

'Really?'

Jack turns to the driver: 'To the shores of the good life my good man.'

That earns him a snigger. He grins at his hands. It could be worse. He could be in the water right now. Closing in on the shoreline he hears music he recognizes. Seeing a sliver of light flashing up on a screen he spies an audience in hammock seats. That's where he'll go.

Climbing out, he falls into the water. Wading up to the beach, ignoring the laughter all around he shakes himself off. Saying his warmest goodbyes to the driver, Jack trudges up the beach to join the cinema crowd, stopping to squeeze water from his trouser bottoms twice, and brush wet sand from his soaked shoes.

Getting to the screening in time the only seats left are in the front row marked VIP. Godfather 4 Jack grabs a place. Looking up he sees what he was just about to miss—Jaws. He turns to a girl seated by him, liking her long dark hair right away as he extends his hand.

'Jack Kimmelon producer, Godfather 4.'

Her initial smile morphs into a sympathetic grimace. When young girls give Jack sympathetic grimaces, age hasn't just crept up on him it's zoomed right over his head and slapped him on the other side. Though he still has the power of charm. 'This the director's cut, sweetie?'

The girl gives him the briefest of smiles.

'Is Steven here?'

The girl glances at him but doesn't smile now, her face not so age-deferential anymore. Jack shrugs. He can't please everyone all of the time. Settling back into his hammock he stares up at the screen, wishing Merryl was there. She hates Jaws, says it's fiction. Horror fiction, he corrected her.

He's asked her to see it with him so many times so he can correct her impressions. One of the greats of our times he's argued more than once. But she thinks sharks are prehistorical miracles not circus acts, so Jack just shrugs. Science is useful, cinema is fun.

'Who needs science telling us when we're going to die all the time?'

The girl ignores him now.

He shrugs re-hearing Merryl saying, If you were any more stupid, Jack, you'd be dangerous. Stupid or not, he'll be dead soon enough, why should he care? Film gives him life. The danger thrills and dreams and schemes all up on a screen. 'Is Steven here, darling?'

The girl grimaces again.

'Did I just ask that?'

Jack can just see the great man walking up to the microphone: 'I'm Steven and I'm glad to be here.' A cheer breaking out everywhere. Security would be needed to hold back the crowd so he can't have made it.

'Remember when he brought ET here?' Jack grins at the girl, getting no reaction. 'All the Jaws figures should be here. Richard Dreyfus. Lorraine Gary. The ghost of Roy Scheider.' Jack stands pulling out his wet digital camera and takes a pic of where they all would be.

'SIT DOWN,' a man yells behind him. Jack can almost hear Steven say: 'Sofia, you there somewhere?' He senses movement on his right. The girl gets up and walks across the sand over to a stage. 'A big hand for Sofia Coppola.' Jack isn't clapping. Damn rude of her.

'SIT DOWN.'

Okay, he's made a gaffe. He didn't recognize her. It happens. She's a celebrity. Jack knows the score. He'll fix it all with his old PR magic. How else did he get a beauty like Merryl? He mentions The Godfather and Francis's daughter doesn't even introduce herself. Wait 'til he meets her father next time. 'I will tell him you know.'

He'll change the production he's working on to Dances with Wolves 2. He practices holding out his hand: 'Jack Kimmelon Producer in development with Dances with Wolves 2. Pleased to meet you.'

'SIT DOWN.' Finally he does. 'Great director.' The girl shifts further away.

'Steven teases his characters out so beautifully.' Jack forms two fingers into an O, someone groaning loudly behind him.

He waves a lazy hand. Nobody on this beach knows this movie like Jack knows it. He can almost taste the salt air, feel the chill of the waters off Amity Island. Shivering, swirling seawater around his ankles, Jack's so far in the zone he's out in the water with that girl swimming all alone, seeing Bill Butler getting the shot of the first bite.

'I could have got the rights to this. Steven got them. Fair dues. He deserved them. He's today's John Ford.'

'SHOOSH!' a voice behind says. The girl gets up and moves three seats down.

'OKAY. COOL IT,' he says back over his head.

'KEEP QUIET.'

Jack swivels around: 'Can't you just enjoy the movie?'

Still, he knows better than to start a full-blown argument with ignorant sorts. And he doesn't want to embarrass the girl who was once by his side. Up on screen, the shark is slipping below the surface inside the channel, Jack holding his breath, hearing the music signalling the beast is stalking. 'GOD,' he shouts. 'LOOK OUT.'

'Stand up and tell us the whole story,' a voice right behind says now.

'If you want I will.'

'BE QUIET.'

Jack waves a hand to the back again, shaking his head and closing his eyes. Philistines every one of them.

He can't look at the screen now. The moment he opens his eyes again he prays he'll see Roy Scheider, Roy the boy, a man after Jack's heart. Family-man. Great wife. Great kids. Lawman with a conscience. From the first frame Brody's every move is on-song. He even drove a Chevy.

'I love a Chevy pick-up. A beautiful truck.'

He wipes away a tear of admiration. Even the props in Jaws get him emotional.

'Did I say I could have had the rights?'

'Stop, please.' The girl three chairs down is showing her steely side now.

'No need to get lippy. I get it. You're an ageist, right? Hate your dad. Poor Francis.'

She purses her lips as Jack leans back and stares up at the screen. Murray Hamilton's mayor Vaughan is up there, the bastard that always gets Jack's goat. When he hears the words: 'Martin you going to shut the beaches on your own authority.' Jack can't help himself. 'WHAT A PHONEY.'

'BE QUIET. '

'WHAT A PHONEY! '

'SHUDDUP. '

Jack has had enough, and swings around. 'NO, YOU SHUDDUP.' Standing, he staggers off waving his arms silhouetted against the screen. Boos and hisses follow him on his way to the water. He gives them all a two-fingered salute. Jack doesn't care. The night-winds over Amity Island have revived him, transported him back to where he belongs. Grinding his teeth, he hears the mayor's sly threat: 'Martin this is your first season here.' Jack's fists are clenched. He's ready to shout. He's as mad as hell and he won't take it anymore. Standing facing the screen he yells at the top of his voice: 'YOU YELL SHARK WE'VE GOT A PANIC ON OUR HANDS. '

'BEDTIME OLD FELLA.'

Jack gives another two-finger salute and stalks down to the sands, several voices urging him to drown himself. And speak of the devil, there it is. His dinghy.

He breaks into a trot, finds clothing sitting on a seat neatly tied. Picking up the package, he turns it over in his hands. Looking up and down the beach he yells: 'ANYONE LEAVE SOME CLOTHES?'

When nobody answers, Jack carries the bundle up the sand, places it where the tide won't reach. Going back to the dinghy he pushes it out too fast, half-falling in again.

He manages to get inside his boat without getting any more wet. Pulling the engine's chord, it starts right away. A miracle. Jack looks up and down the beach expecting someone to yell THIEF. Steering away from the muffled sounds, he stands up: 'YOU YELL SHARK AND...'

The boat begins rocking so much he nearly goes in the water. He grabs a gunnel just in time to stop himself going face first overboard. Scrambling back to the driver's-seat, he opens-up the throttle. He's back on track, breathing in the sea-air, shivering and laughing in utter disbelief.

PUSHING THROUGH THE NIGHT CROWD with her cameraman behind her Marceline Alles can't help smiling at all the energy all around. The cineastes without a seat in any theaters, even down at the beach cinema, walking the streets holding flowers are shouting: 'Free Larry Linsteeg. Free Larry. Free Larry Linsteeg.'

'What else do you want?'

'Democratic revolution in the festival.'

The cineastes shake flowers at Marceline practically drowning out her next question: 'Do you want to make trouble for the festival?'

A girl steps forward. 'We want the festival's structure for choosing prizes to be reformed immediately. Let us vote. Let everyone vote. Why not? Every year we spend money at the festival, yet we have to go and stand outside cinemas so far away from Renne. They literally send cineastes miles away to see films in cinemas plenty haven't even heard of. They stop the trains and buses so we have to walk for miles to those cinemas. When we get there sometimes they're full, there's so many of us.' Marceline is impressed. Not only is the girl's English good, her accent is perfect.

'The festival is meant for professionals and sellers first isn't it?'

'Without audiences there is no cinema. Without us the film industry goes bust. Without us every film festival will die fast.'

'Isn't this just an excuse to get free tickets?'

'Of course we want tickets. Many films in the bâtiment are shown to half empty half-asleep audiences while we who really want to see them have to queue for films in cinemas out of town.'

The girls behind her recite: 'We bring business here.

We buy supermarket food. We fill up all the cheap hotels. Without us the festival would go bust. YEAAHH.'

Voices sound loudly all around Marceline.

'Let me get this right. Getting tickets, would that be enough to make you happy at least for this year?'

The girls talk over the top of each other now until the spokes-girl regains control.

'Getting tickets for seats in the main cinemas is symbolic and just the beginning. We want to be involved in all stages of the festival selection of films and prizes.'

'Why?'

'We the public ultimately decide whether a film succeeds or not. We should have a say. Most reviewers get favours for doing favours. Yet we make or break the box office.'

'Cineastes are treated like idiots,' shouts another girl.

'Many of these reviewers only pay lip-service to big media and big money. Larry Linsteeg said as much.'

'Larry said that? Isn't he big money too?'

'He's broke!'

The girls start singing again. 'FREE LARRY LINSTEEG. FREE BROKE LAR-RY. WE WANT BROKE LARRY LINSTEEG FREE NOW.'

'Why aren't there any boys with you?'

'Oh, they're too frightened. They think they'll be photographed and then banned from screenings forever.'

'YEEEEAHH. THE BOYS ARE SCAREDY CATS.'

'Larry's a boy too isn't he, well an aging boy?'

'Larry took the festival on by going public. He said it like it is.'

Holding her earpiece Marceline has to shout to be heard. 'There you have it Severine. The average cineaste boy is on the nose while Larry Linsteeg who was a boy once too if I remember correctly is now their saviour.' From the studio Severine smiles at her reporter.

'If elections were held for the position of administrative delegate would Larry Linsteeg win?'

Marceline turns to the crowd. 'Would you vote for Larry as festival chief?'

'YEESSS. LARRY POUR DIRECTEUR.'

Smiling, surrounded by a sea of shouting, singing, cheering and waving girls, Marceline covers her earpiece with her free hand. 'So, it seems the still absent Larry Linsteeg can do no wrong. At least for these young cineastes. Back to you.'

The studio anchor smiles at a camera. 'Renne-sur-Mer's young cineaste protesters vote for more democracy at the troubled Renne film festival, while their hero, American producer, Larry Linsteeg, who is in unofficial custody somewhere, still cannot be found. No-one knows quite what authority has him. No-one knows when or if he will be released. And no word from management on what they plan to do for the rest of the festival, or whether they will close-up for the year. That's the state of play tonight.'

THE SOUND OF AN OUTBOARD MOTOR brings Merryl out onto the back landing. She looks down to see a shivering Jack staring up at her from his dinghy. 'I'm frozen stiff, Merryl. Give me a hand.'

'Two in a night. It's spring Jack. You should have come back earlier.'

'Two in what, Merryl?'

'What happened to you?'

'I asked first.'

'Don't be childish.'

'Somebody hijacked my dinghy Merryl. I had to take a ferryboat with partygoers to shore. I had no way back, so I saw a film. I thought I'd have to sleep on the beach. When I came back down onto the sand the dinghy was right there.'

'Were you going to swim back if it wasn't?'

'I thought of it.'

'Then you are truly crazy.' Merryl helps him up on to the landing.

'I'm freezing.'

'What film was it?'

'Jaws.'

'My god. Perfect. Why didn't you stay on Ivan's boat?'

'I was there to talk business with him. Imagine if he found me the next morning sleeping on the deck.'

'And did you talk business?'

'Yes of course I did. We had a great discussion. We made startling progress.'

'I'll get you a towel.'

'Get my robe.'

She doesn't answer, heading inside and coming back with a fluffy towel. 'You will catch a death being out like this.'

'I was warm when I took the ferry.'

'It's spring Jack and of course you're drunk.'

'So was everyone else.'

She helps him out of his wet clothes. 'What is wrong with you.'

'I made it back didn't I. Get me my robe.'

Merryl keeps helping him off with his shirt. She towels him dry. 'Wrap up.'

'My robe is much warmer.'

'Get dry.'

'Why can't I have my robe?'

'It's being washed.'

'Now?'

She doesn't answer.

'Get my robe, please.'

'A guest is using it.'

'What guest?'

'Quiet. He's asleep.'

'HE. Asleep where?'

'You are not the only man who had trouble in this bay tonight. He was injured.'

'What happened?'

'It's a long story.'

'I bet it is.'

'I had to help him. I'll tell you everything later.'

'Tell me now.'

'Quiet. He's asleep.'

'He who?'

'You'll wake him. He nearly died.'

'I want to know who he is and where he's sleeping?'

'You're impossible you know that.'

'Who the hell is he?'

'The guy who was swallowed by that shark.'

'What? Where is he?'

'In our bed.'

'What the ... MERRYL.'

'It's not like that you fool.'

'Where am I going to sleep?'

'With me in the galley.'

'On those narrow benches?'

'He nearly died.'

'What if I had swum out in the dark? I would have been exhausted and found him in my bed.'

'If you swam out tonight you'd probably be dead.'

A coughing behind them turns them both around. Jack sees a man standing at the door to the boat's galley. He takes off Jack's robe and holds it out.

'He's even wearing my silk pyjamas.'

'Jack.'

'I'll take your runabout back.'

'You won't Fred.'

'It's Fred is it.'

'I can bring it back tomorrow.'

'It was stolen once tonight so I guess it makes sense. Take it. It's clearly not mine.'

'Stop it Jack right now. Fred, you are staying. And we're sleeping in the galley. We'll all talk about this tomorrow.'

'I'll go back to the beach and bunk there if you want.'

'JACK.'

WHEN THE PRÉSIDENT OF FRANCE appears without any warning on late night television and speaks soberly of an outbreak of troubles forged by subversive groups in the deep south, shackling this to a boiler-plate discourse on matters of national security, emphasizing more than once that what is happening in Renne is also happening to the nation, an unseasonal cool-change blows in from the far west Mediterranean.

Nobody is quite sure how it all came to this so fast but that a very cool change has arrived is now a meteorological fact. And soon the western winds of change are blowing at greater than eighty knots, with hats, scarfs and a miscellany of untethered objects loosely stored on balconies flying all over Renne's seafront. Dogs bark, cats moan, schtum seagulls gather in fluffballs of feathers, and the usually unflappable cohort of festival journalists stand hard liquor in hand opining to audiences or in digital and print outlets how flabbergasted they are.

'Why has the Président become involved?' one journalist asks finally, managing only to say this in a hoarse whisper in a bar. 'Did Daniel Martin contact him? Did the Président contact Martin?' Whatever, everyone now knows that the Renne film festival is now a matter of national security, with an older correspondent gravely tagging the moment politically, culturally, historically, as Renne-sur-Mer's greatest crisis ever. Journalists called into a hush-hush meeting chaired by Madame Maire in the mairie's boardroom are handed printed briefing materials which are passed around with top-secret strict embargo orders stamped on them in bold, the maire saying that hastily drawn-up contempt of the République legal sanctions involving the country's highest court are now in place—a not so tacit threat to all invitées that they are all sworn to absolute secrecy, or else.

Within half an hour the festival's journalistic fraternity has let practically all of the rest of France know everything that has been proclaimed down to the last syllable in the last sentence of the last page of the document, a document riddled with typos throughout.

Only one writer in town, Larry's, knows absolutely nothing. Snoring in his sloop, somehow he slipped off everyone's list, or as a screenwriter he didn't qualify, or someone thought him untrustworthy. Whatever the reason, he simply is personne, nobody, a nothing, even though many other nothings and personnes in town were invited by the maire's press-team. F and Martin attended, so too a subdued général, learning from Madame Maire that several platoons of infantry and military police armed to the teeth are being trucked to Renne as she speaks. Combat vehicles and troops are on tinderbox standby.

And as soon as the winds abate, patrol boats armed with missiles will motor over. Even the airport 32 kilometres to the east of the coastal town has been surrounded, though nobody quite knows why.

Day 3

Sitting in Le Magnifique bar intern Cindy Turper is waiting for her boss to come down from his room. So far in twenty or so minutes, she's managed to experience more journalism than her entire two months in the London Sentinel office. With several guys looking her over, Cindy was hoping she might be offered a coffee and croissant or cake for breakfast. After the cheap-skate early morning flight from London to Renne right now she could eat and drink anything, though not one of the scribes staring her way will dare say a word to her.

One thing she won't dare do either is move from her listening post on these steps in the middle of everything. The bar debate is lively, with Larry Linsteeg, the man many are accusing of creating chaos in Renne copping a lot. So far, he's been described as a turncoat, a self-serving hypocrite, a liar, cheat, thief, half-baked blancmange, blaggard, bankrupt, and an utter fool, and that's only Cindy's shortlist of Linsteeg's crimes so far. One man at the bar even said he should be in prison.

'He was wasn't he?'

'Well he should have stayed there,' says the first man, summing Linsteeg up coldly with: 'When your career is in the toilet pretend to have political beliefs.'

Only one man present way down at the end of the bar is even a touch sympathetic. 'Going out on a limb isn't Larry's style. Believe me, I know Larry.'

Bent over her pad Cindy is battling with a half-working pen to keep up with all the negative comments. And she's disappointed that nobody so far has mentioned rumours going around about his relationships with young female staff. Cindy thought of bringing it up, or at least offering: Can we leave our opinions on Larry generally to one side for a moment and concentrate on some of the facts? But everyone in this bar is too concerned with expressing themselves generally. It seems specific details and facts can wait. Larry Linsteeg's direct connection to the current terrible situation is the only matter that is relevant right now.

Cindy knows protesters have disrupted the festival to the point of bringing it crashing down, but nobody is saying anything about the paralysed management, the uncertain cops, or the dithering Mairie. And as the man at the end of the bar has quite reasonably offered: 'The demonstrators just want their concerns to be heard.'

Cindy still doesn't know Renne-sur-Mer from a polymer yet from what she's heard she's beginning to think the authorities have completely blown it. If getting control of the current mess is the objective, litter was everywhere driving in from the airport, so even the standard clean-up services are not working.

In the middle of scribbling, her boss appears by her side and with a tap on her shoulder and a curt, 'Let's go', Cindy is forced up and out of the hotel by her paper's main Renne correspondent, Steve Botchwell, to walk in a stiffening breeze without breakfast, following him on what he calls the 'mission' — to be two London-based witnesses to Renne-sur-Mer's demise.

The protests have been happening already for days. They've already missed plenty. Cindy wishes she had the courage to say: well, if we have missed so much couldn't we just miss a bit more and have coffee and a croissant first before heading off to discover more mess. Would a five-minute breakfast change anything? But this is her first day in the field and she hasn't yet mustered enough courage to challenge Steve on anything, not even the obvious: without food it's hard to walk. So on she goes following him with a hollow stomach holding up a light head, her hair blowing everywhere. With her pen and pad in hand she feels more like a journalist from seventy years ago than a twenty-first century film reviewer. She sure as hell wishes she was in the 20th century. If she were, she would have her grandma's biscuits to munch on and her mother's 1960's tape-recorder to record Steve's gems, like: We're in the crotch of time. Duck the bottles with burning linen. Give all missiles a miss. Never eyeball a hardass in a balaclava.

The only hardass in a balaclava Cindy's eyeballed so far is up on a billboard. In truth it's a bandanna. Still, she won't argue with herself, or Steve.

Feigning attention, dead-panning responses to each pronouncements, she's learned fast that short pot-bellied aging white journalists can turn nasty when second-guessed by tall slim better-read multilingual black girls.

A brown colleague in the London office whispered before she left: 'Don't backchat Steve. Nod, grin, if you want to keep the job.' Cindy's not sure she wants to keep this or any job if it means working for Steve Botchwell.

On the plane over France, Cindy prayed day one would be an acclimatisation. After breakfast, a quick walk-around in pre-storm conditions, then witnessing Steve doing celebrity interviews. Certainly not running bent-backed through streets littered with what Steve claims are unexploded shells.

They are rushing apparently to get a taxiboat in order to meet a rogue Russian with a reputation almost as dubious as Larry Linsteeg's. Some film protesters, or whatever they are, trot by them shouting, 'la légitimité cinématographique est morte' punctuated by loud bangs way down the street. It's scared the hell out of Cindy.

She threw herself to the ground after the last explosion lying on the hard bitumen thinking: what's an African-French girl with a MA distinction from King's College London doing lying on this road in the middle of a live-to-air cultural revolution? Confused and dazed by hunger, she gets back to her feet, stars rotating at the edges of her vision as she endures more of Steve's laughter.

'Only a firecracker girlie.'

Cindy grimaces her appreciation of another of his great wisecracks. If she had a pound for all Steve's bad jokes, his 'girlie' or 'don't go studenty on me' comments, she wouldn't have to work again.

With a panama glued to his bald head, that bitter glint in his eyes, what would he be like to live with? Lucky Mrs B doesn't get to see him too often, his assignments mercifully keeping him away-from-home a lot.

Her hair blowing across her face, Cindy watches Steve taking pics of protesters gluing posters over official signs. She hopes like hell the Russian lays on some food. Her blood sugar is rock bottom. A protest-boy with cute bedroom eyes reminiscent of the young Ashton Kutcher smiles her way, giving her spirits a lift. She smiles back. 'Qu'est ce que voulez-vous arriver?' she asks half-expecting Steve to embarrass her again with: I ask the questions girlie.

'Le festival est corrompu.'

'Avez-vous la preuve?'

'On n'a pas besoin de preuve. On le sait.'

'Vous savez?'

'Oui.' By his accent, he's not French. She walks over

and examines his artwork: CULTURE EN LUTTE and LA FORCE C'EST NOUS and then one in English: CORRUPT JURY OUT NOW.

'Qu'est ce que voulez-vous?'

'C'est notre vision démocratique d'un festival du futur.'

Steve cuts off her first live interview with a brusque: 'The boat's waiting. Let's go.' The kid grins, calling out as she totters after Steve: 'DOWN WITH ALL CORRUPT SUGAR DADDIES.'

Cindy frowns. 'He's not my... BONNE CHANCE,' she yells back, her Kutcher lookalike demo-artist giving her the thumbs-up.

'They're not your friends,' Steve says, his head-teacher voice back again.

'I was being ironic,' she manages to say. 'The protesters could make a great interview wouldn't they?'

Steve doesn't answer. He won't let her even do interviews. Yet born in the Congo, speaking English, French and Italian, she's more than qualified. She certainly saw enough street violence as a kid. Everything around her feels thick and gluey all of sudden, Cindy wondering how she'll be able to put-up with Steve for seven days, if she and him even make it through day one.

Watching his middle age waddle to the wharf she's wondering how she got an internship with him in the first place. Looking up the road she sees men in balaclavas coming down from the western pier. By the way they're walking she doesn't need to know more about them. These guys are way different to the kids and their posters. As an Italian journalist said this morning: 'I ragazzi sono infiltrati.'

The town could well be infiltrated. She runs after Steve as a voice down the street echoes in a PA system: 'Le festival est fermé. Nous allons vous tous mettre à jour à nouveau à six heures et trente minutes,' the woman's voice followed by wolf-whistles. Cindy doesn't need years of experience to know the festival is in real trouble. Catching up to Steve she hears him give his name to a boat driver who nods and starts his engine. Getting down into the speedboat, Cindy decides to accept that Steve knows something. Glancing at his profile, she needs to respect that about him. He definitely knows his hardasses in balaclavas from the big talking kids in jeans.

Sitting near the bow she tries meditating her hunger away, thinking on what she can possibly do today that's useful.

So, what does she know? The festival has been wound-up by demonstrators demanding rights, ticket rights apparently, which led to windows getting broken and the kidnapping of a Hollywood producer. A shark fell from a helicopter. This last bit she doesn't understand at all. Together it all led to a collapse in the usual order of things. So she's been told.

Motoring out through luxury cruisers and large sail boats Cindy wonders how long before a rich guy's yacht gets vandalized. Maybe Steve is right. Hell is about to break loose. Whatever the truth of Steve's pronouncements, Cindy doesn't look like getting even a late breakfast anytime soon.

'How does a film festival break down like this?'

'Riots start in the blink of an eye.'

'Yes, but this is France.'

'Happens everywhere.'

'These protesters say there's corruption and they want to stop it. I asked them if they have any proof. He said the festival's corrupt. I asked how they know. He said they just know.'

'They don't care about the truth.'

'Do you think the jury could be corrupt?'

'I have no idea. Anyone can be corrupt.'

'If we repeat a lie, that make us responsible for the lie?'

'Record what's going on. Follow the story. At this moment it's just a possible element in someone's narrative.'

Yeah, someone's narrative, Steve sounding almost postmodern. At least he didn't call her girlie again. And he seems to have dropped his headmaster tone. For the time being. Maybe he did appreciate her asking questions.

Exiting the marina, she stares up at the clouds, feeling raindrops beginning to fall, Cindy wondering if the real story is back at the bâtiment, not out interviewing a porn filmmaker on his floating flophouse.

THE WRITER JACK HAS IN MIND for Ivan's new project is watching a speedboat chauffeuring a short pot-bellied guy and a sassy tall black girl out of the harbour. Heading no doubt to old pot-belly's private yacht, where he'll have his way with her. 'Film Festivals, go figure.'

The rain starting up drives him back inside his rental. Larry's writer doesn't know where the taxiboat is going or if any offence is about to take place, but the sighting sure annoyed him. Ditto for what's happening over at the bâtiment, on TV, radio, and in the streets. It has Larry's writer wondering if his anger is due to the fact he's out of touch with life or his writing. All he really knows right now is his essential services on this boat are not working. His cell phone only functions every now and then and his laptop's internet connection blips-out. More than anything though the sloop's john is blocked up. Having no sailing experience Larry's writer doesn't know a Nature from an Air Head. But he knows trouble when he smells it. The agent told him it was a state-of-the-art foolproof composter system separating liquids from solids. The only thing it's separating out right now are the gases and they're filling his galley. He's called the agent twice and left messages. No answer. Going up top for some air his mobile rings down inside. He thought it was dead. Flying back down the stairs he trips and nearly goes face-first down the stepladder. He manages to save himself by throwing his knee out in front of himself which he bangs hard. Limping across the galley he gasps 'Hello' into his cellphone.

'Jack here.'

Larry's writer vigorously rubbing his knee, squints as he asks: 'Who are you again?'

'Jack.'

'Jack who?'

'Jack Kimmelon, producer of Dances with Wolves three, son.'

'You are doing Dances three? As what?'

'Producer in development.'

'I didn't know there was a Dances 2.'

Larry's writer wonders why he's even struggling to put a face to the name. Nobody appears in his memory. Maybe it shouldn't. He squints at his mobile screen, getting nowhere there either. 'Have we met?'

'Ivan's boat. The director Ed Gobong Olay whatshisname was there.'

The writer thinks a moment. 'Edgar Gordon Olles.'

'Bingo.'

Larry's writer can see him now. A little old guy dressed like a seventies disco try-on, harassing girls all over the decks, banging on to him about all the great films he had seen.

'I was expecting someone else.'

There is a silence at Jack's end. 'A producer?'

'An agent.'

There is another silence.

'I have a proposition to put to you son. It's a writing job. No agents needed.'

Larry's writer stands up straighter. 'An assignment?'

'Can we meet?'

'You have somewhere in mind?'

'Bar des Poissons, a mariner's bar from the forties. You know it?'

Larry's writer has a sinking feeling. He knows he doesn't want to go back there and tries thinking of an alternative, but none comes to mind. 'The forties?'

'The roaring forties, the way back when era.'

'The roaring forties are trade winds, Jack. You mean the roaring twenties.'

'Yeah. Fish. Hemingway. Boats. Cuba. All that ocean-stuff. Off market street. Say three o'clock? You good for a beer son?'

'Any time.'

'Done. See you at three. On the dot son.'

'Jack, could I ...'

The old coot has rung off, leaving Larry's writer staring around the rental cabin trying to recall what film they talked about on Ivan's yacht, wondering if Jack said he liked Fellini or Spielberg. Larry's writer remembers both directors turning up in the shouted exchanges, but in truth he could barely hear him, Jack making about as much sense as Ivan's reasons for holding the party. Still, whatever was said or whether there was zero chemistry between them or not, Larry's writer knows he can't afford to look this gift horse in the mouth. It's meet Dances with Wolves three in the roaring 40s then. Now normally, a writer would ask a question or two about any job offer but Larry's writer has never understood how that process worked in the first place. The producer has all the power. That's where all questions begin and end. He has very little time to prepare anything. So, what has he got to lose? Go, talk, take it from there, wherever there is. Larry's writer needs a break and to get one he needs to be positive. Whistling and rubbing his hands he moves around cleaning up the mess inside the sloop and there's plenty, just in case Jack whoever-he-really-is invites himself back to discuss matters more. He sounded like the self-inviting kind. The trick in the creative world, as Larry's writer sees it, is to be ready for whatever and go wherever the whatever takes you. Hope is more than half any opportunity. Whistling as he washes dishes, he then stacks his papers, wipes tops and mops the floor. He's sure of one thing, the boat agent will be impressed. If he shows up. Now if Larry's writer can get the blocked toilet fixed and the meeting with Jack works out, today will be his best festival day so far, by some margin.

He will negotiate like a Pro, walk in and take charge right away, get his ideas into Jack's head and start running the show. He'll set the rules. Inform himself. He'll stand tall. He's already seeing everything in a different light.

Showering and drying off, he dresses and grabs his things—watch, passport, notepad and practically empty wallet. Still, he feels good right now even if he's limping from his latest self-inflicted bruise. He's ready to face the world. He doesn't lock up, as usual, leaving the hatch ajar and portholes wide open to let out the stink. His neighbours must love him. Outside rain is coming down. His mobile rings. The writer checks his screen, rain drops all over it.

'Hello.'

'You called, monsieur.'

'Monsieur Leblon, thank god, your state-of-the-art composter is all blocked.'

'What?'

'The loo's broken.'

'Have you been stuffing your writing down there?'

'I don't write on paper,' Larry's writer lies.

With a pay day looming, Larry's writer feels he can afford to be bold, argue even with a seasoned French boat agent. In the agent's own language if he has to.

'I could come by tomorrow.'

'The plumber and you or just you?'

'I'll come by first.'

'Bring the plumber as well.'

Leblon lists the things he must do, where he must be tomorrow.

'I am planning to relocate.'

Leblon chuckles. 'In the middle of a festival, you may find it hard monsieur?'

'You don't know the people I know. I am meeting a producer. It's tomorrow or I'll have to find somewhere else. Tomorrow at the latest. With the plumber.'

'I'll do my best,' Leblon says without conviction.

The phone is dead. Limping along the damp wharf Larry's writer is glad he was rude. He's within his rights. Living with a backed-up boat-loo is nervewracking. He woke in the night thinking: I'll swim out to sea. A shark'll take me. I'll end it. They'll find my pages. I'll become posthumously famous. Writing's Vincent Van Gogh. In odd moments the idea doesn't seem that unattractive. Larry's writer stares at the hills day-dreaming of a spacious comfy place with a pool. The wet anonymous hills stare back at him saying: forget it. Jack sounded keen. If he's in with Kevin Costner he's a player. With the porn king involved, there's probably money. If Larry's writer can dump Larry's job he'll throw a party. Passing Pizza Palace he decides he'll have it there. Invite everyone.

He sees a large crowd ahead waving placards. Have the ticket beggars formed a union? Getting closer he realises it's big, hearing real anger in their voices. What looked like actors far-off isn't so fake close-up, Larry's writer impressed by how real it all really is.

ORDERED TO REMAIN IN THEIR VANS gendarmes whisper in low voices, the younger ones wondering when they'll be sent into battle. Their commander can't take their anxiety any longer and climbs out in the rain to stand by his truck calling his captain for some sort of order he can pass on. Nobody higher-up is telling him anything.

Lieutenant Corot wouldn't mind being on the other side right now. The protesters look like they're having fun. All the cops in town are hated. Corot and his men are in a front line, nobody daring to mention the blueline that melted away on day one. His captain answers finally, the lieutenant asking his superior what his orders are. His captain says to be patient. Corot explains that his men are anxious. The captain tells Corot to tell them to stay calm.

'This protest is getting worse. The crowd's getting bigger every minute.'

'Do they have weapons?'

'They're carrying flowers.'

'There you go.'

'Flowers are powerful symbols, captain.'

'Better than missiles or flaming bottles, lieutenant?'

'There have been a few missiles too. Someone's providing these flowers, captain. It's growing, I'm sure of it.' To support Corot's point, a demonstrator goes by him with a bunch of sunflowers and whacks the side of his van.

'It's not what it seems, captain. Check the TV. See for yourself. The people and the media are on the demonstrators' side. If we do nothing, it'll turn out to be more than nothing. We need clear orders.'

'I will get back to you, lieutenant. Stay calm, cocked and ready.'

The captain rings off, leaving Corot staring at his phone, sure he heard a snigger on the line before it went dead.

Why did he call? Shaking his head, Corot starts climbing back inside the van but demonstrators pouring out of a side street stop him. He makes a note then phones another commander, asks what he is seeing where he is. Corot says he doesn't want to overreact but can't help worrying about what is coming. 'A mood-change is happening. In case nobody believes me I have my diary.'

'For all the good it'll do you,' the commander says back.

Corot rings off, seeing different kinds of people turning up, not just young cineastes and students. Ordinary older men and women are here, some in nice dresses and pressed shirts, twin sets and pearls right out of the 1950s.

It's a broad church of agitation, he writes. Pleased with his description he looks for more signs of troublemakers. He writes-up what he analyses. He thought he saw two troublemakers, but they turned out to be cops in plainclothes.

Still, Corot is sure there are hardasses in the protest. A mature age woman goes by with a sign: BEGGARS CAN BE CHOOSERS. The appearance of a liberal styled sentiment worries Corot. The protesters are winning the psychological battle. The crowd is now completely sympathetic to the original marchers. If things get nasty who knows what'll happen. Ordinary people might join in, and even steal tickets from legitimate film-people. Corot relates more ideas in more mobile calls, telling other commanders about his analyses. He gives up when some of them begin laughing. Seeing a photographer taking shots he runs over to him. Initially the photographer isn't keen to be seen with Corot, grimacing at being questioned.

Corot does his best to give an impression of being a friendly flic. Finally, the man relaxes, shrugging as he says that some are rappers, others older demonstrators, rock and rollers reliving a long-gone past. Some are just carrying signs: tickets please, or can you share your leftovers, or something like that.

'Tickets? That's all they want?'

'Every year this happens. Ticket holders don't bother showing up. Seats are empty meaning there is always room for others. Free tickets are never given out'.

'In the main, who are the protesters?'

The photographer grins. 'Cineastes and those in the industry who are not getting into film showings because they're not a producer or something.'

Corot frowns at what the man is saying.

'Where did they get their signs?'

'They are making them from market leftovers.'

'What about the flowers?'

'The stall holders gave them away.'

'The stallholders gave stuff away?'

'Nobody's going to the markets. Stallholders are not making too much so they are giving stuff away. Food too.'

Corot shakes the photographer's hand and thanks him, then calls his captain and relates what he has heard. The captain thanks Corot for the heads up, saying he will pass on this intelligence up the line.

Corot returns to his van angrier than he was before, wondering why he even made this call. If it turns out to be good intelligence the captain will take the credit. If it is bad, then it will be Corot's fault for being a nervous nellie. Still, he senses big trouble coming. Climbing outside again he checks the crowd. Leaning on the side of his van he sketches protesters, wishing he had stayed with his art studies.

'Why do kids please their parents?'

His mobile rings.

'More men are arriving, lieutenant.'

'Not more vans captain?'

'Yes.'

'More vans with more nervous flics is not a good idea.'

But his captain has rung off. So much for Corot's intervention. His superiors used what he had said to justify reinforcements. Corot rubs his face. This will end badly. He just knows it. Looking down the road he sees the shape of the big commander, the man's bow-legged gait pushing through the crowd towards Corot's van.

'Oh Jesus.' Corot opens the door. 'Outside. In formation on the double.' Corot salutes his most senior commander as his men stumble out of the van to fall in.

'What are you lot doing, sleeping?'

'Waiting for orders sir. We were told to stand by.'

Général Pilot studies the men. 'Why have they got sand on their boots?'

'I told them they could have lunch on the beach.'

'This isn't a picnic, lieutenant.'

'I know sir.'

A wave of singing erupts from some kids waving flowers in the air near the bâtiment: LAR-RY LAR-RY GIVE ME YOUR ANSWER DO. I'M HALF CRAZY ALL FOR THE LOVE OF YOU. IT WON'T BE A STYLISH PICKET. WE CAN'T AFFORD A TICKET. BUT WE'LL BE SWEET IF YOU CAN GET US A SEAT IN A FESTIVAL MADE NEW BY YOU.

'What the hell are they singing?'

'I think it is an old english song, sir.'

'What english song?'

'I think it goes: It won't be a stylish marriage. They changed it to, it won't be a stylish picket.' Corot sings it in translation: 'Lar-ry Lar-ry donnez-moi votre réponse, faites-le. Je suis à moitié fou tout pour l'amour de vous.'

The Général stares back at the lieutenant without a trace of a smile.

CLAMBERING OFF THEIR TAXIBOAT Steve and Cindy are met by three members of Ivan's crew. Following them up three flights of stairs they are led into a reception area for the scheduled meeting with the already infamous, at least in some circles, Ivan Dzershinzky. He greets them warmly and then introduces a short stocky white-headed man he names as his new partner, Jack Kimmelon.

Jack takes over after that mentioning the startling fact, at least for Cindy, that he is the producer of Dances with Wolves 2. Cindy nearly asks him for clarification of this because she's heard nothing of Kevin Costner following his American frontier film with another, but her voice gets lost in the loud exclamation by an aide: 'No recording equipment.' Cindy holds up her pad.

The same crewmember steps forward indicating with hand-signals that they have to lift their arms. He frisks them both thoroughly, but Cindy a little more so, who holding her breath tolerates the liberal Russian investigation of her chest. Steve's mini-recorder is discovered and removed. Rosy in the face, he starts speaking quickly as he often does in moments like these, describing the London Sentinel and his position in the organisation, its global reach and readership etc.

Witnessing this Cindy was thinking, nationalist more like it. That's how the meeting that changed Cindy's life all got started. Coffee tea and biscuits were brought in and passed around. Cindy somehow managed not to rush the biscuit basket, as Steve began in his usual earnest way, using his usual earnest spiel, one that Cindy notices had Ivan smiling less and less.

'I know The Sentinel, a trash rag.'

Trash rag? Cindy thought, that's elevating the daily a touch.

'What do you really want to know?'

'What is the Society of Friends for Russian Cinema?'

This is where Steve's interview, as Cindy sees it, went right off the rails into haywire territory and never got back on track. Ivan said nothing, showing her boss the thinnest of smiles. 'After what I have been through you think you can probe me with some phoney agenda?'

Why this broadside reply didn't phase Steve, Cindy doesn't know, because if it had been her she would have been on the floor. At that point, at least for her, if the writing wasn't already on Ivan's cabin wall, then it wouldn't ever be, even if it were thrown up there using a whole can of paint.

'Do you have films in the pipeline?'

'In the where?'

Steve soldiered on like he was neck deep in a swamp. Cindy's seen dogged types make fools of themselves but Steve that day really took the cake.

'I've heard one is a film on Aldrich Ames. Anything you can tell me on that?'

Ivan said nothing, leaning over and pouring himself some tea, for a second smiling to himself, Cindy almost leaning over to her boss to say: listen up tin ear.

'That's one project. Viktor's. He's not here.'

'Does he want to say something?'

Ivan paused again. 'More than say what the Hollywood director wanted to say in Enemy of the State?'

'So, is there a message in the Ames film?'

Why Steve, an experienced reporter, would take this line in questioning was a mystery to Cindy. Did he want to be thrown off the boat? Physically. It was at that point that Ivan turned to Cindy. 'What do you like in films?'

'She's an intern.'

Ivan continued on ignoring Steve. 'What do you prefer?'

'Anything that makes me think or laugh.'

'Any films you can mention?'

Cindy glanced at Steve before answering. 'Six Degrees of Separation and The Paper.'

Steve cleared his throat loudly. 'Mr Dzerzhinsky.'

Ivan continued ignoring him.

'Will Smith.'

'Ah! Then you know Six Degrees?'

'A Fred Schepisi film. Donald Sutherland, Will Smith, Stockard Channing, Ian McKellen, Bruce Davison, Mary Beth Hurt.'

Cindy glanced warily at Steve as he leaned forward saying: 'Could I just come back to Aldrich Ames?'

'Wassily Wassilyevich Kandinsky. Chaos control. You like, you like.' Then Ivan speaks in Russian, finishing with, the translation is: 'Art is born from the inner necessity of the artist in an enigmatic mystical way through which it acquires an autonomous life. It becomes an independent subject animated by a spiritual breath.'

'Wow, I'd like to use that.'

Steve cleared his throat. 'Where exactly?'

'For a journal paper, not the Sentinel, Steve.'

Her face was warm now too. A touch lightheaded, she turned back to Ivan, knowing in her heart if not her head that this was a pivotal moment in her career.

'His speech on The Catcher in the Rye was good.'

'Speak to Viktor about Salinger. He has a theory about Mark David Chapman and John Hinckley Jr. and that novel.'

Steve coughed. 'I was wondering.'

That's when Ivan arranged a tour of the boat for Steve. Calling out in Russian, two crewmembers arrived, standing to attention while Ivan spoke rapidly in Russian at them. He pointed at the door. The two men picked Steve up by his underarms, Steve throwing Cindy a thunderous look as they carried him outside.

Meanwhile, alone with Ivan, she had a wonderful discussion on the subject of great films, saying what living in Britain was like for her, adding that in a society run on hierarchy, humiliating your boss was not high on the recommended list. Ivan waved away her concerns.

'I am Russian. We know plenty about people like Steve. I'll help you.'

'How exactly?'

'I will ask my London lawyer to handle it.'

'Don't please.'

Then he spoke of his plans to buy a London newspaper stunning Cindy with: 'You can work on it.' Cindy sat in his cabin not knowing what to say at that point.

They had lunch. She took a deep breath and questioned him on his reputation as a pornographer. Ivan was open with her saying it was: 'A business I once owned, not managed.' Then he talked about sex films being a seriously defining business for many.

'Porn films?'

Watching Cindy writing he said almost in a half-whisper: 'I provided a service for politicians who wanted, needed, many of them, pornography without public scrutiny. We provided a package, no digital traces possible for anyone snooping. We had clients all over the world via our encrypted web sites. Russians are good at this.'

'You must have made a fortune.'

'Facilitating weakness is an easy way to make money. Porn is not the issue. Not even the business. It's a trade based in the weakness in character.'

'The absence of character.'

Ivan smiled. 'Don't let that man out there ruin your judgment. Some men are good at it. Some women too. We know about him. We've known about him for years. Why do you think he came here?'

Cindy stares back at Ivan, her smile frozen.

'Do you understand me?'

'Mr Dzerzhinsky let me explain something to you.'

'Ivan...please.'

'I'm an intern. This is my first trip for the paper. I am a female. I am black. I am a foreigner. What happened to my boss now won't be forgotten.'

'You worry too much.'

Half an hour and some minutes later Steve was returned unconscious with a large gash on the side of his head. Apparently, so Ivan's men said, he had fallen off the back landing and banged his head on an exposed propellor. How, Cindy couldn't understand, because she thought nothing was exposed back there.

She never did find out the truth and soon decided she probably shouldn't even try. When the shock had subsided, after she had heard a thorough run-through of her erstwhile boss's hidden past, Steve and Cindy were returned to shore accompanied by two Russians, one of them who oddly enough spoke fluent English.

Cindy found herself transported to the local hospital and while waiting during Steve's patch up, she received a call on her mobile from her paper's editor in London.

A bandaged Steve was placed on the last evening flight back to London and Cindy found herself elevated to the Sentinel's lone festival correspondent in Renne.

As a frightened woman tries and fails to make a festival update announcement, the bâtiment forecourt erupts into catcalling, scores of cineastes holding up hand-written banners shouting out: TICKETS TICKETS. WE WANT TICKETS. TICKETS NOW. From his position on a balcony opposite F stares down into the street filled with what he would only describe as street criminals—thugs and thugettes—swearing and laughing, as if thinking they're at a wild buck's or hen's party.

'Utter disgrace,' he hisses. If he were in charge, he would have instructed the woman making the announcement not to run, even if there were missiles raining down on her. Stand your ground, he would order, my men will take care of you.

Turning his binoculars east he sees another group of idiots setting up what looks like a speaker system, one particularly immature-looking boy holding a microphone. F counts two large speakers and one very old-looking amplifier. A girl is working a control board. Two television cameramen are waiting to film, record, whatever the boy-idiot is going to say.

The bâtiment management has totally lost control. As F predicted would happen. He scans the scene again, taking in the face of the laughing boy holding the microphone. He wouldn't be laughing if F and his men were in charge down there. The kid grins at the girl with headphones on now, arranging CDs, setting sound levels it seems.

'This is organised.' As F thought it was all along. He takes another telephoto shot.

'GO,' the girl says, her voice escaping from crackling speakers as a very old recording of La Marseillaise starts-up, filling the street, startling the crowd. Clapping begins. The sound of the boy using a radio announcer's voice of the nineteen forties really irritates F, hearing his well-rehearsed delivery spread via two old speakers all down the street:

'With the failure of the nineteen sixty-eight film wars many cineastes turned hopefully or desperately to Hollywood for help and finding none there London became the disembarkation point. With nothing-much except the Beatles to look forward to, the awful weather and even worse food drives the film-loving refugees to set up a new trail down from Berlin over the Alps to Venice, where they travel the northern isthmus to the western coast and walking the Italian and then French Rivieras, moving on to Anglacé by train, car or on foot, camping out on the beaches of the Côte d'Azur, and from there through influence or luck the fortunate or connected are able to obtain badges. Those who are not beg for freebies outside cinémas, begging, waiting, begging and waiting. And if they're lucky, they are given seats in far-off cinémas in La Bouche and other forgotten far-flung places.' La Marseillaise begins fading out, a by now furious F studying the grinning face of the boy as he's congratulated by many around him.

'Why haven't the police moved in? Damn liberal générals.'

BELLA IS IN A RIGHT TIZZ now as well. Using binoculars, she finds her view of the bâtiment is blocked by rows of palm-trees. The bâtiment on riot street is only one hundred meters away but she can't see a thing. It's driving her nuts, her wall TV her only connection to reality.

'What's the point of being a multi-billionaire if I can't see a revolution just outside my hotel? I'm renting the most expensive hotel-terrace in the world and I can't see an effing thing.' Her second-in-charge won't let her go outside, saying he can't guarantee her safety. Bella paces up and down on her rooftop swearing into phones at anybody she finds waiting on the other end and ringing off begins yelling at Jeff.

'Is nobody in charge anywhere?'

'Everyone is home Ms Fibben. When there's a riot that's where people go. Most people are too frightened to answer their phones. During an insurrection you're better off not talking to anyone.'

Sometimes Bella wishes Jeff would zip it but he's her only friend-contact right now. Furious, she presses digits on her mobile. Finally, she gets through to an assistant of the new director. She shakes her phone at Jeff saying: 'SEE!'

Waiting to speak to a character whose name she can't remember, usually a sign for her—if she can't fix the name of a character he or she is pretty certain to be nobody she actually needs—Bella wonders aloud if she's being recorded.

She doesn't want it known she cares about this, but she really needs this new guy right now. Walking around with a hand over the receiver sighing, finally the acting director is on the line. They speak. Matters proceed via Bella's hopeless French and his dubious English making for a linguistic dog's breakfast vis-à-vis their examination of the situation: Larry's place of detention, his whereabouts, and whether he can be freed easily. 'I'll donate to a new bâtiment if you can resolve this. First, though, I want the palm trees taken off the road out in front here.' When Bella tells Martin the sort of money she is prepared to throw in, the festival wheels begin turning. The acting director rings off saying he will be back in five minutes. Five on the dot he's back telling her she'll be speaking to Larry very, very soon.

'They are re-routing the call,' Bella mouths not so silently to Jeff, miming the wringing of a wet towel. Larry comes on the line sounding like he is half-dead.

'They drugged you.'

'I haven't eaten anything.'

'They drugged you in your sleep.'

'I haven't slept.'

'Physical deprivation, psychological pressure. I was briefed on all techniques. Have you drunk anything?'

'Some water.'

'There you go. Drugs were slipped in that. Larry, they want your film for tomorrow night. I spoke to this Martin fellow. He wants me there too.'

'Why would he want it after what Edgar did to him?'

'Trust me he does.' Bella stares across the room at her right-hand man and some technicians working on a trace.

'I'll get your team together.'

'Is Martin serious?'

'He better be.'

'I don't understand.'

'Larry, focus. I said they want your film for the première. Okay. Who cares why, just play the part. You ready?'

'I'll do anything to get out of here.'

'No more going on the bolshy side.'

'Bella, I'm not political. You know that.'

Never a truer word has come out of his mouth. At least the Larry Bella knew once a long time ago but what does she know of this Larry anymore.

'Some gendarme kept asking me why I'm protesting. They think I'm organized..'

'Who were they?'

The line has gone dead. Bella looks over at the men using a portable device to do a trace. Her main man shakes his head. 'You said you only needed a few minutes.'

'Maybe they have a blocking mechanism.'

THE BAR DES POISSONS is as empty as it was on day one, Larry's writer in his same outfit, except for his improvised hat and sunglasses. Everything is pretty well all the same. The same couple is there, with similar drinks in front of them. The same barman is behind the same bar. The same guy down back is lounging against the same mirror, his head probably in the same newspaper. If it weren't for a girl swearing at the cops in civvies Larry's writer would be lying the same as she was on the pavement, wondering the same, where am I? Who am I? As she still is no doubt. If she's alive. Let off by the same hair's breadth by the same cops beating her, Larry's writer looks around himself.

Bars filled with disinterested punters are usually the same. Let's be frank. All the same sorts of things happen to the same sorts of people all too often in bars. Larry's writer tells himself all the same he needs to prepare. For the same meeting he's had so many, too many times.

He orders the same beer he did on day one, using the same voice. Though the same barman doesn't seem to recognize him, Larry's writer guessing he's pretty much the same as any wandering anybody coming in from the hullabaloo outside. Larry's writer's experiencing the same sort of nervousness he always has, tackling it all in the same way he always has: Be cool. Use your front brain. Utter no negatives. Be the same as you always are. It gets Larry's writer sweating, knowing his same current look is not always the same best look he often forgets to use. Writer producer meetings often go bad, without agents, even worse. He gulps the same beer in the same way mouthing the same advice to himself: Aim for nothing. From nothing everything's up. A concrete deal is worth any number of deals in the bush. Larry's writer's giving himself the same peanuts advice he always has. Just the same he can't complain. He sips faster, his hands shaking in just the same way as they always do. Sell yourself. Be Yourself. Sit up straight. Same as it's ever been. Glancing over at the barman staring into space in the same way as he did on day one, then snapping out of it in just the same way, he walks over. 'Vous voulez quelque chose monsieur?' Larry's writer shakes his head. 'Je parle juste à moi-même,' he says adding, 'Avez-vous vu ça dehors? J'ai juste manqué d'être frappé.'

Hearing the same old foreign accent, the barman smiles in the same sympathetic way. Get a grip, Larry's writer mouths, gripping his glass, let's be honest, in the same desperate way he always does when confronted with the same situation. An old guy comes inside the bar, breaking Larry's writer's reveries. The determined spring in his old deft step gives Larry's writer a flash of a shiver of the same old butterfly stomach.

'Jesus H. Belafonte. What the hell's going on out there? Is it always the same as this?'

'I was in the middle of it. In answer to your question, this year is a little different.'

'What were other years like?'

'1968 was like this.'

'Were you here then, son?'

'There then?'

'Here.'

'Then?'

'Yeah.'

'No, Jack, I wasn't.'

Implicit shared recognition of the fact that they probably don't know what they're talking about dominates the silence that follows.

'The boat driver dropped me at the other end,' Jack says not offering his hand. Larry's writer remembers just in time to do the same.

'That pepper spray, son?'

Larry's writer coughs in the same way he usually does when caught out. 'It's raw out there.' Mumbling an old lie: 'I did my best.'

'Were there cops out there?'

Larry's writer doesn't answer too fast. 'Not that I saw.'

Stick to the story, he says to himself. He ducked the same batons as the girl. They missed. She could be dead. Larry's writer could be the same. Count your blessings and don't mention a thing. Fingering his thinning strip of euros in his wallet he raises a hand to get the barman's attention. He and Jack look the same, strangers doing the same to each other when one or both don't want much to do with the other. All the same, Jack's arrival is a step in the right direction.

'Deux cafés.'

The barman nods and walks away the same as he did on day one.

'What're you doing at the moment?'

'More of the same. Researching, writing.' Larry's writer coughs. 'The usual and you?'

'Working with Ivan. Developing Dances with Wolves 2.'

'With Kevin?'

'Who?'

'Costner.'

'Yeah, Kev, Kev Coster.'

The same pause button has been pushed on nothing produced. Smothered in another awkward silence Larry's writer follows Jack's eyes drifting over to the other drinkers. When his eyes come back they are sharper, harder, scanning Larry's writer face with his own brand of a caste-iron grin in support, Jack shuffling back into his this is all-business style, asking Larry's writer what he thinks of his story.

'It's yours if you want it son.'

Some gestures and a couple of glib mirthless grins later, before Larry's writer knows it, it's his. He's on the payroll.

'Okay.'

'We spoke on Ivan's boat didn't we? That party.' The same laugh. Before Larry's writer can do any more other than use one of his nods, Jack gets out his pen and starts writing. 'Done deal, deal done.' Quicker than it's ever been.

'What are we doing exactly?'

'Recording what's happening.'

'Outside?'

'Yep. You play cards son?'

The same pause he knows only too well envelops Larry's writer's mind as he blinks. 'Cards? What sort of cards?'

'Blackjack.'

Jack pulls out the same pack he probably always has on him.

'It's the same as it usually is. Who wins calls the shots.'

The first card is on the bar, Larry's writer staring at a Jack of clubs. Hopeful and hopeless at the same time. The second card though is as hopeless as it always is, a three a two or a four. This time a three. Next, the same old question:

'You buying or flipping son?'

What can Larry's writer do? It's always the same. He pauses just the same as he always does, before murmuring, 'Flip.' It ends the same as it always does. A similar beer and coffee later Jack holds out his right hand using the same old phrase: 'We have a deal.'

'What deal exactly...Jack?'

'I won. I call the shots.'

'Could we discuss this again maybe with an agent present.'

The writer watches old Jack working with his hands talking about agents being parasites, handwriting as he speaks onto a napkin. 'Deal done twixt Jack K and what's your name?'

'Could we define deal exactly?'

'Sign.'

'So, Jack, it's All the Presidents Men meets Disclosure meets Enemy of the State, that it?' Jack tugs at his belt moving his electron eyes the way he did when writing the

contract on a napkin before turning and blasting Larry's
writer with a cough. 'Sign here son.' He checks his watch.
'Ah look, another appointment.'

'So it's the same old corporate collision with the same
deep-state shenanigans?'

Jack's face blanks the same as Larry's writer's seen many
producers do as he backtracks: 'Or corporate politics à la
Disclosure with the same biz-connected politics?' Larry's
writer even does the same old inverted commas.

'Go wherever it leads you.'

'Realistic, some pomo or fourth walling?'

'Some pony-for-wall's all good son, just the same, make it
for families. Something we can turn on at seven at night and
enjoy—the same great movie.'

They sip their drinks in a similar silence.

'Any budget to speak of Jack?'

'The same as it usually is son.'

The word 'writer' is now scribbled on the same napkin
with Jack adding some words as he announces: '7% of profits
to the writer.'

This perks Larry's writer's up. 'Seven per ... well, okay.'

Jack scoops the napkin up in the same way good
basketballers gather up grounded balls, saying he'll clear it
all with Ivan. 'But just the same it's done. He'll go with me
the same as he always does.'

Good-bying out in the alley, Larry's writer watches the
old coot walk off, not pretending to be forgetful anymore,
calling back: 'THAT'S SEVEN PERCENT OF THE NET.'

Old dodgy swings around before Larry's writer can reply,
striding off to do the same to someone else. As usual, it's the
same as it ever was.

Day 4

La ville de Renne-sur-Mer is in lockdown, the bâtiment empty, except for guards sauntering around checking doors, testing windows at the front and back, and staring at the service ramps facing out to charcoal clouds on the horizon. Security is back in its element, everything at a dead stop, the calmest since troubles began.

It was security that lost control of the crisis when demonstrators cut through them day one, and it is security that is now back on top, acting as if they're thinking: crisis, what crisis? The street protest is undone. That's all that matters. More astute observers know better of course but for the ill-informed unthinking going-on in so many minds, seeing demonstrators back off begs and answers a general question—do they really exist anymore? No.

Walking down a restricted-access corridor with F and Madame Maire, a smiling Daniel, convinced now his handling of matters is exemplary, is using his I'm-in-charge gaze on everyone, describing the clearance of Salle Truffaut as an unqualified success. The général walks behind them all saying nothing. Madame Maire, a woman Daniel was fearful of only a day before, is wearing her best confused, irritated expression, saying the usual: 'Without Léo I don't feel good about this.'

'He is not here. I am madame. And we're doing more than just okay.'

'If you had drowned, would you want Léo to forget you?'

'If I had drowned, I wouldn't matter to anyone.' Daniel smiles, grimly impressed by his own hard-nosed cynicism.

'The film distributors in le Marché will take matters into their own hands if we don't do something to re-open.'

'Madame we are doing everything we can.'

'Général, you have men out there. Use them. If not, we'll get our own people.'

The général sighs. Stroppy small city maires, a tin-pot faux director of a protest-crashed-out film festival, intelligence officers without scruples, he's had enough of all of it. 'Private security will only make more mess we'll have to clean up.'

'Clean up the mess out there, and we won't need to bring security in.'

'Madame don't promote illegal methods. You'll be arrested if you do.'

'You arrest me in your dreams, général.'

The général fixes her with his heavy-duty glare used mainly on men, many of whom have trembled seeing down through the years.

'You have to stop them, général.'

'Who are the people that need stopping F?'

'If we can't agree who they are then there's no hope. If you hadn't vetoed my idea of arresting them inside the cinéma we would know who and where they are.'

'Hear, hear,' says the maire.

'What you proposed was unconscionable.'

'They're criminals.'

'Freedom to protest is a right.'

'They occupied a cinema, disrupted a festival, where's the right for that? A film festival is not an excuse for an insurrection.'

'They're kids making a point.'

'Really? Is that what you call it?'

'Nobody in the Compagnies Républicaines de Sécurité under my command will break the law. I haven't forgotten sixty-eight, even if you have. I won't have a Rive Gauche May 10 debacle on my watch.' The général stands his full height looking down at F. 'Never on my watch.'

'Okay. Okay.'

'I have worked out a solution.'

Everyone turns to face Daniel.

'I have arranged a première with Larry Linsteeg.'

'Linsteeg? Daniel, he's one of them.'

'He was kidnapped.'

'Some kidnapping. He gets Stockholm Syndrome in two minutes, pulls his film out and then we put it back on for him. You make him a hero.'

'He's a hero to the protest, F. Let's accept that as a fact, show our largesse, and gain from it.'

There is a silence.

'Well, I have another solution.' Now everyone stares at F.

'This is going to be good.'

'It is général. We do drugs.'

This gets everyone laughing, even the général.

'I have a list of thirty-nine drugs that will work. Adderall to Zoloft, all famous brands, including Halcion, Prozac, Ritalin, Valium and Xanax.'

'Which corner will you sell them on?'

'I am an intelligence officer not a drug dealer.'

'There's a difference?'

'Now, you're really sounding like an extreme leftist, général.'

'So, what's the plan then?'

'We give them out for free.' F grins around at everyone, over the moon at his own political masterstroke of an idea.

'What will this achieve?'

'Put them all to sleep.'

'Then you drag them out and then what? Don't tell me. I don't want to hear it.'

'We take them to a safe place and when they come to, we bus them home.'

The général studies F, his mouth twisted with chagrin. 'What if someone is allergic to one of your drugs and dies?'

'Clinical trials have been done.'

The général shakes his head. 'If by some miracle the protesters believe you—even if nobody is dead or having a fit on a sidewalk—do we want zombies walking around. Tourists will panic, think it's an epidemic.'

'We will have picked them all up.'

'How many thousands are there of them?'

'No, F, I agree with the général. It won't work.'

Taken aback, F swings around to face Daniel. 'What's your solution then?'

'Declare a truce. A premiere with free tickets and a party for afters. No drugs though. The général is right. Anyway there's enough drugs on the street. And they have better sources than we could ever dream up.'

'If it doesn't work?'

'A night of goodwill and a truce for everyone.'

F considers this in a long silence, contemplating the général with a wry grin. 'One of your policemen was shot out there.'

'He shot himself. Accidentally. He pulled out his weapon and his aim failed.'

'I'd like to see the faces of Les Amis de la Gendarmerie hearing you say that.'

'I say no to force.'

F stares back at him. 'Conciliation never works. A gesture of peace will do no good. They jam up the festival and we throw a party for them? My god.'

'A party that I pay for I suppose, général.'

'Daniel suggested a party, not me, madame. Though we could get the hotels and restaurants to cater.'

There's another silence as the maire and F trade looks.

'Why not, général? They are losing a bundle as it is. Why not help them lose more?'

'The bars are full madame.'

'They're always full. That's not the point. People are leaving.'

'Stop them leaving is my point. Change the atmosphere.'

'Change the atmosphere, what with dancing girls too I suppose?'

'There's some in town. The Russian's got girls.'

F sighs eyeing the général's grin.

'I give up.'

'F that's the most intelligent thing you've said all day.'

SHOUTING VOICES ECHOING DOWN THE PIER and a lone gull emah ha ha haaing in the late afternoon sky are the only sounds of life around his rental. Larry's writer stands on top-deck trying to think-up ways of getting out of Jack's deal, the single gull loud above his head drowning out his ringing mobile below. Finally, Larry's writer shakes himself from some dark thoughts, how to kill a deal or the man offering it, and runs back down inside. Scrambling through his papers he finds his old Blackberry, a phone he should have ditched ages ago. Switching on, he hears nothing, then a far-away voice: 'The première is on again. We need to speak.'

'Who's this?'

The call has gone silent. Checking the screen, Larry's writer sees Larry's number, wondering if it's really him. It sounded like Larry. In reality it sounded far too much like him to be the real Larry. Larry's writer really isn't sure he heard him well. It was muffled. Larry's writer stares at his Blackberry. He could say it was stolen. But really he doesn't have a choice and climbing into his shower he stands under a tepid stream of tank water thinking: does Larry know about Jack's deal and if he doesn't should Larry's writer tell him anyway and how can he tell him?

Drying off and dressing Larry's writer grabs his carry-all bag. Exiting the sloop a cloudburst comes down on his head, cooling him and the waterfront. Heading down the pier Larry's writer tells himself this could be the last time he walks it. It buckets down so hard, Larry's writer is soon drenched through to his skin. Reaching the bâtiment he finds police trucks shut up, wan faces at windows staring out.

The red carpet is a lake. The bâtiment's dark. If the première goes ahead it'll be a miracle. Larry's writer finds a group of protesters working under a plastic sheet dripping rain on them. He bends down, asks if they know anything about Larry's film. They don't. He walks on, asking the same question of another sheltering group. They don't either. Next stop three girls sitting huddled under a canvass-awning fixing a sign squint up at him, an Asian girl speaking finally.

'You a gumshoe?'

'I want to know about the première.'

'Which outfit you with?'

'Outfit? None.'

'What do you want?'

Larry's writer hovers a moment, rain pouring down on him, then wanders on trying again to speak to others repairing their signs. One group are singing a Dylan song he hasn't heard in a long time. You walk into the room with your pencil in your hand. You see somebody naked and you say who is that man? He trudges on, slipping on plastic bags plastered to the footpath, rain coming down so hard now he can barely see palm trunks metres away. He comes across a couple in fold out chairs under an awning, eating sandwiches, sheet lightning streaking across the sky, as their vacant grinning faces stare at him. He asks if they've heard if the première is on or not. The woman gives him a toothy grin. Staggering on, the rain is hyperbolic. Out in the bay the sea is boiling. The festival won't re-open. Climbing over a concrete barrier Larry's writer goes up to the bâtiment's windows, makes signs to guards: 'ARE YOU OPENING UP?'

They stare back at him then look away. Larry's writer walks on by overflowing drains, hearing flagpoles clang above his head. Stopping in front of the Antique Galleries at 13 Villa des Fleurs, he stares in at the relic of a building through its rusted gate.

The crumbling façade, dilapidated shutters, half-tilted balconies, water streaming down peeling walls, it has always been a spiritual icon for him. If God lived in Renne he or she would live here.

Larry's writer sees a shape running towards him, a girl, her hair twisted up like steel-wool. Transfixed he watches the only other person out and about getting closer. Is God coming home? Then he recognizes her face. 'Semolina! I was at your press conference'. She stops, squinting fearfully at him. 'I didn't see you.'

'Or I saw you at Ivan's party'.

She shakes her head.

'I wasn't there. Do you know Zucca?'

Larry's writer stares at her through his rain-misted glasses. 'What's he look like?'

'Federico Fellini only a bit shorter with more hair. He's a photographer.'

The writer struggles with the description, the pair blinking at each other in the pouring rain.

'What happened to you?'

Semolina looks like she's been crying.

'My première's tonight. I don't know what to do.' She stares at Larry's writer, 'Can Zucca stay with you?'

He squints. 'Can't he stay at your hotel?'

Semolina shakes her head. 'They will find him there.'

'Who will?'

'I dunno but Zucca says they will.' She wipes away rain or tears, probably both.

'You have a room?'

'I live on a boat.'

'You live on a boat? How wonderful.'

'It's not wonderful believe me.'

'Can you help him?'

'It's a rental. The loo doesn't work. The agent says I have to leave because I asked him to fix it.'

Semolina stares back at him for a moment then wanders off. Larry's writer runs after her and calls out. She doesn't turn-around. 'He can stay on the boat for some days until he finds a place. It's not great. It's on the Quai Saint Jeanne. Happy Days on the side.'

'Will you be there?'

'The hatch door is always open. Just looks shut but it isn't.'

Larry's writer doesn't know why he is even doing this, but he gives her his mobile number. Standing in the rain he

watches her write it into her notebook, ink running down
the page.

'Are you coming to the première?'

'Is it on?'

'Yes, I will save you a seat.'

'Okay.'

'Zucca will call.' She walks away and turning back she
waves and shouts, 'I will get you a seat near the front.'

If he had a dollar for someone saying that to him, he
might have three dollars. Soaked through to his skin he
watches her walk away as she gets smaller and smaller. He
doesn't move, just stands in the rain until his mobile ringing
distracts him. Answering he whispers: 'Zucca?'

'It's LARRY, you fool. Where the hell are you? In a
mineshaft? You were supposed to be here ages ago. What
the hell's wrong with you?'

'It's raining cats and dogs.'

'Who cares. I've a hell of a story to tell you. GET OVER
HERE!'

WORKERS IN BLUE OVERALLS walk up and down in the
rain checking the condition of the red carpet leading up the
stairs to the doors of the Grand Théâtre. Public speakers
sound out a final TESTING UN DEUX TROIS, the voice
echoing way down the Promenade des Rois. A supervisor
gives a thumbs-up. Daniel Martin appears with two aides
close behind him, one holding an umbrella up above her
boss. The second girl in red without an umbrella stands two
paces behind them, Martin tapping the mike and smiling as
he throws out his hands. 'Good evening FILMLOVERS.'

Three TV crews and several journalists holding umbrellas
stand halfway down the steps recording him.

'On behalf of the festival and Madame Maire I am here to announce that the festival will reopen tonight at 7.30 with the première screening of Edgar Gordon Olles's 'A Death of Intervals.'

The girl in red steps forward and whispers to him.

'Sorry, that should be Death at Intervals. The festival invites everyone to tonight's première FREE. No badges. All seats are on a first come first-served basis at all simultaneous showings in the Godard Truffaut Renoir and Rive Gauche cinémas as well as other cinémas in town along Rue d'Anglacé—the Etoile and maybe even the Athena. Weather permitting down at the Théâtre de la Plage as well. All cinémas are open to all people regardless of age, colour or badges. Tonight, there are no special privileges for anyone. No-one. Not even me.'

Martin laughs, his smile lingering in expectation of what his big-hearted offer will bring. When there's no reaction the smile stays in place a moment longer, Martin hoping the applause will grow, and some of it will ripple up. But silence continues and his smile is replaced by a quizzical grimace.

'All filmgoers are equal tonight.'

The crowd stares up at him, silent wet ghosts. Martin frowns, realizing his free première offer is failing as F said it would. Instead of applause a slightly discordant buzz, a rumbling growl beginning to spread up to him from below. The noise isn't friendly. The girl behind him moves in again to say something.

'And yes. Tonight's film is not out of competition. Linsteeg's film is back in contention.'

Still no applause. Except for the rain, the street is eerily silent. Unsure, Daniel waits another moment.

'Film-lovers we had a discussion among ourselves. Won't

this be seen as favouritism? Someone asked, if we bring back Larry Linsteeg tonight, is this fairness or is it something else.'

Daniel is no orator. No empathetic Léo. Why Léo never asked Daniel ever to speak in public. 'I said to them. Tonight, we are celebrating film and cinematic culture.'

The drenched girl in red comes forward again, leaning in close to whisper for a few seconds. 'And yes, tonight's film is followed by a STREET PARTY. We can thank Madame Maire for it and the contributing hotels who're doing THE CATERING.'

'That hasn't been arranged.' This last whisper from the girl echoes suddenly in his microphone, earning ironic laughter down below.

'Catering will be arranged. The organising is happening as I speak to you. We want to thank them. COME TO OUR PARTY AND DANCE.'

Daniel claps his hands, scraping the microphone which squeals and echoes down the street. Still, he's not giving up or in. 'This is going to all the hotels. So, go home and dress up. Phone around. Tell all your friends. Spread the word of tonight's free screening and BIG PARTY. Everyone's invited. This is your festival. YOURS.'

Daniel Martin holds his arms up to the crowd making double-V signs with his fingers. After a moment the crowd responds with a few ironic cheers punctuated by one set of hands loudly and slowly clapping, followed by another man yelling: 'Yeeeeahhh.'

'Christ,' Daniel whispers into the open microphone, staring up at the sky and then way down the street.

'The weather will clear up soon. Let's see Edgar's film and then get right down and PARRRT-TTYY.' His voice breaks on the last word.

Still no response. Martin stops, aware now a no-show for
his festival intervention is a real possibility. A lose-lose for
all as he sees it. The fear of failure slips back into his voice:
'LET'S SEE EDGAR GORDON OLLES'S FILM. THEN LET'S
PAARRTTTTYYYY.' Silence reigns. Daniel finally turns
and half-tripping on the wet carpet heads back inside the
bâtiment, a voice from the street following him.
    'WHY DID IT TAKE YOU SO LONG?'

HER FINGERS TAPPING fast on her keyboard Cindy is
trying to drum up an introduction for her only piece for The
Sentinel so far. Good ideas aren't coming easily. At first, she
thought she could play around with reports from French
television, imitate Tim Robbins as Joe Flynn in Prêt-à-porter
and do a translation, but all she can think of now is that
she's stealing from Robert Altman's film. Reading her first
draft back aloud she draws a slow ragged-breath as it begins
sinking in what she's doing. This is not a festival round-up,
or a movie review. This is real-life plagiarism.
    'You are The Sentinel's woman in Renne, the paper's chief
and only correspondent in town.' Just hearing herself say
this starts a coughing fit, tears starting up in her eyes. 'I'm
not a reporter, not even a reviewer.' She's certainly not a
correspondent. Her heart thumping, seeing it is practically
time to start to get ready for the resurrection première she
stares at her screen. She has nothing for tomorrow.
    Opening a file on her desktop: Notes on a festival, she
reads through her diary jottings, a list of inconsequential
ruminations, a crude attempt at a hip jaunty commentary.
She hasn't been around long enough to make anything like
this sing. Though she does have the story of her boss falling,
pushed more likely, off the back of Ivan's yacht, then flying

home with his head in a bandage. That'd go down like a bomb. The city desk would never print it, tinged as it is with hints her boss was probably a government spy his entire journalistic career. God only knows what Steve would do if he saw such a take-down. Probably do a revenge piece about Cindy cosying up to a communist pornographer, a Russian everyone in Renne hates. Seeing herself in the mirror, Cindy jumps up. 'Okay, walk time.' Leaving all her room lights on, she grabs her phone and runs out of her room.

Skipping downstairs her panic growing she catches her feet nearly going face-first on the steps, grabbing a railing just in time as she receives a call.

Looking at a number she doesn't recognize she drops her phone on the marble entrance floor and arriving in the street stands wondering if the thing still works.

Taking some breaths of the night air she manages to return the call, hearing a voice she doesn't know from Timothée Chalamet, her heart skipping a beat when the voice says: 'Can we meet?' Could it be Timothée Chalamet?

'Who's this?'

'A friend. Let's say behind l'Hôtel Sublime, by the cinéma.'

'Who are you?'

'I have some good information. Five minutes enough?'

She thinks for a moment. 'How will I know you?'

'I know you.'

The voice rings off and Cindy stands staring at her phone. 'Right Timothée.' She remembers the old saying her grandmother always used. Don't look a gift horse in the mouth. It could be an actor, a director, a conman, a thief all rolled into one. You never know your luck in a seaside town at festival time. Heading off through the streets she's wondering how big a scam or set-up it will turn out to be.

Rain or no rain there are heaps of people out. She's
sure any number of men out and about would be ready to
help her. She replays his voice in her head, wondering if
he sounded genuine. Actors know how to convince. That's
why they are actors. So, who got her number and how?
Getting to the open mall street facing the said cinéma she
stares all around. In seconds a young guy in faded jeans and
a white t-shirt comes out of a doorway. Not quite Timothée
Chalamet but not so un-cute. He extends his hand. 'Pierre
Corot. Two demonstrators suggested you.'

'Parlez-vous francais?'

'Oui.'

'Qu'est ce que vous voulez?'

He looks around. 'Speak English. And not here. I know
a place.'

He walks off, Cindy following him after a moment,
recalling the demonstrators on day one. Was it that special
one who spoke about her? She follows Corot across a square
and over the big road to the waterfront. They end up on a
poorly-lit wharf Cindy really wondering now if she should
be doing this. Fortunately, Corot stops before it gets too
dark. They stand in a dull pool of semi-light near a pontoon
jetty leading to moored motor launches. Is one his? 'Why so
secretive?'

'I can't be seen with you.'

'No-one knows me here.'

'Are you kidding? Everyone's talking about your
interview with the Russian.'

'What?'

'Someone even said you threw your boss off the Russian's
boat.'

'Who's saying this?'

Corot hands her a piece of paper. Cindy stares at the sign the demonstrator made on day one, seeing his eyes and face again pasting posters over the official notices, the first day again in her mind.

'He said all this?'

'No, not him.'

'Who else knows?'

'They have a network. Look, my commanding officer is away for the night, and an intelligence officer here wants us to clear the protesters tonight at one o'clock. What he is doing is illegal.'

'Your commanding officer?'

'I am a cop.'

'When is it happening?'

'We report in an hour during the film première. The protester said you'd help.'

Cindy gets out her notebook. 'Give me the details.'

THE TWO SECURITY TEAMS meet on a floor below Bella's terrace for a late-night discussion on protection plans for the première. Jeff Westbridge introduces himself, describing his role of foreman and chief security officer for Bella Fibben.

'I'm her right-hand man.'

Beginning his briefing to Larry's Chinese kick-boxers Jeff starts with, 'My plan is foolproof.' The mood in the room is tense, the Chinese staring poker-faced back at him. 'Combined, we have twenty men. With everyone armed, carrying linked mobile phones, working with my code tags, we have the beginning of a good programme of action.'

Westbridge holds up a booklet. 'It's all in here. Take one, pass the rest around.' He hands a stack to the first Chinese in the front row who frowns when told to distribute them.

When he stands up, he's way taller than Westbridge. 'I'm in charge of Larry's group. What is this?'

'It explains how we maintain positions at the locations I outline in the booklet. You're all on call—as of now. If there is a repetition of the events we have seen recently we may need to modify our plans somewhat but first-up if Bella wants to locate Mr Linsteeg or he wants to contact her, or he or we need to find either or both of them, from now on we'll use these trace methods I have written-up.'

'Whose idea is this?'

'Bella's. She's worried about communication. She asked me to draw up a plan. Whether we're watching-out for Larry or Bella, it would be good if we combine forces. We communicate trouble by texting in code, GAME ON. If there's a serious problem it'll be: NO BETS. It's all in the booklet. If for any reason we have to pull out it'll be: FOLD.'

Jeff writes the words on the white board, the Chinese kick boxers staring at them and then at each other.

'Hopefully no-one will be listening in. When we wrap I expect you to be on your designated site we agree on within five minutes. The main objective is to keep Mr Linsteeg or Ms Fibben from any danger at the coming première. If the première is on. Any questions?'

The main Chinese guy stands again. 'Yeah about twenty.'

He introduces himself as Hubert Chen, telling everyone that before being Larry's head kick-boxer he worked on many security projects. 'For twenty years.' He pauses, raising his voice more than a touch. 'From experience I think the police seeing Chinese men standing on street corners all over town they will wonder why. They'll think a triad is in town.'

Some of his men snigger when this is translated. 'Like a Hong Kong movie,' one says.

'Well, maybe they'll think you're promoting a film.'

Hubert speaks in Chinese. They share looks and shake their heads. 'I think your men could be doing the same as us. Why don't we reverse roles, and your guys wait on the street corners, do an Italian mafia movie if you like? We drive around in cars. When we know we have a situation, we all go together.'

'Guys, we need to cooperate. We need eyes on the street able to pinpoint people, people texting saying, they're moving him. He's gone north. They've gone east on this route, et cetera.'

The Chinese team's main man remains stoically unimpressed by Jeff's ideas.

'If we have no car to follow them how do we know where whoever it is is really going anyway? The car could park around the corner or change directions, double-back once out of sight and go the other way.'

'We'll be in vehicles. Our drivers will be nearby.'

'Why don't we sit in the cars and your guys stand on the street corners?'

'We think Chinese guys in black SUVs will draw unwanted attention.'

'More than Chinese guys standing on street corners?'

'You have a better idea?'

'Yeah. We all wait in cars when we know where they're going, we all go together.'

Westbridge shakes his head.' I've spent fifteen years in the SAS. Trust me I know what I'm doing.'

The seated Chinese all stare at him as this is translated, then start talking rapidly in Chinese between themselves. Chen stops them, switching back to English. 'We all think this is a bad plan. This is not what we were told back when the agent said: Great job. Piece of cake. You'll be down the beach swimming most of the time. Here we are in the middle of some sort of political mess we still know nothing about. It's not what we signed up for when we came for what Larry still calls a piece of cake job.'

'He's your boss.'

'Okay. Let us look after him. Another thing, none of us have been paid the money we were promised by Larry's agent. All we got are air-tickets and a boat to live on and prepaid supermarket food cards. We have to cook for ourselves.'

The man next to him says something in Chinese.

'And we have terrible neighbours.'

'Boat near us stink,' says the man next to Chen.

Westbridge is unsure how to address their objections. 'We've got a crisis we didn't expect. We're going to have to be calm here because it will get out of hand if we don't, okay. You want money. I am authorised to guarantee you bonus payments. '

'Who's paying?'

'Bella. Trust me it'll be good.'

'The Gold Queen?'

'Yes.'

The Chinese talk rapidly among themselves, one sniggering, then Hubert Chen speaks in English again: 'We don't like it. You do your thing, we'll do ours.'

HEARING A KNOCK AT HER DOOR Semolina calls out softly: 'Who is it?'

A hoarse whisper sounds in the hallway: 'Open up.'

'Zucca, is that you?' Semolina says, leaning close to the door, putting an ear to the wood.

'Of course it's me. Who're you expecting, Robert Redford?'

'Well maybe like forty years ago.'

'You weren't born forty years ago.'

'There's your answer.'

'Open up.'

Why do I bother, Semolina mouths as she pulls the door open. 'I just let my seamstress go and now you show up.'

Zucca barges by her in his wrinkled outfit without so much as giving her cheek a peck. Though even with his crassness she's happy he's alive.

'I hope you brought a smoking jacket.'

Zucca hands her a crumpled cloth bag.

'Do you have a fresh shirt?'

'This.'

'That?'

'I forgot my farfalla.'

'Your what?'

Zucca jiggles a hand at his neck.

'No bowtie, great. I sent you two messages.'

'I saw nothing.'

'Nothing about the boat?'

'What boat?'

Semolina recounts how she met a writer living on a boat that Zucca can stay on, Zucca fiddling with his mobile hardly listening.

'You could say, thanks Semi for thinking of me and my predicament.'

'How much time do we have?'

'About seven minutes before my car arrives. You're a guest, so behave like one.' Semi points at the shower, standing at the bathroom door recounting how she was in total shock when the première was called off, how she suffered an even bigger shock hearing it was back on, adding she waited all afternoon staring at her phones waiting for his call. Zucca doesn't say anything back. Why does she bother? She calls out: 'FIVE MINUTES. I'll do my best with your shirt.'

Her stilettos are cramping her calves, a concreting sensation starting in her ankles. Her breathing problem is back, hyper-ventilating, a series of brain shocks not far behind. Now Zucca's singing in the shower.

'Five minutes only. FIVE. Zucca do you hear me? YOU'VE GOT FIVE MINUTES.'

Semi tries her best to arrange his clothes then gives up. He can go crumpled. If the look suits he's wearing it. She sits heavily down on the bed rubbing her brow.

'Breathe deeply.'

She manages to get him dried and dressed in time to be outside for the Limo pick-up, the stress of all her efforts nearly making her go head over heels down the stairs, grabbing Zucca's elbow just in time.

Inside the official car, Zucca acts like it's Semi who should be grateful he even made it at all. Grimacing out of her window at the spattering rain on the glass she practices her big smile. Her best sharky grin.

Arriving at the Bâtiment, grinning rigidly, all her efforts are now concentrated on making the rest of her come alive. Semolina climbs out into a starry night. Starting up the carpet with old krumplestiltskin at her side, swivelling his head all around, she sees the media throng ahead already clicking and flashing at them. She leans close to him, 'Don't blow this for me.' Reaching for her mother's little helper inside her make-up mirror inside her clutch bag she realizes she left the bag in her room, a man behind her shouting, 'GIVE MR LINSTEEG SOME ROOM.'

Semolina swings around to see her returnee out-of-focus hero-producer being led away from his car. She almost trips over her dress running full-pelt back to greet him, tears starting up, someone in the crowd leaning over a barrier and getting a handful of her outfit, letting go just in time to leave her still in it.

'LARRY.'

Throwing her arms around him, a waterfall of tears cascades down.

'You're the best. Thank god you're here.'

'Don't you start. All I need now is a donkey and people waving palm leaves.'

'I've got a donkey too,' she says, wiping away tears. 'What's wrong.'

'What's wrong? I'm a Jew in a catholic country being treated like Jesus Christ. A couple of hours ago I was a criminal now I am the righteous saviour, my role tonight apparently to save film culture from Thanos. What's coming next? I don't even want to think about it. If I hadn't changed a habit of a lifetime and stayed out where I always have, Pointe d'Anglacés, none of this would have happened. I wouldn't have been within twenty miles of that damn bookshop. Who's this?'

'My donkey, Zucca,' I told you. 'Zucca, this is *the* Larry Linsteeg.'

Larry squints at Zucca's face. 'We've met haven't we?'

'Don't think so. '

'You in film?'

'Don't think so.'

'Funny. I could swear I know you.' Larry shrugs. 'Okay, let's go. Just wave and smile Semi and let's get the hell inside.'

Semolina has to run to keep up with him, holding her dress up which has suddenly started falling off her.

'It's good our film is on isn't it? You couldn't buy PR like this.'

'Yeah, well maybe. If our luck lasts. Just it feels kinda.' He eyes Zucca again. 'He's really familiar to me, Semi. What's your name again?'

'Zucca.'

'That a nickname?'

'He's Italian.'

'I get that, Semi.'

'What's Zucca in Italian?'

'Pumpkin.'

Semolina is shocked. 'Her donkey is a pumpkin.'

'I got it as a kid.'

'Time to lose it as a man.' With all the clicking, whirring and calling, LARRY, SEMOLINA, THIS WAY, Semi realizes Zucca is even more nervy than her.

'You expecting someone?'

He doesn't answer. She decides she's going to have to ignore him and turns back to her saviour, her genius.

'Level with me, Larry, why did you give that communistic speech?'

'I was kidnapped and it wasn't communistic.'

'Right, good old American values, and you just happened to be there, right?'

'I came out of a bookshop. Bang, I was grabbed.'

'Where, exactly?'

Larry gives her a hard look. She chortles.

'All I know Semi is I had breakfast, went for a walk on Rue d'Anglacés, I was kidnapped then dragged across town to the Bâtiment, taken by cops and put in a cell.'

'There is a bit in the middle you missed out.'

'Which bit?'

'Your speech saying our film was out of competition.'

'Was I laughing?'

'You didn't look worried on TV. I thought you were on something, Larry.'

'At ten in the morning. It was an act.'

'How did you get out of jail?'

'Some guy called Martin walked in, said you're free. The police accepted a plea deal.'

'And the bad news?'

Semolina looks every bit the nineteen-going-on-forty-year-old Larry always pegged her as. 'You have nothing to worry about.'

'Why do you look worried then?'

'We're at a première, Semi. Anything can happen.' Larry waves back at some cheering fans. 'As far as I'm concerned this is not over until it's over.'

'You survived. That's enough isn't it?'

He watches her waving. 'You're a Pro Semi. Take my arm. Walk like you own the place, because tonight you do.'

'I can't take your arm. I'm holding onto my dress.'

'You're what? I gave you a dress allowance. You don't have to make your own.'

'I didn't. Someone just tried to rip it off.'

'When?'

'Just now.'

'How?'

'Forget about it. Hold my arm.'

They walk in lock step finding themselves in another blaze of flashing lights accompanied by whirring electric motors, Semi deciding her dress and boyfriend disappointments are off the table tonight. Tonight will be hers with or without clothing.

'What's up with the Italian?'

'He's nervous.'

'About what?'

'It's raining cats and dogs. Rioting kids took over a cinema. A shark fell from a helicopter. How the hell do I know?'

'I thought he's your date.'

'It's a long story but Zucca's sure people want to kill him.'

'Why on earth do they want him dead?'

'I have no idea. I met him first day. He was nice. I thought. Now I don't know.' She turns, finding Zucca half-hiding behind her. 'What's wrong now?'

'Someone's trying to shoot me.'

'We're practically in daylight out here. They need pictures. Let them shoot.'

Semi walks on some photographers yelling out, ICI SEMOLINA. ATTENDEZ. Gliding towards another group she tells herself she's the star. UN MOMENTO MAGNIFICA. ARRÊTE S'IL-TE-PLAÎT. POR FAVOR SEMOLINA.

When Semolina digs her shoes into the wet carpet heading up the stairs one of her heels goes and feeling herself falling she is suddenly caught and guided back to the vertical. Only without her contacts she can't make out her saviour's blurry face. 'Don't let go Zucca.'

'She is under control Laurence.'

'Under control? What do you mean I'm under control?'

'Voilà lui.'

'Voilà who?'

Larry's tell-tale penguin shape plonks over to them.

'Who the hell are you then?'

'Jury President. Geoffrey Leads at your service.'

'NOT THE GEOFFREY LEADS?'

'Thankfully there's only one.'

Such a lovely accent. Semi's saviour takes her hand, leading her up the last of the stairs, introducing her to people along the way, names flying over her head like satellites, Semolina tottering after her latest saviour like a brain-shot disciple. 'I must look drunk.'

'Are you?'

'Not yet.'

'Well, you won't be the last to be drunk at your first première.'

Her face floods with tears. A genteel Englishman is holding her hand and giving her sage advice. 'Stop it,' she hisses to herself. 'You're embarrassing. What are acting lessons for?'

'It's the stress of star billing on the Côte d'Azur,' Leads says, chuckling: 'It's normal anxiety.'

'You a doctor?'

'You need one? What room are you in? I'll bring my instruments.'

Semolina is too lightheaded to question his offer, the details of which she is now receiving in her right ear. His easy-going polite manner didn't give her any warning of the flood of this unrepeatable language. He has her following him like the proverbial deer in headlights, wondering whether what she just heard was what she just heard. Her dress half-falling off her on the pinnacle of western film culture, she sucks in air. 'I need a bottle of oxygen. My first première in the wrong heels with the wrong guy. Not you Geoffrey.' Larry is back by her side again, people yelling her name from behind the barriers, Leads whispering something else in her ear now, words she won't, can't repeat either, not even to herself. The sound of adoring fans, Leads's x-rated enunciations, have worked her to a fever pitch. Was that just the worst wharfie language she's ever heard in her life? All coming out of the mouth of an educated Englishman, too. Who would believe this posh public schoolboy sort learned all that at boarding school.

'I think I am on Mars.'

'Is it good up there?'

Semi throws him a look. 'You're a very bad man.'

Leads grins back at her. She grabs both men's arms saying: 'Let's go inside. See if I'm on the money.'

Everything has wound right down to a snail walk slow-mo. She's not nervous anymore. As if someone just slipped her something. Tonight is suddenly so mysterious, as if all the toys of her childhood have appeared out of nowhere, her brain in an echo chamber, Semolina floating back to herself as a child on rickety wheels of every lost promise. Larry's holding one hand, Geoffrey the other. She tries focusing but she can't see a thing without her glasses.

She just makes out the hazy image of Ivan with a practically naked twenty-something stick-thin blond, a foot taller than Semolina, in spikes too, the ones that nearly broke Semi's left ankle. 'Let's go.'

Larry pulls her back. 'She won't outshine you.'

'How did you read my mind, Larry?'

'I know you, Semi. Remember this is your night. Yours.'

Semolina could kiss him. Tears flow. Why's she crying? Everything's going her way. Seeing Viktor climbing in a black tie and white smoking jacket, looking like a late-flowering Russian Sean Connery, his arctic-snow crewcut brushed back, if she can ditch Zucca she'll get Vik from

Elena's clutches and grab Geoffrey from whomever he's shacked up with and have a wonderful night with a couple of old geezers. It's enough to make Semolina's eyes sparkle. She's not drying them anymore.

Ulyana stalking up the stairs with Edgar in an outfit more crumpled than Zucca's brings her back to earth, but Semi has decided nothing can spoil tonight for her. Not even Bella, who makes it up too, the whole Death team squeezing into a line, Semolina shouting: 'Ladies and Gentlemen, we're Renne's answer to chaos.' Nobody disagrees.

On the summit of French film culture Semolina witnesses a shooting star skate across the firmament. Okay, probably it's only a spy-satellite, one that's broken and spiralling down to Earth, but who's counting. Semi's on Venus.

To ice the moment, more Renaults arrive and a horde of ex-SASers stuffed inside red silk jackets and bright purple cumberbands out-run their Chinese kickboxing comrades, Larry's and Bella's security team hopping the stairs two at a time clad in haircuts cut to a millimetre just for the occasion, their shiny black patterned coats flying, roared on by an ecstatic crowd at the barriers.

'We did it, Larry.' Arms locked, Semolina, Larry, Bella, Edgar, Ulyana, Viktor, Elena, the SASers and Chinese kickboxers, beam at cameras, then wheeling left as if on command they all head inside.

'Good luck,' Geoffrey Leads shouts.

'What's luck got to do with the price of your instruments?' Semolina yells back.

Nobody knows what she means, not even Semi. All she knows right now is she's drifting on her own private magic carpet into the bâtiment holding tight to Larry's hand.

AFTER SCRIBBLING LARRY'S ADVENTURES, Larry's writer ran back to his rental, dressed fast and jogged back to the bâtiment, arriving drenched in sweat, arc lamps doing their best to steam him dry.

Seeing disappointed faces everywhere, he asks one kid and hears his story. The promised seats are a lie. There is no deal. All seats are gone and were gone long ago.

Getting through the crowd and inside the foyer, Larry's writer flashes his phony critic's card and not getting caught makes his way to Semi's gift-seat near the front.

He wonders how long the project of defrauding the dispossessed can go on before the cineastes rise up and launch a revolution. He can't see one person who even looks like a protester, not even in the balcony seats up high. A man sits down by his side, smiling back at Larry's writer's grimaced greeting.

'Did you see any protesters outside?' Larry's writer asks.
'No.'

'I saw many out in the rain a few minutes ago but none of them are here now.'

The man smiles. 'Maybe they don't want to be here.'

'Maybe they were cheated you mean.'

'Cheated by whom?'

'By whoever's using the protest.'

Larry's writer has said too much to someone he doesn't know from Adam. 'Maybe I imagined it. Anything's possible.'

'You think the protesters could be paid agitators.'

'You think that?'

'I've heard a few things,' the man says. 'But we have our seats. Kids, I mean, what can you say anyway?'

Larry's writer smiles back at the man, managing to stop

himself saying any more. Hearing a commotion, they swing around to see a starry-eyed Semolina Pynes coming down the aisle, Larry's writer's sure she's on something.

The festival's acting-director, Daniel Martin, accompanied by a girl young enough to be his daughter arrives just behind them, Larry's writer standing to let them get by, getting no thanks, Martin nodding at the man sitting next to Larry's writer, as the girl pushes by both of them reciting a list of the famous people she's seen. Larry's writer begins scribbling.

'Mesdames et messieurs veuillez prendre vos places la séance commence.'

The lights go down, Larry's writer still scribbling names, a hush descending in the auditorium.

Then the theatre lights are back up again, Larry's writer's pen frozen in mid-air, guests staring at each other as the foyer curtains open. 'Mesdames et Messieurs, veuillez-vous lever pour le Président de la République Française.'

The writer hears Martin gasp, his face staring at the figure walking down the aisle with an even younger woman than Martin's by his side, an orchestrated version of the Marseillaise starting with an unrehearsed vocal support group in the auditorium joining in, guests standing, Larry's writer mumbling what he knows, voices all-around stumbling through a hesitant impromptu rendition of the national anthem that ends up in a vocal riot, shouting voices filling the whole auditorium—

Allons enfants de la patrie
Le jour de gloire est arrivé
Contre nous de la tyrannie
L'étendard sanglant est levé
L'étendard sanglant est levé
Entendez-vous dans les campagnes

Mugir ces feroces soldats
Ils viennent jusque dans vos bras
Égorger vos fils vos compagnes

As quickly as the singing hits a crescendo the voices die down, the Président nodding his appreciation, still waiting for his seat, ushers quickly evacuating a group nearby from their places. 'But these are ours.'

'This row is cancelled, messieurs.'

'This is the first time my seat has been cancelled inside a première anywhere in the world.'

More ushers arrive to help their colleagues empty the furious guests out, the last of them man-handled up the aisle to the sound of an usher bellowing: 'Vite. Le Président de la République est ici, monsieur.'

'Where're we going?'

'Out,' another usher says, a hushed auditorium watching the tense scene play out.

'C'est inédite,' a voice says. Larry's writer slides further down in his seat. It could have been him. The group's manhandled into the foyer. Trudging upstairs, their feet sounding heavily, one woman calls out: 'GET ME A BLOODY SEAT TOO.' The curtains are pulled shut one more time and the lights go down.

'Mesdames et messieurs la séance recommence.'

Two streets away le cinéma Athena is packed with cineastes, upstairs and downstairs. With no system for allocating seats, everyone sitting where they can, Merryl is boxed-in in a middle seat in the lower stalls surrounded by a tribe of pumped-up young cineastes. The excitement is palpable, Merryl guessing what each kid is thinking—who the hell cares about any film première at the bâtiment?

As Merryl predicted would happen, kids all around her are saying they didn't even try to get a seat at Daniel Martin's great reconciliation show. In the Athena nobody cares about the bâtiment. André Philippe's Athena cinéma is the only place to be tonight.

The lights go down, kids sitting in front of Merryl cheering and high-fiving. Sergei Berebanov's Dirt Wars opens with Napoléon arriving at the Nieman River on his all-white steed, surrounded by key cavalry troops. He promptly falls off his horse to cheering throughout the Athena. Merryl stares around at all the smiling faces. They are hip to what is going down here tonight. This film is a takedown of authority and with what is going on in the streets of Renne they are loving every second of it. A montage of the great march north shows the big preparations made by Napoléon and his coalition. The kids begin stamping their feet. The great failure of 1812 filmed in classic spaghetti western style has the kids laughing their heads off.

The invasion gives Napoléon sleepless nights and countless nightmares, as control of Moscow, the great goal, slips further from his grasp each passing day, the kids breaking into howling laughter.

It's like watching a hapless cartoon, Coyote as Napoléon, craving an arrival in Moscow as conqueror, as much as Coyote craved catching Roadrunner.

Everything that can go wrong does. Is his Grande Armée up for the fight? Can Napoléon ride so far and win so little? Can he parade through Moscow's city gates as the faux-emperor of Russia? Will Alexander ever hand over his crown? Will Napoléon open the road to Asia? Can Napoléon ever eclipse Alexander of Macedonia's achievements?

'NO,' shouts back the pumped audience.

The voice-over is winning many admirers, the tone penetrating to the core of Sergei Berebanov's depiction of a conflicted Napoléon—all the planning, thinking and re-thinking, the advising and revising, the kids getting every nuance and loving every word. Berebanov's film is extraordinary. Merryl is amazed.

MEANWHILE OVER IN THE BÂTIMENT'S GRAND THÉÂTRE with pre-film screen credits rolling Semolina is getting ready to slip down under her seat. Hand over her mouth, she's terrified of the thirty-foot close-up of her face that has just appeared. Edgar's over-anticipated reworking of a Nobel prize winner's literary novel is already very hard to watch. Semi's first shot shows her spiky-hair poking out of her cap, her character lifted straight from a Manga comic.

Disaffected, broke, Semolina's playing Death as an unhappy teenager living rough in urban chaos on the wrong side of town. A walking corpse in Edgar Gordon Olles's searing portrait of juvenile despair. Seeing herself stalking through a graveyard Semi is already closing her eyes, thinking, I better get another job pretty quick coz when the industry sees this I won't get another.

Edgar's high-minded reworking of literature, Edgar being Edgar, Semi being Semi, has left a self-destructive, self-harming crazy spiky-haired Goth up on the screen. Edgar told her not to worry. Some judge he is. Semi will never believe a word he says again. She argued with him throughout to no avail. 'That's me up there, not you. Your take of a novelist's take on life is fine and dandy for you, but my film career is over. Kaput.'

What's up on screen is proof. Larry at least expressed some concern, particularly about her clothes. Edgar's

juvenile image of despair equals Semi's future as an actor—
dead as a doornail.

A noise in the aisle startles her. Grateful for any distraction
she watches a huge man running across in front of the
screen, his silhouetted pony-tail covering part of her thirty-
foot face, the heavy-breathing giant shaking off two ushers
whispering: 'Zucca. Vieni qua figliolo.'

Semolina's boyfriend is already barging down their row,
hissing, 'Excusez moi,' Semi watching in a daze as her lover
catapults himself over two members of the President's party,
running for the exit like the criminal she always thought
he was. 'Zucca, devo parlarti,' the big man whispers. Two
ushers whispering as well: 'Messieurs, attendez, s'il vous
plaît!' Murmurs of 'incroyable' and 'qui sont-ils' punctuate
Zucca's progress escaping the big man's grasp, two ushers
chasing them through the curtains and out into the foyer.

'Mais ce n'est pas possible.'

'Is this part of the film?'

'It's performance art, fusing cinema and street theatre.'

'Oh. Screwball comedy then.'

Semolina stares up at the art deco ceiling. She's saved
for now. With everyone focused on the disturbance, few
are remembering how bad she looks up there. It might kill
the film, but Semi's career is not yet quite over. The Chinese
boxers at least are laughing. Others join in too. Still there's
not enough distracted uncomprehending people for Semi's
liking.

'Je l'aime. C'est merveilleux.'

'Which one is death?'

'The big guy?'

'Mesdames et Messieurs, silence s'il vous plaît, le film a
déjà commencé.'

Larry leans over whispering: 'What the hell is going on?'

Semi shrugs, replying in her normal voice: 'Good riddance to bad rubbish as far as I am concerned.'

Two shooshes, a mon dieu and an incroyable punctuate her words. Up on screen, Semolina scuttles back into frame from way back in the shot, a black and white close-up that's even worse. What was Edgar thinking making her look so repulsive? She sinks so low now she'll soon be under her seat, lying there wondering how she can sneak out before being presented to the Président of the République. When the credits roll, she'll run like hell.

SEMOLINA'S NOT THE ONLY PERSON worrying about repercussions and what the Président is thinking right now. Why didn't the security jump that idiot when he ran across the screen? Larry's main fear is not about them, it's about Edgar's vision of law and order. How will Death appear to the man running this country?

Seeing the scene in a police station, Larry covers his face. A cop weeping to a psychologist, who informs him not being able to kill people when he likes is only a freakish occurrence!

'Unlawful killing hasn't gone away,' the psychologist tells his cop-patient. 'Death will be back. Summary execution is alive and well.' The cop in question isn't convinced and neither is Larry. If Death doesn't look like coming back in his director's screen-vision of life, a voice deep in Larry's brain is asking: if hundreds of passengers survive an explosion in a train station, many of them losing limbs after being blown off their feet and torn apart, how come victims start this mysterious process of auto-mending? Climbing back to their feet and looking around and saying, what's happening?

How's this going to look to those who use fear as a daily means of professional control? Some people in the audience are whispering things similar to this, while others just say, 'YES.' Is the audience buying into Edgar's ideas? Larry's main worry though is what will the Président do? He leans over and whispers his misgivings into his director's ear.

'It's in the novel Larry, which you said you read.'

'Of course, I read it, Edgar. I said I did. I did.'

'Every page?'

'At least every third page.'

On screen a CCTV camera reveals a plainclothes cop planting a suitcase-bomb in a railway station, a black & white CCTV shot catching him placing the case by a pillar and not even looking around himself as he walks away.

Some invitees in the auditorium begin hissing SHAME, the on-screen cop running on cue, someone in the audience yelling: GET HIM. Cops everywhere begin panicking inside and outside the story almost as if they can hear this audience's reactions all over France. One-by-one screen cops throw-down their weapons and begin owning-up to recent and past illegal acts and some other unrelated domestic crimes as well.

One cop admits he's a serial wife beater, weeping-wildly as he recounts how he beats his children before breakfast. Before going to work, so he can get ready for maltreating citizens, patrolling city-blocks stopping and searching-out innocents, hauling them back to the station where he beats them inside cells, admitting tearfully that he has been revelling in the life of a bully for over ten years.

Larry's mouth is wide open hearing an undercover cop say: 'I did it. Forgive me.' The too-clever-by-half cop who placed the bomb tries dodging the mob, but even he's finally caught. Beaten black and blue, the more he's hit the more he stays alive.

'Edgar, this is absolutely awful,' Larry moans, covering his eyes, looking through his fingers, as he sees a cop on the brink of death taking a merciless beating, Larry whimpering: 'What will the Président be thinking?'

'It's a black comedy, Larry. A bit blacker than usual but still a comedy.'

'Nobody's laughing.'

'Larry, not all comedies are for laughing,' Edgar whispers back.

'What's the point of making a mirthless comedy?'

'It's a comic revenge satire tale against corrupt and violent cops. It's not wrong.'

'Yeah but in front of the Président and his entourage it's professional suicide. What will this do for our reputations?'

'They're mud anyway.'

'I know but where are the good cops to balance the argument?'

'I am not arguing, I'm making a film. Anyway there are more potential victims than good cops. Am I right?'

'But what about the really bad guys?'

'Career crooks working with cops aren't able to kill anyone anymore either.'

Confused by Edgar's explanation Larry's trying to think now as an unbiased member of the reviewing fraternity might think, which only makes him even more confused. Does Edgar have a point? Larry's so upset now he can barely breathe. He wished he had read the damn novel, even the four-page plot report Annie compiled.

'I should have seen the final cut. I thought I had. Maybe I fell asleep in the screening room. Will reviewers agree this is a satire? Did you go back in the editing room and change everything? What about the public? I'm sure Saramago's version is a bit more nuanced than this.'

'Not according to my reading of the novel.'

'This is an absolute disaster Edgar. It won't sell a ticket. Did Saramago condemn all authorities as criminals?'

'You didn't read him did you?'

'I read a few pages.'

'The title pages.'

'Yes. I thought the font was marvellous.'

'You okayed it on the font?'

'I'm too busy attending financing breakfasts to be reading. Anyway, you read it! And you said it was great. I took your word. Jesus, look at Semolina's character. She has an irresolvable dilemma. Death, the ultimate antagonist of life is impotent.' Larry with even this much understanding is starting to impress Edgar.

'Is that in the book?'

'Not exactly like this but similar.'

'And if guns aren't dangerous why do cops carry them? The disclaimer said nothing about guns being pointless.'

'It comes together in the end.'

'How?'

'Don't worry.'

'*Don't worry*. Okay for you to say don't worry, it comes together in the end. The Président's here. I have to meet him. He might want to know what we mean? And what will the police associations say?'

'It's a film, Larry. What do they care? They're too busy beating people up.'

'Jesus H. Christ. That's your answer. Then don't say anything to the press. That's it, I am not reading any reviews.'

'You don't anyway.'

'Annie puts them all in a drawer.'

Straining to hear reactions as the credits roll, Larry, the great audience-reader, can't make anything out. The audience is silent. All producers want to believe audiences will respond well to their productions but the moment the lights come up in here Larry isn't studying any faces for answers. He's definitely not glancing the Président's way, let alone meeting him.

When the lights finally do come up, Larry's already up and speed-walking out into the foyer. Not looking left or right, once outside he runs vaguely in the direction of his hotel. Let the critics be judge of this film. Which way is he going? Larry has lost his GPS radar. Tonight, he's allergic to microphones, but he is not abandoning Edgar, well not yet.

Day 5

'Is this F's bloody doing?' the général whispers into his phone, waking his wife.

'Henrì it's five o'clock in the morning.'

'Daniel Martin,' the général whispers to his wife his hand over the mouthpiece.

'D'accord. I'm leaving in five minutes.'

Putting the phone back in its cradle the général swings his legs from the bed to the floor.

'What can I do Albì? Martin calls a meeting with panic all over it. I'm still not sure what worries me more, his stupidity or F's ambition. This is a Martin five-star cockup with F's fingerprints all over it. My one night away from the madhouse, and then I'm called back.'

He looks across at Albertine. She's fast asleep, beginning to snore. The général rubs his face. A sleepless night in a Renne hotel would have been better. He and Albì rarely spoke over dinner, the reunion a washout. She prefers the dog. Every so often the général gets the idea he should be at home sleeping in his own bed with his wife, heading down to the village with his, her dog, in the early morning to buy pastries at the local boulangerie. The walk is a romantic idea but in reality what is romantic anymore? He climbs unsteadily to his feet. Looking around for his trousers he knocks over the lamp, Benni beginning to bark.

'Henrì what the hell is going on?'

The général finishes dressing in the hall, their spaniel going around his legs wagging his tail, thinking there's a bonus earlier than usual morning outing. The général shakes his head down at the excited face. 'Sorry, not today.'

Driving west from Biènville, the radio's prognosis for the day ahead is not good. The weather is turning bad and Martin and F are cooking up something.

Reaching the Promenade des Rois the général circles his Peugeot around the western roundabout. Accelerating down along the waterfront he finds nobody waiting for him. Braking, he pulls up, jumps out and leaves his car with its flashers on. Striding up to the bâtiment, seven o'clock gonging on the clock-tower he throws his car keys to a security officer, pointing back. 'Green. Mine. Park.'

Walking faster he heads up the escalator without looking back. Halfway up he thinks again. Turning he yells: 'SPEAK TO MARTIN.'

In the directorial suite there's a low buzz of voices. The général finds a five-star breakfast with all the extras. It makes him feel even more guilty for leaving Albertine. Shoving his domestic problems to the back of his brain he pours coffee, gives everyone a wave as he takes his first mouthful, the brew running the length of his throat and soft-landing in his stomach. Saying, amen, he grabs a croissant, jams it in his mouth. Now he can face the day. He winks at Daniel spraying, 'So, what's so urgent?'

'We have a traitor in our midst. Well, you do.'

AN HOUR AFTER SENDING HER PIECE Cindy received an email from London headed—'What protest clearance? It's great.' She was so relieved she collapsed on her bed and fell fast-asleep. Then checking the local press in the morning she found nothing. After a coffee downstairs it dawned on her that maybe the clearance never happened. The protesters were onto it. In truth she doesn't know either way, but the intelligence guy wanted to clear them, that was her point.

She wrote back to her editor explaining all this and how she got all her information. Cindy said she didn't think Corot would change his colleagues' minds. Maybe the cops were not sent out in the end. Or did they go and then find absolutely no-one? Not knowing either way she sat in her room waiting, biting her fingernails wondering what sort of reply she'd receive. He came back almost immediately.

'Great insight. Keep on it. Just don't forget who's banging whom at the festival, and what the women are wearing or not.' Cindy grimaces reading the last line. Even in her third read-through of his email, the thought of getting all-activated over celebrity sex leaves her cold. Now if she wrote a story saying nobodies were having great sex on the beach, that would be far more interesting to her than cataloguing the sex acts of stars imprisoned in their hotel rooms biting their fingernails over whatever image they're going to project when next outside. Would the Sentinel print something like that? Anyway, either way, yes or no, it's irrelevant because she wouldn't write it, her troubled thoughts spiralling right back to when she first wrote-up her idea of the clearance, which was a real story to her then, and only became a half-a-story in the end. Finally, she dared to look online—The Sentinel did print her! Page 2. Wow.

Call the cop right away and tell him. Get the number of the demonstrators from him. See if it leads to an even bigger story.

THE ON-THE-DOUBLE ORDER for all men to assemble in their makeshift brigade headquarters at the back of the bâtiment has all seats filled inside two minutes. Walking up and down two aisles the général studies the faces of his men.

Pacing back and forth at the front, the général takes a blue felt pen and writes one word on a white board in capitals: TRAÎTRE

'Anyone wish to say anything?' He stares around the room. 'I will give you a hint. It's about informing on F's plans to round-up demonstrators.'

He stifles a smile saying it. At the back Corot can't imagine what would happen to him if he owned up now. Public humiliation? He knows enough about disciplinary procedures and how they go. A sheen of sweat is on his forehead, but he won't dare touch it. It's hard to breathe in the tiny room, nobody daring to ask for a window to be opened.

'I am not angry. I just want to know.'

From his words, face and demeanour the général seems too calm, almost chipper really, but Corot knows there must be an issue attached to this, even if it doesn't concern the brigade itself. Whatever, Corot isn't owning up to anything.

'Okay, you are dismissed.'

Every officer stares back at their commander.

'Await further orders.'

Sighs are heard as the officers file out into the fresh air, Corot hearing a whisper: 'Who was it?' Walking back to his van he mouths silently: 'J'ai mis les pieds dans les plats maintenant.'

If his mobile phone's checked, he's done for. Corot is no traître, and he wouldn't ever betray his brigade, definitely not his country. He would defend la République always. He loves all the liberté, égalité, fraternité, loves the whole shebang. F's ideas are absurd. Standing by his van, Corot's hands are shaking. 'What if the général already knows it was me who spoke to a reporter?'

Looking around he begins to relax. Maybe he caught a break. Maybe the whole town did. The weather is holding off. No more rain and no demonstrators anywhere. His mobile rings. Without looking at the screen he answers.

'Lieutenant, it was printed! Page two and everything.'

'What? Who is this?' Knowing exactly who it is, Corot drops the phone. It clatters hard into a curb. Ashamed of himself he runs over and picks it up. 'You still there?'

'Did something happen?'

'No, it's okay. So, you got it done. That's great.'

'Yeah. Isn't that amazing? Do you have the number for that ... ?'

'Don't say any more. Let's meet. Same place same time tonight.'

'I'll be there.'

CLIMBING OFF A TAXIBOAT Franck is startled by an elegant, striking woman standing totally nude under her muslin dress.

He takes her hand, stumbling over his prepared apology for telephoning her out of the blue.

'I am very glad you did inspector. I'm going stir-crazy out here.'

Perhaps he doesn't like to admit it but the thought of an attractive older woman out alone on a comfortable boat going stir-crazy has instant appeal for Franck.

'I thought that living out on a boat in a bay like this in the Mediterranean with no neighbours was the ultimate dream.'

She gives Franck a look he is not entirely sure about but upon reflection does not mind all that much either.

'Why are you in town alone, madame?'

'I am not alone. My Jaws 6, Dances with Wolves 2, Pulp

whatever husband brought me with him. So, why are you here, inspector?'

'I really don't know.'

'We are a pair then.'

'Only your husband invited you here. Paris forced me to cancel my holidays.'

'If you don't know why you're here, can't you make it a holiday?'

'No.'

'So you are here on assignment?'

Franck nods. 'I have to solve something. What it is in truth I really haven't a clue.'

She laughs a throwaway half-giggle he is not sure about either. 'Jack convinced me it was a good idea to be here. He's good at that. Well, first we came to France. That's another story. Before I knew it he was selling me a broken Model T Ford as if it were a twenty-first century Bentley.'

Franck frowns at her quizzically.

'Don't worry about it. My husband sells things. He's always banging on how he is developing Jaws 6 or 7. I can't remember which. As a producer he's in development.'

'Aren't we all in development?'

She stares at him, smiling at this. 'Only Jack's looking for the bargain of the century in sequels. I'm sure you're not doing anything like that. Or are you?'

'Depends what bargain we're talking about, madame. Anyway, a Jaws sequel doesn't sound like the deal of the century.'

'Jack's a good businessman who made money with VHS and DVDs then with entertainment systems. With my help mind you.'

She does a little shimmy that makes Franck smile.

'How we got this boat. So, he might get Jaws Six done. He certainly knows how to scout favours. So far he just can't seem to get a feature film made, well not at the moment. But he bowled me over on Venice beach. Literally. He ran into me. He's half-blind. I got hit by Jack's truck.'

'Twice in upstate New York.'

She laughs. 'California. You watch movies, inspector?'

Franck nods, laughing now with her as if they've been friends for years.

'I can't complain, Franck. It's been a hell of a ride.'

She laughs harder this time though it comes out less-convincingly. 'In the process of dealing with Jack, I learned what the key to this business is.'

'Which is?'

'Film is ninety nine percent fantasy for ninety nine percent of the people ninety percent of the time.'

'I'm a French guy who hates American films so much I see an awful lot of them. Too many if I'm honest. I don't know why. I guess I must be a ninety-nine percent fantasist.'

'You sound like my kind of guy. Almost a total American. And you even look a bit like that actor, what's his name...?'

'People in Paris say I look like Maradona. After a hard night.'

'Maradona is dead, isn't he?'

'He is. I mean a young Maradona before the drugs. After a hard night.'

'You like some tea, inspector? Or something stronger?'

'Stronger sounds good.'

'Wine?'

'Okay.'

Franck watches her swishing a little going inside the boat's galley, Marc wondering where this might be heading.

She comes back with two bottles. 'Okay I have an Italian red and a French southern white if you prefer local, something frooty-tutty. So I'm told. I'm no expert, except at the drinking bit.' He smiles at another shimmy.

'Fruity sounds great.'

She pours two glasses and downs hers, pours herself another. Seeing Marc's surprise, she shrugs. 'I had a brush with a shark a couple of days ago, so I'm celebrating I'm still alive. Twenty-five-foot Great White brushed against me.'

'Jesus. Do the authorities know?'

'Do the authorities ever know?'

They laugh. 'How did it happen?'

'I went down diving after dark checking on someone's take on that dead shark show a few days back, and out of nowhere this huge fish appears. It bumped me.'

'There's a monster in this bay? Someone ought to know.'

'If they did this whole place would be shut down.'

'You're not going to say anything?'

'I only got bumped.'

'What does only got bumped mean?'

She throws a hip out. 'It bumped me.'

She laughs raucously. Marc takes a swig from his glass.

'I didn't know there were any great whites to bump anyone here.'

'They opened another Suez Canal. Any number of big fish could be coming up from the Indian Ocean. Just a theory of mine. Populations are changing even in this ancient sea. Big sharks are so unpredictable.'

She pours them fresh glasses. 'Near California not long ago a killer whale attacked and ate a great white. She throws the glass back.'

'To defend itself?'

'Offence is the best defence, but no, the Orca only wanted to lunch on the white's liver. You know what an Orca wants, and how they'll get it, but sharks, they're tricky. When it happened, great whites for miles around took off.'

'How do you know this?'

'We know because some are tagged.'

'Sharks scare that easy?'

'Wouldn't you be?'

Merryl throws her arms out, giving him another see-through look. 'I am a marine scientist Franck. My obsession is the carcharadon carcharias. And the more I study them the less I know. The festival director here has disappeared. He could have been taken.'

She eyes Franck.

'Here I am rattling on about my shark obsession. I spend so much time thinking about them and I understand nothing.'

She looks hard at Franck to see if he's with her on this. 'Another glass?'

'Wouldn't say no.' He watches her pour, her hands quite steady.

'And your husband leaves you out here by yourself. '

She stares at him.

'He's busy on shore trying to sell feathers to the Indians. Don't worry I can look out for me ... most times.' She grins broadly, then startles him with another off-the-wall laugh, thinner higher and louder this time.

'Did you think of speaking to the press?'

'About what?'

'The shark.'

She shakes her head. 'I am a marine biologist, not a gossip who sluts down film festivals. Shuts down festivals. A gossip slut at a shutdown festival, now that has a ring to it.'

She laughs with raucous abandon, laughing so hard this time Franck's ears are almost ringing.

'I'm too old to drink so much so quickly but I still can compete. She pulls her shirt dress tight around herself. Do I still have the chops for the catwalk?'

'Well...Definitely. '

When she pulls her shirt dress right up over her head, Franck nearly drops his glass.

'You know a good body when you see one, inspector?'

'Well, I'm no ...'

'But you know a good body when you see one.'

'You can compete.'

'Like a refill?'

'I won't say no.'

Suddenly she's kissing his mouth so hard, before Franck knows it they're rolling around on a deck mattress with a blue sky staring down at their already partially naked selves.

INTERMISSION

Day 6

SPECIAL GOLD EDGED INVITATIONS were printed up and
sent out to all members of Larry Linsteeg's team, as well as
some notables in Renne, saying: 'Join me at my special soirée,
in my suite, today.' Larry has never used such expensive
cardboard for any invitations before but today he feels he
needs to celebrate Edgar's success, even if, judging by his
demeanour, Larry's director isn't sharing his producer's
up-beat mood. Edgar's been downright gloomy since the
première of Death, so much so anyone might believe the
heavy career curtain had fallen with a Renne-wide thud.

Yet in truth early reviews of Death have been good if
vague, definitely kinder than Larry expected. Faint praise,
but better than nothing, Larry is saying to everyone. He is
also telling everyone he doesn't care what the Président of
the République thinks of Death. The man left town right
after the show with his girlfriend, nobody apparently even
seeing the line of Limos disappearing fast into a darkened
surrounding countryside.

And one day and some hours after the première only
one media outlet has predicted a backlash for Death. So far
nobody has joined them in this opinion. It's true no-one has
yet offered to take on distribution, and this news has been
passed around with more than a hint of schadenfreude, still,
without confirmation that this is an industry-wide trend,
Larry is urging Edgar not to take rumours to heart.

Quite a few in his inner party think Larry's timing for
a celebration is a touch premature, even insincere, if not
downright insensitive, given Edgar's state-of-mind.

Though Larry, being Larry—often trying a touch too hard to be believed—he has mending bridges high on his to-do list right now, even if his heart isn't really in the mending. Privately, confirmed by more than one set of ears, Larry predicts Death is ripe for tanking. Publicly, he does what most producers do. He's banging tables and yelling: 'We're in this fight to win.'

Overall, Larry as usual is employing a schizoid strategy but when has Larry ever been less than schizoid. It's his main defence, with hacks all-around reporting hush-hush that Larry is off his-own-off-script and his real meaning on Death's box office is that it's as good as DOA. As dead as you get in the business.

Yet in his suite ce soir Larry the partyist par excellence is playing the bon vivant jubilant producer so well he could get a bit-part playing in an after-dinner repertory production of a producer holding a last-chance saloon party. But his: 'I'm 100% behind Death and Edgar' is convincing nobody especially when he declares: 'I'm only here to do good for my people, especially my director.' Whichever way you look at it, even given Larry's tendency to hyperbolize everything, today is quite a performance.

In his welcoming address to invitees, Larry begins by announcing that he's managed to get a miracle done. 'This is the best picnic I have ever conjured-up.' Working with the hotel staff, Larry has, in his own words, managed to create a culinary masterpiece—moving some guests to share looks, wondering whether Larry is having a dig at his director. Negative speculation on the nature of his relationship with Edgar aside, nothing will stop Larry enthusing over the taxonomy of culinary delights on any day or night. And today he is geeing-up everyone's midbody expectations, listing with glee what he's offering — salmon poached in Provençal white wine grown in the commune de Cassis, cured Yak meatloaf from Ulaanbaatar, homemade French breads, salads, seasonal fruits with all manner of sweets all topped off, he says with a wink, by 'the *best* champagne you're ever likely to taste.' Seeing a group of kids collecting on the waterfront across from the hôtel, revellers Larry would have normally described as society's refuse, he calls out with the air of a diplomat on an international friendship mission, 'Come on up and join us.' Embarrassed by the largesse of a fat foreigner getting footsy with them from the safety of his expensive hotel balcony, the kids say nothing back at first, one using quick sign-language to indicate they might join Larry later.

'We will keep your seats warm.' Earning Larry a look and one inaudible comment. Still, his mood rolls on unchallenged. Heading down the stairs Larry greets late-arrivals in person, jauntily leading them through the Mélodie's foyer and on up the stairs calling out for 'Champagne, mon prince.'

Meanwhile out on his balcony guests murmur platitudes as they ogle his view, Ivan and Ulyana standing with a nervous Edgar, who, in holding hands with Semolina, doesn't join in the consumption of olives, breadsticks or special water, as everyone awaits the special champagne and main menu deliveries. When the doorbell finally sounds, Larry shouts: 'All's well that eats well.'

Going to his door with large-denomination banknotes in full view Larry ushers the waiters in pushing trollies laden with hot food, champagne ice buckets and trays of sweets. Tipping each one a fifty in plain sight, Larry insists on serving the champagne himself. The first bottle exploding its contents out over his balcony, a grinning Larry walks around filling flutes, apologizing that so much of the special contents has splashed onto the breakfast terrace tiles down below. Everyone gripping his and hers, Larry raises a flute. 'To the street party AND US.'

Nobody quite knows what he means, still most present manage to mumble his or her agreement, Bella sipping loudly, then staring at her glass—'What the hell is this?'

'Hiedsieck 1907 Diamant Bleu cuvée madame à votre service.'

Ivan stares at Larry for the first time without an ironic smile. 'The shipwreck in the Baltic sea? The Jönköping freighter sunk by a German submarine in 1916 on its way to Russia to deliver wine and other goods to the court of Tsar Nicholas II?'

'The very same.' Larry smiles in all directions.' I bought some cases at an auction in 1999.'

'How many did you buy?'

Larry smiles even more broadly. 'Two hundred bottles.'

'Two hundred...'

'Are you out of your mind?' Bella blurts out, other murmurs of disbelief joining her, everyone studying their glasses as if half-expecting the word priceless to appear in the bubbles. 'How much did you pay for it?'

Larry holds his glass up to the light remaining coy on this. 'Divers found the wreck back in 1997. It had been lying in freezing temperatures at sixty-seven meters for ninety years. Two thousand bottles of perfectly chilled champagne.'

He winks at Ivan. 'I thought it time to crack open a bottle as we are getting ready to make history together.' He raises his glass again. 'To future projects.'

'To future projects,' everyone says, not quite in unison, each guest sipping carefully. Smacking her lips in the aftermath, Bella swings around to Ivan. 'What do you think, do we have a future together?'

Ivan smiles enigmatically. 'Don't ask me anything while I'm drinking champagne as good as this.'

Semolina grabs Larry's arm. 'This is like swallowing diamonds.' She hugs him.

'So says Madame Death.'

'Bella.'

Many are surprised Bella chose this moment to launch an attack on Larry's star. In the moment of stunned silence that follows her witchy comment, Larry is seen signalling to a waiter to refill flutes from now on with the contents of cheaper brands.

'Anyway let's make a toast to all our big deals.'

Guests raise their glasses and join in the muted shouts of hooray, Edgar wandering out onto the balcony, then coming back quickly inside. 'Speaking of big deals, Larry, one is happening out there.'

'That's what we're here for,' Larry says, grinning even harder.

'No Larry, right here in the street.'

A HEAVYSET REPORTER waddling back from a long lunch on the western wharf gets a call on his mobile. He starts running as well as he can, others following suit, laden down by lunch and wine, one yelling: 'What the hell is up?'

Glancing back over his shoulder, the reporter with his phone still up to his ear shouts back: 'The bâtiment.'

'What about it?'

'Protesters are heading there.' The post-lunch race starts for real. Arriving at the red-carpet middle-aged journalists in various states of physical distress stagger around on the bitumen, the heavy-breathing heavy-set reporter completely bathed in sweat. His shirt out, just managing to stay upright, gasping for air, he says finally: 'I'll never ...ever... make ... my deadline like this.'

Bending over double he empties the barely half-digested contents of his recent meal onto the road. A colleague grabs her mouth seeing his beanbag body heave violently in and out.

'For godsakes Barry couldn't you vomit in the harbour?'

'The harbour is polluted enough,' another colleague suggests.

'Look what he's done to my new trousers.'

'Look at what he's done to my legs.'

Barry staggers about gasping, his face chalk white. 'I've lost ... an expensive lunch.'

'I don't remember you paying a centime, Barry.'

Rumbling noises down the Promenade silence them. Turning east, they take in the size and roar of a march getting closer and closer. In an instant each journalist, even the hardest drinker among them is sober. The wait for a real story is over.

From Larry's Mélodie balcony on the Promenade des Rois, with bodies now overflowing its boundaries, it's a startling picture of a demonstration two steps from completely getting out of control, kids barrelling down the boulevard. As the marchers begin sweeping by Bella's Hôtel des Belles Sables only a hundred meters east, closing in fast now on Larry's hotel, the chanting is beginning to get so loud everything else in the waterfront zone is silenced.

Studying their progress with a pair of Larry's binoculars, Edgar begins recognizing faces and seeing one kid who asked him to join their group he drops Larry's binoculars in a canvas chair and runs through the suite without saying a word.

OUTSIDE THE BÂTIMENT two of the semi-recovered journalists stare balefully at the crowd surging down towards them. The group stands frozen until Barry's whine wakes them up. 'In truth I'd prefer to be elsewhere.'

'UP THE STEPS,' one woman shouts, the lot moving at least at first with the discipline of a herd of elephants under control of their matriarch. Annalise at her safe halfway-point up the red carpet is furious seeing them coming her way. Men in black uniforms and black helmets are already pouring out from side streets with masks down and batons held high. With riot shields out in front of themselves they run straight at the protesters, their battle chants and thudding of leather boots on asphalt stunning everyone. Some of them seeing a small group of journalists cowering up the red stairs, start to come up towards Annalise's position.

'Oh Jesus, they're going to kill us as well?'

The main detachment of men in black meanwhile collide violently with the marchers on the road, clubs savagely bloodying the faces of screaming kids who at first scatter in all directions. Two electric helicopters in silent mode appear in the sky, men with rifles at both open sides. Squinting up at the attack helicopters, Barry does the thinking for all again. 'Are they shooting to kill?' Throwing up again, this time over his shoes, he asks meekly in the aftermath: 'What's the objective now?'

'Objective?' asks an irritated Annalise. Seeing another horde breaking away and heading back to join their brothers still climbing the stairs, clearly seeking to make the journalists the bait in a protest sandwich, Annalise yells: 'TO THE BÂTIMENT.'

'HOLD YOUR GROUND,' the other woman shouts. For a moment the group is rooted to the spot, stay or go, until a man replies, 'Tu es folle' and the troop obeys Annalise and runs helter-skelter up toward the bâtiment windows.

Finding chairs and tables mounted against the glass from the inside, they realize in a second that all is lost, seeing security men waving their fingers, the terrified reporters scattering in all directions like rabbits under gunfire.

SHOUTS AND CHANTS echo off the buildings. Joining the front line, Edgar somehow squeezes-in and links arms with the Japanese artist without being knocked down and trampled on by the protesters pressing up behind him. Glancing back, he sees no end to the demonstrators, the kids starting to sing, M-iki and Edgar joining in, many voices out of tune singing as loud as they can: 'We don't need no starry-eyed actors. We don't need no police patrols. Give us seats in the cinémas, give us culture we can control.'

A rolling thunder review of festival democratisation has begun, one marcher using a megaphone, Edgar repeating: 'WE WANT REAL FILM,' M-iki and Edgar yelling with them all.

Coming alongside Larry's Mélodie hôtel, Edgar sees his production team up on Larry's balcony staring balefully down at him. He knows what he looks like to them—a traitor. But as he sees it, the Renne waterfront is experiencing a long-overdue revolution, Edgar thinking insiders with privileges need to get up to speed with change. Movie professionals need to refocus their beliefs. Caught inside a vortex of a struggle against a moribund film culture, as it has been for far too long, he wants the cineastes to get everything they want.

Seeing a cameraman on the pavement panning up to Larry's balcony signalling: Can I come up? Edgar notices Larry's rude gesture back. Edgar wants to yell, Come on Larry, but it's a bit late for come ons. The champagne-happy I'm-everyone's-friend Larry Linsteeg is getting real as he sees it. One moment he was with the kids now he's against them. He is being an intelligent, prudent businessman. By Larry's side Bella glares down at Edgar too. If only he had a telephoto lens for a shot of her face. Moments earlier he was drinking champagne with her, but you drink with the mining class at your peril.

In the street kids scream for democracy—power over decision-making—the resignations of festival managers—a wholesale rethink of the system.

Whistling missiles fly-by to crack bits of cement. Rocks go through windows. Car windows shatter. History is evolving, truth showing up and not before time.

Up ahead Edgar sees tourists caught in the middle of the road, unable to go back or forward. They're not the only ones who don't know where to go, moving about in slow motion like stick-creatures stuck in the glue in the sudden wave of political heat, the whole march sweeping across the boulevard like a boiling monsoon river of political lava.

Mesmerized Edgar tries communicating his thoughts via hand-signals to M-iki her arm binding tighter to his. The noise has increased three-fold, the protest now a tinder box flash from a total frenzy, someone only needing to throw a match at them and the marchers would all fly up in the air like so much furnace confetti.

Elena tries stopping Viktor rushing outside to see what's going on. Leaving her door open, she goes down nearly two flights after him, calling down repeatedly for him to come back up. Hearing nothing back except the sound of Viktor's shoes echoing in the stairwell and then out into the street, she shrugs and trudges back upstairs. 'He'll find the Promenade far worse than on TV.'

And he does. Helicopters circle above Viktor's head as he stands in the street studying buildings for snipers. Protesters are hard at defending themselves against riot-police, cracks, shouts and screams sounding all-around him.

The two heavily armoured helicopters are now strafing the crowd, men with weapons visible at doors, rifle-fire continuing to bounce off objects everywhere, Viktor wondering if the real shooters are on the ground or in the air and who really has the real and who has the rubber bullets. Wherever the kill shots are coming from, there are motionless bodies in the street to prove it.

This is way beyond manufacturing fear. The on-ground riot police in black, armed with sticks are striking out viciously at demonstrators. The kids are fighting back, their bravery startling Viktor. Yet their casualties are remarkably low. Some parts of the battle are at a critical stage with demonstrators grabbing anything they can—rocks, car mirrors, dustbin lids, anything they can use to fight with. One group with pipes outflank some black uniforms who panic as the pipe-wielding cineastes beat at them not caring if there are snipers anywhere near.

Viktor sees two marchers fall one after the other. A black uniform takes a head shot from what could only be friendly fire. Hidden in a doorway Viktor finds the ferocity of the battle shocking. He rubs his face telling himself repeatedly that this is not Prague in sixty-eight. This is way more violent, worse than anything he has experienced. This battle is a street fight on horse-steroids.

PROTESTERS SHOUT: LE POUVOIR C'EST NOUS, Edgar joining in the chanting, his voice growing hoarse in seconds. LE POUVOIR C'EST NOUS sounds behind and in front of Edgar now, soon morphing into POUVOIR POUR NOUS, tightening into POUVOIR-NOUS, with voices everywhere rising until the sound of the chanting is bouncing off building facades and filling the Promenade end to end. Marchers surge by Edgar yelling wildly as they charge the men in black, the protesters fighting with such conviction and intent, the black uniforms are beginning to form a blanket of fallen bodies on the bitumen. More marchers rush in, Edgar asking himself if he were making a film could he have imagined these bloodied screaming devil-may-care freedom fighters. With everything bewilderingly unclear on who's actually winning, the protesters continue on in their battle to the death for democracy.

'THAT'S IT. THE FUN'S OVER! Get back to the place where you're safe,' the général shouts at nobody, because nobody is listening to him anymore. Running around in circles in his denim civvies he tries herding some terrified spectators caught out on a traffic island. Gesturing at them to run over to him, Cindy sees they won't even think of moving. Caught up as they are in a state of panic, why should they obey some crazy old bloke in ill-fitting denim jeans?

'HE'S A COP. HE'S A COP' Cindy yells, but the women either can't hear or don't want to listen to her, fused in utter fear. Darting in behind the général and pointing, Cindy yells: 'HE'S THE GOOD GUY' immediately realizing that in playing the général's movie sidekick she isn't really gelling well with these stranded tourists or whatever-they-are. She's just another hip black chick with a blonded-Afro, side kicking for an old white guy who's gesturing furiously and saying nothing they can understand.

A couple of centuries of African history is replaying before her eyes. An old-fashioned colonial coup d'état from back in the old time, a bunch of hate-filled white men on horseback with dogs terrorizing black people.

'Have we been infiltrated?' she shouts at the général but it's pointless asking him anything right now. The général can't hear her, doesn't want to hear, his face a portrait of a man who could be on another planet.

As for the women they will not leave their only safe haven on Cindy's or the général's say so. They are sticking with their plan of clinging to a palm tree in the middle of a road in the middle of a riot. They won't, can't, interpret anyone's hand signals. They read what they see. A blur. By their faces they're condemning themselves for even being anywhere near this boulevard. An out-maneuvered old fart, no matter how smart he thinks he looks in his jeans, aint convincing them, his waving arms and shouting voice inspiring nobody. The stranded women can't do anything except remain stranded. Would you, would anyone, obey this old man's orders given what they are facing right now? So, Cindy doesn't blame them. The idea of giving up the ghost and running the gauntlet across this wild street is out of the question. Then one woman falling over on the very road they should be crossing changes everything. Funny that, a small thing changes everything. Cindy runs out and gets the fallen woman upright and dragging her off the bitumen splinters her shirt buttons finally inspiring the women to act, all of them making it into the safety zone by a whisker. The saved woman lies weeping her thanks under a broken window. How murderous this will get Cindy has no idea anymore. She knows only one thing—the popping sounds, the shattered windows, the fallen shapes, the obliteration of order, this is not a political science lesson happening before her eyes. This is a COUP. She points: 'QUI SONT CES MECS?' The still shocked général shakes his head. The look in his face tells Cindy all she needs to know about how much he knew about this. Absolutely nothing. He might not be back to know any more about it either not even as an ex-général after this. The men in black aren't his men, the whole thing so ugly, the général finally has to react. 'PAS DE GENDARMES CRS ET CE NE SONT PAS DES BALLES EN CAOUTCHOUC.' She nods, not knowing what he'll do or what he really means by what he just said.

THE FALLEN MARCHERS are taken by support women as best they can drag them back to a square they have created.

The last men in black charge scattered protesters all around Viktor. From his position in a doorway near the centre of the fight he has seen black uniforms regroup and charge at the demonstrators four times now. Each time the protesters managed to drive them back, a counterattack was mounted by the men in black taking a further toll of the marchers, their frontline disintegrating three times. Viktor saw the young director he only knows as Edgar just missing getting knocked senseless by a metal bar by pure luck alone, a girl holding on to him pulling him backwards just in time. The pair fell sideways out of the mêlée sliding out near the waterfront, Viktor losing sight of them.

These marchers seem to be a different kind of protester in Viktor's experience. Kids, yes, but really tough, with the men in black looking at each other more and more as if saying: We are not paid enough for this.

Viktor witnesses what he believes is a sea change of thinking. It is happening before his eyes. The black clad riot police turn en masse, in an instant. One very strong charge from the protesters forces a complete change of heart. At first some of the men in black start running away from their duties, then the rest follow in a full tilt retreat.

Stepping over bodies of protesters a dazed Edgar half-drags the Japanese girl behind him. They clamber over a barrier, going down some stairs to the beach.

He tries a door. It is open. Edgar finds himself staring at glass cabinets in an empty restaurant, rows of stacked shining glasses, a coffee machine, ceramic cups, two fridges, bottles of liquor stacked on shelves.

Walking around he stands in the semi-darkness staring back at his partner. The girl is not M-iki. 'I thought that's it, I was dead.' Edgar laughs seeing her face. It breaks the tension.

'They left the door unlocked?' she says, the woman shaking her head in awe, Edgar taking in her French-accented English.

'Maybe they left in a hurry.' Edgar looks down at his torn knuckles bleeding from something he can't recall doing. Coming down the stairs didn't seem a very good idea at first. Now it does. 'How did you get mixed up in all this?'

'It is a long story.'

'I'm a director who likes long stories.'

The woman smooths the sides of her dishevelled outfit

with trembling hands. 'Merde, mon sac!' she barks and starts for the door. Edgar pulls her back.

'You won't find it.'

'I must. My phone is in it. My purse. Everything.'

'It'll be trampled.'

The street noise above rises to a crescendo for a moment as if to make Edgar's point crystal clear to her. Forcing a cabinet open he takes a bottle of whisky and unscrews the top. Pouring whiskey on his hands he reads the black label on the face of the bottle. Handing it over to the woman she shakes her head.

'It'll calm you.'

She grimaces and taking the bottle hesitatingly, then lifting it gingerly to her mouth, as if it might cut her tongue, tentatively she takes a short swig and hands the bottle back to him. Edgar drinks more and hands it back to her. This time she lifts the bottle right up high and tilting her head way back pours whisky down her throat.

'Easy now.'

Pulling it away from her mouth she gasps. Edgar takes the bottle back and drinks more, already feeling the effect. Blinking at her he asks how she's feeling.

'We were lucky.'

From her eyes, he can see she doesn't believe in luck. Edgar suddenly has the urge to kiss her. He can see them landing on the wooden floor and tearing each other's clothes off. What a moment it would be, Edgar imagining them yelling and screaming as loud as they can, with a wild street riot going on right above their heads.

He takes a step forward. She takes a step back.

'My husband is up there.'

Two of Bella's security men stand out on the pavement by the hotel's side entrance, wearing sunglasses and earpieces. Watching for any change in the shouting and screaming still going on along the waterfront only yards away the pair are ready to say: Mesdames, Messieurs, this is not an exit.

Sweating colleagues are doing the lifting of boxes out through the hotel's side door, their expressions telling the world that the riot is none of their business. Using free arms to stabilize the weight of the loads they dump box after box onto the flat top back of a small electric truck—the only sign of nerves being an occasional glance to the road on the seafront or up around at windows above them.

Shifting metal in boxes from Jeff's room to a service elevator then down and out through the Sables' side exit the operation takes less than ten minutes. The protest's a perfect cover. To an outsider, the work is carried out with admirable efficiency, the driver climbing in next to his boss, four men sitting on the back of the truck.

Two lookouts in a SUV follow behind, the electric flat top going up Rue Strasbourg, the two vehicles in a tight convoy. Turning right into Rue Pourbelle they head east down Boulevard Général Victoire where the traffic is heavier, much more than Jeff Westbridge expected.

His concern is real but without room for any change to plans he can only cross the middle and index fingers of his right hand and close his eyes for a second or so and hope for the best outcome. Trust there will be nothing left of the protest near the eastern end of the Promenade des Rois and then leave all the rest to fate. This part of the plan should take maybe six minutes. At a maximum seven. For the drive from the hotel to Port Mipento harbour, the driver takes Avenue de Seville and says to Bella's righthand man beside him, 'We'll make it.'

They still have two and half minutes left. Sweeping into an underpass the driver takes them right towards Pointe des Rois, which turns them right again into Avenue Triste Berne. Motoring into the carpark on Quai Bruno Latour, his passenger says under his breath, 'Bravo. Let's hope they're here.' Jeff studies the marina wharf, looking for a white mid-size flat-top with an in-board motor, an open back-landing flying a French flag on the stern.

THE ROAD AND SIDEWALKS of the Promenade are strewn with barricades, projectiles, pick-handles and dead and alive bodies lying flat out on the road. Surveying the scene Inspector Marc sees men and women huddled on top of some bâtiment steps, one woman with an American accent calling out: 'Est-il bien, maintenant?'

Marc waves that it's okay for her to come down. Silhouetted by the headlights of an ambulance caught in a boulevard dust cloud he makes out the shape of a tall man in workmen's jeans loping his way, a tall black girl with bouncing hair behind him.

He recognizes the man wearing faded 501 Levi's and manages in time not to smile. Getting closer the man calls out: 'Do you have a gun, detective?'

'Now that's not the usual question an inspector gets asked in a street.' He smiles at the général's look. 'Back in my room, général, yes.'

'Take this then.'

Marc stares down at the Browning automatic in the général's hand.

'It won't bite.'

Inspector Marc accepts the weapon, wanting to ask where has it come from, where has it been, turning it gingerly around in his hands.

'I said it won't bite.'

'Yes, but has it bitten already.'

'It's clean. You have my word.'

Slipping it into his belt Marc pulls his shirt over the extra weight and follows the général and the young black woman, keeping a few paces behind them.

'Are we off to make an arrest, général?'

The général stops and squints hard back at Marc. 'This is a request from a fellow professional. This is not an order, inspector. You can leave any time you wish.'

Marc nearly says back: And where would I go? He is barely tolerated in Renne and hated in Paris. 'I'm happy to help out. I don't wish to leave, sir.'

'Don't call me, sir. Général, if you must.'

The big man comes close, whispering, 'Inspector, I asked you because I need someone I can trust. An officer who knows what's what, to see procedures and rules are followed and will report to that.' Marc nods. 'I need a witness to what's going on.' Marc nods again. 'Oui, général.'

The général looks at him for a moment then walks on. Marc decides the général's face is of a man on a mission from god or as close to being on a godly mission as those who believe in god believe a man on a mission from god can get.

Marc once thought he was on a mission from some higher authority as well, once in Paris, only he's pretty sure now he's never been on a mission and he certainly isn't anymore. Climbing some steps into a building across from the bâtiment he stays close but not too close to the big man.

Two sentries block their way. After a brief stand-off the men step aside. Walking inside a large old apartment the général shouts, 'WHERE IS HE?'

'Who?' one man asks, facing up to the général.

'You know who I mean.'

The girl jumps back just in time to avoid the général's swinging arm. One of F's mercenaries takes a blow to his head and crashes hard against a door. Marc waits a moment before stepping over the figure, following his new boss, if he could ever call him that, heading further down a hallway, treading carefully on a creaking parquet floor, turning to the girl. 'Are you on the général's staff?'

'I am a reporter.'

'Watch yourself, then,' Marc mutters.

Mouldy-looking mattresses, sleeping bags, clothing lie strewn everywhere. Marc sniffs the air twice and determining it is the stink of chaos, shakes his head, speaking from cinematic memory: 'My, my my, what a mess.'

The place is a mini barracks of sorts where discipline never was or was quickly lost. Sullen, unwashed men, a corps of defeated soldiers lie about in a dishevelled scene Marc believes might actually be some sort of headquarters. Given their numbers in the street there has to be more places like this one somewhere. He walks on tapping the weighty Browning. If these men have guns he hasn't seen any, but he's trusting nobody or anything. Axe handles, batons are lying around. Disorganized or not these mercenaries have the numbers to launch some sort of resistance anytime, though resistance seems to be the last thing on their minds.

Marc's new commanding officer checks room by room, walking the long hallway as any victor will engaging in a mopping-up operation. It's as if Marc is following him back in some tunnel of lost time walking into the aftermath of a long-past battle, men with their wounds undressed, some injured infantrymen, half-clothed showing an interest in Cindy, as men of any age will, but mostly ignoring the intruders, sourly tasting the air around their makeshift beds.

None of them are in any real condition to mount any kind of action, but Marc is still wary. These are not police officers. They are soldiers, barely trained mercenaries only perhaps. They are not French. That much is clear.

At the end of a corridor, they enter a room with a mirror with an ornate gold-corniced antique border. In the middle is a table scattered with empty bottles, dirty plates with remains of food, used food tins acting as ashtrays filled with cigarette butts and stale baguette pieces. A wine bottle with a typed note tied on its neck boasts, Compliments of the bâtiment. In English no less. Franck picks up a flip-open set of matches and stares at a word handwritten there.

On the opposite wall is a painting of another infamous military scene: La Redoute 6 Septembre 1812, the général shouting now: 'Does anyone know where F is?' Nobody replies. He turns to one of his men. 'Call headquarters.' The lieutenant stares back at his commander, his face a picture as if resisting the urge to say, which headquarters? One of the soldiers speaks up in accented French: 'We don't know where he is.'

The général studies the man. 'Sir.'

'Sir.'

'You are in uniform. What uniform I do not know but consider yourself all under arrest. I am the commanding officer of the national police in charge here. You will obey me at all times. Whatever this insignia is on your shoulder, whatever country you are from, you are part of a foreign force operating illegally in my country.' The général takes a step closer looking more closely at the markings.

'Is this some sort of fascist badge?' Marc's right hand strays instinctively to the grip of the Browning automatic, his middle finger feeling for the handgun single-action trigger.

Given the number of men in the rooms around them Marc would have advised against questioning anyone in this way.

'What on earth is this utter fool doing? Corot, put out an order in my name. F is to be arrested on sight. He is a fugitive from French justice.'

Lieutenant Corot salutes and turns to go outside to carry out this order. How Marc doesn't know, and neither does Corot by the look on his face. Still, Marc can see just what the général is doing, even if Corot can't. Military theatre, and it's working. The général stands staring at a face a foot below him.

'You will follow protocols in this country. Where is your boss, that bloody civilian? Speak up man. Where is he?'

'I don't know... sir.'

'How long ago did he leave?'

'I don't know exactly, sir. Twenty minutes.'

'Did he take a vehicle?'

This confuses the man. 'I don't know sir.'

'Are you in charge of this rabble?'

'I am the sergeant on duty, sir.'

The général nods, walking on around the room, glancing at papers on a desk up against a wall. Going out on to the balcony he studies cameras on tripods, their lenses pointing at the bâtiment.

'Bloody mercenaries.'

The sergeant with the insignia on his shoulder stands to attention staring at a French général in baggy 501 Levis.

With an even baggier denim shirt tucked-in to show an automatic pistol at his belted middle the général looks more like a mercenary. A puffy-faced man joins them out on the balcony, bowing as he offers the général his hand. The général doesn't shake it.

'Capitan Artebaschov at your service.'

Staring at the général's outfit he apologises for the chaos, Marc noticing the man's fluent even elegant French. 'Discipline has broken down,' Capitan Artebaschov explains. He drops his voice to a whisper leaning in conspiratorially, alcohol or bad breath making the général grimace and pull away. 'These are all students from officer training schools. Boys only. They can be a little messy at times.'

'Who are you and where are you from exactly, Capitan?'

Capitan Artebaschov ignores the question and showing no flicker of embarrassment asks the général: 'Any of you Americans?'

'This is France.'

'I would like to join the American army. With bases around the globe military-professionals like me can have a good life. Could you help me with a visa?'

Cindy brings Marc back to Earth by whispering: 'If these are the hard-heads we saw in the streets, they could be dangerous, right?'

'Tell that to the boss.'

They watch the général as he grabs captain Artebaschov's collar. 'Where is F? Tell me everything, capitan. Lie to me and I will not only not help you get to America I will have you placed in a Marseille dungeon where you will remain for the rest of your miserable life. So, where is he?'

Marc now switches off the safety on the Browning.

'He left one half-hour ago.'

'Which way did he go?'

Artebaschov shrugs. 'I didn't see.'

The général raises his hands as he speaks to his men.

'Listen up. Our target has been on the run for thirty minutes. Average foot speed over missile strewn ground is three kilometres an hour. Barring nature or ice-cream stops that gives us a radius maximum of two kilometres. I want you to search every flop house, hen house, whore house, alleyway, doorway, hallway, over-way, byway, laneway, throughway, underpass, back garden and building stairwells. Our fugitive's name is Doctor Hugonot Fugard. Go get him.'

THE TENDER COMES ALONGSIDE the seaward pointing stern of Ivan's huge boat which idles in the off-shore breeze. Jeff's men clamber off onto the wooden slatted back-landing, the huge bow facing Renne. This offloading operation is virtually invisible from land. Nobody in the town can see the metal cases being placed on Ivan's back landing. With all that is happening on the Promenade boulevard, even someone who isn't distracted and there aren't any, or even if there were someone knowledgeable about Ivan's boat and its habits, and if he or she were using binoculars pointed directly at the Soraya, he or she would have great trouble determining that anything out of the ordinary is going on.

The electrics are switched off, the men below working in the ambient light. Out to sea is another proposition, but lookouts are taking care of any approaching boats, and there are no boats anywhere near the Soraya's mooring.

'Do we need to bother with all this secrecy?' asks one of Jeff's crew. 'It could attract attention in itself, no?'

'Stop talking. Grab that box.'

The man shrugs at his boss. Two other men are sweating in the hold, stacking cases one on another, panting heavily in the confined space.

'Can the sub take this weight?'

'The manual says so.'

Bella's main man up-top is not worrying about these boxes either out here in daylight. He doesn't know why this is happening and he's not asking questions. If Bella wants something done he does it. The last box packed, his boys come back up on deck laughing as they wipe themselves dry. They step on board the transport, the tender backing away from the Soraya's wide stern, swinging around and heading back for shore towards Port Mipento. Nobody says anything as the electrics on Ivan's launch come on again, the runabout driver upping his throttle.

TENDING TO THE FACES OF THE INJURED Semolina tries to determine serious from non-serious wounds, searching for holes from phantom bullets that officially did not rain down from helicopters that nobody saw in the sky. Some wounded are delirious. Going from shape to shape it isn't long before Semi is almost delirious herself, the features of the firing squad victim Philippe Baucq appearing in every face. Semi so-wanted to play Edith Cavill in that TV series, a character she was born but never selected to be and soon she's weeping as if she never left the series she was never cast in, playing the role she trained so hard for in her apartment and didn't get, waiting for the casting director's call that never came. She's never wept so many tears over missing anything in her life, those tears of despair raining down again here. She practiced reality-rehearsals in her London flat, kneeling beside a pillow treating the victims, lifting each casualty, a papermache-head, onto her pillow-prop. It was at least not wasted time or effort, with the re-stimulation of the manufactured emotions she so cleverly created, informing her in this sphere of reality, the actress experiencing the same devastating emotions, fiction blurring into fact. No time spent on an imaginary set is ever wasted. Simulation has its place in time.

A woman's voice in her ear brings her back to a very thick present, asking Semi if she can help out. Looking up, Semolina can barely make out the face. Then gradually she begins to see her. 'You're the inspector's wife.'

Marie squeezes Semolina's shoulder. Taking water and a towel from her, Marie walks off to work on another of the injured. An eerie calm has settled in the road, the two women only yards away from each other yet not looking each other's way as they work on one prostrate form after another. A woman limps over. 'There a Marie Marc here?'

'C'est moi.'

Marie stands and takes the cellphone from the woman without saying anything or asking questions.

'Franck?' she says even before hearing the familiar voice speak. 'I am on the waterfront close to the Mélodie Hôtel.'

Finding out she's okay, Franck replies that he's okay too but rings off before Marie can find out where he is. She stands a moment staring at the blank screen sitting in her hand. Moving on she sees an Asian girl, deciding that she is someone best left to the professionals, a human being too peaceful to spell any good, though Marie can't just leave her. She wipes blood from the top of her head carefully cleaning muck from a wound in her hair, the face way too calm, Marie swaying saying, 'Franck, Franck,' flinching as Semolina cries out behind her, 'Somebody get me a stretcher.'

MARIE AND FRANCK MARC. Why are they even in Renne-sur-Mer? Marie pointed out Semolina to Franck even before they knew anything about her. Sitting alone at a table looking scared and vulnerable, it was the very night of their arrival on day one of this assignment, at what Franck and Marie thought was a welcome dinner for them. It wasn't. It was for the stars, actors, directors, producers, to show off in, with Franck and Marie seated well away from everyone who was anyone. Close to Semolina as it turned out. She looked so lost, Marie made a point of going over to say hello. Marie knew she appreciated her gesture. The girl was almost in tears. Coming back Marie whispered: 'She's so young.'

Having arrived at midday, Marie boating over from Bastia later, then swept into Renne in a hire car, they settled into the apartment overlooking a market square that Martin provided for the entire festival. A story in itself.

Forget the parcel with champagne and tickets etc, a straight-up bribe as far as Franck is concerned, he wanted to send it all back, but that would have meant a confrontation and Marie wouldn't get to see any films or go to any private parties. Like the dinner on night one.

So, at 8 pm, precisely, Franck being good with time, they headed down from their okay place overlooking it has to be said a cute market square.

Only let's be honest. They were quite some way from the sea, and you would have thought, as Marie did, they at least deserved a view of the water.

Arriving at the famous beach front restaurant where again they thought they were going to be, perhaps not honoured guests, but at least pretty welcome. At least on the list. Standing in a line at the door of La Carré d'Argent,

Marie and Franck weathered the looks of others all dressed to nines trying not to smile at Marie and Franck's outfits.

Luckily a few name actors dressed down too. Smiling, broadly at first at the waitress, they gave their names. Then they said them again and then again. They couldn't be found anywhere, Franck mumbling about who he is, and why he was there. Finally, Marie stepped around her man to confront the restaurant chief in her best clipped English. The man paid her back with his own.

'We are completely full Madame. This is festival time.'

'Tell me about it.' Marie's English was more than solid. She could give as good as she got in any language and she spoke four, apart from her native French in which she topped her class in her final year at lycée. The queue behind them started murmuring. But Marie wouldn't be deterred, doing a second more fulsome description of Marc's Parisian position at Quai des Orfèvres, how he had solved more crimes than the Maître du restaurant had seen hot dinners.

'That's quite a few, madame.'

Forget that the Président had asked specifically for someone like him to be in Rennes. Franck was chosen by reputation. He stood behind her embarrassed by what he thought was an unnecessary inflation of his worth. Still, Marie wasn't stopping or letting go, her voice loud enough to be heard down in the street. The Maître du restaurant remained unimpressed until Franck got through to the new festival director by mobile, who came out pretty quickly it must be said to sort it all out, full of apologies. The maître du restaurant apologized as well, Marie showing both of them just what she thought of their show of contrition.

It was why Marie marched today. She understood in a flash why the cineastes were demonstrating. She and they were marching against privilege. The absurdity of the concept and weight it placed on society. She was marching against privilege today, even if she had had a privileged life herself, her grandmother leaving her a two-story apartment in the 5th arrondissement without a cent owing on it. Franck always laughed off that fleck of a flaw in her politics.

Of course, the dinner invite was unnecessary anyway, and more than ironic, because if it had been up to Franck he would have been happy with a take-away pizza and paper cup of wine, decent wine of course. Eating and drinking on a bench facing the sea would have done him fine. Two-star Michelin restaurants leave him cold, especially when filled with actors, especially foreign actors.

In truth Marie's show of her character made him somewhat angry, not at her at all, but at all that had already happened to him and her on that day. Gulping down his second, third and fourth glasses of champagne he began mentally composing his resignation letter. He had had enough. His blood sugar was up. When Marie nudged his arm to say, 'Isn't that Steven Spielberg?' he snapped at her, 'You're the expert.' He apologized. 'This is just crazy.'

When Geoffrey Leads, as président du jury, the man Franck had already met upon arriving in Renne sitting in the back of Martin's official car facing boats in a marina, hearing a completely bullshit story about voting corruption—when Leads walked in with a super svelte stunning young actress on his arm, Franck told Marie it's time to leave.

'I'll get you some bread.'

She managed to steal a bread basket from another table. Accepting the breadroll, Franck stared into space chewing it, only realizing Marie was trying to get his attention again when she squeezed his left bicep hard. 'Your phone, Franck.'

Checking his screen he saw Chief Inspector Dessilin's number. Mouthing, the boss, he half-stumbled getting up and heading over to the window stood facing the water.

'So how's the Côte d'Azur treating you?'

'I'm at dinner with the stars what's not to like.'

Turning, Franck saw Marie in conversation with a young actor-type now leaning across at her from the other side of their table.

'What am I doing here, exactly, sir?'

'Investigating on behalf of the Président, as I told you.'

'Investigating what?'

'A corruption issue.'

What crap, Franck nearly said. 'Shouldn't someone in the local force do this?'

'They can live without that.' Who can live without it? he nearly said. But he knew what was meant. The festival was covering up its filthy laundry.

'Pretend you're on holiday.'

Marc pulled the mobile away from his face and stared at it. I was going, Marie and I were practically there on holiday, he almost said. Corsica, remember. Before your call, but as usual he said nothing, exhaling, thinking on the first call he received early that day on the wharf on Biènville, followed by a depressing walk back to get the car, how it turned upside down all his and Marie's holiday plans.

'Keep your eyes peeled. Let me know if you need any help.'

Franck opened his mouth to ask for just that but Dessilin had already rung off. He took the phone away from his ear and stared at it again. Glancing over at Marie still happily talking to this young handsome talkative guy, Franck returned to his seat. He was introduced to the young actor, forgetting his name right away, who in seeing Franck's face found a reason to return to his own table.

'Everything okay?'

Franck squeezed her thigh. 'Couldn't be better.'

'The food is good.'

He noticed she had barely touched her plate.

Strangely, after this awful beginning, and it was a bad start, the first night at dinner in a hoity-toity restaurant turned out to be a really pleasant affair, until the very end when it went bad again. Perhaps Franck drank too much. During their second course Geoffrey Leads came over, Marc managing to bring the man to the attention of Marie without any irony in his voice. Another stack of party invitations and film tickets were presented. A tall gregarious American stood with a hand on the back of Franck's chair, giving him an impromptu lecture on French crime procedurals and their connection to American cinema, mentioning all films he'd seen in the process. Franck managed to converse with him in English without making too many mistakes or sounding disingenuous. In fact, he laughed a lot, really enjoying himself for the first time in the night, hearing the man's list of achievements and not feeling anything other than admiration. Wow, so many films, Reservoir Dogs, Pulp Fiction, Jackie Brown and Chill Bill, his new pal leaving eventually, saying he hoped he and Franck got together again. The goodbyes were warm.

'Stick to your guns,' Franck called out, Quentin jerking his head around and grinning, Marie later deftly pointing out the unintended irony in the phrase. Franck thought it was just like saying: be firm.

'It is and it isn't, in this context.'

'I guess I should go back and study more.'

Another reason why he wondered why he had been sent to Renne. His poor English. After some more drinks, an actress whose name he also misplaced in seconds got him going on the subject of French democracy, a pet subject, the conversation heading into truly weird territory when she asked how he stayed in character.

'A detective not good at his job, you mean?'

They laughed over that. He liked her eyes and getting close enough to sample her perfume it wasn't long before he found himself under the table helping her look for a lost earring, her foot ending up in his mouth.

Staggering back upright, ten champagnes into the night, or was it fifteen, he discovered the delightful Jennifer had been stolen away, Marie staring over at him.

On the way home, going down to the beach for some air, she let him have it. Coolly at first, then not so coolly.

'I am not angry you drank so much and talked to every actress in the room. You looked wonderful on your knees under the table kissing the blond's foot by the way.'

'Was she blond? She dropped some jewellery.'

'I bet. Alone is she?'

'Marie, I was being patronized. She even kicked me in the face.'

'Not much of a kick as I saw it, more like you were chewing her toes.'

'I was pretending to enjoy myself.'

'Try a little less next time.'

'You weren't having such a bad time yourself.'

'Only I didn't have twenty-seven glasses of champagne.'

'Twenty-seven ... I was socialising, as Dessilin said I should.'

'Did he?'

'More or less.'

'Less than more I bet.'

She left him on the beach, Marc managing to get up the steps without tripping over his feet. 'Wait!' She didn't.

Maybe that was really why she marched. Marie was really angry over the lost holiday and she had a way of staying angry, sometimes for days on end.

VOOR'S NOT GOING ANYWHERE. In the middle of a spreading mist of an eighth or tenth cognac, he smooths his pony-tail listening to F explain why the extra add on to the job is necessary, a job Voor already feels is done, F saying it needs to be done a little more.

'This is a major cultural revolt. An attack on French culture.' F leans across the bar table, whispering a name. Voor stares back at him, his mouth drying.

'I always knew you were crazy. The coast will be crawling with gendarmes, probably the army too in five minutes.'

'You have two helicopters to help you out, and one of our guys is even on the Russian's boat.'

Looking over the square Voor struggles with what his next move should be. F has just now changed their original agreement. 'You fucked it up and you want me to fix it.'

Voor studies F and his out-of-date teardrop sunglasses then looks over at some orange trees in a square searching for CCTV cameras, microphones, bringing his gaze back onto his boss. 'Give me another piece and all the cash you owe me, and I'll do the guy.'

'I can't give you anything until it is done.'

'I have already had expenses.' Voor shudders, the several cognacs he'd already had repeating on him now. 'I'll meet you halfway.'

A waiter arrives with more coffees, no cognacs.

'No half-ways,' F says, 'one full way or no way.'

F and Voor sit sipping their espressos staring into the same square. Clear. Restart. Method. Focus. Voor thinks of standing up and does with some difficulty, draining his coffee cup, ransacking another fog from his head, trying to get his mind to slide into meditation-mode, let the old training kick in. Somehow he manages to stay upright.

'Leave a hundred for them and let's go.'

'I can't do that. I need a receipt.'

It is almost dark by the time the necessary paperwork is in F's pocket, the pair walking across the road and standing in the open air under orange trees and palms fronds, seeds on the ground, Voor asking again, 'Does it have a silencer?'

'Not here.'

Voor's thinking a Glock 21 45 acp federal hollow points, extreme accuracy, light recoil, with legendary stopping power. 'Thirteen slugs?'

'Ten.'

'Traceable?'

'It's from Albania.'

'Originally. Does it have a history here? Is there a tube? Give it to me.'

'Stop it. I said not here.'

'Does it HAVE a fucking tube?' Voor points to a laneway. 'Over there. We can make it look like a drug deal.'

'You've been watching too much television.'

Voor smiles seeing F lick his lips, and makes a move to remove the guy's glasses.

'Stop it.'

Voor leaves the glasses and gets hold of F's satchel, dragging it out of his hands. They struggle and bang into a palm trunk, F's head thudding as if it is a full coconut falling on hard ground, his voice rising several octaves: 'STOP IT.'

Voor manages to wrench the bag from him.

'For a weak shit you sure got one helluva of a grip.'

Voor pulls the flap open. Rifling around inside he finds wrapped wads of notes, fifties and hundreds by their look. 'How much is there?'

'Not here.'

Voor pulls out the pistol. People in the vicinity duck, a man yelling: 'HE'S GOT A GUN.'

'For godsakes do you have to make a scene.'

'Who cares over here.'

F folds himself from the waist as if suddenly wanting to tie his shoelaces, Voor staring: 'You know I could shoot you right here in the back of the head.'

That gets F back up fast. 'Take it all. We're square.'

'No, we're not square'. Voor points the weapon. A woman screams.

'Don't worry madame. We know each other. Though that doesn't mean I wouldn't like to kill him.' Voor grins at her as her second half scream dies.

Suddenly F is on top of Voor, trying to wrestle the SIG from him, Voor going around and around with F on his back, clicking the pistol. Voor finally throws F onto the pavement, and staggering around, staring down at the face of a man he realizes he barely knows, F grimacing up at him.

'You bring people?'

'No.'

Voor pulls F upright watching him hop around rubbing his knee.

'Give me back the satchel. I have changed my mind. Give it to me, Voor.'

'Over your dead body.'

'You're making a scene.'

The buzz is there, Voor recalling every hollow-head moment he's ever been involved in, that old feeling back again. 'Where's the slugs.'

'Put that thing away you fool.'

'I'm the fool. You want me to kill a gendarme general, I'm the fool.'

'Oh, tell the whole world why don't you.'

Voor ignores him, rifling in the satchel and pulling out another plastic bag filled with hollow-head-points. 'Okay, waiting back there I was thinking. I have a better idea. Do you want to hear it?'

'This'll be good.'

'Do you wanna hear it or not?'

'Do I have a choice?'

Wrapping F's left arm up around his shoulder Voor half-drags his boss as they head over to the edge of the square, the man who shouted before staring blankly at them, a SIG heavy in Voor's hand. Voor smiles, nods at the man. 'He's my boss. And you never argue with your boss, right?'

The man half smiles back, rooted to a spot, looking like he might actually try to run for cover any minute. 'Don't worry about it. We're done. You can go back to whatever you were doing.'

Grabbing F's right shoulder, Voor leads his boss, probably his former boss by now, with his bad knee and grimacing face, down towards the train station, saying: 'Now this is what I had in mind.'

Day 7

A<small>FTER THE SUCCESSFUL SCREENING</small> of Sergei Berebanov's feature film Dirt Wars leading to wee small hour discussions in several bars along the waterfront, the owner of the Athena decided to screen in secret a rough-cut documentary of the making of Berebanov's film, demonstrating how the director worked. Word-of-mouth goes around so fast ninety percent of the places are gone in several minutes.

Ninety percent of the audience is young, most coming from those who participated in the street protests. Berebanov is a favourite among the young in Renne, Merryl hearing again from her friend, the Athena's owner, that if she went at 2pm, she and her friends could sit in saved stall seats.

While the screening of Berebanov's Dirt Wars was a rowdy event, the making-of-documentary is watched in silence. The take on Napoléon's wild intentions in Russia is striking a huge chord, in particular, the Russians' dig-in defence west south west of Moscow, on a stretch of road, any old stretch of road less than 150 kilometres from the capital, where the Russian and French armies met in a now or never, face and fight, do and die affair.

In the documentary, Berebanov's shooting of his story of the Battle of Borodino was followed by a discussion in the documentary over how to shoot or not to shoot the battle, the discussion visibly dividing and upsetting both the main actor and his director. So much so, they have met to speak about it, Sergei's secret cameras rolling.

'History is what you rewrite.'

'Did they rewrite history in *Elizabeth*?'

'*Elizabeth* has more fabrications than Elizabeth invented for herself in her own life. Then on top of her historical inventions, Shekhar Kapur's film is literally pure invention.'

'How do we make this real then?'

'There's a museum up there. We can go look at it.'

'Let's go.'

Bruce and Sergei visit the village museum, see models, war representations, arms and uniforms. They walk down the street leading down to the Great Redoubt where General Rayevski's artillery was once stationed. Some of the original trenches are still visible, and a monument stands marking the spot General Bagration was mortally wounded on horseback under French fire, his shin shattered by shrapnel. Just beyond this position, a.k.a. les flèches or Bagration's arrows, is the village of Semenovskoye, a position Tolstoy frowned about for hours, trying to give his literary War and Peace representations genuine life and perhaps hope.

Sergei puts a map out on a table, his first-unit camera team filming, letting Bruce begin to speak first: 'This is a nightmare heading downhill from Smolensk. I am a dead duck whatever happens?'

'You are. Napoléon was. He just didn't know it.'

'Really? He didn't know.'

'No he didn't.'

'Why?'

'He had lost it.'

This part of 'the making of' documentary screening ends with a promise by the Athena's owner that all the cineastes can return to see more in two days, with the rest of the making-of film being cut elsewhere in Renne. It is an unusual offer and is well-received, setting off another series of discussions inside and outside the cinema as the kids hit the bars again and the day begins to fade into night.

The young cineastes are adamant. White males, however short or tall, should not be in power anymore. They just make a mess of everything. Napoléon's plan was ridiculous, dragging 690,000 soldiers and hangers-on from so many countries into Russia with no idea where he would even do what he was saying he was doing anyway. Who the hell financed the misguided mission?

Leaving the cinema, Merryl presses André Philippe on why the screening is being shown this way.

'I want kids seeing it while the film is being edited real-time. Then they can go and think about it in the knowledge the real historical reconstruction is being made at the same time. Otherwise, they'll just be in the streets throwing things around. I worry the French army will arrive. Then, where'll we be?'

OUTSIDE DANIEL MARTIN'S OFFICE late-afternoon walkers seem tranquil down on the waterfront. Inside his office the scene is anything but calm.

'Daniel you better start remembering. I want to know where he is.'

'Don't shout, madame.'

'You went along with him.'

'So, did you, madame.'

'Général, I, I didn't know what F was really up to. It wasn't my job to know.'

'He didn't seem completely out of his head.'

The Général smiles. 'I don't think he was ever completely in it either, madame. The drugs party idea, that didn't warn you? I tried telling everyone.'

'You knew everything beforehand. Then why didn't you stop him?'

'I was trying to do exactly that, and you laughed in my face, madame.'

'Don't be so smug.'

'I tried telling you all. I tried but was not getting any help. I remind you, nobody was listening. I didn't expect F would bring in an army of renegades, I'll admit that.'

'You had your men out of uniform, that's all over TV. You certainly were a sight in those jeans. As if wearing a denim shirt and Levi's could solve anything.'

'I was trying to defuse a protest.'

'Defuse it, how? By dressing down.'

'This blame-game won't solve anything.'

Madame maire takes a deep breath. 'What do we do now? We have to find F before he does something worse. Do we call Paris?'

'They will send the army in if we do.'

The maire stares at the two men.

'I want Léo back. That's all I know. Right now.'

In the Bar des Poissons Le Cigaro's film correspondent points at a small model of a wooden sloop on a table and waving his arms recounts how an almost completely eaten body covered in crabs was found on a real boat just like it.

'Are you serious, Charles?'

'A Chinese on a rental next to it reported the stink. The cops went in and found a corpse decomposed beyond recognition. No-one in the press except Annalise has seen it.'

'Who is it?'

'Apparently it's a writer nobody knows. He was living on it. Annalise went on board and came off right away. Word has it she slipped on the body fluids and fell face-first on this hyper-toxic bacterial soup of a thing. It went right up her nose and crabs started crawling in her hair.'

'You're lying.'

'A cop I know saw it happen. If you got off your stool once in a while and walked over there, Charlotte, did some real research, you would actually know something, have something new to write about sometimes.'

'Look who's talking. Your bum is glued to that stool 24/7.'

'My bar's not open 24/7.'

'Michel, I was being metaphorical.'

'Jesus, look at the time. I have to do something. I'll be back in ten, maybe thirty. Mind the bar, you lot, okay?'

The three of them watch him go. 'Make that an hour, if you're lucky,' Charlotte says.

'How the hell do the crabs get inside a boat?'

'Apparently they climb nets, Bernard.'

'Is that what happened? There were nets there?'

'Yes apparently.'

'Then someone put them there deliberately. Which writer is it, Charles?'

'How the hell do I know, Bernard? I don't even know which boat it is.'

'It's somebody whatshisberger's sloop. Look here's a photo of that guy,' Bernard says.

'Which guy?'

'The guy I met. He's here in this pic with the guy who saved the Russian from drowning.'

'You met him Bernard?'

'On the Russian's boat, that night he nearly drowned.'

'It happened on whatshisberger's boat?'

'Charlotte, try to keep up.'

'The body has decomposed completely, Bernard. So, it can't be him. It would have been dead for at least a week.'

THE SLOOP SITS UNDER AN OVERCAST SKY the unidentified body still below. Madame Maire stares at the wharf, then at the traffic below her window. The Promenade des Rois is gridlocked from the red carpet down to the western pier, the whole waterfront at a standstill. From her Hôtel de Ville office with binoculars she studies a long white boat at the end of the quay, calling out to her assistant to ask the police to shut down the entire waterfront. A police moratorium on traffic in the western sector of the city would be a start to bringing some order. In the strung-out line of vehicles in the not yet no-go area there are: one broadcast truck, some SUVs, a host of white vans, two 4x4s, and countless other small vehicles all neutered to a dead stop on Mairie Corner.

When a TV's white van mounts a curb, the driver yelling at everyone to get out of the way, furious pedestrians form a ring around it, a man ripping off a side mirror, an officer witnessing the fracas calling for back-up.

Nobody blames the flics for not wanting to get involved. The whole scene has grown ugly very fast, vespas zipping in and out, ferrying camera-people to the site of the current news-cycle's holy grail.

When a large motorbike with a cameraperson on the back overtakes some walkers and slips sideways careering across the footpath and narrowly missing a screaming woman pushing a baby in a pram, traffic police finally wake up and call a halt to everything. The press and convoy of the curious, having crawled a meter an hour towards Marcel's Pizza Palace, are now stopped in their tracks for good, furious journalists exiting their vehicles and without leaving notes on their windscreens heading over to the sloop on foot only to be blocked by a double blue line of cops. Sensing a bonus, municipal traffic cops move in with their parking ticket pads. The frazzled police lines block infuriated press, disaster junkies, some footloose tourists, a couple of grinning cineastes, and one bewildered ancient duo stuck midway down Quai Saint Jeanne in an immaculate maroon and black 1948 original Citroën 2CV deux chevaux, Cindy Turper writing everything down in her pad. Today is shaping up to be a journalist's moment in heaven.

Waiting her turn to go aboard she has enjoyed every minute so far. Is this when the whatsit hits the fan? She doesn't quite know but today she's wearing the Sentinel's Our Woman in Renne badge with real pride, and even if nobody coming off the boat is showing the sort of satisfaction Cindy is anticipating, she is still dying to find out what kind of strange creature from the sea is down there, or not, as the case may be. This is her first major story. And Cindy can just taste getting a chunk of it. She's got the bug, gridlock-chaos only adding to some newly-found ambitions.

This mêlée opportunité has also stranded the Citroën couple who in climbing out of their vintage vehicle stare at the whole scene in disbelief, making for Cindy's photo-offer for page three. She gets to interview them as well. And with hubbie going off to buy them all ice-creams, Cindy stands, nodding and laughing listening to his wife recite their wonderful travels so far.

'We're off to Anglacés.'

'Not yet.'

'No. That's right.'

The husband returns with three cones, a blue topped one for Cindy, which slips nicely into her stomach, to sit on top of her free lunch. She tries not to burp, thanking the couple, and excusing herself heads back to her spot at the top of the queue, the Citroën owner beginning a conversation with a rotund journalist on the pier introducing himself as Charles to the couple, the correspondent of a Parisian paper Cindy doesn't quite hear the name of.

Seeing a freshened-up, re-perfumed Annalise de la Forêt striding down the dock, Cindy leaps over to ask her esteemed senior colleague if she would do a short interview.

'Who're you with cherie?'

When Cindy mentions The Sentinel, Annalise makes no effort to mask a grimace, but Cindy won't let a small thing like professional contempt ruin her day, blaming her former boss, Steve, for any bad image the paper seems to have.

Asking for an appraisal of what's going on, explaining why she wants to ask her this, knowing her question is already too long, unnecessarily filled with preamblics, as she calls them, Cindy finally gets to the point, closing her mouth long enough to hear: 'My turn cherie?'

Cindy apologizes for gushing, getting a tight grin in reply, Annalise explaining that the festival this year is comparable to Venice's famous Carnevale every year, though Venice's Carnevale costumes are sexier, Annalise's litmus test for quality in any festival, Cindy scribbling the quotes verbatim from her esteemed colleague. Considered la dame de haute style of Renne's annual event, Annalise stands a foot taller than Cindy by one pair of stiletto spikes, a choice which tells Cindy in one fell swoop that Annalise has no intention whatsoever of going back on board the boat. 'Why are you back? Something you missed, Annalise?'

With one leg splayed out like the model Annalise seemed always to believe herself capable of being, she stares Cindy down with undisguised superiority, angling her body around in front of the lowering western sun, engineering a shut-down of Cindy's vision asking: 'Why do you think I'm back cherie?'

Cindy blinks hearing her question swatted back at her.

'To find out who it is?'

'Bingo. So, cherie, be a good sport and go down and find out for me.'

'Some say it's an unknown writer.'

'Yes but which unknown writer? How many unknown writers do you know?'

'Quite a few come to think of it.'

'Maybe it's a somebody with a forgettable name, or a nobody who'll never be known? Find out for me will you when you go down.'

Cindy has more questions but a man on the sloop calling her name gets her attention. 'C'est moi.'

'There you go. Have fun.'

Annalise smiles, waving Cindy off on her mission to find the truth, Cindy hurrying over the gangplank like a sailing pro, the man in white telling her to be quick and touch nothing while down there.

'The général recommended to me, I should go down.'

'Terrific.'

Cindy grins her thanks. 'This is my first crime scene.'

She follows the man down the sloop's inner stairs. Two minutes later she is back on deck staggering over to clutch at a mast stay with both hands, barely able to stay upright, her stomach shuddering. What follows is predictable. The wonderful lunch the général bought her—a lobster salad and bread roll topped in Tuscan oil and herbs, washed down by a delicate Provençal white followed by an espresso and a tiramisu—goes with an ooooooohhhh and a watery slush over the side. Seeing her leather notebook slipping from her hand, Cindy grabs at thin air, a metal stay dragging off the family diamond ring her mother gifted her, Cindy staring at the book and ring floating on the surface in her stomach muck, sitting there for a moment before it all slides below the surface.

As a rotund man tries before his allotted time to get on board via the gangplank, and for his sins slips and goes head-first into the old port's waters, a woman wharf-side screams and Cindy's legs give way. Banging her funny bone as she hits the deck hard, a photographer on the pier documents her fate, Cindy's lazily lifted hand thanking him as she drops into a dead faint.

Two BLACK SUVs glide by, Marie getting a glimpse of a face she thinks she knows. She waves, hoping the man might help her find Franck but the convoy keeps going. In her call to him moments before, he just said, 'It's awful.' Marie has already heard that a body was discovered. On her fifth attempt she gets through again. 'Who is it?'

'Nobody knows.'

'Franck please'.

'Some writer, apparently, that's all anyone's saying.'

'Writer-director or just a writer? Is it a he and is he famous? Even sort of.'

'Nobody knows. We don't know. Odds on it's a guy. Famous, haven't got a clue. Probably not. What is sort of famous anyway?'

'Can I come and see?'

'You wouldn't want to.'

'FRANCK.'

Marie stands in the street staring at her phone. Did her battery die? She switches off. She hasn't seen the young director for a while. In mad moments, anything's possible. Marie studies the road out in front of her, seeing nobody she knows. She switches on her phone again, pressing Franck's number this time getting through right away. 'Who is it Franck? I promise I won't say.'

'They think it's an author, that's all I know.'

Marie puts a hand around the phone: 'Is it a murder?'

'Someone's dead in strange circumstances.'

'How strange?'

'Very.'

'Franck, please.'

He half-laughs. 'All I can say, you couldn't make this up.'

First Franck gets an assignment without any clear line of investigation, then the promised movies and parties don't happen. Now this. All Marie has done so far is play an unpaid street nurse in a real-life protest. And today a lurid murder-tale on some boat is forcing an unwanted mystery on her. 'I miss our holiday.'

'Me too.'

'It's not your fault, Franck.'

'I know.'

'Make sure they don't say it is.'

'I haven't time to worry about this. I'll call you back.'

He rings off in her ear, Marie standing listening to the sound of dead air, imagining bone-white beaches, lying back on a warm deserted sand in western Corsica, swimming with Franck in the blue green seas. Instead, she's in this seaside town nobody wants to be in anymore. Franck was right. This assignment had trouble written all over it.

Franck knows he needs to be cool. The call from Marie hasn't helped. Down inside the sloop again, after escaping the scene for some air he studies the shape. It's about five-foot long, more than three quarters consumed, by what exactly he's not yet sure, all making for a scene of death defying all his professional experience.

Box-shaped crabs with their eyes out on stalks crawling on what's left of the flesh are the main culprits, moving about like bloated barbeque guests at a Sunday picnic their claws exploring the bits of flesh and exposed bone. But they didn't kill the thing. Instinct tells him that.

Where skin should be on a head there is no flesh. Where the eyes should be, there are only holes. Where a brain was, nothing. A set of grinning teeth exposes cheap dental work. There are no sexual organs and almost zero muscle tissue left on the hips, thighs and legs. Any ligament that once covered the throat has evaporated. Franck sees it all but doesn't comprehend anything anymore, his mind racing to find an explanation.

A writer has been mentioned who once rented the boat, but Franck knows better. The day after the night before the forensic team say it happened, he met the man some think this is, not so full of beans, but alive and well enough to speak.

Rushing upstairs and out on the deck, he pulls his mask away from his face and stands to windward drinking in sea air, as much fresh air as he can get inside himself. The wind changes and the stench wafts back over him once more.

Holding on to a single mast stay with Daniel Martin vomiting on the other side of the boat, Franck belches, acid rising in his throat as he suffers a bout of vertigo. He closes his eyes for a few seconds. Only a few people have been allowed on board yet a description of what it looks like and what it represents is all over town.

Franck walks over to a man in white protective clothing and shows his ID.

'Do you mind if I ask you some questions?'

'If you are quick, inspector.'

'How did the crabs get up inside there?'

'There's a net extending down from a forward starboard porthole.' The man points at the bow.

'That is how it happened?'

'Officially.'

Franck nods his appreciation for the honesty. He needs to soft pedal with this witness. He might not get another chance at this, so can't afford to blow the interview.

'I'll keep this short.' His mind already coursing through several possibilities, from murder to accidental death, using his training Franck corrals his questions inside his head into an order he can manage. 'Being objective for a moment, from the point of view of a crab.'

The man laughs, Franck joining him in laughing. It lightens the moment.

'A crab learns of food, what, by smell?'

'I'm no expert on that. But yes, I imagine crabs find food first by sensing putrefaction.'

'How long could a body be lying down there before a crab learns of it? One day, two days, more. Am I close?'

'We're not sure of the time-frame.'

'Did the crabs find the body after death or before it?'

The man glances around himself. 'It was a death by a thousand cuts.'

'Crab cuts?'

The man in the white clothing stares at Franck.

'It was mutilated before it was dead.'

'Before.' Franck knits his brow. 'Someone cut it up while the body was alive?'

'We think death came after cutting, but we're still not sure.'

'The cutting killed him?'

'We don't know yet.'

'He bled during it.'

'Substantially. There are scalpel cuts all over the corpse.'

'So he was tortured.'

The man looks around himself. 'You're not recording me?'

Franck holds his hands out. 'I promise.'

'I didn't tell you this.' The man takes a breath. 'A medical professional or someone similar who knew what he or she was doing and who wanted to accelerate the autolytic processes cut open everything. All major organs were exposed. The muscle tissue was dissected to aid a massive invasion of microorganisms. Everything was sped up. The body must have been cut up then drenched in water and radiators left on to allow an invasion in all parts of the body. Heat, water, bacteria, fungus, insects, putrefaction cellular self-produced enzymes, all helped the process of the body's self-digestion and decomposition. The interior of the boat was very hot, as high as the heating could go.'

'How long has he or she been dead?'

'This should take at least a week but we are pretty sure it isn't much more than a day. It's a dump site of fly larvae, fungi, insects and bacteria.'

'A day. And the crabs?'

'Crabs in triplicate. All sorts. The portholes were left open we think to give the impression the invasion was natural. They didn't climb the net. Some maybe, but only after they were thrown down into the water below the boat. Most are from a species you can find naturally on the sands along the Mediterranean.'

'The net is a diversion.'

'To anyone looking, quickly, they came up from the seabed.'

'Jesus,' Franck says quietly. 'What kinds of bacteria?'

'The body is covered in clostridium welchii, always present in the advanced haemolysis, but streptococci staphylococci and B coli are also present as well. Don't touch your mouth or nose or anything.'

Franck stares down at his hands in silence. 'And the actual cause of death?'

'We may never know. The decomposition is way-too extensive. A DNA test could identify who it is but that will take at least a week.'

'Who reported it?'

'Some Chinese on the boat alongside called the gendarmes. One of them woke up in the night and said he saw a seagull trying to get in through a porthole. He thought someone had died. A colleague saw movement on board the night before and thought it was the writer.'

'What department are you with?'

'I can't say.'

'Security?'

'I've said too much already.'

'My lips are sealed.'

'Don't touch them.'

Franck thanks the man and walks over to where Daniel Martin is clinging on to a mast-stay. 'Don't touch your eyes, nose or mouth. This is an infection trap.'

'God, I have touched them several times.'

'Go and have a long, hot shower. Use lots of soap.'

Franck follows him off the sloop, Martin almost in tears nodding goodbye. He watches the distressed deputy walking along the wharf towards the bâtiment. The quay is almost empty, Franck amazed how quickly the gendarmes cleared the area.

MADAME LA MAIRE STANDS BEFORE THE WORLD biting her lip, people watching at home seeing traces of blood appear on their screens. Television cameras and photographers close in on her face outside Hôtel de Ville. The death on the sloop is just one example of several catastrophes that are happening all over her town, even if the news about the state of a corpse on the writer's sloop has shocked the town's population more than anything else. From their expressions here, people in the street support their maire, believe in her, knowing they are seeing a woman who believes in herself. So much so, many believe she's the only person who can resolve the mess in Renne right now. People agree with her. This boat body is the final straw. Yet, instead of making any enemies by breaking protocols and throwing unwanted stray cats of accusation among the pigeons of local politics, the maire only whispers, with convincing regret, that it is with great sadness that she is here to announce the death of a writer. 'An unspeakable crime has occurred in our treasured old port.' Her eyes glaze over, staring out over le vieux port, taking in all the magnificent possessions of these wealthy political patrons who sometimes even reside in this great summer holiday town. But these examples of how the wealthy know how to float themselves on the shimmering mirror-like waters here, isn't any argument against them, and nobody is going to tell this maire these resulting rewards of their hard work and commercial ingenuity makes what she is seeing just a bunch of aging plastic monsters registered in Kingston or wherever in order for her town to be the ultimate place for tax-dodging. This is not what her town is for, rich people. It's for all people.

In truth, the maire prefers making speeches with broader political positives in mind, speeches for those who voted for her, not standing here defending the rich but today some crucial recent conversations have convinced her that the privileged class who own these boats and have given generously to her political campaigns in the past need her help right now.

Today the maire knows she must be politically objective, quite practical in terms of her career. She is not planning on being an also-ran from a small town forever, an anonymous forever dot in a chamber of five hundred and seventy-seven députés— she is aiming at the highest office in the land. And for that to happen she needs the help of these people who own these boats.

To her mind, at least, it is time a woman got to the highest position in the land. So now at this critical moment in time, her main political responsibility is not to deal in a down in the seaweed sort of way re-describing a tragically grotesque crime, but to somehow use the moment to prepare herself for future political victories. She knows she can't let any odd cats out of this bag, and she has told her secret backers that she won't.

Refocusing her gaze over the heads and cameras, Madame Maire stares at her other audience, the hoi polloi. She knows she needs to reassure them that she's on message with them as well, taking to heart their needs. Scouring her mind for an apt quotation from history, a word or two on the value of writers to humanity, she lets her good eye waver over this scene, struggling with how to express how utterly bereft she is at the cruelty of this act.

Perhaps a week ago the maire might have used this moment to tear one off in Polispeak-terms, something like: If the maniac responsible for this effing eff-up thinks he can ruin my town he'll have to reckon with me. But she doesn't say anything like this. Instead, she blinks down at her prepared text, speaking in a restrained voice.

'We want the restaurants open. We need Renne's visitors walking, laughing, eating and seeing fine films. Let the festival be up and open again. I urge the festival to put back-on all films. This city is a jewel of French and world culture and must be again.'

Her closest personal aide moves closer, alarm bells no-doubt ringing in his head as Madame Maire is sometimes known to slip-off message at the end of at least some of her addresses. She is not letting go of the microphone. Oh god.

'THIS MUST STOP OR I WILL BRING IN THE ARMY.'

With this sudden exclamation of righteous political anger delivered, Madame Maire whirls away from the street and speed-walks inside the Hôtel de Ville building.

'Madame Maire!'

Hearing a reporter's voice she recognizes, a journalist she rather fancies if the truth be known, the maire stops, her eyes re-focusing a face.

'Yes, Marceline.'

'The army's here.'

'I haven't seen any army.'

'You haven't...? The trucks are outside the town.'

Madame maire isn't just annoyed Marceline couldn't find the right question, she is beside herself with fury.

Disappearing fast inside, she leaves her aide-de-camp to adlib her last words into some sort of palatable press release, his voice far too high for comfort yelling: 'No further questions, merci.'

'TESTING ONE TWO THREE' reverberates throughout the half-empty ballroom of the bâtiment, a showered but still-nervous Daniel Martin half-whispering into a microphone attached to an echoey PA system. The audience so far is made-up of film and related professionals still in town, journalists, producers, directors and writers, actors, hangers-on, those without any meetings to rush off to, or interviews to give, make-up film-sessions to attend. With the festival at a stand-still this makes the potential audience just about everyone left.

Festival reporters, affiliated and unaffiliated, still filing inside, take up seats in twos and threes, here and there, nodding at each other, trading eye-contact, as if saying: Here we go again.

Some put their heads together, remaining that way whispering as other colleagues arrive. Uninitiated unknowns such as Marie sit alone staring around the room. Up at the front, a pale Annalise de la Forêt is remonstrating with another journalist and a member of the festival staff over some matter, the details of which Marie tries to understand but isn't close enough to hear clearly.

Three rows behind her, Ivan, Ulyana, Jack, Bella and Larry sit with two members of Larry's Kungfu protection team. Behind them on either side are several of Bella's security men sharing jokes in low voices. Marie keeps on turning around in the hope Franck will turn up. When she sees the général walk in and stride down the aisle she almost gets-up to ask him about Franck but checks herself, sitting on the edge of her seat watching the big man climb the steps to the stage with difficulty, smiling as she hears the jeering after a clearly anxious Martin welcomes all in the microphone.

Marie knows Martin doesn't just divide opinion. He is the problem, 100 percent the cause of everything, well almost for everyone right now. It's now practically-official—the barely out of short-pants Daniel Martin is so far out of his depth he is practically speaking scraping the sands of Tunisia, many festival attendees saying openly how they always distrusted him. Old hands grin ironically, reminding listeners that they were the ones first on record as saying the new acting director was a complete joke. Hearing Martin ask one more time if everyone can hear him, an irritated man yells back angrily: 'IF ONLY WE COULDN'T.' Glancing back nervously at the général Martin points at the mike. The général shakes his head emphatically. Taking the microphone from out of its holder, the still acting director Daniel Martin holds it close to his mouth.

'Is this okay?'

'OUI,' shouts a weary voice from way back.

Annalise calls out: 'Is this a murder inquiry now?'

'A body has been found dead on a boat.'

'TELL US SOMETHING WE DON'T KNOW.'

Marie slides down in her seat sympathizing with everybody's frustration.

'SOME PEOPLE HAVE BEEN ABOARD,' calls one man. 'THEY HAVE SEEN IT.'

'I've seen it. Who's going to pay for my dry-cleaning?'

'Annalise, you know full-well we don't accept extra-curricular bills from anyone and certainly not the press corps.'

'We're doing you a favour. If we told the truth the town would be shut down.'

'That's not going to happen.'

'Some maniac's loose.'

'Who's in charge?'

Martin doesn't speak for a moment. 'I am in charge.'

This is met with room-wide laughter and jeering. 'Tell us who's responsible.'

'Tell us what happened first,' calls-out a woman.

'Someone is dead, madame.'

'Who's dead?'

'WHAT DID HE OR SHE DIE OF?' yells a man at the back. Martin pivots around to the général who shakes his head again.

'We can't say. We don't know what the cause of death is yet.'

'Do the police have a culprit?' a man asks.

Martin glances behind himself again.

'We have no likely suspect as yet.'

'What about the crabs?'

'We have no crabs in custody either.' Martin gives a nervous smile when his off-the-cuff joke is met with silence. A uniformed gendarme runs down the aisle and up on stage, whispering to the général, who steps forward to speak for the first time. 'We have to leave it there.'

'Has there been an arrest?' yells the woman behind Marie.

Annalise de la Forêt stands up. 'WAIT A MINUTE. I WAS THERE. I KNOW WHAT HAPPENED.' She stops, wavering suddenly, sitting down quickly, placing a pale hand on her pale forehead as if remembering all over again how bad it was. 'Where's Léo?' she says, her voice barely audible. 'We need him. Somebody real...'

Blinking back tears, Daniel Martin stares down at her. He turns again to the général. 'You tell them,' he says, his voice caught on microphone. Loud voices erupt throughout the auditorium. 'GIVE US SOMETHING WE CAN PRINT,' a rotund wet-haired man wrapped in a blanket yells out from the back, several people yelling OUI almost in unison. Martin grimaces having great trouble placing the microphone back into its metal holder.

'Tell us something,' Annalise says half-coughing up her words. 'We have to write something. Is it the writer who was living on the boat?'

The room breaks up into an uproar.

'DOES THE THING AT LEAST HAVE A NAME?' a man at the back yells. Martin stares out at the audience then quickly follows the général off stage.

'Personne,' Annalise whispers. Marie thinks she heard her say that word, the général and Martin walking down the aisle surrounded by gendarmes, a stream of journalists rushing after them, each one on a mobile. Marie tries again to catch the général's eye, Ulyana, Ivan, Larry and Bella standing-up, trading glances and shrugging as they too file outside. Her first attendance at a festival press event without Franck present has left Marie over and underwhelmed in equal measure. Arguing journalists block her exit. Marie is the last outside. She stands alone, her hands shaking, wondering if it is from rage or dismay.

'TELL US ANYTHING,' a man yells at the disappearing figures of the général and Martin. 'IS IT TRUE IT'S DISGUSTING?'

'WHO THE HELL IS RESPONSIBLE?'

'WHO THE HELL IS *F*?'

WALKING BACK TO HIS AND MARIE'S APARTMENT a pensive Franck sees a man on a chair speaking to a small crowd. Staying on the perimeter Franck stares around at the people there. The evening spring air and atmosphere here is a huge respite from what he has just experienced, so he loiters a little listening to the speaker.

'If they withdraw all their forces we will stop this protest as a gesture of peace. Any peace settlement will need to be ratified in a meeting with all our comrades. For the moment though let's offer say a three-day truce to the cultural imperialist forces so the festival can re-open.'

The man puts up his hands against the crowd's objections.

'Yes, we want a real peace but that doesn't mean we are afraid of conflict. If necessary we will march again.'

Franck notices many in the crowd are wearing bandages.

'Free all Culture,' a man yells. Another yells: 'LET'S MARCH NOW.' There are cheers. Franck blinks when someone yells: 'THIS IS WAR.'

'Is it a war?' he murmurs.

The man up on the chair tries to calm the crowd but when they won't listen to him, he gestures to some musicians. Music starts up, the band singing l'Internationale.

It's a strange choice for calming a crowd, Franck joining in so people around won't wonder about him. Hearing English accents it's very odd, Franck singing a song with those whose ideas are not his, singing something he does not know from Adam. If they did know who he is they might yell: 'Kill the plant.' Then what? Has it come to this? Franck knows colleagues who carried out undercover work, some caught and beaten up, one yes even killed. Franck knows the audience is angry. They are outsiders to all that is going on and they are not hearing any truth. He understands the frustration. He's been an outsider in Paris for so long he can't remember being anything else. One day someone even put a DVD copy of The French Connection in his locker. He tried to joke it off, went around the office saying: I am Popeye, doing Gene Hackman Popeye impressions. He keeps on singing with the crowd, the man on the chair waving at the musicians to stop.

'Culture is created for and by people. Regarding all films at this festival, they are forthwith confiscated from producers and control given to the workers on the films. All producers must hand over film rights to the Festival's Cineaste People's Collective Committee—and we will give them to the workers and if they don't want them, to the protesting cineastes. Collective ownership. Private ownership should be abolished, all titles transferred to public-ownership, with screenings and tickets all free. Billboards should be in our hands as well.'

The crowd is quiet now. Franck looks around. Then a voice yells: 'DOWN WITH ALL CORRUPT ENTITIES. DOWN WITH THE CULTURAL-GENTSIA. DOWN WITH AUTEURS, DIRECTORS, PRODUCERS, MOGULS AND STARS. DOWN WITH FILM'S PHONYGENTSIA AND ALL LACKEYS.' Franck has heard enough. The man on the chair is crazy. Marie is dead right. He is way too bourgeois for politics like this. He pushes back through the people. He's not a communist or a cultural Marxist. He's a cop. Still.

Suddenly, he catches the eye of a girl. They trade smiles, Franck's one of deliberate bewilderment, hers less-complicated.

'Are you demonstrating?' Franck asks, then wishes he hadn't asked. The girl doesn't seem to mind.

She shakes her head.

'Are you?' He shakes his head.

'Are you in film?'

'Haven't a clue about it. You're in it, though, I bet.'

'A film I worked on is in competition. I'm part of the team. I do make-up.'

Franck almost asks her what she thought of all that has just been said but he might reveal who he really is, and he doesn't want to do that. Especially not to someone he doesn't know. She could be a plant herself. In the background he hears musicians quietly tuning their guitars by the makeshift stage.

'What make up do you do. Special effects?

'No. Basic stuff. Paint ups. Stickies. All the sort of tricks old horror movies used to do once,' she says, looking almost embarrassed.

'You do the actors faces? Wonderful.'

'A bit more sometimes, but yes that in the main.'

An old song Franck's always liked Be My Baby by The Ronettes starts playing, three acoustic guitarists joining in. People standing around drop their bags and things on the grass and begin to dance. Did the speaker arrange this? Smart if he did.

'Come on. Let's dance.' The girl holds out her hand. Franck hesitates, then seeing people all around reacting to the eruption of music he breaks a habit of a lifetime and acts almost spontaneously for once.

So, won't you say you love me?

I'll make you so proud of me

We'll make 'em turn their heads every place we go.

Franck begins remembering what he thought he never knew in the first place if the truth's known, a dance technique he probably tried and gave up on way back in time. Left back, right back, one, two, three, four, swing her around. Soon he's jiving as he thought he never even imagined he could, which probably isn't much now because he still doesn't know the jive. Still his lack of skill doesn't stop passers-by joining in, he and the girl wading further inside the crowd as much to hide themselves and their embarrassment over their lack of skill as to embrace the mood and swing of everyone jiving as well as any one of them ever could. Franck catches glimpses of people of all ages and sizes throwing themselves around to the old favourite. Many could be pros they are so good, giving a proper demonstration of rhythm and style.

Say you'll be my darlin' be my, be my baby.

Be my baby now my one and only baby

'The producer gave us the free trip as a bonus,' the girl manages to say. 'The film came in under budget, so she brought us here. It's my first time.'

'Mine too.'

'But you sound French.'

'I am but that doesn't make me a big fan of film. I like special effects. I'm interested in make-up.' He laughs. 'You must show me how it's done.'

'What do you do?'

'I am finishing one job, looking for another.'

'You sound like a writer.'

'No, I am still a detective.'

Before she can digest this answer, they are jiving hard, twirling, the dancing growing into a frenzy, new people joining in, bopping, swinging and hopping.

I'll make you happy baby just wait and see.

For every kiss you give me I'll give you three.

Be my baby now my one and only baby. Wha-oh-oh-oh.

Then the song is over, something nobody wants or can

quite believe. They stand out of breath, laughing, everyone probably thinking: why did it end? Isn't there another verse?

'I've never danced with a detective before.'

'The dancing detective. Well now you have.' Franck sees Corot in uniform on the edge of the crowd waving at him.

'I think I have to go.'

'Police work?'

He smiles at her. 'Career leftovers, yes. But I don't work with him. I am from Paris. But right now I am on an assignment which is going to be my last, cleaning up a mess I'm not even sure I can call a career. I was just passing by on my way home. This event here is nothing to do with my assignment or me.'

'You don't have to explain.'

'I want you to know I am not on duty here.'

The girl rifles in her purse, hands him her card. 'I'm here for two days.' He stares at the card now in his hand. 'Thanks, Liz, good name by the way. Let's do it and soon. Franck is my name. Franck Marc.' They shake hands. Leaving, he calls back: 'I'll phone you.'

POINTE D'ANGLACÉS HAS LONG FIGURED in Daniel Martin's consciousness, and just the idea of him seeing all the wealth and constructed beauty driving over there again is affecting him. At the outset he was beside himself with fury at the turn of events, but ten kilometres from Renne's waterfront promenade, turning into Boulevard de Novembre 22 and winding south to a point where he knows he will eventually merge with Boulevard Roosevelt, the view out in front of him brings him his first real smile, his first real taste of joy in many days. Daniel could be in a foreign country he is so relieved and just recognizing this helps him relax, the north south winding boulevards leading him on toward la crème de la crème cinq étoile festival residence of Hôtel Grande Pointe d'Anglacés, the second home for all the super rich near to Renne. Daniel has had a lifelong wish-list of goals and one close to the top is to live in Hôtel Grande Pointe d'Anglacés one day. At least for one day. Two and three on the wish list are to get power and live in luxury for the rest of his life. What problem do the rich ever have? Nothing apart from death. Sighing, Daniel studies the villas flashing by, knowing he'll have to go abroad to achieve his last two please-god wishes. The wheels of his life have fallen off.

He finds Barrosi's property on his second try, number 1180 adjacent to Pas du Diabolique, lying well-hidden behind a wall. Daniel is so irritated he missed it he keeps bashing the steering wheel. Why couldn't he have spotted it first try? Before tonight he didn't even know Manuel Barrosi owned an estate on this road. As with all the mansions in the area, Daniel knows Barrosi must possess an utterly spectacular west-facing view over Golfe Géri.

Parking outside the mansion gates, Daniel studies a watery ruin close to shore—an abandoned square of old stones in the shallows across the road. Did Barrosi import it? Placing it there on his waterfront to give his property an architectural edge over other properties along the bay.

It's what Daniel would do. Walking up a path he takes in the clipped lawns on either side of the old winding stone walkway, angry at not knowing how many mansions like this have winding stone walkways? He doesn't know Barrosi's actual worth, even to the festival, or more to the point, to himself.

Daniel needs rich and powerful friends right now. Still

angry that Barrosi expects guests to park in the street—a man as wealthy as Barrosi could share his private entrance with visitors surely, he rings the doorbell, smiling all around where he imagines hidden cameras must be. He hears a Spanish-sounding woman answering the intercom. He gives her his name, exercising his facial muscles, getting caught in the act as the front door opens on him quicker than he expected. The woman stares at him for a moment, then steps aside and lets him inside the house.

The way through this mansion takes Daniel on a journey through several artistic moods, a walk-through a wood-panelled hallway under the gaze of a Matisse-like collage on one wall, a Picasso wannabe on another. It's sobering though to walk into the main room and be met by beige-plastered walls, an open rustic fireplace facing a picture window looking over the bay. Such a cliché. Terracotta flooring even under-foot. The overall effect is so deflating. Daniel hasn't spotted any originals. Even without his glasses he has outed two Picasso lookalikes. A carved mahogany chess-set on a low table is about the best thing on offer. Daniel rates everything as pretty average, the whole room barely reaching a B minus in interior design.

With his renown Montagne de Reims vineyard, Daniel expected more from his invisible host, Daniel's gaze falling finally on two ochre sofas. Dirty mustard both of them. God, Manuel Heinrich Barrosi has made thirty-eight films in his career. All things considered looking around this house, if Daniel had not been forced by fate, well Madame Maire, to drive over he would have given the whole thing a miss.

In an online search before setting-out, Daniel discovered that of the thirty-three feature films and five documentaries that Barrosi released to the public, Daniel noted that none are integral to any part of film history. Only four have figured in competitions. Barrosi's oeuvre never set any one festival alight, Daniel deciding that his decision was entirely justified to eliminate Barrosi from the list of attending grandees this year. With this decision in mind right now, Daniel licks his lips. Shooting glances into room shadows he flinches each second that passes. What mood will the host be in when he appears? What will he even be wearing?

Wait, one sofa is not empty. The top of a white head moved or seemed to move. Is this who he thinks it is? Martin creeps closer and discovers the man he has actually come to see in a dressing gown, no less, the sort of gowns hôtels give away for free. Turning, Daniel and Léo come face to face, Daniel leaping back and exclaiming: 'My god.'

Léo stares right into the eyes of his former junior. Propped up against two cushions, he doesn't acknowledge him with anything like the warmth Daniel believes he deserves.

'There has been some real trouble,' he half-whispers. He grins toothily at the former festival head.

'You're the director now.'

'No. Perhaps you don't understand. Things are really out of hand.' Daniel takes a quick breath. 'Rioters marched on the bâtiment.'

'Voting with their feet. You said you supported democracy.'

'This is no joke, Léo.'

'Let French intelligence handle it if you can't. Or call the général.' Daniel grimaces, hiding his two shaking hands behind his back now, searching his head for something pithy to say, something to clear the air between them.

'What was it you said? Everyone in power over fifty-five should consider their positions carefully.'

'Age is cruel I know. Anyway, I was joking, Léo. You must know that.'

This is not the kind of ice-breaking small talk Daniel was hoping for. Driving to Anglacés, he worried Léo might address their rocky past with all its many fractious moments. Searching his head for ways to break the impasse, Daniel thinks of mentioning that he's planning something on the architectural heritage of the Côte d'Azur, nearly saying: I want to bring you in on that, get your input, have you help us out in the regeneration of tourism and the festival's cultural image. Daniel needs to show Léo what a man of ideas he really is, but right now is perhaps not the right moment. He grins. This reunion was never going to be easy. Given Léo's awkward departure this was never going to be a courtesy call, even if Daniel wants to make it one. He sure hopes Signor Barrosi is on side when he appears. Biting his lip, recalling some bad moments he wishes never happened, Daniel launches into his prepared speech, the way to reconciliation he wrote-up before leaving Renne. 'The reason I'm here, Léo, we need you. The festival has reached a cataclysmic point. Destructive forces are at work.'

Seeing Léo's face Daniel's voice quavers off to nothing. The pair are simply not in tune. 'You didn't swim all this way, did you?' Daniel blinks waiting for a response.

Léo's eyes settle harder on Daniel's face. 'That just occur to you?'

'Of course not. I was petrified for you.'

Léo's gaze is as tough as Daniel has ever seen it. Looking over at the wide-screen TV sitting on a table he thinks of switching it on, give the room some sound and vision to fill in the silences. Something. Anything.

'Léo, look, if I disappointed you.'

'You told me it was time for me to retire.'

'No, you misheard me.'

'Your very words.'

'I really don't recall saying anything like that.'

'Are you suffering from Alzheimer's or just amnesia? The long version of what you said, Daniel, was: "Why don't you just leave for the good of all. You are having memory problems. Leave and die well." I can still see your face saying the die well bit. You even blocked my emails.'

'I don't recall a word of this, but I do remember I was under unbelievable stress.'

'It's what gross misappropriation of power does, Daniel. It brings stress to weak people. If one is as weak as you are stealing power rarely works for long.'

'Is that all you think of me, Léo?'

Léo chuckles. 'There's more to you?'

'I do remember you never listened to me. It is documented in minutes.'

'That you wrote up.'

'I never wrote anything up.'

'There are witnesses.'

'Who?'

'People.'

'Which people?'

'You can't remember? Daniel you are having memory problems now.'

'You've always disrespected me.'

'I let you be my deputy and you undermined me.'

Searching his coat pocket for a tissue, Daniel suddenly realizes he left his pad with all the details of all the new plans he wanted to discuss in the car. When he begins speaking again, slower now, so his voice won't shake, he tries desperately to remember the arguments he wrote down, hiccupping, struggling to stop his voice from quavering.

'I am sorry if I gave you that impression, Léo. People thought a shark ate you. I was very worried.'

'Really.'

'You think that I wanted you dead?'

Léo sighs.

'The festival needs you.'

Daniel watches the trademark irritation cross his former boss's face.

'I shouldn't get angry. No more of this.'

'Léo please.'

Léo waves away any further discussion, Daniel wanting to say he has done his best in trying times forced on him by an unfair externally-inspired situation. He wants to say he's tried to keep the festival afloat at great personal sacrifice. Only his selfless efforts haven't worked.

'Fuck it Léo. Do your duty. The wheels have fallen off.'

Léo swings right around. 'WHAT?'

Luckily for Daniel a door across the room clatters open. A huge man with thick black hair and a greying beard careers into the room, his booming baritone rattling the china behind Daniel's head.

'Bon soir mon bon ami.'

Dressed in a tent-shaped amber t-shirt and blue shorts Barrosi holds out his arms in welcome, Léo making a half-hearted introduction: 'Daniel, the festival's acting director.'

Daniel glances angrily at Léo, nearly saying: I have already appointed myself permanent acting-director. Only he doesn't get the chance, his attempts failing to convert the big man's right hand into a hip handshake, then a fist pump. Barrosi envelops him in a bear hug, crushing Daniel into his chest, tears running from Daniel's eyes. Releasing him the big man booms: 'Wine?'

Daniel blinks. 'Yes, please.'

'Mine or another's?'

'Yours, of course, sir.'

'You must be hungry too after all the troubles I've been hearing of.'

Daniel nods, his eyes filling with real tears, glancing at Léo as he manages to say: 'You don't know the half of it.'

The big man squeezes Daniel's shoulder and heads behind a bar at the back of the room and produces a couple of bottles. 'Vermillia, cheese, olives, dried tomatoes, bread, oil, lemons and crackers. Pronto out on the terrace.'

Tearing off the silver wrapper, Barrosi pulls a cork, announcing the bottle from his estate is his best vintage Pinot Noir Montagne de Reims Champagne.

Three flutes dangling between three fingers on one hand Barrosi leads them out into the night air. Pouring, he holds each flute up to the three-quarter moon.

'In praise of good fortune.'

A cool wind blows in from the bay as Daniel drains his glass, the wine splash-landing into his empty stomach. The effect's thrilling. Unfortunately he burps loudly, a heavy bell sounding off in the distance not masking his faux pas.

'A wonderful year, Signor Barrosi.' Daniel flinches hearing Léo's trademark groan. Vermillia appears with food and lays it on a table. Daniel raises his refilled glass unable to stop himself: 'Signor Barrosi, a toast to you. Gifted man, wonderful host, brilliant director. Here's hoping you'll be with us for the finale. I'll courier your invitation.'

Léo sucks in a breath alongside him. 'Manuel's already invited.'

Daniel blinks: 'Some invitées were crossed-off last minute by mistake.'

'Yours or someone else's?'

'I am here to reverse that decision, a weight lifted from my shoulders.'

Daniel drinks to stop himself from saying any more: 'Signor Barrosi, please join us at the finale.'

As Barrosi's eyes knit into a frown, Daniel soldiers on, 'Even with chaos and shenanigans, we will have a finale. All's...' Daniel catches Léo winking at Barrosi.

Without knowing how or why he drops his full flute splash cracking splintering onto his host's tiles. Reddening, Daniel bends down now to clean it all up, Barrosi bellowing in his ear:

'FOR GODSAKES LEAVE IT MAN!'

Day 8

'GOD TELL ME YOU'RE KIDDING' Annalise shouts, her shaking right hand holding tightly onto her room phone. She's so excited she thanks the caller twice. Switching off she stares at her bedside clock: 'He's back! He's actually back!'

Annalise pinches herself twice realising le revenant directeur's first conference this morning will be historic. Catapulting herself out of her bed she has barely time-enough for a song in the shower and a room coffee. Hurrying up to Le Magnifique to see if the news is really true, she goes around in circles from room to room, smiling at everybody she finds, amazed her worst ex-boyfriend in a lifetime of boyfriend failures has finally gotten his just desserts.

Annalise says she stopped liking Daniel the moment he usurped Léo's position, though her dislike really began way earlier than that. She's ready now to swear she began writing Daniel's obituary not the moment he waltzed into Léo's office, not the moment he stole the paper-cutter Annalise gave Léo for his birthday, but the day he met Annalise. Another effing phoney boyfriend bites the effing dust.

Larry Linsteeg walks in breaking into her thoughts. She manages to get a smile out of him, but Larry doesn't stop, heading over to the coffee table with some haste. He's frightened about what's coming or hasn't forgiven her for attacking him and his director at their first press conference. She heads over now thinking of ways she can be diplomatic.

'Bonjour, Larry. What are you expecting?'

'No idea.'

'Come on, you've heard something.'

He stares at her saying nothing.

'Come on, all's fair in film and journalism. Let's forgive and forget. Friends again?'

Larry gives her a half-smile, a small mean thing that barely creases his mouth and then moves away not saying another word.

Shaking her head Annalise stalks back to her seat. She wanted to ask about the new company he's setting up with Ivan and Bella. Rumours are circulating everywhere. She wants to meet the mystery investors. How else can she write up her story? Someone said there could be a Middle East Sheikh with oodles of boodle. All Annalise knows is that it's all hush-hush classified on the Larry front these days. It could be Russian money too, but Ivan's spokeswoman is zipped-up, ignoring Annalise's texts, Ivan's people hating her as well.

She folds her arms, telling herself she doesn't care. They can all go to hell the fastest way possible. No more free publicity for anyone. Larry's probably angry at her for other reasons. And like everybody else she'll eventually guess who the investor is. The word is Larry's film won't get any awards this year, the favourite now being a Ridley animation. Annalise isn't betting on any entry winning though, knowing everything's up in the air. With all the street troubles she's completely out of the loop. This has never happened before.

More people pile inside, some she knows, some she doesn't. She nods, some nod back. Annalise narrows her eyes. Suddenly, there is Léo himself.

'Bonjour tous.' Looking more rested than Annalise has felt in ages he smiles at everyone around the room. 'I want to apologize for my absence.'

Annalise stares up him. Léo's speaking in English—the first note that goes in her pad.

'My doctor said I should take a break but with some rogue mercenaries committing a terrible crime two days ago attacking a lawful protest, I am back to hopefully fix things, put things right.'

Annalise half yells: 'Yeahhh.'

Léo grins down at her, nodding his gratitude for a positive response. 'I am not Arnold Schwarzenegger or Charles De Gaulle but better than nobody. I am back with reform in my heart.'

Larry Linsteeg glances at his lifeless mobile, again seeing nothing from Bella. What? He looks up. Did Léo say reform? Annalise and Larry are thinking the same thing, Annalise doing a quick scribble in her diary, before swinging around to see if her reaction is the same as others. She sees faces everywhere as stunned as she feels.

'We are having this conference because my office is being used by policemen.'

'What?'

Larry's phone vibrates. Glancing at it he kills the call. He has been on the telephone all morning seeking financial justice, but that can all wait.

'Why I am here today is to tell you that for this year I am retiring the festival jury from all prize selection. I am instigating an open vote from today. Voting on all entrants is now free for anyone who attends the screenings. A ballot will be handed out to all, even those seeing films on the beach.'

'Democracy?' someone murmurs.

Hearing him say it, Annalise barks, 'DEMOCRACY?'

Larry's head yanks up, something like spanners clanking

all over the parquet floor all about him. 'What do you mean democracy?'

The sound of creaking chairs plays back-up singers to some very loud murmurs.

'Friends, democracy, it's just that, democracy. A democratic selection of prizes.'

'But this is a film festival Léo,' Annalise exclaims. 'What's democracy got to do with a film festival?'

A man appearing at a side door signals to Léo. He nods back. 'I'm sorry, I have to go. As you can imagine there's much to do.'

Annalise is on her feet before anyone else, rushing after him. 'That's it? What about details? How is this going to work?' She screams as her feet catch a chair leg and she trips, falling in an aisle. Struggling to disentangle herself she slips again, her bag strap catching around the chair leg. She calls out: 'Léo, Léo,' but he's gone.

Upright again she's lost her chance to get Léo on tape. She slaps her bag against the guilty object, the most recent cause of her troubles this year.

In the past, no festival director would have dared ignore her. Nobody came to her aid today either. If someone ripped her panties off in broad daylight, she wouldn't get any help. She writes this in her pad. Léo's already halfway down the street, Annalise scribbling: he will learn of my feelings.

For Cindy, several rows back, the resonating word was Democracy. Renewing the political vibe of 1968 in her head. She wasn't even born then but the year moves her like no other. She sits still smiling at Léo's bombshell speech, awake to all the possibilities suddenly, glad she was there to witness it. She's buzzing, over the moon. After the boat-body trauma this is truly a welcome change.

This year is no longer a festival but a political event, Cindy imagining cineastes getting out to lobby for votes now. She walks out into a brand-new spring air. Whatever the outcome of Léo's speech, nothing festival-wise will ever be the same in Renne again. Not in her short intern life has Cindy ever seen people leaving a press conference so surprised. Something truly amazing has occurred.

And what a change Léo makes on Daniel Martin. Chalk and cheese. Finding a bench, Cindy sits still quite stunned, staring out to sea. What a difference an idea makes. Cindy's already a paid-up believer. She doesn't want to seem naïve but why worry even if she does. This is not just so good, it is epiphanous.

She stands again, walking with the sun shining right into her face. Stopping a man she recognises, a conference attendee hard at scribbling his own notes, she asks what he thinks of the changes.

'It's a confidence trick.'

'What?'

'Has to be. Someone wants their film to win. The decision has been hijacked from the jury. This vote will be stacked with votes by street criminals.'

'You mean the demonstrators?'

'I mean the street hooligans.'

'Those protesters weren't hooligans. I am in the street. You're in the street. Does that make us hooligans too?'

The man grimaces at Cindy, mumbling about liberal nonsense as he walks away. Cindy realizes now how divided reactions will be. Some out lobbying for votes will see only danger, others seeing a brilliant opportunity. Cindy hears producers, actors and critics already talking walking remonstrating with others that Léo's plan can't work.

'Too many films haven't been seen. There's a hidden agenda behind all this.'

'There are not enough voters for this to be effective.'

'Democracy can't work here.'

'Why weren't we consulted?'

'Why is it happening anyway?'

Cindy wants to tell them Léo's here to fix everything, not blow up the festival. Some producers say their films are being manipulated out of prizes. Others show sympathy for the ditched deputy. 'Poor Daniel, it's a disgrace Léo throwing out the man who threw him out like this.'

Léo's supporters see the upheaval as a much-needed recipe for a whole new way. Naysayers are in a funk, saying chaos will be the only result. If democracy happens, the old system is completely finished, if democracy's happening now at all.

Walking on to get other viewpoints, Cindy realizes the system must have been ripe for collapse for a long time to have this sort of effect on so many. Get used to it, she wants to say to Léo's critics. Democracy is here to stay.

She scribbles her analysis: It's a cultural epiphany. Moving on, she seeks out more reactions. Two are heartening but even more are disappointing. Few seem prepared to give Léo the unconditional love Cindy feels for him and his democratic project. The only people convinced by the new system and its capacity to work are Cindy, two young cineastes she's only just met, one producer, and Léo, so far. Cindy writes: Can Léo really make this happen?

Seeing Larry Linsteeg walking ahead of her staring at his mobile, she follows him up inside the Mélodie terrace bar where a loud debate is going on. Cindy wonders what a troubled Larry might do if she gate-crashes him. Dodging between tables, squeezing here, shimmying there, she calls out: 'Oh Mr Linsteeg.' People look up, their eyes lingering on her. 'Get used to it guys, I'm the new girl in town.'

On her second yell, Larry turns and stares at her. Winding her way over to him, she finds him in a tête-à-tête with a girl scribbling fast. A busy Linsteeg might be her only chance. She's not going to let him off the hook. Getting to his table she launches herself: 'Cindy Turper, London Daily Sentinel. What's your take on the voting changes? Death a shoo-in this year, what do you think? Can we do that interview I texted you about? Now okay?'

Larry squints up at her, fear and loathing floating around in his face. Is he pretending to be embarrassed? Larry's troubles are already a net mème, his only way back as Cindy sees it, winning with Death at the very end.

'I need a story. You need good press. Two minutes?'

With dealmakers everywhere rubbing their eyes like they're all waking up from a fifty-year industry coma, surely Larry can't turn her down now. He needs her more than she needs him. He offers her a chair.

'Tea? Frutti di Bosco. Biscuits?'

'As long as they are not your dog's.' Cindy chortles after saying it. Larry's smile back, barely a tiny crease. Checking the notes in her pad, she tells herself to nix the fox paws. You're in. Be cool. You could get slapped if you don't.

'Democracy's the byword now, the new voting regime's electrifying debate. What's your take? You mind me calling you Larry? What winners will it throw up? Which directors, producers, actors are in for a shock?'

Cindy stops, telling herself to calm down. 'You happy with the changes, Larry?'

'There hasn't been any yet.'

'Democracy regime change I mean.'

'You can never tell with an idea like this.'

'Léo's guess is as good as yours you mean? Death is still the main stayer of the festival many are still saying. Your director might be the favourite. You see opportunities?'

Larry looks at her sideways and doesn't answer, finally mumbling, 'Maybe.'

The waiter comes back serving up a hiatus that does nothing to settle Cindy's galloping nerves. Taking deep breaths, she sips some tea, hearing liquid land in her stomach. Stifling a burp, she glances at her jottings.

'We're lucky to have Léo back.' She burps for real now. 'Martin wasn't up to it.'

'Is that a question?'

'Who's better, the upstart or steady hand?'

Larry sizes her up. 'Steady hand.'

She notes this down, her eyes darting down her list. 'You've been around, seen a few festivals.'

'I have experience, is that a question?'

She grabs a biscuit. 'Can I take you back to sixty-eight?'

Larry shifts his cup around in its saucer.

'First time wasn't it for you?'

'What?'

'First time at a festival in France for you?'

Larry nods.

'Do you feel empathy for the protest?'

'Because of '68? I understand the feelings.'

Cindy splashes tea on her lips, biscuit crumbs going everywhere down her front as she launches her next question.

'You saw Godard Truffaut, Forman and Saura make a stand, they must have impressed you?'

'Not only them.'

'You were close to all of it?'

Larry nods, his eyes straying to something behind her head, Cindy resisting the urge to look around.

'They took down a festival.'

'Interesting choice of words, Larry. Are you with the students then? Do you agree with them?'

'Up to a point.'

'So, you're siding with them politically, or see them as disruptive because you now have a chance of winning?'

Larry frowns.

'Do you agree overall with them?'

'Now or before?'

'Shutting down a film festival's a drastic way of making a point.'

'Then or now?'

'Both.'

'I saw their need then and I support some ideas now.'

'Do you think the jury would have selected Death without this protest?'

'You can never tell what a jury will decide.'

'Without a jury, would festival politics be against Death winning?'

'What do you mean?'

'Edgar punching the former acting director.'

Larry rolls his eyes, shakes his jowls. 'Minor derailment. That's three-day old fish anyway.'

'What's your point, stink or irrelevance?'

'The latter.'

Cindy watches him drink some tea, then glance down at his watch. The needed follow-through rapport from her shock-awe first appearance isn't working.

She needs to launch something. 'One more thing, if that's okay.' He nods.

'I heard that in 1968 you were working for the American government.'

She sits very still, her face and throat tightening as she waits for his counterattack, Larry staring back at, well, really right through her. 'Who said that?'

Non-denial denial, Cindy's mind almost screams, but she doesn't dare write anything.

'Someone said it to me.'

'Said to you here?'

Glancing left Cindy sees Lennie Facteur in a conversation. Further away there is a smart-ass actor who fobbed her off only a day ago when she asked for an interview. Both are reasonable choices. Seeing Larry yelling at that actor might be fun but she comes back to the obvious, Lennie, so Larry-like in so many ways, but she can't lie.

'I can't remember.'

Larry leans close. 'Who?'

'I plead the fifth.'

'The fifth?'

'You're an intern, a subject of England, what's the fifth got to do with you?'

'I'd be revealing a source.'

'I'm a producer. I'm giving you time. My advice is this: learn how it's done before you start getting up on your hind legs. Was it Lennie, was it him?'

'I didn't say it was Lennie.'

I saw you look at him. 'Was it him?'

'I was told you were working for US intelligence from sixty-eight right through to now. You even get a stipend.' Cindy's hands are shaking. 'True or false?'

'That's defamation.'

Cindy stares back at him. 'Did you inform on people?'

'I'll sue your paper and you personally.'

Cindy's heart's thumping. 'That's a non-denial denial Larry.'

'I didn't do it. Get it.'

'There's a report with your name in it.'

Larry narrows his eyes. 'What report?'

'Official Report on Cultural Surveillance Activities.'

'This interview is over.'

Larry stands, his big angry face looming above her, getting Cindy thinking she should stand up too. She's as tall as he is, only slimmer, a lot slimmer if you ask her.

'So, is this a non-denial denial or a straight denial you were an informant?'

Larry points, his lips quivering, his cheeks blotchy red ringed in white now.

'You print any of this I'll....' Larry sprays her with fruit tea and chewed biscuit matter. 'I'll ruin you.'

'You'll do what exactly?'

Larry Linsteeg's face goes purple. 'You're recording this. You cunning bitch.'

Cindy holds up her pad. Larry grabs her t-shirt, shaping to rip it off or slap her, probably both. She ducks in time and he gets a handful of her hair. She screams, falling backwards, losing a curl or two in the overturning of her chair. Crawling out of reach under the table she's now thinking: He's gonna kick me. She's saved by a young kid with long blond-hair coming up the steps and announcing: 'ELECTION TIME.'

Oblivious to a black girl under a table or Larry frozen above her, the smiling new arrival goes around handing out voting papers. The distribution done, the visitor stands for a moment in the middle of the terrace yelling: 'On the top of the page is how to Vote for Your Film choice, followed by a list of films and candidates for various categories going over on to the back. At the bottom are instructions on how to fill in who you are, then how to return it to the bâtiment. Thanks for your attention. Happy Viewing and Happy Voting a Tous. Merci. Thank you.'

INSIDE THE PACKED GRAND THÉÂTRE the festival's rebirth is etched in each and every face, standing room only, film lovers cramming the aisles. Salle Truffaut is a symbol for Léo and his face tells Cindy how much this is true.

So much has happened in a few hours she is breathlessly filled with hope. She still can't believe what happened on the terrace. People clapped when she got back up to her feet. She hopes like hell that the tireless illusion everyone clings to, hope, will lead people to act in a fair and just way during the vote.

This is where Léo's festival fortunes sprang back to life. This is where everything got back on track. With so many hopeful film professionals now accepting Léo's ideas, recognizing the invasion by protesters was a necessary drama for them in order to be sitting here again, they confirm this belief in nods and smiles.

'Mesdames, messieurs, in this place, the festival went off the rails. In this place I will put it back on track. What art form is so comprehensive in its presentation and representation. What art form has the capacity to teach us how to live better according to what we see in two hours of projected images on a screen? What art form explores societies, politics, gender, race and culture so viscerally with such immediacy? What art form is so inclusive, combining writing, performance, direction, cinematography, editing, dance, song, music, set-direction, choreography and costume?'

'Théâtre,' a man shouts out and is promptly told to shut up—booing starting up not so much against théâtre, but on the timing of the man's intervention.

'With théâtre there is an indelible shared history. I love théâtre and so do many of you here this evening. I know that. Film loves théâtre and owes théâtre so much. La comédie-française fed cinéma, but cinéma is more than théâtre. Not better. More.'

'OUI,' several voices shout out, foot-stamping starting-up that soon becomes regimented.

'Taking all art in all fields of creativity think for a moment what you can get for a few euros entrance price. In cinemas near your home, or in your home via streamed transmissions or on DVDs you can participate in today's most widespread cultural treasure—film. It's my belief that film and democracy stand shoulder to shoulder.'

Shouting erupts everywhere, Cindy watching the euphoria outside feeding in from all cinémas. Léo has his arms up but he can't stop the fervour now. Cindy can see he knows he has gone over the top with his democracy théâtrics but today is 'showtime' before anything else and Léo knows when it's time to put on a show.

Applause filling the auditorium goes on longer than three minutes. A solid three minutes, stopping dead at the end with one woman calling out: 'On y va!'

Watching from the front stalls Cindy is over the moon at witnessing this happen. Léo raises his arms to calm down some new shouts of support.

'Extraordinary things have happened in Renne these last few days. Today the spirit of democracy is alive at this festival. Let's celebrate the most democratic cultural form in the world.' Cheering takes over the auditorium, Léo finally managing again to quieten everyone down but only after many failed attempts.

Barely out of film school, Cindy's experience of festivals is limited to these few days in Renne but she knows the world of cinéma well-enough to say that film is a business-led cultural activity with profit, privilege and nepotism reigning and thriving by the bucketloads. So, her only critique of Léo's optimistic vision is that it is missing a point, that profit trumps everything. The great underbody of the culture of film might underpin the sphere of the imagination at this famed Riviera event, but profit is never far behind. Cindy wants to yell right now, where's the human right of film? Can anything ever be truly democratic in film? She knows if she poses these questions aloud, say to all, Can we define cine-democracy before going on, she can expect heaps of invective in return, starting with, Gimme a break, then some. Perhaps even Léo would start yelling at her.

'What art form celebrates the magnificence of life. What art form explores our times, present past future, with such fascination, with such soul.'

'MUSIC,' the same main calls out. Nobody disagrees this time.

'Okay, point taken. But what art form is universally distributed and shared. I don't speak of theory mesdames et messieurs. What cinéma achieves in every exhibited film is a miracle. Friends we live in precious times and cinéma is the art form of our time.'

Music taking the gloss off his argument a touch, Léo grins hopefully out at his audience. 'Today both French and world cinéma need your help.' Shouts of OUI fill the auditorium. Are they even hearing what he is saying? To Cindy, the cheering is a naked expression of relief that Léo is back. Many are giving him their support unconditionally. The fixer is Léo, their saviour, in an irrepressible uncritical demonstration of affection reigning everywhere for him. People want a democratic festival and Léo is the only person who can make it happen it seems.

Cindy sees a clear and present belief in Léo in faces all around. Many people are in tears. Someone passes around a huge box of chocolates, a man alongside Cindy begins telling her that he was in Renne in 1968, describing how wonderful it was. 'That was the sixties,' he says wistfully. Less than half his age, Cindy laughs with the man, so glad he's prepared to share his reflections. Cindy is a child of a new century and she grew up learning a whole other political, social and cultural ball game. She has only vague ideas what the hippy rock'n'roll let's do whatever drugs times were like.

She's so pleased she's here to witness the energy exploding inside this iconic théâtre, wherever it is coming from doesn't matter. Whatever the truth or falsehood of 'mine was the greatest age' or 'this is the greatest artform' illusions of her adjacent neighbour and the man on stage Cindy simply loves the positive acceptance of Léo's ideals. The man by her side says he thought the Daniel Martin nightmare would never end. Cindy agrees. Now le revenant Léo, Léo the man truly for this moment, is transcending rational thought.

Famous faces now begin appearing without ceremony through a curtain. Directors, actors, screenwriters, cinematographers and producers come out, standing in a line, arm-in-arm, women and men, waving out to an audience that is calling back BRAVA and BRAVO to them.

'We're here for the festival. We're here for democracy.'

'We're here for you Léo,' comes the response in the audience. 'Let the good times ROL,' someone shouts. Return of Léo, ROL is now the acronym of the moment. Let's ROL with Léo.

'WHO WISHES TO SPEAK?'

Hands go up all around in response to Léo's question, and Lennie Facteur is the first to stand up. From her recent cultural studies Cindy knows a thing or two about power and how it expresses itself in culture. Does Lennie Facteur have the juice for this moment? Cindy has real doubts. His film in competition, Helpless, helmed by new rom-commer Sarah Blewitt, boasting an expensive cast, is a write-off. Neutered by a blunt script, the story limping two hours with barely a decent line, penned by a former prize-winner, the by-now out-to-pasture, Javier Booney, a writer without a hit in how many years, Lennie's film is as good as face-down in the drink. So, he's offered to distribute Larry's film.

Word on the waterfront is that Lennie is jumping out of his fat into Larry's fire for that reason alone. Still Death is no done deal for any prizes or box office returns either. Over by an entrance door the late-arriving Larry Linsteeg hovers with his fist in his mouth. More than anyone, Cindy knows Larry knows just how easily moments like this can go off the rails. You have to get your interventions dead right, ad hoc political speeches going haywire in the blink of an eye.

'Two thousand five hundred years ago in Greece,' Lennie says with professorial brio, 'Cleisthenes had an idea. To break the oligarchic control of the four main families he designed a voting system on the basis of a geometrically divided Athens. With this inspired move he created democracy. Léo has done the same for this festival. Now everyone can be heard. Now everyone has a say. One view one vote. No badges, no affiliation, no oligarchy of film studios, producers or distributors. No elite or elitist jury deciding films. Léo has done this for us.'

Larry still stands immobile, his fist not leaving his mouth.

'I am proud to be here to give Léo my complete support. Léo, your inspiration is as brilliant as Cleisthenes' concept of democracy. Brilliant because it is perfectly timed. Perfect because it is right for here and now. Great because it is simple and speaks directly to us all.'

Lennie sits down, a tepid 'oui' sounding. People know who Lennie is and what he's doing. Lennie, as one writer put it: gets the money, chooses the subject, actors, writers and director, the kind of producer who regards himself as an alchemist of the modern mystery, cinéma, with nothing out of his control, a manager whose orchestration of a 'thousand forms' making for a unique Lennie Facteur film. More's the pity, Cindy thinks, because lately, every choice Lennie has made has been a big sack of manure. To be blunt, filmic value emanating from Lennie's company in recent times is in such short supply, maybe Cindy should have said Lennie said it about Larry and they might have had a fight and killed each other on the breakfast terrace. And Lennie wouldn't have been alive to make this self-serving speech.

Cindy can't believe she just had that thought. Everyone here is content to let Lennie speak.

Léo's return has coalesced a generous audience. Cindy sees Larry rubbing his face in relief. Lennie, known for mangling moments, risqué jokes delivered at the wrong moment, actually didn't blow anything or launch any crass jokes from his list of gems. Larry and Léo are visibly exhaling. And now one by one, others get up to praise Léo, Cindy scribbling down comments as fast as she's able. She's relieved to have a positive story to write, one she hopes will have a happy ending when the lottery slips are counted, but the eulogizing is a touch premature. Anything can still happen. And it does with a grey-haired man standing and pointing at the stage. 'How can you talk about democracy? You're a liar.'

Complete silence descends throughout the auditorium, many at first thinking the man means Léo, but then he refers to Lennie by name, people beginning to whisper: who is this guy? The man launches a diatribe, Léo standing his forehead in hand staring balefully out at the speaker, as an expletive-filled invective piles up against Lennie. 'You owe me three million you bastard.' Lennie gets to his feet, tries calming his critic. 'You were paid what you're due.'

'You call what you wrote-up a contract?'

'You signed it.'

'You promised me back end you thief.'

'Read your contract, Phil.'

'It's true Lennie,' yells a voice way back in the théâtre. 'Phil's film was never distributed as you promised.' Heartened by the support, Phil yells louder: 'Lennie, you are one miserable son of a ....' Phil is so worked up he can't get the last word out. Describing now how he was cheated and lied to by Lennie from preproduction to postproduction. Hearing the tale many guests nod their heads. He has support, his predicament well-known. Even without knowing the facts, a distressed creator taken for a fool by a producer is a familiar tale. Sympathetic nods continue, as more take note of Phil's pain. The more he speaks, the more Lennie's victims appear, those who have dealt with him, calling out that they know what Phil means. It's clear a lot have a Facteur production disaster to relate. Creators getting fleeced, bras ripped off.

'C'est vrai,' voices whisper, then the whispers morph into shouts, as film worker after film worker gets up to list a grievance over the unscrupulous producer. Slapping the backs of her seat, a lone woman shouts for a charter of rights for all creators free from bastards. 'The Facteurs of film are too common,' she yells, 'both in the appropriation of intellectual property and in the conning of creators out of their share of the box-office.' The woman stands up and screams, 'LENNIE, YOU HAVE SOME BALLS.'

Suddenly it's become a let's get Lennie Facteur night not we're here for democracy. Struggling to intervene, Léo finds he has to defend himself too, no doubt wondering now why on earth he let Lennie Facteur anywhere near a microphone in the first place. Then Léo starts yelling at guests. 'CAN WE ALL STOP!'

Two big things are clear to Cindy. Lennie has a roomful of sworn enemies and Léo's brilliant initiative has been hijacked. When someone shouts from the back: 'TIME TO GO LENNIE. YOU'RE NOT INTERESTED IN DEMOCRACY. BE HONEST FOR ONCE IN YOUR LIFE,' Lennie momentarily stands his ground in defiance of his critics.

'Come on guys, look at my history.'

'WE HAVE,' someone in the middle yells. Lennie keeps talking, but with so many voices drowning him out, he gives up the ghost, walking up the théâtre aisle to whistles and boos and a collection of choice phrasal expletives as he heads to the exit, where his new partner once was, Larry Linsteeg, who now can't be seen for moon dust.

WHEN QUAI DES ORFÈVRES released him to the général's command Franck knew his sell-by-date as a police professional had finally arrived. Getting to the place on Rue

d'Anglacés where the général asked him to wait, Franck
stands his full height, squaring his shoulders. He could
be an actor. Gary Cooper in High Noon. Burt Reynolds in
Deliverance. Yves Montand in Jean de Florette. Anthony
Quinn in Zorba. He would settle for Humphrey Bogart in
Casablanca, but then who wouldn't? The général's Peugeot
pulls up. Braking hard, the passenger door opens.

'Out of uniform again,' Franck says getting inside. Belting
up, he appraises the général's outfit. A light beige-coloured
check-shirt and mid-blue chinos above tan leather boots.
With a Stetson on his head the général could be a rancher.

'What movie are you auditioning for,' he mutters, Franck
managing to muffle his comment with, 'What the hell is
happening?' his accent almost west Texan.

The général offers no explanation for this either. They
drive on in silence. Staring out of his window Franck tells
himself to stay a step ahead of whatever it is that is coming.
'Do I sense a blame-game starting?'

'We're operational. That's all we need to focus on.'

Before Franck can unpack this last statement, the général
is illegally-double-parking in front of the Hôtel Sublime,
Franck spotting Daniel Martin waiting for them on the
sidewalk. Going into the lobby, the général whispers: 'Léo's
doing. He wants him occupied.'

Franck doesn't try to unpack this either, though the idea
appeals less and less going up in the elevator. Still he knows
enough to know when it is time not to offer an opinion.
They arrive at the second floor. Walking the hallway, Marc
watches as Martin stops at a door, then uses a tissue to open
it. Inside he finds what he expects, something he doesn't
need to know too much about. A fully clothed man lies inert
on a bed, no blood in sight. Franck begins wondering why

he's needed. Pinching the skin between his eyes he tells himself to get into analytical mode, start thinking like the inspector he won't be for much longer. Looking at Daniel Martin and then the général he wonders who's in charge, asking after a long moment: 'Who is he?'

'A Ridley executive.'

'Who discovered him?

'A maid.'

Marc stares down at the inert body, his mind not exactly racing with pertinent questions. He spies an empty bottle on a bedside table. Squatting down he studies the label.

'Ridley LA doesn't want this going public before their film premiere.'

'When is that?'

'On the last night.'

Franck stands wondering if an autopsy will be set up for this man, or the writer, but decides he doesn't want to ask too much about either cases.

'What is your take, inspector?'

Franck draws-in a breath. 'Well, there are only three possibilities. Death by natural causes, suicide, or unlawful killing which could be murder.'

'Look suspicious to you?'

'If you want me to investigate this properly, then ask me properly and I will preside over it.'

'They don't want it investigated.'

'Who doesn't want it investigated?'

'Martin points north.'

'Paris?' Martin nods. 'Then forget I exist.'

Franck doesn't want to know who in Paris isn't interested in this perhaps suicide or homicide. He doesn't care.

'If that's what Paris wants, let them handle it. I suggest

we turn-up the air-conditioning and leave.'

'We can't do that.'

'Why not?'

'It's as high as it goes.'

'Then lock the door. Tape it up. On the basis of what you've just said I'm certainly not putting my fingerprints anywhere near it, or my name on any piece of paper.'

Turning, Franck finds a young actress they all know standing in the doorway. The three men watch Semolina walk inside and stare at the man, two fingernails clawing at her lips.

'He was very unhappy.'

'You spoke to him?'

Semolina nods. 'He was very upset about being forced out of the Mélodie. Larry wanted his suite and the concierge asked him to leave. He was humiliated.'

'This hotel is okay isn't it?'

'He had a suite in Renne's most famous hotel. He told everyone back home where he was staying. He had made it.'

Semolina stares at the bottle on the bedside table. 'What are the odds this would happen in a room next to mine?'

'Meaning?'

'I play death in a film and the guy next door ends up dead.'

'That's stretching your thespian powers a bit.'

Semolina covers her mouth. 'She's here.'

'Who is?'

'Madame Morendo.'

'Here in this room?'

'She's right here, sizing us up. Don't look at me like that. I know something about her. She's a serial killer with no regret.'

The général steps forward. 'You should get some rest.'

Semolina stares at him as if trying to register who he is.

'Are you taking him away now?'

'He stays here for a while longer.'

'And you expect me to sleep with this body next door?'

The général tries to lead her back inside her room but Semolina pushes his hand away. 'Don't drink anymore.'

'How can I not drink with him here?'

The général's face is full of sympathy. 'Nous naissons, nous vivons, nous souffrons, nous mourons.'

'You know that's the lamest cliché I've ever heard.'

The général turns to Franck. 'Maybe you should talk to Madame Morendo.'

'She's here? In the Sublime?'

Semolina nods.

'You want me to bring Madame Morendo in for questioning?'

'Speak to her.'

Semolina sucks in a breath. 'She's here right now is what I'm saying.' Semolina stares resolutely at the général. 'This man is in a black hole of her making, his soul in a perpetual sea of motionlessness, a vortex where all echoes are swept into a stilled sea of light and time. All because of her.'

'Vous êtes une poétesse.'

Semolina relaxes, even smiles briefly. 'I was on a roll for a moment.'

The général tries again to lead her back to her room. Semolina pushes his arm away again, more forcefully this time. Leaning forward she kisses the man's face, jumping back.

'Jesus, his lips are moving.'

'WHAT?'

The général pushes her aside. 'God, she's right. Didn't you call a doctor?'

'He looked dead.' Martin's shock looks phony to Franck.

'Did you check his pulse?'

Martin stares back at the général. 'I'm not a doctor. He didn't look like he was breathing. His face was cold.'

'Of course, the air conditioner is up full-bore. Give me that duvet.'

Franck studies the usurping ex-deputy thinking his face does invite a punch. Shaking his head, the général takes the phone and presses a button, waits. 'I've never heard of such a thing.'

'I only got here twenty minutes ago, and I called you right away.'

The général puts his hand up. 'This is the police. Get an ambulance right away to room 303. Right now, please. It's life and death.'

The général puts the phone down and stares at Martin for a long moment. 'Edgar Gordon Olles was right. We all should punch you.'

'He's right in his film as well.'

The général squints at Semolina. 'About what?'

'One day death simply stops killing. I thought he was crazy but not now.'

Franck sighs. 'Am I needed further?'

'Of course, inspector. If you are still a professional.'

'I am still a homicide detective, général, if that's what you mean. And as this man is not dead, and because there is someone who represents Death here on Earth and is floating around, maybe on this floor, if not in this room, I think I should try to find her, perhaps bring Madame Morendo in for questioning.'

As he heads for the door Semolina takes his arm.

'I am going with the toreador.'

'I like to be thought of like that.'

Franck walks out with Semolina on his arm, an actor and an inspector heading down a Sublime hallway together, neither bothering to look back.

DAY 10

CINDY IS UP EARLY FOR THE FINALS. Showered and dressed and out in the streets, her task is to witness the new regime of democracy happening in real-time. The waterfront is almost dry with the early bright sun warming the whole town fast. Vote City is really waking up.

However fragile, Renne is alive in ways organizers can only hope it'll always be at this time of year, a buzz in the air around cafés and boulangeries. The Carré D'Argent is doing a brisk trade everywhere she looks.

Cindy can't help smiling at cineastes greeting each other excitedly, hearing them trade good-natured arguments and jokes on what films they are going to see. Sipping hot coffee, munching fresh pastries in lines going way down the street outside the cinémas, they cheer a beaming Léo making his way through the snaking queues. Someone yells: 'You're the man Léo'—le revenant hero director broadly smiling and waving back at his fans as he disappears inside the bâtiment.

At eight-fifteen sharp all cinéma doors open up and filmgoers begin filing inside, nobody racing to her or his seat. No breakdown in decorum is recorded in any location, yet every cinéma is full in minutes. Eight thirty on the dot all screenings begin. Cindy is so impressed by the smooth operation she's wondering if Léo is thinking like her that this is how it could have been all along, and would have been, if everyone had been equal in status from the outset.

Checking her watch and smiling constantly she heads towards her rendezvous with the head scrutineer she met by chance in the bâtiment the night before.

And there he is waiting for her, his smile as big as Cindy's. Leading her through the security barrier he says loudly: 'She's with me.' Cindy is with everyone today. In a backroom of a basement office, she stands alongside the manager watching festival workers briskly stacking the voting boxes, something they have been doing from the very first screening at midnight the night before. Cindy sees boxes of the sealed envelopes packed with voting-choices. The counters on nightshift start leaving the room closely followed by the supervisor and Cindy. 'It's so exciting. Let's hope the results are received this positively.' The supervisor grins at her as he locks the door behind himself. He turns to see Léo coming down the hallway. 'Ah, Léo, morning.'

'How's everything shaping up?'

'First boxes already in and recorded.'

'Excellent.' Léo stands a moment looking from the supervisor to the girl.

'This is a journalist from London. I was showing her how the vote is being managed. Cindy Turper, Director Léo Stern. '

Cindy and Léo shake hands. 'Could I get an interview with you on this operation?'

'Come up to my office later if you like. After five?'

'Wonderful. Thank you.'

Giving her his new I've-got-everything-under-control smile, Léo turns and walks off.

'I wish everyone was this pleasant when I asked for interviews.'

The supervisor grimaces. 'I hope he doesn't mind you being here.'

'I haven't created a problem, have I? We haven't done anything wrong.'

'You haven't. Only scrutineers and counters are meant to be in that room.'

'I really appreciate being allowed to see the counting operation.'

Cindy sees the man's fixed smile slide into a grimace. Outside she thanks him again, saying she hopes they'll meet up again soon, her tone perhaps a touch too saccharine given the worry in his face. 'I'll take the blame for this.'

'How?' the man says, still smiling.

'I will tell Léo it was my fault.'

'That'll only make it worse. There's a lot riding on this.'

'Now I feel really bad.'

'Don't.'

They shake hands, Cindy walking away trying hard to dispel her doubts, but she has some misgivings right now. Though witnessing democracy at work can't be wrong. Even if protocols are protocols. She rifles in her bag for her teardrop sunglasses. 'What counts,' she decides aloud, 'is not the doubt you're feeling now but that democratic forces are at work.' In the middle of talking to herself a TV journalist collars her.

'Look here is Cindy Turper the correspondent for The London Daily Sentinel. Cindy you are live on local TV. You look a bit concerned. Something wrong?'

'No.'

'What do you think about what's going on?'

Cindy stares at the girl. 'Who did you say you are with again?'

'Marceline Alles and you're live on French television.'

Cindy stands her full height. 'What counts is democracy is happening and that it's being properly managed.'

'Is it being properly managed?'

'Absolutely. It's a democratized festival.'

'And democracy still includes winning right?'

'Yes, winning of course, but democracy also includes a wider ideal for the filmmaking community, one filmmakers should support.'

'You think filmmakers don't support democracy?'

'Not everyone supports the idea of democracy Léo has created. A lot of protesters were injured trying to set this all up.'

'Where's the recognition of them, you mean?'

'I am concerned about the voting process.'

'Really?'

Cindy can't help flinching. She wonders why she's saying all this. She arrived in town hoping to learn something about reviewing, now she is sounding off like some self-appointed political pundit. 'No, what I am truly concerned about is that the spirit of pioneering filmmakers gets locked together with cinephiles in a sixty-eight mindset, with the support of those who changed our vision and ideas recognising history in supporting this ideal.' Cindy squints, wondering where the subject and verb was in all that.

'Léo's idea may not work you mean?'

'Back in '68 ...' Cindy's mind gropes for an idea to hang on to now. 'At the Cinémathèque, Langlois was a bit of a dictator. Malraux was against him.'

'Langlois had popular support.'

'People protested.'

'What's nineteen sixty-eight got to do with Léo's democracy plan here?'

'Filmmakers down on the coast here came out in support of freedoms being fought for in Paris. They had a single purpose, more democracy.'

'1968 is the inspiration? You think filmmakers here today know about '68?'

'I'm not sure...' Cindy stops in mid-speech, asking herself what the hell is she doing. The streets are a dangerous place with TV reporters lurking everywhere. Cindy needs to stay on message but what message is she on right now? What drug more like it. She needs to shut up.

'You think that filmmakers are not showing their gratitude for 1968?'

Cindy stares back at Marceline, confused over what she's being asked to answer now, thinking: what answer won't trap me? This is not an interview anymore, this is a gnarly back-alley debate, a cliff face interview with sheer drops everywhere.

'Léo's offering democracy,' Cindy says quietly, 'Filmmakers need to know that.'

'You mean where's the recognition for Léo for setting up this vote?'

'The recognition is here right now.'

The reporter frowns, holding her earpiece. 'Thank you, Cindy Turper.'

Marceline turns and walks off with her camera crew, pushing her microphone into the face of someone else. 'You're live on French television. What do you think of this new democracy regime?'

Regime? Cindy isn't waiting around to hear this, stalking down some steps, people staring at her. She should have said: 'I'm with Léo.' Let it go at that. Going towards the bay she tries speed-walking off her dismay at getting caught out like this. Why did she go in to all that crap? She's not the story. Democracy is the story. She jams her teardrop sunglasses back on her face. She is a journalist rookie behaving like some sort of media super-all-knowing-nut-case. Jesus Christ she can't go around expressing her opinions like she's been around for yonks in broadcasting. Is she crazy? Walking down through the merry-go-round gardens she shakes her hair. 'Okay,' she says aloud, 'RESET. The sun's shining. Believe it or not this will be okay. Believe it and it will be okay. It will be.'

Her luck over the last few days has gone pretty well, so she needs to believe in it. 'You are even okay without it,' she says only half-believing her last words. As she goes by a merry-go-round, a man in a cowboy outfit jumps out from behind a bush scaring the hell out of her. 'Hey baby como você está fazendo.'

'Oh please.' Another microphone's in front of her with another cameraman behind.

'O que você achou do filme estréia.'

'You have the wrong person.'

Cindy walks faster, the TV team jogging by her side.

'Nós te amamos baby.'

'I am not who you think I am.'

'Falando Inglês bem estes dias.'

Cindy rakes her sunglasses off her face. 'Am I the Brazilian babe you think I am?'

The man realizing his mistake stops. As Cindy begins walking again, a group of onlookers start to clap. She quickens her pace, smiling, then killing it, unsure if they are applauding her politics or thinking she is really some phony celebrity or just wants to look like one. Everyone wants a piece of her right now. Nobody seems to understand that if she were who they might think she is, and she's not, some actor blipping across their radar, she'd have an army of minders shoving them all away or punching their lights out.

Or she'd be on the phone up in her suite having her nails done, whatever.

She pushes her sunglasses back against her eyes trying hard not to be the ungracious celebrity dismissing her fans which it seems she's playing right now. Just because they have her confused with some famous Brazilian actress, seeing her toss her hair and hide behind sunglasses, she doesn't need to be as rude as the imaginary actor.

People keep staring, two people trying to stop her. A couple runs on to the path in front of her, the girl almost tripping over her own feet taking a photo. Pixing a celebrity she doesn't know from the younger sister of Beyoncé Giselle Knowles-Carter or whatever babe they haven't a fix on or clue about that Cindy clearly is not.

'What if I had to put up with this every day? People reading my mind.'

'Get used to it,' she hears a voice say. Glancing in fear to her right, an old black actor mostly backlit who could be Sidney Poitier stands with a woman who could be Joanna Shimkus. Embarrassed Cindy thinks of asking them both for their autographs, only maybe they aren't the pair she thinks they are. She smiles quickly and walks on heading where right now? Attracting another photo fiend. Veering left she crashes through two people, that guy and girl again, who turn and dash across the road at a crosswalk without looking, forcing an accelerating SUV to break just in time.

'Oh my god I'm going to get somebody killed.'

Killed for tracking someone who's not even sure she looks much like anyone at all. Shaken by the near miss, her fault it seems, Cindy has only one objective. To get as far away from this waterfront madness as quickly as she can.

'Hey beautiful, un momento. One shot, okay?'

'Shut up.'

Now she really is being rude. It's bad karma.

But they don't want to talk to her, confusing her with someone else she's confusing herself with now, some Brazilian she's totally nonplussed about, Cindy speed-walking to her hotel, taking a back route through empty streets, going faster, hiding deeper behind the shades of some Brazilian babe she has become, apparently.

'WE REALLY DO NEED TO DISCUSS THE FUTURE. We've had our differences in the past. Let's bury the hatchet on them now. Times are always tough.'

Jack is on the back of the Sunshine Coast, on the phone, making one of his let's-keep-keeping-on-united speeches into a mobile, a helicopter flying near the other speaker's place forcing Jack to shout: 'WE NEED TO UNITE. WE HAVE TO GRAB THIS OPPORTUNITY BEFORE IT DISAPPEARS.'

When the voice seems to cut-out, Jack switches off, returning to his seat, throwing out his hands in a who-knows-gesture when Merryl asks what the call was all about.

'Couldn't hear much. Helicopters again.'

'Who was it?'

'Linsteeg, I think.'

'Is he coming out?'

'I think he's depressed.'

'Why?'

'He thinks he won't win anything.'

Jack leans back in his director's chair re-joining a discussion halfway through some programme of action. Without Larry there to run things Jack has assumed the managerial role, something he doesn't mind doing, Edgar, Ulyana, Merryl, Ivan, Bella and Jack all sitting around a table on the Sunshine's stern sipping Merryl's herbal teas and munching special biscuits she champions.

'If the writer's dead who'll write the script?'

'What did he do before anyway?'

'A lot for Larry. So, I heard.'

Ivan stares at Jack. 'He was working for Larry as well?'

Merryl is confused. 'Which writer are we talking about?'

'I can't remember his name.'

'Me either.'

'Jack, you met him.'

'Yeah but we never got as far as names.'

They look over at Edgar who shrugs. 'He's a writer is all I know. And he's dead. So everyone is saying.'

'Writer of what? Screenplays?'

'Your guess is as good as mine, Merryl.'

'We're talking about the same guy aren't we?'

'Are there more dead writers in town?'

'Probably.'

'The guy who's living on the yacht?'

'Was living. He's dead Ivan.'

'Is he really dead?'

'He's dead.'

'How do you know? The detective's wife says she saw him the day after.'

'After what?'

'The riot.'

'Saw him where?'

'In my apartment.'

'Edgar, what was the detective's wife doing in your apartment?'

'She got separated from her husband during the riot.'

'Officially? Was the office open?'

'What office?'

'You couldn't separate them with a crowbar.'

'We were, well we ended up in a beach bar during the riot.'

'Who ended up on the beach?'

'We did.'

'The writer?'

'No, not the writer. I was on the beach in a bar with the detective's wife.'

'What on earth were you doing in a beach bar with her during the riot?' There is a silence on board as everyone digests this idea.

'She's cute right?'

'What's her name?'

'Marie. We got away. I took her to my place. She was lucky.'

'You were lucky.'

'I'm totally innocent, Jack.'

'Like the riot.'

'Nooo.'

'So, the wife of the detective saw the writer at Edgar's place?'

'She said so. I didn't see him.'

'Where did she see him? In a dream?'

'She said she saw him. Said so anyway. I wasn't there.'

'Is she nuts?'

'Of course not.'

'She saw a writer who everyone else says is dead in your apartment? She was drunk right?

'No, she wasn't.'

'On drugs?'

'No.'

'Yeah, I bet. Come on, you had drugs at your place.'

'Some hash'

'Oh boy.'

'I don't believe this.'

'Did she speak to him?'

'To the writer? She said so.'

'You questioned her on it?'

'No. She just volunteered it.'

'She's a volunteer for what?'

'But she said she spoke to him.'

'Yes.'

'She was high and saw and spoke to this nameless dead writer.'

'Makes sense.'

'Were others there?'

'Yes.'

'Did they speak with him?'

'I don't know, Ivan. I didn't ask.'

'You didn't see him?'

'I told you I went somewhere. I can't remember what for.'

'You went for drugs?'

'For godsakes it was after a pretty chaotic riot. Maybe I had a spliff or two outside. Nobody was smoking any amount at all. I didn't bring any big stash out.'

'You had a big stash?'

'They were smoking while you were away.'

'Maybe there was some stuff on the table.'

'So, you came back high or were they high?'

'I don't remember.'

'Then you were. It's understandable. It was a stressful time. When I learn about conversations people on drugs had with a dead man I'm sceptical.'

'He went out to buy something and left some dope on the table.'

'Which the inspector's wife and this writer which you never saw probably smoked or baked into cakes, stuff they were enjoying while you were away buying more stuff.'

'How do you know she had a conversation with the writer?'

'Merryl, she told me he had good ideas.'

'That was before or after she ate your hash?'

'She didn't eat anything. I didn't have much. Maybe a loaded muffin.'

'Did she know she was in your apartment?'

'Of course, she did. She wanted to redecorate it.'

'She had a couple of drinks, whatever, then wanted to redecorate.'

'We both had a couple. Before and after.'

'Where?'

'Down at the beach.'

'What exactly?'

'Whisky.'

'Straight whisky?'

'Yes. Black Label.'

'Oh boy. Whisky followed by a hash-muffin.'

'Where did you get it?'

'Get what?'

'The whisky.'

'I opened a cabinet and took a bottle and drank from it.'

'You finished the bottle?'

'No.'

'How much?'

'About half, maybe three-quarters.'

'Oh boy.'

'How did you get into the bar?'

'I'd rather not say.'

'You broke into a restaurant and drank a bottle of whisky?'

'It was a nasty moment.'

'You were drinking on the beach during the riot, then went back to your place, had a couple of spliffs and then Marie had a conversation with a dead writer you think maybe you couldn't see.'

'Didn't see. I went out.'

'When you came back, was she or he there?'

'Both. Neither. I don't know. Jesus.'

'Oh boy.'

'Okay, then on the basis of this I think we can conclude we need another writer. Any suggestions?'

HEADING FROM ONE MEETING TO ANOTHER le revenant directeur speaks to one group after another, walking faster trying to shake off several newshounds constantly trying to collar him with the same questions.

'Where was he?'

'Why did he leave?'

'Was he sick?'

Standing by the escalator waiting to accost the man herself, Cindy sees the stress in Léo's face, especially when a journalist grabs his arm.

'Why have awards at all? Isn't it impossible to compare creative works?'

Léo takes a deep breath, answering with what has become his boilerplate response: 'This is a democratic festival for by and of the people. The people have a right to see films and a right to vote on the choice for best.'

More journalists surround Léo, a man right behind

Cindy's left ear, asking loudly: 'People are saying many voters are political plants.'

'Do you know that for a fact?'

'It will be too late if it is true.'

'If it turns out to be true, we will consider returning to the old ways, next year. Not now though while this is happening.'

'You are going back to the jury next year?'

'I didn't say that.'

'Are you anticipating voter fraud?'

'No, I am not anticipating anything. If this proves not to have worked, then we'll have to think again.'

'Don't you believe it will work?'

'I didn't say that.'

Cindy is now officially part of a group of journalists hounding Léo. She feels so sorry for him as she does for herself just being there. Why's she here? Then Léo shocks her by turning around and pointing: 'We have an interview. Right?'

'Yes.'

'Let's go then. Prior appointment everyone.'

With no apology, Léo takes her arm and leads her towards his upstairs office.

'God, if they didn't have doubts about me they have now.'

'We had an appointment didn't we?'

'They wanted to question you.'

'Don't worry about them.'

Léo leads her to a picture window open area cordoned off by several security guards. They sit in plain view of everyone facing over the waterfront. 'I'm all yours. Fire away.'

'Someone back there said something about fraud.'

'Good ideas turn bad fast if you stoke untested rumour.'

'Some are saying a festival celebrating films without awards is better.'

'It's something to think about.'

'Others say the scrutineers were handpicked by you.'

'And your sources? You won't say. Look, scrutineers are in the bâtiment working hard at keeping watch on the count. I have to go.'

Cindy holds onto his arm. 'I didn't mean to imply corrupt voting.'

'It's okay. It's your job.'

He gets up, walks away.

'I didn't want this job,' she calls out to him. He swings around.

'Then why do it?'

Cindy runs after him. 'Look this may seem like that nice scrutineer manager said this. He didn't. He was really nice and all I did was stand and watch them stacking boxes. I asked to see how it worked and he allowed me to see it.'

Léo stands patiently hearing her out. 'The scrutineers are hard at work keeping a close watch on the count. The counters are counting hard. We need to respect the process. In conversations around town, it's gossip first, facts second. What is the festival's future? Who the hell's going to win? No-one knows. So, journalists start making up who will win, then why. Without a jury, there are no leaks. Without leaks there's no inside buzz. No jury, no story. Without the gossip, courtesy of some inside-buzz merchant, confused old hands sit slumped in lobbies and rooted to barstools. Old hands who once considered themselves privileged enough to receive inside tips are now not on the inside anymore. They sit staring into their drinks, saying: This is unheard of. Recipe for disaster. Bigger than that, it is a disaster. What's the headline: Failed art event. Sub-heading: Three people nearly killed by a promotion gone wrong in the bay. Then in the body-text: Director walks out on his own festival. Rotting body found on a sloop. Unclaimed female swimmer's body in the morgue.'

'What swimmer?'

'Before a screenwriter turned up as crab mornay the biggest scandal here was a star's dress split on the red carpet or some filmmaker trying to get noticed mentioned Hitler or reel three of a film went missing. Or if you really were lucky, a jury man was caught in bed with a jury woman both of them taking polaroids.'

Cindy glances inside her bag. Her recorder is off. 'I forgot to turn it on. Could you just say all that again?'

Léo taps his head. 'Use your memory, it's refreshing. Once we actually knew what a scandal was, Cindy. This year has rewritten the code.'

'Can we talk about nineteen sixty-eight?'

'Ancient history.'

'It's the blueprint for this year. Larry Linsteeg and 1968.'

'Cindy, given what's going on now who cares?'

'Larry cares.'

'Maybe he needs to. End of career crisis or something.'

'That what you think of him?'

'No, and I didn't say it.'

Cindy is jotting down his comments, Larry's name getting a circle around it. Léo touches her hand. 'Listen, I'll tell you everything right after the festival. Just do me this favour. Don't write anything about it until it's over. Then let's talk.'

'When do I call you, Mr Stern?'

'Call me Léo.'

'I will call you Léo.'

He mimes a phone to his ear. 'No, I'll call.'

'You want my number.' She starts juggling her bag and pad.

'I've got your number.'

'Au revoir merci.'

'Je t'en prie,' he says quickly, shaking her hand.

Cindy heads for the escalator in a daze. Did he just hit on her? He was cool. She was tense. He had her cold. She was easy pickings. Be positive girlie as Steve used to say. Seeing the journalists waiting below Cindy knows why she needs to be positive.

'What did he say?' one woman asks.

'Nothing.'

'Sure Cindy. Did he invite you on his boat?'

'Does he have a boat?'

'Interested?'

'NO.'

THE WORLD THIS MORNING was way too craggy and long in the tooth for Larry to find it worth getting up early. From first light he has been filibustering every negative proposition his exhausted brain can come up with—firstly on Bella and her money slipping away from him, coupled to the lingering effect of his jail-time. Peering at the Mediterranean out through his shutters spread-eagled like a shot-gunned pelican in his king's sized bed he has been thinking through everything, interrogating himself over and over. 'All's not lost,' he says without conviction to a spent TV.

A blank screen in Larry's life is a prescient marker in itself. See a dead electronic propaganda-conveyor in an abode Larry occupies, call an ambulance. To win Bella back, he needs to get her, and everyone, impressed with him again.

Climbing out of bed, he showers, dresses and carefully descends the stairs to have two coffees on an empty stomach on an empty terrace. Heading off to find transport for the journey out to the Sunshine Coast, he stands waiting on a wharf for twenty minutes, and when a taxiboat finally does turn-up, he sits slumped on a stern seat wondering why he's even going out.

Clambering off at his destination he waves like the trooper he is, trusting the welcome he is getting back about as much as he would a tail-shake with a stingray.

Mr Sell-through-video is in charge. There has to be a big catch to Jack somewhere. Larry grins his appreciation at Merryl's flag-halfway-up-the-mast greeting.

'Where were we?'

'Tea, Larry?'

Watching Merryl swish off and come back with a fresh pot, grinning as she pours him a cup, Larry trades greetings with others in his usual open-big-hearted-sort-of-guy way. Except for a facial tic on show and his hand-rubbing he's doing okay, as he half-squawks again: 'So, what's on the agenda?'

'Nothing.'

'Promising.'

'Jack was just attacking Edgar's choices on the future potential for his films.'

'I was not, Merryl.'

'Sounded that way.'

'I was just saying it's about choice. I was explaining, Merryl, that Saramago's Death at Intervals along with John Kennedy Toole's A Confederacy of Dunces and James Kelman's How Late It Was, How Late, makes up the best list of film-proof novels I've ever come across, movies ordinary people barely would comprehend let alone want to see in big numbers. They're not our best approach is what I'm saying.'

Edgar and Merryl sitting close together glare back at Jack in tandem.

'What do you think, Larry?'

'If I were Jack's age I would be happy just to get out that film list without falling asleep.'

'What the hell does that mean?'

'Just a joke Jack.' Larry waves his hand in a 'forget about it' gesture. 'Serious bit. You make money in this business by looking like you don't want to make money.'

Jack studies him. 'Like you're doing with Death?'

Touché, Larry almost says wiping his mouth down with a napkin, labouring on like the fighter who knows he is two seconds from a knock-out punch. 'The days of making money by looking like you are trying to make money are over. Audiences are way too smart.'

'Says he who can't take his own advice.'

'They see through the BS, Jack, is all I am saying.'

'Yeah yours. I'm seeing through yours. Everyone is.'

Jack glances around to see if everyone is with him on his Larry = BS verdict. Larry dodges Jack's slight, again by a whisker, using his only weapon left, his broad if crooked grin. 'The slick lines, Jack, the trumped-up fantasies, audiences are sick to death by all of it.'

'What do you think works?'

'What does work mean?'

'What it says on the tin. Tickets sold in theatre entrances. Films that speak to people.'

'We've had talkies for nearly a century, Jack.'

No-one laughs, the small audience on Jack's boat getting the picture. Larry's losing this.

'I don't mean something from CGI bonkers-ville.'

'From CGI where?' Jacks barks staring hard at Larry. 'Ridley runs the world with CGI.'

Merryl pats her husband's wrist. 'Jack, he means films that are about reality. What is going on for real in the here and now.'

'Why I am pursuing Jaws 6, Merryl.'

'I thought it was five.'

'You too,' Jack murmurs back. 'Thanks.'

'What I am saying, Jack,' Larry says emboldened by Merryl's timely helping hand, 'is we can't keep going down fantasy rabbit holes hoping to score the big bucks.'

'Is the Jaws franchise too much fantasy for you? It made a fortune.'

DAZED AND CONFUSED kids congregate on Promenade des Rois across from 13 Villa des Fleurs. Riding in from Biènville and Marseille, and further west, they are milling about with others who have TGV'd down from Paris, greeting each other without any enthusiasm.

Franck doesn't blame them for being skittish. From comments he is hearing they expected to be met and have their mission fully explained and told how it can be achieved. All they've heard so far is the protest is over, finished. They came all the way to Renne to be part of a decisive something on democracy and their leadership and purpose has disappeared. Nobody from the Grand Cinephile Protest Central Committee was on the station platform to greet them. Now, standing on a wind-blown waterfront they are spooked. From his bench, his eyes closed as if he's asleep, Franck listens to them whispering about unexplained new ideas and secret plans and spies everywhere. Through his eyelashes he sees their frowns, glancing around at people staring down at them from balconies.

'Perhaps we could wear insignias like the men in black,' one says, sniggering at his own comment, only increasing the general dismay. Very few of them know who F's men in black were or what they did over the last few days. When one boy says maybe they could observe a minute's silence for the dead writer, another kid snaps back angrily: 'It might help if the guy had a name'.

Another kid coming back from buying a cigarette lighter at a Tabac a few streets away has them falling silent again as he recounts how a shop owner told him the French army is in town.

Gathering into a tight circle to speak quietly, covering their mouths, Franck unable to get a clear idea what they are saying anymore, they make some sort of agreement, the whole group nodding their heads.

WALKING DOWN TO THE BÂTIMENT for the grand finale on a still rainless evening, Larry's writer is feeling good for once. In fact, he is cock-a-hoop at all the blank faces he's seeing all around him. Secret lobbying is out the window. The power cliques add up to zero. The malice of anyone but him or her, please god, has given way to an eerie silence. The swagger of the powerful is done for tonight. The crème de la crème of the know-all-about-everything in the sell-through suit brigade is in hiding or has given up and left town. Those who are left know nothing on who'll win or lose. Executives hoping to snare a bonus are out of the loop. No jury to milk for insider tips, they can't get their heads around what Léo's democracy will mean to their box-offices. Everything's up in the air. The raison d'être of the principle of film bankability is on the brink of going on the blink. Profit the only principle and measure anyone can properly understand is now impossible to predict. All the weighing-up and calculating in all the markets around the world tonight adds up to the horror of the unknown. A nobody that nobody has a share-in or a handle-on could win.

Nobody knows what kind of deals lie behind a door or under a table in such a world. Cue Larry's writer's kind of festival. He's over the moon seeing uncertainty reign. Climbing the carpeted stairs, he's dying to get inside to celebrate, seeing an unruly off-the-wall film win.

With two possible paying writing jobs on the trot now, even if both Jack and Larry are about as financially trustworthy as the weather, Larry's writer almost feels as if he's on solid ground, even if everything on his horizon is unclear. Especially now, after the riot and now this horrific boat death, murder really, because it sure looks like murder to Larry's soon-to-be ex-writer. It could be him down there. Is he now a ghost walking around in his final days on this earth? Rumour says death herself is in town. Just as in Edgar's film. Did he just hear a mosquito go by his ear? Larry's writer takes a deep breath of the humid night air. Still, he has to believe that where there's mayhem there's hope. He better believe it because the opposite is just too terrifying. Getting eaten alive by three-inch crabs. He shudders. Okay, fortune favours the brave. So even if his enemies are sharpening their claws to cut him out of whatever deal is left on whatever table that hasn't yet been overturned, Larry's writer's career careering from bleak to awful is still surviving on half-chances. Shaking himself from the awful fantasies in his head, he edges into a place between photographers, a vantage point from where he can spy stars, producers and directors as they climb the red stairs in this great return to film showings in a blighted festival.

Larry's writer is ready and willing to be witness to the improvisations the famous employ in dangerous moments. He's back on watch on a so far rainless night. With an intelligence officer still on the run, Larry's writer is hoping something unique will happen. Maybe the police will arrest someone right in front of him. If not, who will be the author of the night's big story? What will it be? A wardrobe failure. A footwear foul-up. A cat fight between two performers in unequal films. Larry's writer stares down the slippery red stairs of film fortune hoping that something, anything, will appear that he can write home to somebody about.

'OPEN UP RIGHT NOW DANIEL or we will kick the door down. What the hell do you think you can achieve doing this?' The général waves a voting slip at the doorhandle.

'He can't see you.'

Hearing this, the général throws Léo's assistant a withering look. 'LÉO, CAN YOU HEAR ME?'

There is a pause, then Léo speaks. 'Yes.'

'Have you counted all the votes yet?'

'I'm not in charge of that. It is all done independently.'

'I know that you didn't count them yourself Léo, but have they been counted?'

'Yes.'

'Who has won?'

'It's under festival embargo.'

'Does Daniel know?'

'No.'

The général turns to the assistant: 'At least he's not reacting to that.'

'Why would he?'

'If he's working for someone he could.'

'Is that likely, général?'

'We can't be sure of anything.' The général squints and grimaces. 'OPEN UP DANIEL RIGHT NOW.' The général takes a deep breath. 'Daniel, look, let's talk this through okay. I have a solution.'

There is another long moment of silence.

'What solution?'

The général whispers, 'We're taking you to the nut house.'

A security officer grins.

'I heard that.'

The général grimaces, whispering behind himself: 'How the hell did he hear me?'

'He probably heard something and filled in the blanks.'

The général stares at Léo's assistant as she says this then looks back at the door in front of his face. 'Daniel you know you can trust me.'

'Sure, général. You're whispering about me.'

'People are waiting on Léo's announcements.'

'I'm supposed to care about that.'

'OPEN UP NOW.'

'I'd rather kill myself.'

The général mutters, 'There's an idea.'

'I heard that.'

The général shakes his fist. 'You're going to jail.'

'Not if I'm dead.'

'Is there someone you will talk to?'

Silence. The général shakes his head. 'Is there anyone?

The général waits for an answer.

'Annalise.'

'Annalise?'

'Yes.'

'Can we find her?'

Léo's assistant points down the hall mouthing, press room.

'Go find her. DANIEL, WE'RE LOCATING HER.'

A few moments later the assistant comes back, shaking her head.

'Jesus, you talk to him then.' Léo's assistant points at herself. 'Yes, you.'

'What do I say to him?'

'Ask him what he wants.'

'Isn't it obvious? He wants to be let go.'

'Talk to him. Pretend we're not here.'

'Daniel it's me. We can't find Annalise. We're trying to find her. She could be anywhere. Will you talk to me?' There is a silence. 'They want to know what you want.'

'Who's they?'

'The général etc.' The général waves his finger.

'No, some others.'

'Tell him to go away.'

The général walks out into the corridor and stands there.

'They're going away now, Daniel.'

'Have they gone?'

'Yes, they've gone.'

'I don't believe you.'

'Daniel, I hardly think it matters. Léo's in there listening to you.'

'He might not be for much longer.'

'Don't do anything stupid.'

'Tell them to go.'

She waves her arm at the général who moves back a few more paces.

'They've gone, Daniel.' There is a silence. 'Daniel let's do this please.'

'Listen, I want you to do something for me. Tell Annalise for me. I want you to tell her when things started going badly for her, I should have been more supportive. I should have been behind her ... Tell her that.'

Annalise comes down the corridor. The général sees her and puts a finger to his lips, pointing at Léo's door.

'Tell her ... I want you to...I want you to say...tell her that I am ... I am sorry.'

Annalise steps forward. 'Yeah, okay I get it Daniel. Listen we went out for about a week. Now open this door now. NOW goddammit. NOW.' There is a short silence followed by the sound of the lock turning. Impressed by Annalise's capacity to resolve the standoff so quickly the général jumps forward to hold the door open for her. He follows her inside. They find Léo sitting in his old director's chair wearing his usual resigned expression. Daniel stands alongside him pointing a gun at his head. Annalise marches over to Daniel.

'Give me that you fool.'

Daniel jumps behind Léo's chair, putting the gun to his own head.

'Put that down. You're not shooting yourself.'

Sighing, Martin steps forward and places the gun on the table. 'I've been under a lot of stress.'

'You're not the only one. I have a deadline tonight. I haven't written a word.'

The général takes the gun.

'Where the hell is Inspector Marc when I need him.'

STARING SOUTH FROM LARRY'S BALCONY Ivan sees his boat's lights flickering on and off at its mooring. Phoning a trusted crewmember out of the boat to check if all's well and getting no response Ivan immediately phones his boat for transport. Preparing to abandon Larry's pre-awards cocktail party, he tells everyone he is sorry but he just has to leave. Something has come up suddenly. Knowing he can't show any obvious concern now, he grins around at everyone, saying he'll be back soon. 'I promise.'

'He needs to change into a new tuxedo.'

Ivan laughs heartily at the joke.

'What is more important than the dressing up for the final night.'

'Here, take this just in case.' Larry hands Ivan one of the special invitations he has prepared for everyone. The guests watch the Russian head out into the hallway and then from above watch him walking down the street, giving each other knowing looks. 'He's maintaining a Kremlinesque silence.'

Using his binoculars, Larry studies Ivan's speed-walking technique heading off towards the old port.

Down in the street where Larry's binoculars are focused, Ivan's mind is in complete disarray. Walking, mentally calculating the cash he has in several currencies, passports and other secrets he keeps out on his boat, he is so absorbed by all this he heads right by the road to the wharf, finding himself suddenly at Pizza corner.

Furious with himself Ivan rushes back the way he came. What he has stashed out in the bay in lucre and weapons and Bella's loaded cargo is more important than any social impression Larry's guests might be conjuring up about him. But still Ivan hopes he seemed light-hearted enough to have convinced them there wasn't any problem. Glancing anxiously out into the bay he sees the lights on his boat go out again.

Jostling his way through the evening crowd, he arrives at the pick-up point on the wharf and drenched in sweat he sees someone he doesn't recognize at the runabout's wheel. It doesn't improve his mood.

On the verge of losing his temper, he stares down at a Russian version of Mike Tyson at the wheel of the twin-outboard tender, pinching the bridge of his nose between his eyes, trying to avoid any public meltdown.

'Who are you?'

'Vlad.'

'Vlad, why don't I know you?'

Vlad shrugs. 'I'm Vlad. From the engine room.'

Ivan has met all the crew. He doesn't recall any Vlad in the engine room. 'Why haven't I met you?'

Vlad stands shrugging back at Ivan, a placid expression on his face.

'You're Vlad the Impaler, right?'

The man grins, hearing the nickname he's probably had thrown at him all his life. Ivan hesitates, silently debating what to do.

'Where's Federico?'

Vlad shrugs. 'He's busy boss.'

'Busy doing what? I want Federico on duty when I need him on duty.'

Vlad slaps the wheel. 'Well, I'm here boss. We going?'

Ivan hesitates then clambers down into the tender telling himself to focus. He needs to concentrate his mind on the lighting out on the Soraya. Cursing himself silently, Ivan wonders whether he should call Ulyana but he will have to speak about Vlad in front of Vlad. The who's who question about this crewmember has to wait.

Motioning to Vlad to get moving, Ivan grabs a centre-bar

with two hands, his arms getting straight quick as Vlad ups the throttle.

Forced to hold on tight, the tender's speed is soon up over the old port's limit. The wind already hard in Ivan's face, his sweat is now dry.

Ivan studies a white launch secured at a long finger end of the wharf, a French flag on the stern, remembering what Viktor said about the port being alive with intelligence operatives. Hiding in plain sight.

'Great,' Ivan mutters.

The big white boat could be the floating headquarters of a mobster, or some CEO's lifestyle choice wrapped in a tax dodge, or some sort of louche mobster's heirloom, an ill-gotten gain, a borrow, a rent, a pre-inheritance meant to impress girlfriends, dull-witted tourists—a boat idiots mistake for real money. Instead, it's most probably as Viktor said, a cover for French agents. Ivan counts the communications bubble apparatuses on top. Even more than on his own boat.

Shivering, he tells himself again to focus. This is France, their country. They can do as they want with whatever boat at whatever mooring.

He smiles for the first time and signals back to Vlad to speed up, with engine-room Vlad accelerating so fast Ivan is thrown off his feet. Falling-over again getting back up, Ivan stabilizes himself on the wood-slat flooring, glaring back at the crewmember he really needs to get a CV handle on. Vlad's every move spells menace and with his hand on the wheel, the other on the throttle, he has all the power out here.

Silently cursing the situation, Ivan with his hands hard on the bar, stares straight ahead, keeping his expression out of Vlad's eyeline.

The last thing Ivan needs is Vlad thinking Ivan's panicking.

Splintering the runabout out through three fishing boats at anchor, Vlad bounces the light tender into a cross-chop blowing-up out in the bay, Ivan having to hang on with all his strength now, silently rehearsing the choice words he will use when he next sees Federico.

Ivan weathers the port exit like the Russian he is, has always been, a man from the steppes. In America Ivan would be a rodeo bronco icon, a grin welded tight to his mouth, daily surviving the anger of raging bulls.

Further out in the bay as the chop gets worse and going at this speed, Ivan has trouble focusing anything. Is his boat still at its mooring? Are the lights back on? Ivan pulls out his binoculars and trains them one-handed on his boat. The postcard picture of the vessel is welcome—even if he can't see it that well. Bouncing around as he is, everything looks as it did when he last left it.

Did he over-react, come out too soon? He almost tells Vlad to ease off some, but then he sees figures moving about all over the decks. Looking again, Ivan decides it's not gently bobbing up and down at anchor, it's heading out.

Swinging around Ivan yells at Vlad to accelerate more, Vlad winding up to full bore, throwing Ivan off his feet again, nearly clean out of the runabout this time.

Somehow Ivan manages to clamber back up to his feet, fuel-soiled and wet, he re-takes the centre rail bar yelling: 'I said accelerate, not flat out.'

Vlad grins. 'That isn't flat out. THIS IS.'

Vlad winds the tender up to its top speed and they leap the choppy swells like flying fish on amphetamines.

'SLOW DOWN FOR CHRISSAKES.'

A SECOND LIMO BRINGS SEMOLINA and as she exits into the open air clad in a coat, with Edgar, her escort for the night close by her side, she looks extremely nervous. From his position halfway up the stairs Larry's writer sympathizes. As Death's best chance in the award-spree for this year this moment must be daunting, especially with the vote so wide-open. Everyone and anyone is pretty-well in with a chance tonight, so there's no shame in a moment of panic, Larry's writer wants to call out.

'No false steps tonight, Semi,' he whispers.

He can see by her grave face she's probably lugging the hopes of a film that deserves few in the eyes of many and could well mean a downturn for the careers of her producer and director. To carry that on her shoulders it has to be tough on a neophyte star. And as she begins walking the carpet, appearing in the next Renault is Francis Ford Coppola, a man of past glories, yes, but still a big star of cinéma nonetheless, and that only adds to the pressure on Semolina, so new as she is to the game.

Still Larry's writer doesn't place any of that at the feet of Francis C. He can only stare with admiration as the hero of the Godfathers manhandles his considerable bulk out of a Limo. Is Coppola's position now the backseat of cultural power? How does he now see his place in film? If he can see anything right now with all the camera flashing and exploding going on around him.

Most so-called greats of cinéma lose their lustre over time, some faster than others, only somehow this seems not to be quite as true for Francis Ford Coppola. He has to be today's most relevant older director and look who is with him, Jean-Luc Godard. Where did he turn up from? You couldn't make this up. Two of the best from France and America standing and smiling arm in arm together for the cameras. The past is prologue for Francis and Jean-Luc, the two cinematic greats showing a remarkable respect for the future as they quietly wait their turn, watching Semolina scaling the bâtiment's red-carpeted north face.

Without so much as a backward glance, Semolina ignores the directors of The Godfather, Apocalypse Now, The Conversation, The Outsiders, Rumble Fish, Breathless, Contempt, Bande à part, Pierrot le Fou, Une Femme est une Femme and Vivre Sa Vie to name just a few of their collective achievements. Seeing her stare almost maniacally at her escort, Larry's writer is wondering if in the thick present of awards night the young star isn't completely overwhelmed.

Awards nights can have a petrifying effect on the young and new, and Semi who is both now looks even more nervous than she did a minute ago.

Closing in on his position, Larry's writer is almost beside himself with anxiety for her. Semolina gulps in the night air, a pure distilled fear in her face.

Larry's writer feels like leaping the barrier and taking her hand, helping her up the stairs, her expression telling him just how determined you have to be to make it and take it in this game.

Semi's arrived, this is her night, her road to perdition or pure stardom paved by Death. Larry's writer is crossing his fingers now. If he could, he would cross his toes.

'Walk with style,' he murmurs, 'you deserve this.'

With her ingénuité and astonishing beauty Semolina seems powered by an inner light, her nerves making her even more mesmerizing.

A young actress in her prime with Francis Ford Coppola in her wake, her gleaming eyes seeming to be saying it's now or never. It is, Larry's writer almost yells. IT IS. This chance will never come again.

The uncertainty, the glamour, Semi must know she's right at her pinnacle tonight. And it's not the outfit because the beige trench coat isn't doing her any justice. Larry's writer wants to call out: Bask in the glory. It's you that counts. Nothing else matters. How long does anyone have to shine? How many chances do we ever really have to seize our destiny? 'This is your moment, Semi,' he calls out. She doesn't hear him. Occupy every square millimetre of your power under the lights, Larry's writer wants to add and then finally manages to shout again: 'Tonight, the whole spectrum is yours.'

With so many photographers from so many countries firing their flash guns her way, instead of enjoying herself Semolina seems to be holding her breath.

Then off comes the trench coat, and Larry's writer nearly falls over. For a moment there's nothing but unadulterated nothingness all around her. No sound.

What the hell is she wearing? A bodystocking? Should he salute? Gliding shoeless on the carpet to the tune of a zillion orbiting spheres above her head, cameras respectfully whirring in unison at her, Semolina Pynes is as bone naked as she is in the shower.

FROM HER POSITION twenty feet higher Cindy Turper believes Semi will now take some beating for best actor in the female category. On this performance alone, on the back of another's vision, because the self-reveal looks to Cindy like a canny reworking of Prêt-à-porter. Edgar's female lead has just fluttered herself close to the edge of mythic status on the red carpet.

Her escort, a man whose name everyone has forgotten or never knew in the first place and probably never will, at least not for his part in Semi's performance tonight, bends down and retrieves the coat, his probably, Cindy imagines, as well as anyone can under these circumstances, carrying the crumpled damp thing as he follows the star.

Cindy sees Francis and Jean-Luc winking at each other, wondering what either or both are thinking right now?

Silhouetted by a jungle of flashes Semi is radiant, her face not grave anymore suddenly, like, dammit I've done it! I'm etched into history. If Cindy were Semi, she'd be replaying this part of the tape tonight over and over, perhaps over dubbing Alec Guinness' words from Bridge on the River Kwai: 'What have I done?' With: I did it.

Semolina isn't collapsing on any explosives plunger or getting herself stabbed. She is climbing the red stairs nude in spikes as if she does this every other day, her escort catching her up at the doors, wrapping her up in that damp cloth, the pair leaning in to share a word. Were they in one mind on this? More power to them if they were, some reporters near Cindy yelling out to Coppola and Godard for their reactions.

'Everyone needs re-invention,' Francis yells back.

'And fatal beauty,' adds Jean-Luc. The moment over, two iconic old film guys from two continents link arms and locked into an upstair climb, photographers calling, ARRÊTEZ UN INSTANT S'IL VOUS PLAÎT, they head for the bâtiment's entrance. If Semi didn't steal their old breaths away, nothing will. 'Brilliant, if a touch chaste,' Cindy will write, as if she were making a comment on Amazon. On timing, personal courage alone, five big stars in a row.

THE SORAYA SWINGS EAST with Ivan deciding to drop any more objections to Vlad's assumed captaincy, giving him the thumbs-up to winding-up to flat-out, Ivan holding on to the centre bar in a straight-armed grip using more mental strength to remain that way than he's used in the whole week in Renne so far.

'WHO'S OUT THERE?'

'CREWMEMBERS.'

'I know that,' Ivan hisses. 'WHICH ONES?'

He knows Vlad is not the right person to ask anything but as he's the only crewmember on board the runabout, who else can Ivan ask? He was hoping the Soraya was moving away to re-anchor but that's all garbage-out right now. His boat is leaving, where to, who knows? With thieves everywhere, owning a big boat these days means nothing. Even with his high-tech defences and mostly loyal crew apparently it isn't enough to stop the techno-head thieves out and about. Ivan knows what he's talking about. He's done a bit of techno-head-thieving in his time. He knows the scene, many aggrieved owners' faces coming to mind. The people Ivan's robbed in his career, which karma is accounting for right now, is enough to place him on Interpol's most wanted list, if they knew of him which they don't. Still, Ivan's not giving up, thief or no thief, on feeling mightily aggrieved.

'GET CLOSER.'

'OK.'

'STAY FIFTY METERS BACK.'

'OK.'

In the count-down to this new world reality he's found himself in, one where floating apartment blocks get hijacked early evening even on the low seas, Ivan finds himself getting furiouser and furiouser with the situation.

C'est complètement fou. And Vlad's grin isn't helping. Ivan should have known about Vlad and who he really is.

It might not help Ivan much in the current situation, but if he were steely-eyed Pierce Brosnan on this tender right now, Ivan would be hard at giving Vlad the best of an artistic comeuppance.

Pulling out the sacred device from his satchel Ivan extends its small aerial with his teeth. He doesn't want to use it. He is aiming it in the air out in front of himself as he imagines James Bond would do, all without an oiled strand of hair out of place.

Ivan gets his boat in his device's sights, and searching for the tiny prized laser signal bouncing around under this darkening sky, Ivan is close to getting a fix on his big boat's bouncing future.

It's choppy, the moment is maddening. Ah, contact made, only the light that should be green is not a colour he can recognise. It's like threading a needle on a roller coaster, the light flickering red, orange, anything but what it should be.

'SLOW DOWN.' When nothing happens Ivan glances back and gives Vlad his best Brosnan: You might have the wheel but I'm in charge here glare.

Vlad gets the message. The tender slows-up. With one bouncing Brosnan eye on the Soraya's progress, binoculars nearby, clutching the iron rail in the crook of an elbow, Ivan knows when he's in trouble.

When the launch turns seaward, seeming to increase its speed rounding the point at Port Mipento, Ivan swings around letting go with one elbow crook to yell: 'HAS IT SEEN US?'

He promptly falls over, seeing in between bounces, Vlad shrugging. A shrugging Vlad is all Ivan needs right now.

'CATCH-UP THEN STAY BEHIND FIFTY METERS.'

Vlad obeys immediately for once, speeding up because he likes speeding up. Dropping his spyglasses into a tray in front of him Ivan manages to get out his mobile. With his boat motoring further away he keys in a number just as Vlad decides to up the throttle again a notch more, Ivan losing the cell from his grip, the phone bouncing once then twice then out into the bay. Seeing Vlad's grinning face Ivan glares Brosnan-like again at his driver. Vlad smiles.

Ivan has a glare spare and he uses it. Again, Vlad smiles. They are fifty to sixty meters behind the launch which is already up to what looks like its own full throttle.

'There's only one chance now,' Ivan pointlessly yells, adding louder: 'IT'S GETTING AWAY.' Vlad indicates he can't go any faster.

His biceps aching now from all his hanging on, the twin-outboards flying the tender over larger chop, Ivan bends trying to get the arcane device working, but with the tender bouncing around, coupled to the fact he only has one spare arm, the green light coming and going ever-so briefly, first it's red—amber—green—then amber again. There's no purple. What the hell? What is wrong with technology today? Ivan pulls out a spare phone. Always have a spare.

Managing to press a call with his small finger at the end of his spare aching arm he hears what he thinks is a voice saying hello, and yells: 'It's heading out RIGHT NOW.'

Then the call goes dead. Did he get through? Was it a wrong number? Bouncing like he's on a roller coaster inside a merry-go-round Ivan switches devices again and somehow manages to set up the sacred signal. Then the tender hits cross-chop or swell or a wave or even a rock the bashing so hard now Ivan again loses his footing, the device this time slipping from his hand, and he helplessly watches it bouncing down to the back of the tender.

Vlad doesn't move. Crawling crab-like back to where it's wedged under a board Ivan sees Vlad moving from his end. He beats Ivan to it. Picking the phone up and passing it back to Ivan, the driverless flat-out runabout hits more chop, nearly flipping, as Ivan sees the light change red to green. He'll swear black and blue he never saw any purple.

WAITING ON HER TERRACE for her transport to arrive, the limo ferrying her to the bâtiment for the festival's grand finale, Madame Maire stares at the dark sea wondering what crisis awaits her in the wings with tonight's winners.

Lifting her head to drain another flute of champagne she thinks of F and his crazy sidekick. She's never met anyone like Voor. In a blink of an eye, the earth's lower atmosphere all-around her explodes, going up with such power the flute flies from her hand and smashes onto her terracotta tiles.

'WHAT IN THE HELL WAS THAT?'

When something flies right by her head and crashes through her lounge room window demolishing her brand-new widescreen wall television set she's ready to strangle the guy who did this. The maire of Renne has met too many crumby festival officials, seen too many fireworks displays, to be fooled by this one. Fireworks are never this brilliant and never so short. So, what goes up in the bay and comes down flying through her window? If she paid anything for this she wants the money back. All of it. What blew up in nanoseconds, died in milliseconds. Her heart thumping, the Maire of Renne treads light-headed on her crackly terrace. Blinking in fury she stares up at the sky. 'The son of a bitch!'

Manuel Barrosi's laugh fills his garden all the way to the fence overlooking Golfe Géri. He and his maid just saw the sky go every colour under the sun then billow black. He stands waiting for more. 'That's it?'

When nothing more happens he takes a deep breath and summarizes what he just saw in his even-toned reassuring voice: 'A boat rounded the peninsular and headed over towards Pointe d'Anglacés, then went BOOM....'

Something thudding in the grass about two metres away stops him. Walking over to it, Barrosi stares down at a metal block embedded in the grass. Bending down for a closer look, he sees what would make an interesting tile in any swimming pool. Standing again and speaking slowly he asks his personal maid of twenty-five years: 'What's yellow, oblong, twenty-five centimetres long, with four hundred Troy ounces stamped on its face?'

Vermillia screams and runs up the slope. 'I'll call the police.'

'STOP.'

She swings around, her chest heaving, two shocked-eyes trained on her employer.

'What should I do then?'

'Bring some good champagne and two glasses.'

She nods as if this makes perfect sense, wading up the rest of the lawn onto the patio before disappearing inside the mansion.

Turning back to the strange night visitor, something else in the yellow brick now gets Barrosi's attention. Struggling back down into a squatting position he looks intently at several small cracks in its face.

THE SKY LIGHTING UP in shimmering variables of red, blue and yellow up and down the coast, boatloads of witnesses begin thinking and speaking in several languages. When everything in the sky goes black again, one man begins telling his friends that only a large meteor could do this.

'Then it just landed on a Renne beach,' his wife says.

A lone sailor, his senses in pharmaceutical overload claims into an answering machine he saw an x-rayed image of a giant human in the sky for two minutes. Staggering around on his deck he yells that God is attacking the earth, as molded decking, teak interiors, metal engine parts bits and pieces, together with chunks of hull begin hurtling back down all around him.

At the speed of a failing light bulb, pieces of Ivan's former boat return from hundreds, perhaps thousands of feet up in the air, with large pieces of the Soraya finding a new home on even larger pieces of real estate from Pointe d'Anglacés to Renne La Bouche.

Reports of direct hits circulate on social media, one lone radio-announcer claiming the skies over Renne are playing host to a rogue asteroid from a rogue galaxy far, far away.

The sky has certainly rained debris, broken windows, carved divots and destroyed rooves and coming from wherever it has exhibited an awesome display of destructive power.

Hosting a dinner for Viktor and Elena out on the back of the Sunshine Coast, Merryl, Jack and guests hear a splash only feet from their table. The hostess draining her glass promises to go down for a closer look a.s.a.p.

All four stare at each other for about a minute digesting the event, before Viktor stands up, saying he sees shadows of Prague everywhere, Merryl murmuring, it's spring too.

'Is Ivan's boat up in smoke?' Jack says finally.

'Is he dead?'

Pacing the deck, Viktor taps his mobile's screen. There's no answer. Running inside Merryl switches on the boat's radio and they sit in muted silence listening to garbled reports of sightings and goings-on coming in from all directions.

Objects landed on beaches. Things went through decks. A gold brick splashed in a hotel pool. A family of six received a shiny brick visitor through their ceiling, the bowl of steaming seafood soup on the table distributing second degree burns. Miraculously nobody is blind. And there are no reported deaths. One brick apparently missed a drunk by millimetres. Guests returning to Hôtel Grande Pointe d'Anglacés heard something hit their helicopter, the object 'pinging the undercarriage,' the pilot explained over the intercom. Near-death experiences pile-up electronically, morphing into shouts across balconies, in an expanding narrative of shock and awe. Nobody is yet able to say what is true or not, or who did what to whom, or why or how so many might have been in the kill or injury zone. One self-styled reporter, desperate to be first, emails his account from an old desktop computer, headlined: Skies Rain Porn Gold.

Realtime a savage debate starts up online, one stunned caller in Golfe Géri phoning a talk radio show host to swear he saw the skeleton of a man out on the Soraya shine gold in a charcoal sky for two solid minutes. Sceptics pout and cynics laugh as callers swear on their mothers' graves as to what they are sure they saw. One very well-lubricated journalist on a barstool goes one better than all, explaining that a recently towed-in dead dwarf-star, being used for an inner-space disaster movie, has unfortunately just blown itself to bits.

ONLY BELLA DRIVING in her SUV isn't taken in by any of
the palava she's hearing. Pulling over she listens to crashing
sounds all around her, something heavy landing in a nearby
restaurant resulting in loud shouts and screams. She knows
what it means. How could she not? Pointe d'Anglacés is
raining her gold. She sits in her rental, her mobile up against
her ear. It won't protect her. Neither will her steel-plated
SUV. It can take a hit but not from a gold brick flying at the
speed it must be going at. Finally, she gets through. 'What
the hell are you doing in Marseilles?'

Switching off, she throws her phone on the passenger's
seat side. 'He said he was going to Golfe Géri.'

Wheeling her SUV right around she drives like the
clappers the way she had come in the first place, pushing her
SUV to the limits of its brochure description as she careers
down a darkened Péage, turning off finally into empty
streets, sirens sounding in the distance.

It's not long before she turns into the Sables drive-way.
Applying the brakes, scattering a doorman who dives into
a bush. Leaving her door wide-open she throws her keys
at his upturned shape still tangled up in green, yelling:
'PARK.' Flying through the lobby, barrelling across what
now seems like acres of marble flooring, she scatters guests
in all directions yelling: 'CLEAR THE BLOODY LIFT.'

TUCKED INSIDE A TUXEDO for the night, Larry shifts his
heft faster than he ever has done in his middle-ages. Dabbing
sweat from his forehead he pants his way along a hallway
one floor below Bella's rooftop, breathing: 'it is time to get
back in the gym.' A moment later Bella emerges from the
floor-to-floor-people-carrier yelling expletives with a clarity

he hasn't heard in ages. Pushing him aside she sprints the length of the hallway and bangs on a door, 'JEFF! OPEN-UP!'

Opening up, her startled manager stands in his underwear staring back at his boss, then at Larry, Bella saying between her ragged breaths: 'We ...have ...a problem.'

Bella barges inside pushing Jeff aside. 'HAS ANYONE BEEN IN HERE OTHER THAN YOU?'

Jeff looks at her then at Larry. 'Except you, no.'

'Everything's here then?'

'I think so.'

'Larry you're my witness.' Through gritted-teeth Bella whispers at her manager. 'Have you checked the vault?'

'The cupboard? No. Why should I?'

Following Jeff and Bella into Jeff's bedroom Larry watches her throw open a door muttering about her secret stuff. She bends down, checking the seals and markings on each of the five metal boxes left.

'I have been robbed,' she yells. 'Ten trunks are missing.'

Larry has seen first time auditioning teenagers give more convincing performances.

'Larry, you are my witness.'

'To what exactly?'

STUNNED BY THE EXPLOSION Léo's face cuts off any discussion of whether it was, sabotage, an accident, or whatever. He doesn't want to hear any more on possible conspiracies. Léo only wants to hear ideas on how to get the guests back inside the Grand Théâtre. When Franck suggests the bâtiment's security officers use loud hailers in the streets to call everyone back in, Léo nods his thanks.

'Will you take care of that?'

Unable to refuse to help out on his own suggestion, Franck tells Léo he will. Once out in the forecourt, he stands watching bâtiment security yell at guests to 'COME BACK INSIDE,' a loudspeaker above their heads adding, 'Mesdames et Messieurs la cérémonie commencera au Grand Théâtre en quinze minutes.'

Given the curiosity over what went down out in the bay the disruption is over remarkably fast, guests filing back inside the Grand Théâtre, showing their support for Léo. Many of them discover their seats occupied by others. No-one shows any anger. Everyone is content to sit where he or she can, on the floor if needs be. An atmosphere of stunned acceptance now reigns everywhere, the notables sitting with the hoi polloi, the famous with the unknowns, everyone smiling blankly at each other.

Three rows behind Semolina, Cindy is keeping close tabs on everybody. She has a good view of Francis Ford Coppola sitting alongside Jean-Luc Godard, the two men still like old buddies, someone nearby whispering that a man in a wheelchair is being brought in. Cindy turns to see a figure in a hat and sunglasses, accompanied by the Japanese artist leaning on a stick, hobbling by his side, the pair she thought were dead, coming down the aisle. She writes: Does this signify the rebirth of cinéma in Renne? A tired looking Léo slowly walks out tieless in a rumpled smoking jacket and receives a rowdy reception.

'Bon soir. Bienvenue. Benvenuti. Wilkommen. Welcome everyone. I'm so glad and grateful to be with you here on this extraordinary night.' It sounds a bit boilerplate but he's trying, Cindy making a note that no mention is made of the recent disruptive explosion, Léo raising his hands as he says: 'Tonight is cinématical history lessoning.'

Faces around Cindy are too much in shock to question any grammatical glitches in his English, Léo's welcome, inspiring a collective sigh of relief spreading throughout the auditorium, as if the whole audience was just knocked unconscious and is just coming around, cameras feeding people's faces in the Grand Théâtre to a big screen behind Léo's head. The Cinéma de la Plage, Truffaut and Godard cinémas are shown now too, Léo waving wanly out at the many cheering audiences.

'We are alive. Bon soir tous. What do we look like?' he asks.

Shouts in the main auditorium are matched by those outside. 'Tonight is about us.'

'YES,' people yell back in several languages, Léo waving to all spots in all cinémas, rocking on his heels, laughing as best he can, clearly wanting to show that he is grateful for the audiences severally giving their support to him.

'I will dispense with niceties and all formalities and get down to tin tacks.'

MC or clown, Cindy can't decide, it's too much, a woman close by yelling: 'VOUS ÊTES FRANÇAIS. PARLEZ FRANCAIS. S'IL VOUS PLAÎT.'

'Madame, I am speaking to the world. La France will understand if I use English as the lingua franca for this occasion.'

His use of English idiom, tin tacks, brings shrugs and acceptance of the language of the old enemy across the channel. The effect of the woman's comment extends itself when she shouts: 'La France is wiser than l'Angleterre,' ironic smiles from many guests showing that most want to shut down divisiveness: 'Non, rien de tout ça ce soir.' A culturally-inclusive mood quickly gains the upper-hand with Léo also closing down more disagreement: 'There is enough history in France to be generous over language tonight. This event shows films from many places in many languages.'

'OUI, YES, SÍ' sounds around Cindy. The majority in the still shell-shocked audience is solidly with Léo.

'There will be no cultural xenophobia here tonight.'

Nodding heads and a few cheers indicate Léo's on the right track.

'My sincere thanks first to the jury for stepping aside. It is a pleasure to see you all here, sharing the cultural spirit of this annual event which outweighs any attempt to shut it down. This is a celebration of film democracy tonight.'

'OUI, YES, SÍ. SPEAK LEO SPEAK.'

He smiles out the 'LET LEO SPEAK. LET LEO SPEAK' soon becoming a mantra spreading throughout the theatre. 'LET LEO SPEAK. LET LEO SPEAK.' Léo puts his hands up and finally gets the clapping, shouting and foot-stomping to stop. 'I am grateful for your support.'

'I love you' a woman's voice rings out.

'Never too late to hear that, madame.'

Shouts of OUI, SI, JA, YES and DA are shouted out to him. People cheer and applaud loudly, the clapping dying down only as Léo continues speaking.

'I am of course Léo Stern this festival's returned director and glad to be.'

Le Grand Théâtre erupts into wild cheering and it goes on until at his fifth try Léo manages to cut it off briefly. Smiling, he holds up his hands giving up only when cheering and clapping refuses to stop, going on and on until it turns into a regimented foot stamping in all cinemas.

Cindy imagines people stamping their feet down at

the open air Cinéma de la Plage as well, wishing she had managed to have a better interview with him, hoping he will remember their agreement for a proper sit-down affair with him later. She hasn't much time to do it, with Léo fast closing in on megastar status.

'Mesdames et messieurs I am so happy experiencing your goodwill here and now. This is a time for everyone involved in the whole process of cinéma to congratulate yourselves. We need positive support of cinema and you have given it.'

There is another very long round of applause.

'This is truly wonderful because tonight I get to renew a very old ideal, Democracy. A secret democratic ballot has been held with all awards chosen by you. My idea was always to open up the whole process this year. We are all winners tonight.' There is another burst of applause.

'The audiences attending the films have made their choices and without holding you in suspense any longer, I want to announce the selections the voters have made. First I must say how I am indebted to the Mairie and the volunteers who did the counting. La société des scrutateurs who have done a marvellous job to make sure the voting process has been fair.'

Yells of OUI SI and YES from the audience drown him out, followed by cheers and not only in the main auditorium, outside as well. Cindy's sure she can hear the crowd watching the big screen in the street, or is she only imagining the thunderous applause is drifting in from all the cinémas.

'I won't hold you up any longer.' Léo pauses, then says: 'So on to the awards.' He looks off-stage waiting, then moves a few steps towards the side curtains.

'Just a minute. The results have been in the process of being collated. It should only be a moment.' Léo stares off into the wings. His assistant runs back on stage to whisper in his ear for some moments, Léo looking at the floor, nodding as she speaks. Waving at the audience he says: 'I will be back in half of one minute.'

Watching him walk off stage murmuring starts-up, voices growing steadily louder the longer he is away. When one minute becomes two, then five, conversations soon begin everywhere, guests standing up and heading over to friends and colleagues seated elsewhere, with many speaking and waving their arms about. Groups form in aisles, below the stage, congregate at the back making comments like: 'Should we be surprised? Democracy is never easy. Come on, let's not be critical. It's remarkable as it is. As it was, as it was.'

Cindy grows more worried every few minutes that passes by, the next few minutes only seeming longer than the minutes before. After fifteen, or is it thirty minutes, Léo finally reappears, walking back on stage with his head down, the silence in the audience showing just how much they know what he will say.

'I am afraid I have bad news.'

This announcement is greeted by stony silence. Then after a moment a voice yells: 'IT'S OKAY LEO. WE CAN WAIT.'

People applaud. 'YES. YES. HOWEVER LONG.'

The last man's voice, spoken in English, clearly not his mother tongue, breaks the gloom. People smile encouragingly at each other applauding and saying 'oui' a sensation of relief growing which turns into more shouts of support. 'OUI. YES.' People yell out words of support and clap their agreement.

'What's happened is that the machines collating the voting slips have broken down. I thought we had it under control but apparently there has been a problem over the last few hours I didn't know about. We are going to do the count manually.'

The announcement stuns everyone, followed by several 'mon dieus.' At first a stoic acceptance maintains itself in the audience until everyone properly digests the news.

'How long will this take?' a white-haired woman shouts, 'I have rebooked my flight for tomorrow. Recounting will take days, isn't that true?'

Léo nods and sighs. 'You are right. Two days at least, madame.' Deep dismay spreads throughout the audience. 'I will make calls to the main hotels. I hope they will agree that if people booked out you can all go back in and stay on.'

'WILL WE HAVE TO PAY?'

'We will begin negotiating right now.'

'WE HAVE FLIGHTS BOOKED.'

Léo raises his hands. 'We will call all the airlines and enlist help from hotels. As far as it is possible, we'll make this as easy as possible. We will try for everyone.'

'BUT WHO IS GOING TO PAY?'

Léo holds his hands up against the avalanche of protests.

'I realize that this will not help you all but please bear with me on this. We will hold the awards ceremony two nights from now at the same time. Thank you. I must get to work.'

He hurries off stage to exclamations of growing distress and anger now. After all the build-up, the disappointment is real, the anguish is deep. A few just sit and laugh. Others shake their heads. Many guests are just so stunned they can't say anything. One woman sits alone quietly crying. Some throw up their hands. People get up, standing in groups debating, voices calling out to each other across the auditorium. 'IT HAD TO BE LIKE THIS.'

'WHY?'

'DEMOCRACY NEVER WORKS IN A CULTURAL EVENT LIKE THIS.'

'YES, IT DOES.'

'THIS IS ONLY A LOGISTICAL PROBLEM.'

'A LOGISTICAL NIGHTMARE YOU MEAN.'

'DO NOT LOSE HOPE,' someone yells. Only, way too many have lost hope already. And for the next half-hour many in distress wander around aimlessly, ushers running around telling all they must leave.

Finally, the last of the disenchanted drift out through the foyer doors continuing to discuss how disappointed they are and just how hopeless festival-life is right now. Conversations like this continue on the outside steps, then in the forecourt—so many people walking through the streets arguing.

Cindy tries asking them what their greatest fear or bone of contention is, Léo, the organisation of democracy, or democracy itself, but most guests are far too disillusioned to give her anything that is quotable.

She does find one man who is willing to express himself, Cindy now getting the news she's wondering whether she can believe or not.

Apparently, during Léo's speech, a team of thieves broke into a jewellery shop on the waterfront. Climbing through a broken window they emptied display cases stealing a unique Louise Duv collection of rings, necklaces and earrings worth hundreds of thousands of euros. The volume of the TV in the police station was so loud, officers glued to Léo's speech never heard the shop's relayed alarm sounding out in the police station's front office. Cindy laughs, not knowing if the man is joking or not.

Late news reports also described an incident in the Porte de Marseille near the Terminaux de croisières. A man wanted for questioning and fitting circulated descriptions was spotted by plain-clothes officers who were checking boarding passengers on a cruise ship. The général and some gendarmes helicoptered over to confront the man.

The général and the crack-force gendarmes in three unmarked cars chased the fugitive along the waterfront road for eight kilometres at break-neck speed until he screeched to a halt at Gare de Marseille Saint-Charles, where the officers chased him with the hip-damaged général some ways behind trying to catch up.

Confronting the desperado, they had no other option but to draw their weapons in self-protection.

The man later described as a Dutch national of Russian origin fired indiscriminately until he succumbed to a volley of return fire, several bullets severely wounding his upper body and lower legs.

With street lights out in towns, urban and central city areas all over the country, the président appears suddenly live on late night television to present a second national address to the nation in as many weeks.

Delivered from his official residence the address had an ad hoc feel, especially as the président focused on the subject of insurrection in the south. With so many southerners, as with practically everyone else all over the country, being for the most part asleep, the président wasn't speaking to the south but to some particular off-shore territories that would be waking up, territories often associated with harbouring extremist views. What the président had in mind wasn't at all clear at first but that he was sending an important message seemed obvious to those who saw the address. Was he speaking to friends and allies in off-shore pockets of political resistance he hadn't yet conquered at the ballot box? Was this about his own political survival or someone else's demise?

Then the président grew poetic mid-address singling out an explosion on a luxury boat in the south, describing the event as a grievous crime.

The lateness of the delivery and the thrust of its meaning had some keen observers of politics searching the internet. Sure enough, it was discovered that F had once lived both in the south and in an offshore territory. Were members of the idle taxless in other time zones and overseas territories receiving a warning?

For a président to deliver an emergency address to the nation was highly unusual in itself, but at this late hour it was unheard of, the président finishing with: 'Those responsible for this crime when found and charged and convicted will face the full penalty of the law as it stands.'

Going on to mention that new legislation for criminals of this kind was also being prepared as he spoke.

Day 11

Sitting out in the sun on Elena's balcony the morning after the failed final night, an argument broke out between Ivan and Viktor in Russian over the meaning of the présidential address. Morphing into a more local discussion regarding the vote in Renne, the voices grew louder and louder, with Elena beginning to wonder what her neighbours were thinking, and whether the cops would be called pretty soon.

Viktor continued asking, almost shouting at times, why doesn't anybody know what is going to happen after all this, and what does this all mean to a restoration of order, and what are the Russians in Renne going do when it's all done.

'It is only a film festival, Viktor.'

'Rubbish!'

Their conversation is brought to a halt by a loud-hailer making an announcement from a vehicle in the street outside Elena's apartment: 'Hear Ye, Hear Ye, Hear Ye, News from the Mairie. Results will be released at the bâtiment very soon.'

Unnerved by everything he's experienced in recent days Viktor is quickest to his feet shouting out, 'Что за херня! Russian elections were never like this.'

A wide-eyed Elena agrees. The time is certainly as strange as she's ever witnessed even if she hasn't experienced a Russian election in her life. 'But I'm sure it'll be sorted out.'

'Elena, you always think everything will work itself out.'

'You have to be positive.'

'Go,' Ivan says. The recovering guest in Elena's second

guestroom at the back of her Belle Époque apartment twirls
his cane in the sun listening to Viktor and Elena rushing
about dressing themselves, before heading off and leaving
the door wide open. Viktor comes back and slams it shut,
their voices echoing down the stairs as Ivan sits soaking up
the morning sun thinking again of his miraculous escape.

'I dived in before the explosion? Or was I blown out of the
runabout after it happened? It can't be both.'

He recalls feeling like he was paralysed, mesmerised by a
collection of misty lights shimmer-jiggling on the horizon as
he tried to get his muscles to work again, two wooden legs
that had forgotten how to make sense of movement. Ivan
smiles at how frightened he was, thinking he was actually
taking his last breaths. His clothes so tight all over him, he
kept praying that someone would arrive. The pain in the
right side of his neck was excruciating. He can feel it now.
His right arm was loose, warm liquid exiting near his mouth.

'Somebody help me,' he croaks again, then laughs looking
out from Elena's balcony to see if any one heard him.

Swallowing seawater, his calves cramping, what it took to
get what was left of his brain power to pass simple messages
to stricken parts of his body was extraordinary. His knees
wouldn't answer. His ankles were stone deaf. His hips and
chest muscles were throwing fits. He tried yelling at them. It
didn't work. Ivan moans again in anger at the fear and pain
he experienced. Who did this to him? He has to find out.
Seeing what he was sure was the ultimate predator coming
at him again, the thin shape turning into an aerial, Ivan is
almost as delirious as he was then, proof to him that he
was truly hallucinating at the time, certainly when a yellow
submarine surfaced, and a hatch opened. He thought what's
next, The Beatles!

'Boss, we saw you on the periscope.' The voice of the man Ivan forgot, the man who took a shark in the head for his boss. Seeing Federico's face again Ivan's guilt rises in his throat. Did he deserve such good karma? The throb is back in his neck, pain reappearing throughout his body. Croaking the line again: 'Get me out, Fred' he actually sees the ethereal figure of Federico sliding into the water, Ivan moaning: Is it you?

'That's enough,' Ivan says. Only, he can't forget.

DEEP INSIDE THE CROWD milling around outside the bâtiment Cindy stands alongside several journalists listening to Annalise recount some recent troubles in Marseille, with Cindy piecing together a narrative from what she's hearing going like this: Twenty gendarmes under the command of the général arrived in time to shut down a stand-off with two fugitives from justice who were apprehended on a Marseille Saint-Charles train platform and taken in by police after an altercation including pistol fire, with a conductor taking a bullet in the hip. Travellers scattered in all directions when gendarmes started firing back in order to stop a crazy Dutchman before he shot anyone else, Cindy hearing a woman whisper to a man by her side, 'What crazy Dutchman?'

Annalise goes on to recount how the rogue black-ops led by security agent code-named F, acting on his own orders, have done a deal with police, a man next to Annalise asking how she knows all this.

'I got it from a good source.'

'The général?'

'Close.'

'Let's count our lucky stars he arrived in time.'

Murmurs of agreement spread together with expressions of thanks for the général's existence.

'Is this all about the cultural revolution people are talking about?'

'What revolution?' another voice asks.

REACHING THE PROMENADE Viktor and Elena join the crowd circulating with varying degrees of purpose and displays of reason outside the bâtiment's entrance. Sidling into a position not far from the edge of the red carpet, a puffed-out Viktor, with a heavy-breathing Elena close behind, hear the words 'what revolution' spoken in the crowd.

Determined to get as close as he can get to the action, Viktor pushes through several bystanders, Elena hurrying after him, catching-up in time to hear him whisper that there are hardcore-types everywhere.

'Viktor, not everyone is a hardcore type,' she says, her French far too good to be misinterpreted.

Reddening visibly, Viktor stands grinning rigidly, accepting her rebuke, pretending people are not turning his way, staring off into the far distance with twitching eyes. Desperate to change the subject, he points at a face watching from a high-up window, half-yelling: 'Look, it's the returned director, Léo whatshisface.'

'At least the director knows what is happening now. That's good isn't it?'

'It doesn't look good to me,' Viktor whispers back.

'Stop seeing Prague everywhere.'

Elena falls silent as people turn to stare at her now as well as Viktor's crimson face. Viktor can barely breathe he's so angry, but he knows when it's time to argue with Elena in a public place and when it's not. Standing with his stock-standard fixed grin he uses in moments like these, everything is at a complete standstill, his two eyes staring with unusual intensity up at a young man who has appeared suddenly at a microphone.

'This'll be trouble, big trouble,' he can't help but whisper.

'Viktor, how do you know? He's just standing there.'

'You will see,' he can't help himself whispering back.

'Mesdames et messieurs, I want to congratulate everyone. You brought changes. Changes we all know were needed. It's a victory for all.'

'Thank god for amplified microphones,' Viktor mutters, the blood having drained so fast from his face Elena wonders if he's now going to faint.

'Viktor, you're very pale.'

Viktor's fixed smile reappears on his face as if painted there.

'WHERE IS LEO?' a voice yells.

The young man at the microphone raises his hands. 'This democracy movement has changed history profoundly.'

'WHERE'S LEO?'

'YEAH, WHERE'S LEO?'

CINDY CAN HEAR THE ANGER IN VOICES all around her, wondering whether the people nearby also haven't a clue who the speaker is. Looking lost when his microphone stops working the young man stands trying for a moment to speak without it, but he can't make himself heard.

'WHAT HAPPENED TO THE ARMY?' a man yells.

'The mafia hitmen, you mean,' someone says.

'Has anyone read the riot act?' says another voice. This gets people laughing and more jokes start up on what the neophyte at the microphone is up to, some men deciding to find out. They climb towards him, the kid nervously backing up a few steps as the men close in on him. Going backwards faster, he turns quickly and nearly trips over his feet running to the top.

Dashing flat-out he makes it to the doors and inside the bâtiment just in time for security officers to lock the doors behind him and place a table against the glass. The chasing men gesture through the door but don't do anything else, grinning as they saunter back down the bâtiment steps to cheers from the crowd.

Cindy watches all the laughing, handshaking, fist-bumping, as the returning steps-climbers greet each other, executing male chest bumping and hugging rituals.

She has no clue what's going on and won't dare ask anybody. She still doesn't know who it was at the microphone or what he really wanted to say. Looking around it seems to her as if all the cops have vanished. There isn't one left in the street. Hearing Annalise speak again to journalists by her side, saying a deal must have been made, Cindy gets closer, hearing: 'I am going to find out.'

Annalise climbs the stairs with Cindy and others close behind their esteemed senior colleague. Arriving at the locked doors first, though it was a close-run race for a moment, Cindy nearly overtaking a panting Annalise, Annalise bangs on the glass with her fist.

'JE VOUDRAIS PARLER AVEC LE DIRECTEUR.'

A security man wags a finger: 'On est fermé.'

'POURRIEZ-VOUS LE DEMANDER VENIR ICI PARLER AVEC NOUS.'

The man shakes his head, turning away.

'Jesus, we are in the dark again. So much for Glasnost.'

Annalise stares up at the sky. 'It's going to rain soon as well.'

'Maybe we can call Léo,' Cindy offers.

'Good luck,' Annalise says. 'He's not answering his phone. We haven't even heard who the winners are yet.' Annalise throws up her hands. 'This is what everyone wanted, democracy.'

This annoys Cindy who turns away, not wanting to get into a heated argument with the doyenne of the local press corps on a subject close to her heart. It's certainly a bit rich of Annalise, considering the big show in support of democracy she turned on when Léo first came back. And she encouraged Cindy to go on board the infected sloop without saying what she knew. Cindy doesn't much trust Annalise anymore.

Choosing the old city seemed like good cover for Franck and even Marie to discuss personal matters that had gotten out of hand, so when he suggested that they walk up to a spot called Place Mantille, abandoning the idea of a coffee in a café where people might listen in, on the morning after the day of the prizes night, Franck saying, nobody needs to be recognized, especially not a cop, Marie accepted the idea without giving it a second thought.

They walked the streets of the old quarter until Franck found the square. Standing close to an old wall covered in creepers it seemed to both of them a safe enough out of the way location to have a discussion. And as long as they were quiet, who would or could bother them at this still reasonably early hour? But before they were even three minutes into their pow-wow, a woman appeared at a second floor window right above them yelling they should go somewhere else do their drug deal.

'Drug deal?' Franck said. 'We're only talking.'

The woman glared at Marie. 'She your floozy.'

Before either Franck or Marie could respond, the woman disappeared, coming back holding what looked like an antique rifle. She pointed it at them demanding to know why they were still there.

'It's a free country.'

'Is she your whore?'

Franck and Marie stared open-mouthed at the woman, Franck telling her to mind her own business. It was a bit tame but with a rifle pointed his way he wasn't keen to get the woman anymore riled than she already looked. Then she took aim and fired at them. She wasn't such a bad shot. Franck grabbed Marie in time before the woman got off a second shot, coming so fast it had to be some sort of automatic, the pair just getting out of her line of sight in time. Flattening themselves together in the front door ingress right under the woman's window in the two-story early 20th century apartment building, they wondered what to do.

'Jesus, that was close, Franck.'

Telling a still very frightened Marie to wait where she was, Franck went in through the street door and climbed the stairs to the first floor. He could hear the woman speaking loudly so he didn't have to decide which apartment she was in. Was she still at the window trying to get a shot off at Marie? Taking out his browning, he knocked on the door. 'OPEN UP.' He didn't say, police.

The woman came to the door lugging her gun. He could see what it was now. A Fusil Automatique Modele 1917. Franck knew the gun. Gas-operated, semi-automatic rifle placed into service by the French Army during the latter part of World War I.

Grabbing the barrel with his free hand Franck yanked the gun out of her hands. She screamed but still managed to fire it. And she didn't miss him by all that much this time. Franck dropped the rifle with a clatter on the wooden boards of the entry hall and pointed his browning at the woman's head, backing her up, and who was sitting in there, not saying a word at a kitchen table—F.

Calling for back-up, it wasn't long before a car with the général's men arrived. The woman, F's aunt as she turned out to be, said she was protecting her nephew in a house where little F grew up.

People in surrounding apartments stood in the street, several nodding knowingly, not particularly sympathetically either, as they watched the gendarmes march F and his sobbing aunt down through the cobbled streets, taking them on foot through the now heavily-trafficked tourist quarter, getting plenty of startled looks, the gendarmes placing the pair in the back of a police vehicle, and driving both off to the local lockup.

Meanwhile Franck and Marie went on foot to join the général in Leo's office, nodding their thanks at the clapping crowd.

'You stirred up a hornet's nest. Going to be in the damn newspapers tomorrow. All we need, more bad press.'

'The woman fired at us, what was I supposed to do? Stand there and get shot. She nearly hit us both.'

'You pull your gun on every person who points a gun at you?'

Franck stared at Léo wondering if he was joking. 'Generally, yes, and if you had been in my position you would have too. I know plenty who would have blown her head off after what she did but I don't fire if I don't have to. I didn't have to, so I didn't. But she fired twice, no three times at us, and I didn't fire once.'

'How did you know where F once lived?'

'I checked it out online, général.'

Marie stood studying Franck saying nothing as he recounted all this.

'The day we were in F's headquarters with all those soldiers I picked up some matches off the big table, one of those light flip flap kind of matches. Mantille was scribbled inside. I put his name and that name into a search. His aunt came up. Maybe he wrote it down unconsciously. He lived with her aged ten to fifteen.'

'He might have wanted to burn her place down.'

'The woman thought we were drug dealers.'

Léo laughs hard. 'Where is this again? I work in this town every year and I don't know where anything is.'

'A small square just below the old Church, off a street that comes through the old city. There's a wall on one side a tree with big branches and leaves. We were standing there.'

'Amazing you found it.'

'Yes, wasn't it,' says Marie.

There's a knock at Léo's door. 'No interruptions.' The knock happens harder.

'YES.'

A security officer opens up. 'Sorry to bother you, monsieur directeur, this young lady was trying to force her way inside the building at the back. She insisted she has an interview with you.'

'Who is it?'

Cindy pokes her head around the door and throws Léo a rueful look. 'You promised me.' She stares around the room. 'Am I interrupting something?'

'Come on in. You know the général?'

Cindy smiles warmly. He returns the smile. 'This is the Inspector Franck Marc. Hero of the moment.'

Franck throws the général a look as he shakes hands with Cindy.

'We met that day at F's mini-barracks.'

'How could I forget.'

'My wife, Marie.'

'I saw you at the demonstration.' Cindy shakes her hand, then hugs her.

'Cindy was extraordinary during the demonstration,' says the général putting his arm on her shoulder, 'It was like she had been doing this her whole life.'

THE COUNTING DONE the scrutineers are satisfied. Junior staff are sent out on foot, Zeena relishing walking from hôtel to hôtel yelling, 'Hear ye, hear ye, the awards will be presented on the red carpet in three hours. Be there or be square.' The last phrase was her idea. Nobody she meets is complaining. Almost everyone is over the moon there is now a result even if doubt lingers in many minds, especially the older festival attendees still in town, who keep on saying: 'until I hear it from Léo's lips I'm not believing a thing. Not a thing.' Some people are too disillusioned to listen to any news anymore and are up in their rooms with headphones on, the volume up full, packing their bags. Still, Zeena walks around, saying to anyone who will listen that winners have been decided, walking into bars and hotels, Cindy right behind her witnessing Zeena's discomfort when people raise their voices, shouting: 'This one is part of the corruption that's been withholding the disinformation all along.' Still for all the cynicism, heading back to the press room, Cindy finds the bâtiment forecourt overflowing again with streets full of happy people waiting to hear the news.

Collecting at the barriers several photographers tuck into their usual positions, their faces staring up at the bank of microphones at the top of the steps. TV cameras are everywhere, with word on a result finally being at hand spreading fast. 'A nobody won the main prize.' 'Which nobody?' someone asks. 'Why have winners at all?' says another. 'Why can't there be winners?' another voice snaps. 'This is a complete farce. All this angst about winners.' 'Without winners, life is a circus.' 'With winners it's not?'

Most people standing around have no energy for arguing the toss anymore, saying the big names will hoover it all up as always anyway. Pockets of people nod their heads as if welded into a group that can't debate the increasingly pointless points anymore.

For the most part people just stand around quietly realizing nobody knows a goddamn thing anyway. The best kept secret in town is still the best kept secret in town. Annalise knows nothing. Cindy knows nothing. The journalists in bars know nothing. Apart from the nobody who won and the rumour the usual know-everythings are spreading—the concierges, drivers, photographers, security men, festival insiders admit they know nothing too. Even Léo says he knows nothing.

'He is saying that because he has to say that. Léo chooses the counters. The counters choose the winner.'

'What else is new?'

'At least there was a vote.'

A new thread of argument starts-up on the hopelessness of change in any cultural setting and this spreads like a grassfire in high summer, nobody adding any insights to what Léo knows or doesn't know or wants to know or could know. 'He knows what he has to do.'

'Let's hope so.'

'He delivered democracy. Who could do that, if not Léo? The corporations?'

'The corporations manage Hollywood. Hollywood manages democracy.'

'You're always criticizing Hollywood.'

'Hollywood is a corporate rehearsal for irreality. Without Hollywood, life on film could be meaningful.'

'You should hear yourself.'

'What irreality are we talking about?'

Conversations like this continue circulating as the afternoon breeze strengthens, the waiting crowd getting more restless by the half-minute, voices lifting, dying, rising and falling like the gliding birds above their heads. When somebody says he'll kick the bucket in this street if he doesn't hear soon, Cindy realises she could fall over in the street any minute herself. Then, Léo and a small team of extras appear in a sudden burst of sunlight, cheers erupting everywhere as clouds miraculously suddenly drift south.

Waving at everyone as he taps the microphone, Léo asks if he's on. He is told by many that he is.

'So, this is it,' he says, 'what we have and you have been waiting for. First, I need to thank all those who have worked so hard to get it done.'

A groan ripples through the crowd. 'Not another speech. Tell me I'm dreaming.'

'TELL US,' a man shouts.

'I won't keep you in suspense, I promise. But I want to thank you all for being here. I must say that I don't know anything of these results. So, I am as excited as you. The counters have been sleeping in the voting room watching the ballot boxes.'

'Really? Is that the honest truth? Watching each other?' one man shouts.

'I heard they slept in shifts.'

'With each other.'

'Shut up.'

'You shut up.'

'With no electronic voting it meant the count was arduous. So, a round of applause for the counting staff and scrutineers.'

Applause happens, but without too much enthusiasm.

'COME ON. TELL US. NO MORE WAITING. PLEASE.'

Handclapping starts up and down the street and right in front of the steps, rising then dying and rising again as Léo hesitates. Staring down at the awards sheet he seems suddenly tense, aware perhaps, Cindy is thinking, of his responsibility being the messenger here today.

How will the crowd respond to: Best film. Best actress. Best actor. Best director. Léo's special award. And the special write-in award, where voters chose their own candidate to win. The People's Choice. How will they, it, all be received?

SQUINTING UP AT THE IMAGES on her widescreen wall TV Bella bites her lip. The meeting with Larry, her French lawyer, and her legal team online back home in Sydney, is really getting on her nerves. 'It doesn't matter what an insurer thinks in London. They are insurance people and they have to handle it, okay.'

'You've been told that?'

'Yes.'

'Madame, my experience of English insurers ...'

'Don't start with this Brexit and insurance crap across the channel thing. We know you all hate each other.'

'Madame please, it's not about Brexit, this is simply business.'

'Insurance business, which we all know is a scam.'

There is a silence. 'Madam, that's a word I would forget if I were you.'

'Larry, if this were your boat, or your gold, would you accept this?'

'For the boat, maybe, Ivan has a case. Not you. Your cargo, no. Bella, you can't claim you were guarding the stuff when you didn't have it under your control.'

'It was under Ivan's control.'

'He agreed to that?'

'Yes.'

'You have that in writing.'

'It was a verbal, but people heard him say it and saw it all go on board.'

'Who Bella?'

'Lots of people. Crewmembers on board for starters.'

'Who are all vapour in the ether now?'

'They were seen in binoculars. I saw them.'

'What, going up in bits, or coming down as humidity.'

'Damn it, I saw them.'

'Who else saw them in what binoculars?'

'Lots of people.'

'Do you have a photo with a written-up sound bubble by their heads, saying: what Bella Fibben is saying is all true?'

'Ivan's my witness.'

'Ivan who is up to his ears in his own claim.'

'Someone else must be alive who heard him say it.'

'Say what?'

'I'm looking after Bella's gold, which I checked brick by brick. Even if they didn't hear him say it, how can they deny it? My word against theirs.'

'Bella...I think...And then there's the tungsten in the blocks?'

'It was policy, 99% tungsten was in some bricks.'

'Which ones?'

'Some.'

'Bella if it looks like a con, it is a con.'

'Bullshit, Larry, this is my business and I carry it out as I want.'

'That's the case you are taking to court?'

'Come on Sydney, say something for godsakes. Don't just sit there in your chairs halfway around the world. I am paying you.' The lawyers sit mute side by side in their Sydney office half-grinning.

'London will put two and two together and say all the bricks were phony.'

'Larry, whose side are you on?'

'All they have to do is find one brick.'

'There aren't any to find.'

'You can't be serious.'

'If you found a gold brick would you hand it in?'

Bella turns back to the screen and seeing Léo with a sheet in his hand turns up the volume again.

'And that concludes this announcement. Thank you again for your patience.'

Léo takes off his glasses and walks back to the top of the stairs and heads inside, leaving a stony silence in the street.

'Damn it, Larry, now I've missed the winners. I wanted to hear that.'

'*You* turned it down.'

Inside Bar des Poissons the usual suspects leap to their feet shouting in unison: 'NOOO.' Charlotte grabs Charles.

'A WRITE-IN WON!'

Bernard laughing down at the back yells, 'I told you this would happen.'

'Rubbish you told us, Bernard. When did you say it?'

'I said, Expect the Unexpected, Charles.'

'Thus spaketh Bernard Zarathustra after the event.'

Le Cigaro's film correspondent sits by a dismantled plastic mock-up model launch staring mournfully at the barman. 'Drinks, Michel. Very strong and very tall.'

'It's democracy Charles.'

'Shut up Bernard.'

'It's great.'

'How's it great?'

'The voters were alienated. The festival got what it asked for. That is democracy speaking. It's great.'

'Alienated from what?'

'Alienated from money, power, marchers, themselves? How the hell do I know? Maybe they felt sorry for the Russians.'

'Exactly, that's what communists do, Bernard. They feel sorry for each other.'

'Are you kidding me Charles? The Russian's boat blew up after everybody had voted. Maybe they thought Dzerzhinsky got a raw deal.'

'Well, did he, Bernard?' Le Cigaro's reporter takes off his glasses, rests his head in his hands. 'I'm finished. Why did I write that? I sent my story an hour too early.'

'Don't fret, Charles. It always was going to be like this.'

'Charlotte, nothing was going to be like anything.'

'It's the weight of circumstances. Like Tolstoy said. It had to be like this.'

'You an expert on Tolstoy too, Bernard. I bet a thousand euros on Death.' Charles rubs his eyes, shivers and sneezes.

'Didn't you hear that the kids hate Linsteeg?'

'Bernard, they made him their hero.'

'They woke up and realized they were being manipulated and rebelled.'

'You sent yours off before you heard?'

'I know, Charlotte, I thought, God, I have never done this before.'

'What did you write?'

'Death was the protest kids' choice for the Poisson.'

'You actually wrote that, Charles? Which festival were you at?'

'Okay, what did you say then? Have you sent yours off?'

'I sent my piece off twenty minutes ago. After I heard.'

'Incredible that Dirt Wars won best director.'

'Shut up Bernard. So, what did you write then?'

'Death couldn't win in the end. I was right, except for the nudist show.'

'I didn't pick the write-in. Damn, I'm finished.'

'Okay, even if you're finished, there's always next year, Charles.'

DIRT WARS IS THE GRAND POISSON WINNER says the man on TV—From Homer to Shakespeare to Sartre writers set out to tell 'the truth.' A reclusive Russian writer-director Sergei Berebanov wins the main prize, a man who never turns-up at festivals or promotes his films. Described by his French publicist as more than a little influenced by everything, filmmaker Sergei Berebanov is prepared to die in the process of bringing truth to the screen. Yet Dirt Wars is a fantasy set in the Russian snow from a Russian filmmaker who somehow forgot history. Can we trust his portrait of Napoléon? If we are Russian. The film is in the first-person, the writer-director setting out to deceive us, trying to convince us that by using the first-person throughout that we are closer to reality, that his main character is telling his truth, transferring any doubt over the facts to the filmgoing audience..'.

Pointing the remote, Edgar switches off.

'I was watching that.'

'David Hardon wouldn't know Napoléon from his own raggedy arse.'

'You don't like Hardon because he gave you a bad review. And you didn't win. So, you're jealous.' Semolina stares at Edgar. 'Hardon gives everyone bad reviews anyway. So he said, you took extreme liberties with the original novel. That's what all filmakers do.'

Edgar won't even look at her now. 'He said I was so egotistical to do that with a famous writer's novel.'

Marie and Ulyana sitting on the other side of the room smile grimly not saying a thing.

'Anyway I'm really pleased for you, Semi. You deserve a Poisson. I am pleased for us. I am pleased I directed you so well. We won something.'

'*I* won something, you mean.'

'You won, Semi. Happy now?'

'Did you hear the comment, complex handling of the most difficult role ever attempted.'

'I won't get another job.'

'Edgar, you'll get plenty of jobs.'

'Ivan wants you to do his film.'

'If it happens, Ully. Now I have to show my face out there. I'll be eaten alive.'

'Don't worry what people think.'

'An action movie wins The Grand Poisson in Renne. Can you believe that? A write-in won three awards. I didn't see that coming.'

'Nobody did.'

'Is Bruce even in town?'

TWO DAYS LATER

SEAGULLS CALL TO EACH OTHER in a stiff breeze, the sun hitting Elena flush in her face, her hair blowing everywhere as she leans over her balcony studying her courtyard.

'Viktor what on earth is that man doing down there? Is he making that damn car?'

'I doubt he's trying to make a 1959 Peugeot 403 Cabriolet,' a voice behind her says quietly.

'Oh, you are an expert on cars now, Ivan?'

Grinning from a directors' chair near the balcony double doors Ivan turns his knees to let her push by him.

'You should be in bed.'

'I like a place in the sun.'

Elena goes into her kitchen and comes back with a chocolate cake, putting it down on the edge of a laden table with a thud. 'Viktor, there's no room for anything.'

'Then leave all of it in the kitchen.'

'Shut up, Ivan. VIKTOR.'

'WHAT?'

'I need more to drink.'

'You're not the only one.'

Elena stares around her sitting-room. 'Can't I even have my own things? Edgar, you're a director. Direct this man to remove his furniture.'

'Most people would be happy having my antiques in their home.'

'Yes, they're yours Ivan not mine.'

The front door swings open and Larry walks inside.

'Well, Bella is held up.'

'Expect the worst and it happens. No news is good news.'

Ivan waves his cane saying: 'I have never understood this no news is good news. Is it, hearing no news is good news, or no news is ever good news?'

A light tap sounds at the open door followed by a voice. 'Bonjour à tous.'

Zeena Zatters, Semolina and a woman in black almost dance inside, Semolina throwing out her arms. 'Mesdames et messieurs les trois mortiqueers.'

Edgar goes down on one knee: 'Semi, Semi it is you—really you.'

Viktor heads over to the table and picks up a bottle of champagne, stripping the foil off the cork. 'Let's make a toast to La belle du Cinéma.'

With Viktor pouring glasses Ivan studies Larry. 'You look pale.'

'Democracy, it's nothing but a lottery.'

'Democracy... nobody's talking about anything else.'

'In Russia there's no such thing,' Elena says from the kitchen.

Ivan ignores her. 'Have you heard something, Larry?'

Elena brings another cake, telling everyone to make some space for her on the table.

'For you or the cake?'

'Viktor, stop it. You have been mean to me all morning and you're not helping me at all. Neither are you lot. Standing around with long faces, moaning about democracy. What's the news?'

'Léo's been betrayed by his love of democracy.'

'Who betrayed him Larry? A Russian film that wasn't anyone's choice has won best director, best actor and best screenwriter? So what.'

'It won on a write-in.'

'Which is democracy writ large. Good choice.'

'It's populism.'

'Funny democracy throwing up the very thing no-one wants.'

'I don't see anything funny in that, Elena.'

'Then get the jury back.'

'You'd prefer a dictate by a committee?'

'The count is finished. Now people are saying the count is phoney.'

'Which count is phoney? Viktor don't open any bottles until everyone is here.'

'Elena, will you relax. She's worried that her soirée won't turn out well.'

'And Viktor is unhappy because Sergei Berebanov won so many prizes.'

'Sergei Berebanov's film only won three awards.'

'Only three, that's all.'

'Wasn't Bruce great as Napoléon?'

'He was gloomy.'

'He played Napoléon in Russia. How could he not be gloomy?'

'He was being ironic.'

'Don't start on political irony, pleeeaaase. Viktor is unhappy because a Russian director he doesn't like won best director.'

'Elena, I respect the vote.'

'Sure. Mr KGB respects the vote.'

'I am ex-KGB.'

'You know what they say.'

A WEATHER WORN 2012 model 208 GTI Peugeot with the général at the wheel pulls up below Elena's apartment block on Rue des Nations-Unies. Idling the motor, the général looks over at the entrance to her building, seeing a girl standing by the door holding a bag. Switching off, he speaks rapidly to Franck beside him. 'Laisse ta ligne ouverte, d'accord?'

'Si elle essaie de courir, que dois-je faire?'

The général gives him a look from under his brow, then glances back at Bella in the back of the two-door sedan. Switching back to English, the général says quietly: 'I'll go and warn them.'

'Warn them about what? I have official legal immunity. On two counts. I am a billionaire and I am a foreigner.'

'You're helping with our inquiries, madame, you're not under arrest.'

'Then let me speak to my lawyer.'

'Under French law I can hold you garde à vue for twenty-four hours.'

'24 hours? I'm not eating prison food.'

'I am holding you only until a magistrate decides.'

Ignoring any further complaints now, the général climbs out of the car and walks across the road as briskly as his bad hip will allow him.

'Don't hitch yourself to that bitter old fuck. He doesn't know who he's dealing with. I'm not just any foreigner.'

Franck sighs and says nothing.

'You don't need to do this.'

Franck asks her in rapid French if she would like to be interviewed formally.

'I don't speak French.'

'Then I can't help you, madame.'

'There's something in this for you if you keep your mind open.'

'What does that mean?'

'You're a smart guy.'

THE SHARP KNOCK AT HER DOOR startles Elena. Wiping her hands down her dress she sidles over to it. Looking like a cat in a strange place she touches her hair and slowly opens the door. She comes back very relieved, the général walking behind her.

'Look what the cat dragged.'

The général raises himself to his full height, nodding around at everyone. 'I can't stay. We have Ms Fibben downstairs.'

Hearing this, everyone in the room crowds around him asking questions, all except the recently arrived M-iki and Ivan, who sit quietly conversing, Ivan tapping his cane, M-iki's injured leg stretched across the floor.

'She under arrest?'

The général shakes his head at Semolina.

'Where was she found?'

'At the airport.'

'Getting on a plane?'

'Waiting for her Dreamliner to fly back in. I should say her rented Dreamliner.'

A few knowing ah-hahs are expressed in unison.

'Inspector Marc traced her out there via a good contact who also heard there had been a shooting at the Marseille Saint Charles train station.'

'That's a roundabout way of finding out isn't it?'

The général looks over at Ivan. 'Intelligence is intelligence.'

'Anyone dead, général?'

The général flashes Viktor what looks like a victory smile.

'Two injured. Nobody dead. Another stroke of luck because after Franck caught F redhanded he's been singing like a canary.'

Elena looks confused. 'Who sang like a canary?'

'Keep up.'

'Ivan I will have you and your furniture out of here if you speak to me like that.' She touches her hair. 'You should have killed them both, général.'

'Which both?'

The général's smile drops into a professional grimace.

'We don't carry out extra-judicial murder in this country.'

Ivan eyes the général. 'What was F's sidekick doing in Marseille?'

'We don't know. He's unconscious.'

'We think F intended to meet up with Madame Fibben after his Dutch fix-it mechanic tried to abduct him and drag him in the opposite direction. It seems F wanted me dead.'

This news inspires several intakes of breath.

'How do you know that.'

'Piece of paper found in the fix-it's pocket.'

'Are you charging him?'

'F?'

'The Dutch guy.'

'Yes, and F, if he told him to do it.'

'F really wanted to murder you, général?'

'Voor will probably say he was ordered to do it, if we get to question him.'

'Are you going to torture him?'

'Madam, we don't torture people in this country.'

Ivan winks at Viktor, the général catching him do it.

'You can count on that under my command.'

'How did you catch the Dutch guy?'

'An Alerte d'urgence was out for them. A team of gendarmes were waiting on the platform. Voor saw them and went berserk. The gendarmes shot him in a leg.'

'Then in the chest for good measure?'

'That part I don't know.'

'Meanwhile F is in the local lock-up flashing his get-out-of-jail pass,' says Ivan.

'Is he trying to talk his way out of all this?'

'We briefed the local officers. They are hearing him out.'

The général looks around at all faces staring back at him.

'The good news is there's enough evidence to put F away for a long time.'

'Would have saved a lot of people a lot of bother if his mechanic had shot him.'

The général eyes Ivan again.

'Why did he want you dead?'

The général places a hand on Elena's shoulder.

'That doesn't matter now, madame. And luckily, F wouldn't pay Voor extra for the job.'

Ivan smiles. 'Do you think this will get as far as F going to jail?'

'Well, as God is my witness, we will try, monsieur.'

'Good luck with God on it, général,' Ivan says quietly. 'What about Bella?'

The général sighs. 'Madame Fibben is a more complicated problem.'

'Something to do with her being a billionaire?'

'What are you suggesting?'

'Glass of champagne, général.'

'I could do with one or three.'

'She give you trouble.'

'We found her at the far end of Biènville airport cursing workers, yelling, Where's my pline? They didn't know what a pline is. They barely understand English, let alone her version of it. As it turned out Ms Fibben doesn't even own the dreamliner.'

'And she accused me of not owning the Soraya.'

'The bad news is she can probably still afford some good French legal assistance.'

'So she's not broke then? Then she can pay for my boat. I imagine you are not charging her for that.'

The général frowns at Ivan again letting out a breath, staring around the room at all the faces staring back at him.

'At the moment that's a matter for the insurers. I don't know the story of that explosion, but I can say some of what I do know now about her background. Due to mismanagement back in her country, false accounting, call it what you will, I am reliably informed that Ms Fibben is in a tax hole for some billions. When Larry asked her to help fund a film company she jumped at the idea.'

'Civil matter.'

'Could be criminal.'

Larry frowns seeing his writer scribbling down notes.

'Général, do you think she needed something new in her life?'

'What, you a writer or a psychologist?'

Larry's writer grins apologetically at his boss.

'Bella told us some interesting things.'

'Such as?'

'F had a spy on Ivan's boat.'

Ivan eyes the général. 'Did F admit he put someone out there?'

'He is yet to be questioned on it, or any issue, but word is he had someone out there. With F's help Bella allegedly set out to load your boat with gold which someone allegedly set out to sink in an explosion.'

'I thought as much.'

'You have insurance?'

'A claim is being made.'

There is some tut-tutting and grave expressions of dismay hearing all this, Larry looking so shocked he can't find any words at first. 'You can prove all this?'

'Proof is a big word in criminal matters.'

Everyone looks at Ivan, seeing real anger in his face for the first time at the party.

'It was some guy called Vlad. And Vlad's probably dead is all I know. If he survived the explosion, then he drowned. I don't think he even made it into the water.'

'Oh dear.'

'For godsakes don't mourn Vlad, Elena.'

Seeing her delightful soirée morph into a wake for Vlad after the général's depressing story and Ivan's aggressive comments Elena grabs a plate of pastries and begins passing them around.

'Please everyone, EAT. Viktor, more full glasses please.'

Going around with two plates, Elena smiles fixedly at everyone, saying: 'Homemade Russian delicacies. Ptichie Moloko special Birds' Milk first cake patent Soviet Union made by Vladimir Guralnik, a legend in his own dessert. Chief sweets maker in a Prague restaurant. Muscovites love them like the French love marshmallows. This gingerbread is from ancient Egypt, in Russia for nine centuries. A legend from Rurik and Oleg of Novgorod joining East Slavic and Finno-Ugric tribes to form one country. Please try, better with a glass of wine. VIKTOR! More vodka. If you like stronger. More cakes in the kitchen. Lots to drink, plenty of bottles over there on the table. Everyone enjoy! More in the oven, plenty more coming soon.'

Elena makes another face at Viktor who picks up two bottles and begins filling glasses and handing them around.

'Why don't we invite Bella up here?'

The général frowns at Edgar's suggestion, then sees several heads nodding.

'You really want her in here? You sure?'

'Yes, invite her to the party with us. Let's meet her, see who she really is,' Elena says.

'We know who she is,' Merryl warns.

The général hesitates. 'I want no trouble. Are we agreed on that?' He looks around at everyone one by one.

'I'm informing you all Ms Fibben is only helping us with our inquiries. That is all. Are we agreed?'

With nodding all around, the général heads outside with his phone to his ear.

'He is bringing her up here now?'

'Brainstorming is healthy Semi.'

'You said that all throughout the shoot. Look what it got you.'

'It won us one prize at least.'

'I won me a prize.'

'My guess is the général is not averse to having an inspirational meeting right now.'

Semi screws up her eyes hearing Merryl say this.

'Inspirational? Like a prayer meeting?'

Before a smiling Merryl can answer, the général is back again leading Bella in through the door, Franck close behind them. Ivan greets Bella with a curt nod, smiling tightly under his brow.

'If the général remembers how to obey French law and lets me see my lawyer this can all be sorted out easily.'

'Like the deaths on my boat? Who's sorting them out?'

'I didn't blow anyone up. I flew here to save Larry's arse.'

'You think I want your money?'

'You did once.'

'If I had known the truth I wouldn't have asked.'

'Ah my money's not good enough for you now. It wasn't long ago you were on your effing knees with nobody on the horizon offering you a cent.'

'You're deluded.'

'If being a billionaire is being deluded I am happy to be deluded.'

'I thought she was broke.'

'If she has any money it belongs to my people.'

Bella narrows her eyes at Edgar. 'You going to start a Land Rights demonstration now?'

'You're wasting your time, général. Arrest the bitch now.'

'Semi, calm down.'

'Larry, for once in your feckless life, will you shut the fuck up. Général, arrest her now!'

The général holds up his hands.

'Nobody's getting arrested. I thought that was clear.'

'Général tell that tart to take off her clothes. At least this dull party will have her showing off her tits.'

'Bella you are one prize bitch.'

Elena nods her agreement.

'I might be a bitch but I know when to keep my clothes on.'

'With your body Bella it would be a crime not to.'

'Semi, STOP.'

'That woman is a fraud.'

Semolina picks up a cream-cake and throws it at Bella, missing her and hitting Ivan in the face. He takes it well enough, licking his lips and smiling, exclaiming: 'My, this is good.'

The général puts his arms up again trying to separate the parties. 'STAY CALM!'

'Viktor do something.'

'Anyone recording this?'

'Where is my camera?'

'Where you left it, Edgar.'

Ivan and M-iki are the only guests left at Elena's party who are remaining silent. With everyone else present so verbally animated by the sudden aggression between the women, the général stands in the middle of the room, his hands high up in the air, yelling now: 'BE CALM. STAY CALM.'

Guests rush the table to grab more cakes which they throw at Bella and then at each other, Bella managing to grab half a chocolate cake and crowning Semi with it.

Frowning at the chaos, Franck stands a moment and then wheels around and walks out through the front door, Marie following him, calling down the stairs. Franck doesn't look back. Marie watches him go, then shrugging comes back inside, heading over to the buffet table to choose a Bird's milk cake. Tasting it, she exclaims: 'This is heaven.'

With chocolate cake all over her, Semolina grabs a Bird's milk cake as well, and munching says loudly through a mouth full of crumbs: 'You're right, these ARE delicious.'

Madame Morendo walks over and takes the last slice of chocolate cake. 'Sugar will be the death of me.'

Everyone follows, grabbing at the sweets that are left on offer, pouring glasses of wine, all except Ivan and M-iki who watch everyone as if a play has suddenly begun, Ivan seeing

Chekhov, M-iki, shaking her head—'No, it's Kabuki.'

Merryl manages to find four cakes, bringing them over for Ivan , M-iki, Jack and herself. Everyone stands munching near the table, Semolina saying: 'These are so good.'

A broad grin returns to Elena's face. Her party so close to becoming a total disaster now has everyone happily eating and agreeing her choices are superb.

'I have more where this came from. Chak-chak from Turkey. Vatrushka and Syrniki. Pancakes if you want. I can make plenty in a jiffy.'

She runs out into the kitchen bringing back two more loaded plates, placing them down. In no time all these are gone, Elena running back into the kitchen for replacements.

Opening a bottle of champagne Viktor moves around filling glasses like the lithe twenty-year old expert waiter he once was. Bits of cake crumble from guests' lips. Hands grip glasses. Everyone tossing back their drinks, the party suddenly is a competition to see who can eat and drink the most and fall over last.

A huge bang echoing in the courtyard has guests screaming in unison, bringing the party to a sudden halt.

'VIKTOR THAT MAN HAS BLOWN UP HIS CAR.'

Viktor walks out on to the balcony, stares down into the courtyard. He comes back inside. 'It's nothing. Just an old car with an even older engine.' He grabs Elena's arm to stop her going out onto the balcony.

'OW!' Elena pulls herself away, rubbing her arm, wandering out into the kitchen massaging her elbow just above the joint, mumbling now about making honey pancakes.

Viktor takes Edgar by his arm now. 'I wanted to talk to you about your storyline.'

Lowering his voice, Viktor leans close as they get to the end of the room.

'You must take Marie away from here. What I wanted to say, her husband has shot himself.'

TEN MONTHS ON

Many critized Edgar for making a film of a troubled chaotic festival so soon after the inspector's incomprehensible demise, but when Marie weighed-in, giving her blessing to his project, one by one the voices of criticism disappeared.

The controversy is still taking a toll on the director who now feels he's carrying the torch for an idea he wasn't even sure he wanted any part in at the outset.

Some press was vicious, inspiring respected observers to speak up in Edgar's defence, important voices, some who said the critique of him and his film was a smokescreen created by friends of owners and major participants in the annual festival business who wanted to find a scapegoat for the troubles.

A way to forget the word democracy altogether, to get everyone back to remembering the historical precedent formed over time—privilege. Privilege that once ruled the film roost would again, the implicit and explicit message, some raucous right wingers joining in and blaming all and sundry for destroying the annual fun spring-time festival partying, and for what—damnable democracy?

Weighed down by Death's failure and hit hard by all this debate, even before he had even started shooting, Edgar began saying he couldn't go on.

Completion of the project was already turning into some kind of slow career-suicide pact. He had so many creative complications on his plate. The dysfunctionalities Renne experienced in its last year affected him far more than he imagined. He is not sleeping well, with a good ending to his film constantly eluding him. Still, with Ivan encouraging him, Edgar is managing to put his fears to one side and concentrate his mind on being the young lion of film that people always used to think of him as being, that guy with the voice trumpet turning up daily with a brave face in film locations all over Renne.

Ivan's battle to secure the finances is resolved, the necessary monies where they should be, where nobody can touch them except Ivan. He's not saying how he managed it, or where the budget is actually coming from, replying to anyone who asks—this film is going ahead like a bullet train. That's all you need to know.

Today, with some of the main cast shivering out in the open together with several technicians and extras on the end of Renne's main pier, everyone awaits Edgar's next command, who of late has taken to controlling his set with the iron-fist of an old studio director, prompting some to mutter—who does he think he is? Followed by the predictable—Edgar B. deMille?

Of course, it's all a front. Edgar's living in terror, with those around him, some of whom should know better, suggesting privately that the job has gone right to his head. Others, further out of hearing, whisper that he is too far out of his head to have a job to do in it anyway.

His story ideas alone have many wondering, what the hell is this? Where's the script? Is it fact or fiction, fantasy or reality, or just a crazy mix of all those things? Where's the plot? Nobody knows, even after a month of shooting. Most have simply given up on questioning the director's methods and motives for anything and started doing this some ways back. Let it lie where it lies has become the phrase of this shoot, coined first by the very soon to be officially ex-général, who is already looking like he might be one of the success stories of the project.

The set is run as a military affair, leakless to the press, after Ivan instituted an embargo on any information getting outside. Everyone on the film, if he or she wants to keep her or his job, is glued to his or her role, shooting day in and day out in a stiff winter breeze, enough to blow off a few hats.

So, on another windy, sunny, cold mid-February morning, the actor playing the still-mourned much-missed inspector is gazing seaward, concentrating on that life-changing moment in his soul, martialling the necessary emotions needed for a reasonably life-like portrayal of the still-difficult to uncover enigmatic character of the man. With his director unable to provide any real help in unravelling the real man under the interminable baggage of a reconstruction, bringing to the large-screen a real-life inspector in inner turmoil, driven to the brink by a career on the rocks, is taking a toll on the actor playing Franck as well.

Recreating an inspector beside himself, with all the misgivings over being in Renne at all, he hears another wave bash the pylons beneath him as he stands trying to recall his Chief's exact words, his mind leaping back to that departure point, the pivotal moment in the real Franck's historicity, indelibly linked as it is to a hammer blow of fate, the kill shot, that's still sending shockwaves up and down the spine of the actor playing Franck.

The actor's recreation of Franck's real-life struggles, duplicating a troubled reality in fiction, is a sudden slow-motion take-over of his thought-patterns, making him float in the stratosphere of simulation—repetitive pain as he imagines it—in the wake of a revolver hammer dropping.

The echoing courtyard scared the bejesus out of everyone at Elena's party, stopping everything on a dime, the mechanic closest to the action banging his head so hard on the inner side of the bonnet of the old Peugeot, he stood swearing like a trooper for a solid ten minutes.

Rocking on his heels, Franck's simulator whispers to himself to get back into character, that of a terminally uncommitted professional. Marie was dead right. From day one Franck was always psychologically unfit for the role he had in life.

'CUT. DON'T TURN AWAY FOR CHRISSAKES.'

Hearing footsteps, the actor playing Franck swings around, seeing only the général loping his way. With the shrug of a veteran he seems soon destined to be, the général comes up alongside his colleague, quietly advising the actor playing Franck to call on Konstantin Stanislavsky's showboat of tricks. 'School your deepest resources.'

The actor playing Franck grimaces his thanks at the général for another pep-talk as he spies Edgar having as much trouble climbing down from his crane rig as the général does traversing flat ground. Does Edgar B. deMille bringing the antique mega-whatever with him have a bad hip too?

'LET'S SEE THE WHOLE THING IN YOUR FACE. THIS IS CINÉMA.'

'I'm ten feet away. Do you need to use that?'

'We need to see more than the back of your head.'

'The back of my head means nothing? You ever see *Witness*? Book in the booth phoning his best friend and hearing he's been killed was the best shot in the film.'

'I hear you.'

'Do you?'

They stand sizing each other up like two end of career gunslingers in a quickly drawn-up B spaghetti western stand-off, Edgar examining the actor playing Franck's head wound in such an exaggerated way the actor imagines Edgar simply doesn't know what to say.

'That make-up girl really did a great job. You're Colombo meets Mantegna. Just don't mumble. Sound's complaining.'

This really gets the actor playing Franck frowning.

'People mumble to themselves all the time. Woody Allen did. It could be the général and me way down the pier in a wide-shot just like in *Annie Hall*. Remember that street shot?'

'Sound's complaining.'

'What's sound got to complain about. Pick it up with a gun mike. It's a great monologue.'

'It's not in the script.'

That script is practically three-day old carp, the actor playing Franck nearly says, but doesn't, not wanting to get into a stand-up fight. 'Well, it should be.'

'Ad-hoc monologues don't work, Franck.'

'I am not Franck. I'm an actor playing him. Anyway, monologues work well in Tarantino, and they work brilliantly in comedy.'

'This isn't a comedy.'

'Maybe it should be.'

'Film audiences don't buy into crazy.'

'What? Yes they do.'

Edgar stares a moment at the actor playing Franck before turning away and yelling into his trumpet thing, 'FIVE MINUTES EVERYONE. THEN SET UP FOR THE GENERAL AND INSPECTOR MARC ON THE BOAT. I DON'T WANT ANYONE GOING INTO THE WATER THIS TIME.'

The général hobbles over to glare at Edgar.

'That gangplank's faulty.'

'The Captain said there's nothing wrong with it. You get your ginger tea?'

'I don't swim until June. I go-in again like I did before I'll get arthritis in my hip.'

'ZEENA GET THE GENERAL A HOT GINGER TEA, PLENTY OF HONEY.'

'I'll be going to the bathroom all the time.'

'You can use the boat's loo. I spoke with the captain.'

'I can't be out in this wind either.'

'I hear you.'

'Let's hope so. For once.'

'LISTEN EVERYONE. WE NEED TO DO THIS ON THE DOUBLE.'

Zeena walks over carrying a clipboard.

'You getting the général's tea?'

'On its way.'

'No more problems okay.'

'I can ignore them if you want.'

'Go on. Tell me.'

'The real estate agent wants to know if we're paying for cleaning up the sloop.'

'Talk to intelligence on the boat.'

'The captain won't confirm or deny his existence.'

'Next.'

'Viktor and Elena asked if they can charge their party to the production.'

'What? Larry's the producer. Get him to handle this.'

'He's gone fishing with his writer.'

'He's my writer.'

'They took out a metal detector.'

'I don't need to hear this. Anything else?'

'Annalise is down the end of the pier. She wants five minutes.'

'No.'

'She says she wants to know why Death got Léo's special-jury after-thought-prize when there was no jury.'

'Anything else?'

'Bella is in wardrobe now and will be in make-up later.'

'We don't need her until Friday.'

'She says she needs to decide if she should wear a tent t-shirt or a tent dress.'

'Tell her to bring both.'

'She wants to know as there aren't any actors' trailers where is she going to change?'

'With a towel on the beach like everybody else. If Larry's not here, give this to Jack.'

'Jack's working on a prosthetic leg for the général.'

'There are no prosthetic limbs in this script.'

'The général says if he has to walk this pier once more he is going to need one.'

Edgar looks over at the général who continues studying the sea.

'We done?'

'Do you want crab or tuna for lunch?'

'Not the crab.'

ANNALISE AND CINDY stand at the barrier near the promenade carpark some distance behind the bâtiment, both staring, seemingly with the same intention of knowing why nothing significant is going on down on the end of the pier. They see Léo coming out of the back of festival headquarters, walking briskly surrounded by junior staff.

'Léo, why can't we go out there?' yells Annalise.

'Edgar needs time to get it right.'

'Let me through this gate so I can go down and see him trying.'

'It's not my decision.'

'I have to write something. I can't wait here all day.'

'Cindy's okay waiting.'

'Cindy's not even sure she wants to be a reporter.'

'More power to her.'

'See you're against me.'

'No, I am for Edgar getting it right.'

'We know that. You even gave him the jury prize.'

'It was given to the film, Annalise.'

'It's the same.'

'It's not.'

'No jury, no jury prize Léo.'

Léo walks off before Annalise can say any more. She watches him go through the barrier: 'COME ON LÉO ASK HIM PLEASE.' Léo doesn't look back.

THE ACTOR PLAYING FRANCK and the général are now stretching and loosening-up around the big white boat with its French flag missing today, the actor playing Franck eyeing Léo greeting Edgar and Edgar taking Léo's arm and speaking into his ear.

'I hear they're appointing a magistrate.'

The général sighs. 'It won't get that far.'

Edgar hurries back over to them carrying his megaphone.

'GET IN TO CHARACTER YOU TWO. FRANCK, YOU'RE TRACKING GOLD THROUGH THE ISLAND'S UNDERWORLD.'

'Would you stop it with that thing, I'm right here. Anyway, tracking stolen gold through a Corsican mafia stronghold isn't my strong suit.'

'This is only a film.'

'They're probably down inside this boat recording us.'

'Relax.'

'You have nothing to lose.'

'I'm the director, the buck-stops-here, remember. It's only a film.'

'Tell that to the Corsican mafia.'

The général sighs and pulls out an envelope from his jacket. 'Come on let's get this done. So, I take the envelope and give it to him.'

'As if you both know it's trouble. When he gives it to you Mr actor playing Franck, you study it. Then the général mumbles something like burn after reading.'

The actor playing Franck tears the envelope open, the général laughing hard.

'You don't open it until you're halfway to Corsica.'

'ZEENA WE NEED ANOTHER ENVELOPE.'

'Not again.'

'Go with the torn envelope.'

'What do I say again?'

'This is my last run. The général replies: You're my right-hand man.'

'If they're listening down there and I bet they are, they will know the général is a cop, then eight hundred metres off this coast I'm fish food.'

Zeena walks over and hands the actor playing Franck a new envelope. 'That is the last one. No more.'

The général takes the envelope and shakes it.

'I don't get it with this. If he's deep undercover why would I give him a hardcopy? I'd verbal him, use facial signals if necessary.'

Swinging around, Edgar walks fast back to his dolly rig calling out over his shoulder with his megaphone: 'DO WHATEVER YOU FEEL IS RIGHT.'

'Edgar, what do we do with the letter?'

'IMPROVISE.'

'Some director. That's all we've been doing.'

The actors study their director climbing back up on the rig and placing himself in his seat by the camera operator.

'How the hell are we going to do this?'

Holding up his megaphone, from his seat on the crane Edgar yells: 'FIRST POSITIONS ON THE DOUBLE.'

The actor playing Franck shakes his head. 'Zeena, shouldn't the first assistant be saying all this?'

'Bella crossed all assistants off the crew list.'

'Why?'

'Apparently her main guy tried getting through Biènville airport with four gold bricks in his hand-carry. They caught him at the metal detector.'

'Going through?'

'No he handed it around the machine to the security guy who dropped it on his foot.'

'On Bella's guy's foot?'

'No, on his own foot.'

'Jesus.'

'LISTEN UP EVERYONE. THE HELICOPTERS AND SHARK ARE COMING OVER IN ONE HOUR. LET'S GET THIS DONE. I DON'T WANT ANY MORE SCREW UPS. ANYONE GOT A PROBLEM WITH THAT?'

'Looks like you've got a problem already. They're coming across right now.' The actor playing Franck points east over the bay. Everyone on set stops to watch two choppers flying in tight formation low along the empty beachfront, then swing out and head across the bay, the chopper in front carrying a cup dangling underneath.

'TELL ME I'M DREAMING. ZEENA!'

'What?'

'CALL M-IKI OR THE HELICOPTER PEOPLE. FIND OUT WHAT'S GOING ON. I SAID TWELVE O'CLOCK.'

'You tell her yourself. She's up there on the promenade with Viktor and Ivan.'

'WELL, THAT'S SCREWED EVERYTHING. IT'S HALF-PAST ELEVEN. THAT'S IT FOR THE MORNING.'

Zeena runs over. 'I have M-iki on the line.'

Edgar climbs down. 'Ask her if she wouldn't mind asking them kindly to put down on the beach. Land on the sand and just wait there.'

Edgar lifts his megaphone. 'LISTEN UP EVERYONE. WE'RE BREAKING FOR LUNCH.'

Zeena waves her free-hand at him. 'M-iki's asking if you mean the pilots land it on the public beach? The choppers usually land on tarmac. You mean on the sand?'

'On the sand and invite them for lunch.'

'They're already invited.' Edgar stares at her. 'They came early specially.'

'The sons of bitches.'

The crew and cast walk down the pier towards a row of parallel trestle tables with chairs, catering staff throwing tablecloths in the wind and putting down plates of food to hold the tablecloths in place.

The first helicopter lands the cup and shark, releasing its cables on the sand, making a soft-landing alongside the cup, managing to blow sand all over the tables.

'JESUS.'

'You said to land on the beach.'

'Put a guard on that shark.'

'I don't think anyone's going to walk away with a ten-foot shark.'

'Did you invite M-iki?'

'Léo, the journalists as well, and Ivan Viktor and Elena.'

'They're here too.'

'It's one big happy family, Ed.'

'Great.'

WHITE TUFTS OF VIKTOR'S CREW-CUT blow as he moves about playing a drinks waiter again this time for the cast and crew, pouring the wine and water that the caterers provided. When the crew and cast and friends begin converging on the buffet table, making choices, filling their plates, seagulls glide above observing what's happening below.

The two pilots seated comfortably smile as if nothing happened on their watch back on day one. For them it seems nothing did. Speaking to Léo, Manuel, Larry, Cindy and Annalise, one pilot jokes about the show-cup, miming the shark falling at the swimming platform, making a demonstration of his shock reciting his take on it, all in a tone as if he is telling a children's story. The younger pilot grins broadly listening to his colleague, then pitches in as well, starting on what he saw that day, both pilots with every word and gesture absolving themselves of any culpability.

Ivan smiles at how they are managing not to look his way, keeping their gaze on members of Edgar's team only, the spread of cast and crew, the actor playing Franck and the général at the far end laughing at something between themselves, the whole film production team eating, drinking and enjoying themselves on Ivan's dime.

The good-life without end it seems which Ivan is paying

for. Tapping his shoulder, Jack Kimmelon breaks Ivan's train of thought, asking him how he is, kicking off another one of his career stories, telling Ivan and everyone nearby holding up his thumb and forefinger: 'You know I was this close to getting the rights to Jaws.'

Jack includes everyone around him, recounting the rest of an old story, a well-honed narrative journey of life as a video-store sell-through operator as if they haven't heard it, relating again with his thumb and forefinger how close he is right now to getting the rights to Die Hard 7.0, raising enough laughter to compete with the seagulls above their heads. 'We're a shoo-in for an Oscar if I do.'

Ivan holds up his glass. 'Good luck to shoo-ins. What is it you said Edgar?'

'We live in a thick present.'

'Yeah, but before that.'

'Einstein was wrong.'

'No, before that too.'

'It's all quantum. Everything is up for grabs. It's the luck of the electron draw.'

'Yes.' Ivan laughs, holding up his glass. 'To our genius director.'

'And to democracy,' Merryl says leaning over to touch her glass to Léo's. 'Here's to Léo's greatest achievement. Long may it last.'

'As long it doesn't create more chaos.'

'Democracy didn't bring any chaos. F and Daniel did that.' Merryl glares at Bella, the two women facing each other in a tense stand-off.

'If only you were as good at making money as you are talking up democracy.'

'Bella, what is that supposed to mean? I'm for making

money. Democracy belongs at the heart of societies so people can make money, the right way.'

'Try making films people want to see.'

'What are you talking about?'

'How much box-office has Death done?' Bella holds her fingers in a zero.

'Well, for starters Bella, I didn't make Death.'

Guests roll their eyes at Bella's words.

'Why don't we change the subject.'

Many nod their agreement at Ivan shutting down the argument, the général saying 'hear, hear' from the end of the table. Stretching one leg out, the person Ivan has always believed to be the sanest member of his project, the soon to be ex-général Henri Pilot, starts up a new debate on an even trickier subject. 'How on earth did a crab-eaten dead body end up on the sloop?'

'Who cares,' Bella says. 'He's dead and not coming back.'

Cast and crewmembers stare at Bella as she rakes in another mouthful of lobster.

'Someone must know something about him.'

Ivan hits a table leg with his cane. 'Or her, général.'

'Someone somewhere surely is missing somebody now. Maybe a room's empty, a voice asking when is he coming home? There has to be a story or a theory at least.'

'I wrote one.'

'Oh pleeese.'

People grimace at Bella's put-down of Larry's writer. Most ignore her as they turn their faces to Larry's writer giving him all their attention.

'Tell us your bloody story then,' says Bella.

'Yes out with it,' agrees Jack.

'Take it from me there is a story. And it is bloody.'

'What is it?' asks Merryl.

The général grins saying nothing. Many at the table stare down at him, wondering if the général shouldn't be doing the telling. 'Let's just say your guess is as good as mine,' he says. Bella barks down the table, 'Well if général whatshisface doesn't know then none of us do.'

'Let Larry's writer tell us what we are all missing,' says a smiling Ivan. The général sits upright in his chair not saying anything anymore.

'Yes. Let's hear the story.'

'Yes, speak son.'

Larry's writer grins wanly back at Jack, the man who convinced him into taking on this current mess-to-clean-up screenwriting job in the first place. And now he's pushing him into answering to Bella of all people.

'Speak son.'

Larry's now dual contracted writer looks for a moment as if he's really not going to agree to Jack's order, especially when he catches Semolina staring at him. He hadn't seen her giving him the mean eye before. His mind racing now on an idea that a select few really don't want him saying anything on this, everyone looking at him, he takes a deep breath and launches himself into pure fiction. 'Well, it all starts with this surgeon novelist who after many rejections from many publishers out of the blue gets an offer from a producer.'

'Which producer we talking about? I hope this isn't about me.'

'It's not you, Larry. Or Jack. Or any particular producer. It's just a producer.'

'What's his name?'

Larry's writer takes another breath. 'Nailly Gingbones.'

A name he somehow produced out of nowhere.

'A producer who's not well liked, shall we say.'

'Is this Neil Gingham?'

'The guy who produced all Claude Zatters' films?'

'Didn't he have an affair with that Belgian actress?'

'She went to the press and said no.'

'The rumour I heard from a French camera operator, Claude went to console her while Gingham was having his way with her and then ran off with the actress himself. Sorry Zeena.'

Hearing his tale hijacked and driven sideways into industry gossip, Larry's writer stares at everyone around the table. 'Should I stop?' Quite foolishly adding: 'Or should I go on?' Several people reply back: 'Yes.' Emphatically enough to drive Larry's writer to go on. 'Well, this producer Nailly Gingbones kept promising.' Larry's writer looks over at Semolina, her face still pleading with him. 'I'm calling the producer Nailly Gingbonés. As in cojónes. No confusion with real people. Gingbonés contracted the surgeon novelist to write for him.'

'Who's this surgeon novelist?' Merryl asks.

'He has aliases going up the wazoo. The police are probably at his property going through his house.'

'Up there now?'

'It's fiction.'

'Let's hear this story.'

The writer nods over at the général. 'So, we have this surgeon novelist who when the movie of the book he wrote starts making a shedload of cash he finds out he's getting next to nothing, and he heads to Paris to confront Gingbonés.

'Over what?'

'His contract.'

'Was the contract phoney?'

'The contract was legit but he was getting seven percent of the net.'

'Nothing in other words.' Larry's writer sees Jack staring at him, and quickly shifts his gaze to other listeners.

'Nailly Gingbonés has a security system that's the envy of présidents. There are cameras in trees. Over doors. Everywhere. Other writers had made threats too. With a couple being crime novelists, Gingbonés was an expert at handling his own security.'

'The surgeon novelist knew?'

Larry's writer nods. 'He took his time walking the streets around the house for a week discovering the right time to confront Gingbonés was Thursday nights.'

'I like that,' Merryl says. 'Thursdays are always bad.'

Jack shooshes her, getting her silent rebuke, Merryl's long stare, which has him putting his hands up in mock surrender, earning a knowing smile from the général.

'On Thursday nights Madame Gingbonés plays bridge, the bodyguards driving her and her dog, practically a wolf. The surgeon novelist sprayed all CCTV in the streets nearby. Then he charmed his way into the house saying he had information on some actresses who were planning to sue.'

'Gingbonés fell for that?'

'Producers have achilles heels. Gingbonés knows some women have the wood on him. He has problems with actresses.'

'Sounds ropy to me.' People turn and stare at Zeena.

'The surgeon novelist brought rope too and a bottle of Pinot Noir. The surgeon novelist opens the bottle and Nailly Gingbonés drinks it with added chemicals.'

'You ever add chemicals, Manuel?'

'Never.'

'Gingbonés was catatonic in minutes.'

'Wait a minute, the surgeon novelist didn't drink with him?'

'No.'

'Gingbonés didn't notice this?'

'He thought the surgeon novelist being a doctor didn't drink.'

'Why did he bring the wine in the first place?'

People around the table roll their eyes. 'Let him finish.'

'The surgeon novelist trusses Gingbonés up, cleans up, turns the lights off and gets Gingbonés outside and into his car, drives all night, then wakes him, takes him to his boat ties him to a table and does the gruesome deed.'

'This is a lurid story.'

'The film of which is going straight to Youtube.'

'Was he conscious?'

'The boat isn't soundproof but at night the marina is empty, so, after finishing the surgeon novelist off, being a deep-sea fisherman, he planned to dump Gingbonés's remains out to sea.'

'How does he get caught then?'

'Driving back with the dog from bridge Madame Gingbonés first dropped off security. She got home late. The only entrance accessible on Thursdays is a side door. Seeing everything is dark she decides to phone first.'

'Why?'

'With the streetlamps and house lights off she is scared her husband has a girl inside. But even with her mobile screen close to her face she can't work her phone out. Instead of phoning she takes a photo. Then the phone works and she makes her call. There's no answer. She walks around for a while then goes in, finding the house is empty.'

'What about the bottle with two glasses?'

'One glass, and it's gone. She thinks Nailly's out with a girlfriend. The wife shrugs and goes to bed but next morning Nailly's still not there. This goes on for days. Then raking through his online accounts, she finds no withdrawals. She shrugs that off.'

'She shrugged it off?'

'Producer, producer's wife you know what it's like.'

A few guests tut-tut.

'One afternoon she's fiddling with her phone thinking of calling the police.'

'She waited so long?'

Larry's writer puts up his hand. He is in control, Ivan seeing for the first time what he's like when he's in full story telling mode. 'She finds a photo she didn't know she took, one of her husband roped-up over some guy shoulder opening the back door of his car, the number plate in full view.'

'She sees what just happened.'

Larry's writer nods. 'She goes to the police. They check it out and running through phone records they find out the surgeon novelist and F are friends.'

'Birds of a feather.'

'But with no further leads the investigation stalls. Then the sloop-murder happens in Renne and the police think again. They pick up the surgeon-novelist.'

'This is a ridiculous story.'

'Truth usually is, Semi.'

'I thought you said this was fiction. Edgar, fire this idiot.'

'Semi calm down.'

'If you want me to act in your film get another writer.'

'Semi he's just telling a story.'

'Yeah that's what he told us.'

Larry's writer hearing Semi denouncing him is about to say something but his participation in the discussion over the reality of his fictional tale stops when a couple walks up to the tables.

'Who owns that shark?'

Edgar stands. 'You can speak with me.'

'It's yours?'

Edgar glances at Ivan. 'As much as it's anyone's.'

'Is it legal to keep an animal imprisoned in this way?'

'It's an art piece.'

The man stares at M-iki. 'You could say that about almost anything.'

'It's not alive.'

'Looks alive to me.'

M-iki swings around and stares down at the tank on the beach, while everybody at the tables stares at the couple, Merryl throwing the woman a wry look. M-iki tries to get up but has trouble standing without her cane and has to sit down again. 'It's mine. You don't like it. You want to argue with someone, argue with me.'

'You're happy doing this?'

'Would you have questioned Alfred Hitchcock's use of birds?'

'If he were here now, yes.'

Guests share looks and on cue two seagulls dive down at one table, screeching as they snatch chicken pieces from two plates. A film-extra eating next to an attacking bird screams and leaps out of her seat. This gets others standing up and sets the birds off which attack en masse. Only Viktor, the général, the actor playing Franck and Ivan remain seated, birds flashing all around as guests knock over their chairs getting out of the way of the dive-bombing birds.

'The animal world is staging a revolution.'

The complainer realizing what he might have set off quickly takes his embarrassed partner by her elbow and heads back down to the beach. Catering staff rush over to put up net coverings over the tables using several bamboo props as supports. Viktor lifts the net on his side and throws out a chicken wing.

'Don't encourage them Viktor.'

'Calm down, Elena. If you feed your enemy you know what he's doing.'

The général laughs. 'I'm not sure of the logic of that. How does feeding a psychopath work?'

'There's a difference between intelligence and police work.'

'Clearly.'

With many birds circling showing increasing intent, nobody moves to sit back down again.

'They are not giving up, Edgar.'

'Nor am I.'

Seeing the couple down by the tank the général whispers to the actor playing Franck, suggesting that he pretend to be an inspector, walk down and speak to them. The actor playing Franck is reluctant but heads down the slope.

Edgar follows him down there. Soon the complainer, now claiming to be an important animal rights campaigner and the actor playing Franck are in a shouting match, their argument growing fierce fast. With Edgar joining in, the three men face each other a foot apart, the animal-rights-campaigner yelling about the rights of sharks under French law, and foreigners sticking their noses into matters where they don't belong. Telling the man that he is French, the actor playing Franck and Edgar shout at each other until Edgar gets into a wrestling match with the man, a crewmember trying to pull them apart, the woman struggling to help her partner, Merryl running down to help out as well, followed by other members of the production, one shooting the whole scene with a small camera.

The général starts a slow descent down the hill as well but with his bad hip worse today the going's very slow, the now plain Henri Pilot watching his every foot-fall on the slippery slope.

The lunch abandoned, the seagulls attacking the table in earnest, one bird pecks its way under the netting. An exceptionally large seagull, it parades up and down on the plates, now in charge of the lunch table. Two caterers appear again pulling all the netting off but then have a hard time shooing the big bird away.

The général's descent now complete he finds Edgar standing over the complainer prostrate on the sand, his wife yelling to anyone who'll listen, 'He hit him. This foreigner hit my husband.' Two local policemen approach the scene, the général studying them. 'Where did they come from?'

The actor playing Franck points up at their vehicle in the carpark. 'They've been watching us for some time.'

One of the officers apprehends Edgar who unsuccessfully tries to disentangle himself from the cop's grip, and yells over at Larry's writer with real venom in his voice: 'SEMI'S RIGHT. YOU'RE FIRED.'

'What's he done?'

'If he had refrained from telling that ridiculous story, général, we would've finished eating by now. We'd be back at work.'

'I can't remember such an entertaining lunch.'

Seeing Ivan standing alone twenty feet away, the général struggles across the sands to speak to him.

'Did you see this happen?'

'I saw the animal-rights man fall.'

'Did Edgar hit him?'

Ivan shakes his head. 'Edgar raised his fist but the complainer got in first and did a striker's special.'

'He dived?'

Ivan nods. The man's wife begins yelling: 'This bastard hit him. The bloody immigrant hit mon Michel'.

The général swings around and yells at her, 'Edgar's not an immigrant. He's a guest in this country.'

'Like I am a guest as well I suppose général,' Bella yells.

Ignoring Bella, the général wades across the soft sand waving at the police. Reaching them he tries introducing himself, but being so short of breath he can barely speak properly. 'Give him to me ... officers. I'll make sure...he shows up at the station ... Tomorrow... okay?'

'Général. We have orders. We have a complaint on the books.'

'What complaint?'

'Daniel Martin wrote a letter.'

'What? He's going to be arrested himself.'

'All we know is we have an assault complaint against Edgar Gordon Olles.'

'Martin is up to his ears in accusations. He'll probably go to jail himself.'

'Sorry général. Anyway, you're retired now.'

'That's not finalised.'

No matter how hard the général tries to convince his former fellow junior officers they keep shaking their heads.

They march Edgar to their car, the général waving to the

cast and crew to gather around, and then turning to Zeena.

'Can you get the caterers to put more lunch out?'

'Why?'

'I need to talk to everybody. I want everyone together.'

'With those dinosaurs flying around?'

'If necessary, yes.'

Zeena eyes the général and storms off, leaving him waving his arms. 'Listen up everyone,' he says. 'Back to lunch. I need to fill you in on some facts.'

With the lunch tables more or less under control once more, some crewmembers sitting uneasily, though most refusing to reseat themselves, standing up ready to run if the seagulls begin attacking again, glancing sideways at Merryl the général puts his arms in the air.

'First-up, the electronic shark was F's idea.'

'WHAT!'

END NOTES

When Jack returned from the film's wrap party sporting facial gashes and two black eyes Merryl read him the riot act, ordering him to sleep out on a roll out mattress on the Sunshine's back deck. To his credit Jack took his punishment without a word of complaint.

The following morning over breakfast, the pair made a truce, Jack swearing he would begin therapy. He was a happier person in subsequent days, while Merryl was left incurably melancholic, her actions making her weep.

Sipping herbal teas, she interrogated herself for hours. Was she right to always pull Jack up? She couldn't forgive herself.

Returning to their south LA beachfront bungalow she left Jack in the house and walked the Pacific-facing beach sands end to end rethinking her whole life.

What began as a reasonably actionable shopping list of self-improvement promises miraculously ended-up as a treatment-reworking of *Invasion of the Body Snatchers*, retitled *Reinvasion of the Body Snatchers*.

When Jack learned of the title he was sure Merryl somehow had it in mind to document his condition. He told her he didn't mind. In fact, he welcomed the critique. So, he said. Merryl told him it wasn't like that at all.

In her reinvention of Walter Wanger's much-admired 1956 Sci-fi movie, tiny aliens in the form of microbes entered humans via various orifices.

Within hours they were controlling their hosts all according to life-instructions packaged inside nano-digital message-systems, jettisoned during circulations of their hosts' bloodstreams.

As with most sophisticated AI, the digital devices immediately began writing their own code, reconfiguring brain messaging systems, the miniscule body-sitting invaders soon determining the desires and action of more than half of humanity.

Victims would often go mad but not before setting out under micro-instructions to perpetrate a host of the most egregious crimes which Merryl with the aid of a flow of gin and dry vermouth kept conjuring-up.

With Ivan producing and Jack associate-producing Merryl took on her first role as writer director. It was a gamble for all and costly, but production and post-production went well. Merryl performed brilliantly throughout, with the film completed on schedule and under budget.

Without a skerrick of prepublicity the completed film was released at midnight in a single near-empty LA cinema with only friends, family and sympathetic critics invited to the première. That way at least Ivan could get paid. Having the film appear at least in one place, crucially, given his complicated deal with a hedge fund, meant they shouldered the production costs, letting Ivan off an onerous financial hook. By chance an unknown critic also found his way inside the cinema that night—some say it was Rob le Riche. Others said he was not even in the country.

Whoever it was, the unknown visitor watching Merryl's film, decided she was eminently bankable. When his commentary posted anonymously late-night on a film-blog website, Reinvasion began what looked at first to be the oddest word of mouth travel ever recorded in the history of American cinema.

Merryl's film made it big with the horror film devotees. Inside a month film-buffs all-over America began campaigning online, demanding that *Reinvasion of the Body Snatchers* be released everywhere, Merryl's film suddenly becoming the biggest post-virus re-imagining of the LA wide midnight cine-circuit set.

One venue became two, then five, soon jumping to ten. Word then spread to general audiences with kids of all ages wearing WW1 gasmasks flocking in to see Merryl's neo-gothic tale of biological horror.

Hearing the news, cine-experts fell over themselves getting into cinemas as well, accepting standing-room places at the back, texting each other on the audacity of the storyline, a reworking as if it weren't a reworking.

Critical accolades out did each other identifying manifold themes. One review became two, then fifty. Film-writers from major magazines rushed down to see Reinvasion at the reopened Rose Tinted Theatre in East Hollywood, offering astoundingly positive commentary as well. Before anyone knew why or how, a nationwide buzz spread from the west to east coasts.

When Merryl's film invaded the malls, she became Youtube's latest star. Using her now-famous Vlog monologues to comment on her methods, she explained her motives and screenwriting techniques, pleading that she never intended to strip humanity of any moral culpability.

One critic wrote that: 'The no-big-stars box office hit has morphed into the film smash of our era.' Merryl's 'masterpiece' gathered support exponentially in the oddest quarters. The Pope sent her a congratulatory postcard.

Hitting big in the west, ticket-sales rose even faster in the east, the film swamping malls in the mid-west.

Reinvasion headed south in the middle of the night, then spread overseas unhindered by subtitles.

On a dollar spent to dollar earned, Merryl's film became the biggest single film success story in the history of cinema, restoring American cinema to what it was in the 1940s.

In one year, *Reinvasion of the Body Snatchers* took well over two billion at the box office all on a modest budget of 2 million, give or take an Ivan-accounted-for dollar or so. With practically speaking no advertising, the numbers spoke for themselves, record-breaking results following Jack everywhere, leaving the reformed one unable to say anything except: 'I couldn't be prouder of my Merryl. I should have taken her to France sooner.'

As the principal investor Ivan is over the moon. The film ran for ten months non-stop in the French quarter of New Orleans alone, connecting up with a newly opened Blues Pomo Cabaret act playing next door which in turn kicked-off another word-of-mouth nationwide spread of rave notices all-over again.

Merryl's master-hit re-crisscrossed the country three times, breaking down even more geographical and community divides each time, with conservative, liberal, black, white, Asian, Hispanic, Wasps, Jews and Muslims applauding her talent.

With Reinvasion now the most talked about directorial debut in two centuries of cinema, Merryl's style continues jolting audiences and garnering critical plaudits wherever her film happens to show-up.

When she heard members of the Academy were whispering her name and then she won a brace of Platinum Globules, followed by nomination for an Oscar for best original screenplay it felt as if she had dived that night and gathered up a gold brick instead of tungsten at the bottom of Renne's mysterious bay.

Not many know this, but sometimes in her bath Merryl daydreams of F's electronic shark and how it bumped her.

She is not saying this in public, but for her, everything was due to mad F and his even madder electronic shark, shaking up Merryl's inner self in such a way that her extraordinary good fortune found a way into the lives of so many.